Praise for

A Question Mark Is Half a Heart

"A warmhearted portrayal of family and forgiveness."

—*Kirkus Reviews*

"Readers will soak up the suspense as they search for the truth alongside Elin up until the end."

—*Publishers Weekly*

"Elin is a complex character with a compelling story, and Lundberg avoids the obvious resolutions that readers may expect in favor of a deeper exploration of the meaning of love, forgiveness, and family. This satisfying novel will appeal to fans of Lisa Duffy and Patti Callahan Henry."

—*Booklist*

"With graceful prose and an artist's eye, Lundberg returns with a powerful and illuminating novel that navigates the channels of the human heart and the secrets that threaten to tear it apart. A poetic and haunting read, I was captured from the first page to the last."

—Alyson Richman, bestselling author of *The Lost Wife*

"Such an engrossing and affecting story of love and loss—and the inescapable shadows cast on the present by the past."

—Joanna Glen, bestselling author of *The Other Half of Augusta Hope*

A
Question
Mark
Is
Half a Heart

⇒ ◆ ⇐

Sofia Lundberg

TRANSLATED BY

Nichola Smalley

HARPER ◉ PERENNIAL

NEW YORK • LONDON • TORONTO • SYDNEY • NEW DELHI • AUCKLAND

HARPER ● PERENNIAL

FIRST HARPER PERENNIAL EDITION PUBLISHED 2022.

Library of Congress Cataloging-in-Publication Data
Names: Lundberg, Sofia, 1974– author. | Smalley, Nichola, translator.
Title: A question mark is half a heart / Sofia Lundberg;
translated by Nichola Smalley.
Other titles: Frågetecken är ett halvt hjärta. English
Identifiers: LCCN 2020023895 (print) | LCCN 2020023896 (ebook) |
ISBN 9780358697374 (paperback) | ISBN 9780358450221 |
ISBN 9780358450429 | ISBN 9781328473523 (ebook)
Classification: LCC PT9877.22.U535 2021 (print) | LCC PT9877.22.U535 (ebook) |
DDC 839.73/8—dc23
LC record available at https://lccn.loc.gov/2020023895
LC ebook record available at https://lccn.loc.gov/2020023896

Book design by Greta D. Sibley

22 23 24 25 26 LSC 10 9 8 7 6 5 4 3 2 1

We are all in the gutter, but some of us
are looking at the stars.

—*Oscar Wilde*

Now

⸺ ◆ ⸺

NEW YORK, 2017

It's dusk. Outside the industrial windows, the sun is setting behind the tall buildings. Stubborn rays wedge their way between the facades; like golden spearheads they penetrate the encroaching darkness. Evening again. Elin hasn't eaten dinner at home in several weeks. She won't tonight, either. She turns to look at the building just a few blocks away, where she can see the luxuriant vegetation on her very own roof terrace, the red parasol, and the barbecue that's already been lit. A narrow column of smoke rises toward the sky.

She catches a glimpse of someone, probably Sam or Alice. Or maybe a friend who's come over to visit. All she can see is a figure moving about purposefully between the plants.

They're sure to be waiting for her again at home. In vain.

Behind her, people move back and forth across the studio floor. A gray-blue backdrop hangs from a steel fixture, swooping from wall to floor. A chaise longue upholstered in gold brocade has been placed in the center. On it, a beautiful woman reclines, with strands of pearls around her neck. She's wearing a wide, flowing white-tulle skirt that spreads across the floor. Her upper body is glossy with oil, and the chunky pearl necklaces cover her naked breasts. Her lips are red, her skin smoothed to perfection with layers of makeup.

Two assistants are correcting the light: they raise and lower the big light boxes, click the camera shutter, read the meters, start again. Behind the assistants stands a team of stylists and makeup artists. They carefully observe every detail of the image that's in the process of being created. They're dressed in black. Everyone is dressed in black, everyone but Elin. She's wearing a red dress. Red like blood, red like life. Red like the evening sun outside the window.

Elin is torn from her thoughts as the beautiful woman, growing irritated, begins to make dissatisfied noises.

"What's taking so long? I'm not going to be able to hold this pose much longer. Hey! Can we get started now?"

She sighs and twists her body into a more comfortable position, and the necklaces fall to the side and reveal her nipple, which is hard and blue. Two stylists are on the spot immediately, patiently and carefully rearranging the pearls to cover it. Some of the necklaces are stuck down with double-sided clear tape, and the woman's skin rises in goose bumps from the contact. She sighs audibly and rolls her eyes, the only part of her body she's free to move.

A man in a suit, the woman's agent, walks over to Elin. He smiles politely, leans toward her, and whispers, "We'd better get started, she's getting impatient and it won't end well."

Elin shakes her head vaguely and looks back to the window. She sighs.

"We can stop now if she wants. I'm sure we have enough pictures already, it's just a spread this time, not a cover."

The agent holds up his hands and stares at her hard.

"No, absolutely not. We'll do this one too."

Elin tears herself away from the view of her home and walks toward the camera. Her telephone vibrates in her pocket; she knows who's trying to reach her but doesn't respond. Knows the message will just play on her conscience. Knows the people at home are disappointed.

As soon as Elin gets behind the camera, a thousand tiny stars light up in the woman's eyes; her back straightens, her lips pout. Her hair falls back as she lightly shakes her head, and it ripples in the gentle breeze from the fan. She's a star, and Elin is too. Soon only the two of them exist, they're absorbed in each other. Elin shoots and instructs, the woman laughs and flirts with her. Behind them the team applauds. The rush of creativity pounds through Elin's veins.

◆

Several hours pass before Elin finally forces herself to leave the studio and all the new shots requiring her attention on the computer. Her phone is full of missed calls and annoyed texts. From Sam, from Alice.

When are you going to be here?

Where are you Mom?

She scrolls through but doesn't read all the words. She hasn't the strength. She lets the taxis pass her in the vibrant Manhattan night. The asphalt still feels warm from the sun's heat as she crosses the street. She walks slowly, past beautiful young people who laugh loudly, intoxicated. Sees other people sitting on the street, dirty, vulnerable. It's a long time since she walked home, even though it's so close. A long time since she moved beyond the walls of the gym, the studio, her home. The paving stones are uneven beneath her heels and she walks slowly, noting every detail along the way. Her own street, Orchard Street, lies deserted in the night, empty of people, empty of cars. It's grimy and rough, like all the streets of the Lower East Side. She loves it, the contrast between outside and inside, between shabbiness and luxury. She takes a step into the lobby, passes the slumbering doorman unnoticed, and presses the button for the elevator. But when the doors open, she hesitates and turns around. She wants to stay out, to linger in the pulsating night. The others have probably gone to sleep anyway.

She unlocks her mailbox and takes the stack of letters to the restaurant a few doors down, the local she often goes to after late shoots. Once there, she orders a glass of 1982 Bordeaux. The waiter shakes his head.

"Nineteen eighty-two, we don't serve that by the glass. We have only a few bottles. That shit's exclusive. A good year."

Elin shifts uncomfortably in her chair.

"Depends how you look at it. But I'm happy to pay for a bottle. Give me the wine, thanks — I'm worth it. It's got to be the 1982."

"All right, you're worth it." The waiter rolls his eyes. "We're closing soon, by the way."

Elin nods.

"Don't worry, I drink fast."

She fingers the letters, laying aside the sealed envelopes until one catches her attention. The postmark is from Visby, the stamp Swedish. Her name has been written by hand in capitals, carefully spelled out in blue ink. She opens the envelope and unfolds the sheet of paper within. It's some kind of star chart and on it her name is printed, in large ornate type. She holds her breath, reading the Swedish words above it.

On this day, a star was named Elin.

She reads the line again and again in the unfamiliar language. A long string of coordinates denotes the star's precise whereabouts in the heavens.

A star someone has bought for her. Her very own star, which now bears her name. It must be from . . . can it really be . . . him, who sent it? She puts the brakes on her own thoughts, doesn't even want to pronounce the name to herself. But she can picture his face clearly, his smile too.

Her heart is hammering in her chest. She pushes the chart away. Stares at it. Then she gets up and runs out into the street to look up at the sky, but she can see only a dark-blue featureless mass above the buildings. It's never truly dark in New York, never enough to see the meandering muddle of the stars. The tall buildings of Manhattan almost touch the sky, but down on the streets it just feels distant. She goes in again. The waiter is standing by her seat, waiting, wine bottle in hand. He pours a splash into her glass and she downs it without noticing how it tastes. With an impatient wave of the hand she indicates that he should refill it, and takes two more large gulps. Then she picks up the star chart again and turns the shiny paper this way and that. In the bottom corner, against the dark background, someone has written in gold marker:

> I saw your picture in a magazine. You look just the same.
> Long time no see. Get in touch!
> F

And underneath, an address. Elin feels her stomach cramp when she sees the place of origin. She can't stop looking at it, her eyes filling with tears. She follows the contours of the letter *F* with her index finger and mouths his name. Fredrik.

Her mouth feels dry. She reaches for the wineglass and empties it. Then she calls the waiter over, loudly.

"Hello! Can I get a large glass of milk? I'm so thirsty, suddenly."

Then

≡ ◆ ≡

HEIVIDE, GOTLAND, SWEDEN, 1979

"One cup each. And no squabbling now."

Small hands gripped the red-and-white milk carton that Elin had just placed on the pine table. Two pairs of children's hands with dirt under their fingernails. Elin tried to take the carton away from them, but the brothers barged her out of the way with sharp elbows. They were both talking at once.

"Me first."

"You're taking too much."

"Give it to me!"

A stern voice rose over the quarrel.

"No squabbling, I can't take any more. Oldest first, you know the rules. One cup each. Listen to Elin!"

Marianne was still turned away from them, bent over the sink.

"See? Listen to Mama now." Elin pushed Erik and Edvin aside roughly. The boys fell off the kitchen bench without letting go of the milk carton. Silence filled the room as they took a brown china plate along with them. As though the air had suddenly become thick and time stood still. The crash and the splash that followed as the whole mess landed on the floor drew forth a roar.

Then silence and wide eyes.

A white pool of milk spread slowly across the linoleum; it dripped from the table, and white rivulets made their way down the rough table legs. And then another roar. The rage in that cry sliced through the room.

"You fucking brats. Out! Out of my kitchen!"

Elin and her brothers took off without hesitating, running out the door and cutting across the yard, chased by the curses that continued to fill every corner of the kitchen. They curled up close together behind a heap of junk by the wall of the barn to hide.

"Elin, will we get no food now?" her younger brother whispered in a voice that barely carried.

"She'll calm down soon, Edvin, you know that. Don't worry. It was my fault the plate broke." Elin stroked his hair tenderly, held him tight, and rocked him.

After a while she let go of her brothers, stood up, and walked tentatively back to the house. Inside she could see her mother's hunched form picking the dirty pieces of china up off the floor, saw her taking each one between her thumb and forefinger as a pile of fragments slowly grew in her other hand.

The kitchen door was ajar, and it creaked loudly in the strong wind. A few raindrops fell from the gutter. *Plop, plop.* Elin listened carefully. The house was silent. Marianne stayed crouched, head hanging, even when all the pieces had been picked up. Their dog, Sunny, was nosing around on the floor in front of her, licking up the spilled milk. Marianne paid no attention.

Elin was steeling herself to go in when suddenly, the bent figure straightened. Elin's heart leapt in her chest, and she turned and ran back to her brothers. Quick across the gravel, followed by more shouting. She crouched behind the junk heap. Marianne rushed over to the door and threw out the shards, sharp projectiles.

"Stay out there, wherever you are, I don't want to see you anymore! You hear me? I don't want to see you anymore!"

When there were no pieces of china left, Marianne turned around and around, looking for the children. Elin curled up in a ball, putting her arm around her brothers and letting them burrow their heads into her. They were afraid to even breathe, listening carefully for the slightest movement.

"There'll be no more food this month. You hear that? No food. Fucking brats! Filthy fucking brats!"

She whirled her arms around, even though there were no more shards to throw. Elin watched her forlornly through gaps in the rubbish heap. Old furniture, planks, pallets, and other things that should have been thrown away a long time ago but had piled up instead. In the end, Marianne turned and went back into the house, her hand to her chest, as though her heart was contracting inside. Through the kitchen window Elin could see her rummaging impatiently in her handbag and the kitchen drawers until she found what she was looking for. A cigarette. She lit it, inhaled deeply, and blew smoke rings toward the ceiling. Perfect round rings that turned to ovals and then dissipated into a haze and vanished. When only the butt remained, she'd throw it into the sink and it would all be over.

The siblings stayed where they were for a while, close together, Edvin with his head bent forward. He dragged a stick across the ground, drawing lines and circles, as Elin sat still, with her eyes fixed on the house. When Marianne finally, after a long, silent pause, opened the dirty kitchen window, Elin stepped out and met her gaze. She smiled cautiously and lifted her hand in greeting. Marianne smiled weakly in response but with her mouth closed and tense.

Everything was back to normal. It was over now.

On the windowsill were two dry primroses with wrinkled little flowers. Marianne pinched out a few of the most shriveled ones and threw the rubbish out into the flower bed.

"You can come in again. Sorry. I just got a bit angry," she called. Then she turned her back to them again. Elin saw her sit down at the kitchen table. Elin crouched and played with a few pebbles on the ground, throwing them into the air and catching them on the back of her hand. One stone stayed there awhile, but then rolled down and fell with the others to the earth.

"You're not going to have any children," Edvin teased.

Elin glared at him.

"Shut it."

Erik comforted her. "You might have one — one of them stayed a little while."

"Oh please, do you really believe a handful of stones can predict the future?"

Elin sighed and walked toward the house. Halfway there she stopped and waved at her brothers.

"Come on, you two, let's eat now, I'm hungry."

When they came back into the kitchen, Marianne was sitting at the kitchen window, deep in thought. She held a cigarette in her hand, the loose ash hanging, waiting to be flicked off. The ashtray on the table was full, butt after butt crushed down into the sand at the bottom. Marianne's face was pale; her eyes stared emptily. She didn't even react when the children took their seats on the kitchen bench.

❖

Elin, Erik, and Edvin ate in silence. Baloney, two thick slices each, and cold macaroni stuck together in big clumps. A huge dollop of ketchup helped separate them. Their glasses were empty, so Elin got up to fetch water. Marianne followed her with her eyes as she filled three glasses and set them on the table.

"Are you going to be good now?" Her voice sounded thick, as though she'd just woken up.

Elin sighed as the brothers jostled for space on the bench behind her.

"We spilled it by accident, Mama, we didn't mean to."

"Are you answering back to me?"

She shook her head.

"No, I'm not, but . . ."

"Quiet. Just be quiet. Not another word. Eat your food."

"Sorry, Mama, it wasn't on purpose. We just spilled a bit, it was my fault the plate broke. Don't be angry at Erik and Edvin."

"You're always fighting, do you have to fight? All the time. I can't take it anymore." Marianne groaned loudly.

"We don't need any milk today. Water's fine."

"I'm so horribly tired."

"Sorry, Mama. We're sorry. Right, Erik? Right, Edvin?"

The brothers nodded. Marianne leaned over the pot, scraped a little, and put a spoonful of pasta in her mouth.

"Do you want a plate, Mama?" Elin got up and walked toward the cupboard, but Marianne stopped her.

"There's no need, you eat. Just promise me you'll stop fighting. You'll have to drink water the rest of the month, we don't have any more money."

Erik and Edvin pushed the food around on their plates, their forks screeching against the brown glaze.

"Eat properly."

"But Mama, they have to stir their food. The macaroni's cold and sticky."

"It wouldn't be if you hadn't been fighting. Eat properly, I said."

Edvin stopped eating; Erik hung his head and impaled pieces of pasta carefully and quietly with his fork. One on each spike.

"Why do you have to be so angry?" Erik whispered, turning his eyes to Marianne.

"I want you to be able to eat with the king. You hear? Any child of mine should be well-behaved enough to eat with the king any day."

"Mama, stop. That was just something Papa said when he was drunk. We'll never get to eat with the king. How would it even happen?" Elin sighed and looked away.

Marianne grabbed Elin's cutlery and threw it hard onto the table, so it bounced and fell to the floor.

"I can't take it. I can't take any more. You hear?"

Marianne took Elin's plate and carried it over to the sink. She banged the pots and pans loudly as she washed up. She got this angry only when she was hungry, Elin knew that. She stopped her brothers when they reached out to get more pasta.

"We're finished, Mama, there's some left for you."

Elin glanced at her brothers sitting there at the table in despondent silence, with their plates scraped clean in front of them. Edvin with thick blond curls that still hadn't been cut, even though he was seven now and had just started school. They cascaded down over his ears and the back of his neck, like a waterfall of gold. And Erik, only a year older, but so much bigger, so much more mature. His hair had never had even a suggestion of a curl. Marianne shaved it regularly with a trimmer, and the bare scalp emphasized his ears, which stuck out.

"We're full now." Elin looked at them, imploring. They nodded reluctantly and slipped down onto the floor.

"May we get down from the table?"

Elin nodded. The brothers vanished upstairs. She stayed where she was and listened to the clattering of dishes, watching the bent back leaning over the too-low sink. Suddenly the movements stopped.

"We have it good, right? In spite of everything?"

Elin didn't reply. Marianne didn't turn around. Their eyes didn't meet. The clattering resumed.

"What would I do without you? Without your brothers? You're my three aces."

"You'd be a bit less angry, maybe?"

Marianne turned around. The sun was shining in through the kitchen window, catching the grime on the lenses of her glasses. She met Elin's gaze, swallowed hard, and then walked over to the pan and scooped cold macaroni into her mouth.

"Are you all full? Are you sure?"

Marianne squeezed her way in beside Elin on the kitchen bench and stroked her hand gently over Elin's head.

"You help me so much, I could never manage without you."

"Do we really not have any money? Not even for milk? You buy cigarettes." Elin mumbled the last few words with her eyes on the table.

"No. Not this month. My cigarettes will be gone soon, I can't afford to buy any more. I got the car fixed, we need it. You'll have to eat what we've got in the larder, there are a few tins in there. And there's water in the tap, drink that if you're hungry."

"Phone Grandma, then. Ask for help." Elin looked at her, pleading.

"Not in a million years." She shook her head. "What help could she offer? They're as poor as us. I'm not going to complain."

Elin stood up and dug down into the pocket of her skintight jeans. She pulled out two bottle tops, a yellow pencil stump, two dirty one-krona coins, and two fifty-öre coins.

"I have this." She piled up the coins one by one in front of Marianne.

"That will buy us a liter. Go down to the shop tomorrow if you want. Thank you. You'll get four krona in return once I have the money. I promise."

Elin sneaked out of the house into the cool dusk. Marianne stayed at the kitchen table, a fresh cigarette in her hand.

❖

Elin counted the drops that fell from the drainpipe. They filtered slowly through the pine needles that were clogging it. There was a muted *plop* as they landed in the blue plastic barrel Marianne had dragged home from some neighboring farm. It had contained a pesticide called Resistance. *Resistance.* Elin liked that word and what it stood for. She wished there was a little Resistance left in it, which she could borrow when necessary. She cast an invisible spell on the barrel, hissing:

"Resist now. Come on, resist it all. All the bad stuff."

❖

There, behind the corner of the house, she had her secret place. At the back where no one was interested in going, where the junipers grew right up against the house and where the pine needles were sharp against her feet when she went barefoot. She'd hidden there for half her life now, since she was five years old. When she needed to be left alone. Or when someone was angry with her. When Papa was slurring. When Mama was crying.

She'd made a chair with some branches from the forest and it was always there waiting for her, leaning against the wall. There, she could sit and think; she could hear her thoughts so much better when she was alone. The plastic roof and gutter sheltered her head from the rain, but only if she sat close to the wall. She tilted her head back, closed her eyes, and let the drops soak into her worn jeans. They grew speckled with dark spots and the chill spread across her thighs like a blanket of ice. She stayed like that, her legs out in the ever-heavier downpour, letting them get wetter and wetter, colder and colder. The drops falling into the barrel pattered faster and faster. She focused on the sound, counting and keeping the figures in order. It was harder at school. The sounds were never pure there, not like here. At school there were always other noises to disturb her: shouts, talking, rustling, bodily noises. Elin's brain registered it all, heard it all. The figures in her head merged into one; she lost the thread and couldn't concentrate. *She's hopeless,* she'd heard Miss say to Marianne at parents' evening. Hopeless at mathematics. Hopeless at writing neatly so Miss could read what she'd written. Hopeless at most things. And what's more, the daughter of a criminal. They talked about it, all the children in the school, and the teachers too, when they thought she couldn't hear. They whispered as she passed. She didn't even know what the word *criminal* meant.

The only one who always defended her was Fredrik. He was the strongest, smartest boy in school. He'd take her by the arm and pull her along with him, telling off the others for being mean. Once she'd asked him what that word meant, but he'd just laughed and told her to think about something else instead. Something that made her happy.

She thought it must have something to do with them coming to take Papa away, the police, and him not living at home anymore. She missed him every day. He never thought she was hopeless; he didn't see the point of being good at school. She used to help him in the workshop, and she was always good at that. He said so, anyway.

But now she probably wouldn't get to help him anymore. Ever.

◆

It felt good to sit behind the house. There, where the only thing you could hear was the muted *drip-drop* of the rain on the water in the barrel and the murmur of the wind as it rummaged about in the tops of the pines. There, where she could hear her own thoughts.

She needed the time. The silent time. To think. To understand. Mostly she thought about how things must be in jail, where Papa lived. She thought about how sounds must sound there. If he was completely alone with his thoughts behind the bars that protected the world from him. If there were bars, or just normal doors. Maybe they were impermeable, made of thick iron. The kind that no bombs in the whole world could break down. Doors that would stand firm even when the world around them was collapsing.

She wondered how it felt when Papa got angry and punched the door with his fists. If it hurt, if it got holes in it, like at home.

Sunday was visiting day; she'd read that in a letter Marianne had received. So every Sunday she waited for them to take the trip to the boat. For it to take them to the mainland, and the prison there on the other side of the sea. For the guards to take out their great big rattling bunches of keys and unlock the heavy metal door and let Papa out into the open. So she could run into his arms and feel the warmth of his big hands as he stroked her back and whispered *Hello there, Number One*, with a voice that was gravelly from too many cigarettes.

She waited in vain.

They never went. Marianne had had enough, that's what she told anyone who asked. She said she didn't miss him, not in the slightest. One time, when a neighbor had inquired, she even said it would be good if he was left to rot there in jail so she wouldn't have to see him again. That filled Elin's head with terrible images, ones that refused to go away. She saw his body grow green with mold, slowly decomposing into a pool on a cold gray concrete floor.

It was lucky she had her magic place. She'd sit there, day after day, in the company of the drips, the wind, the sun, the clouds, the trees, and the ants that bit her feet. She often wondered what he'd done that was so awful, they had to lock him up. If he actually was a bad person.

❖

Drip, drop, drip, drop. Four hundred and seven, four hundred and eight, four hundred and nine. She counted and thought. Time slowed down a little. Maybe that's how it was for Papa, there in jail. She wondered what he did with all that time. If he too was counting the drops falling from the roof.

Now

NEW YORK, 2017

The cold, white liquid feels harsh chasing the wine she drank before. She clicks her tongue against her palate. The inside of her mouth has a sticky coating. The restaurant's milk is so fatty, so different. Not at all like the fresh milk she remembers and longs for. She pushes the half-full tumbler to one side and takes hold of the base of the wineglass, sliding it toward her without picking it up. In front of her lies the envelope, with the star chart folded back inside. She runs her palm over the handwritten address.

Inhales. Exhales.

He's there in the lines of the pen; his fingers have formed the letters that make up her name. He hasn't forgotten her. She breathes more and more rapidly. Her heart beats within the red dress. She's suddenly cold, goose bumps puckering her skin.

"We're closing soon." The waiter's there again, demanding her attention. He nods to the bottle, which is still more than half full.

"Come on. This is New York. And you know me. Let me sit here awhile, I don't want to go home yet," she mumbles. She downs the contents of her glass in two great gulps and fills it again. The hand holding the bottle shakes, and she spills a few red drops on the white paper tablecloth. The liquid spreads, soaks in. Her eyes follow the pattern.

"Tough day at work, I'm guessing?" The waiter sniggers quietly and clears plates from the next table.

She nods and turns the envelope over and is faced with the name she hasn't spoken for so many years, a name hardly even in her thoughts. Fredrik Grinde. Fredrik. She says the name again and again, feels her bottom lip move against her teeth.

"OK, you can stay while I close up if you want. I'm not going to throw you out. But just because it's you."

The waiter disappears behind the bar. He changes the music. A solitary saxophone is accompanied by the clattering of dishes from the kitchen. The ceiling lights are switched on and the restaurant fills with glaring light. Elin hides her face in her hands. A tear falls to the table and lands on the red stain, which spreads farther.

Her phone vibrates against her leg and she pulls it from the pocket of her dress. Yet another message. It's from Sam, just two words:

Good night.

They promised each other that when they got married, they would always say good night, would never go to sleep without making up. She's broken that promise many times. He never has. It's never him who lets her down, it's always her. It's always her job eating up all the time.

She breaks the promise this time too. It would be so easy to reply *Night night.* And yet she doesn't. She swipes his words away and goes instead to the search engine, occupied with thoughts of another. She types in Fredrik's first name, almost expects to find his freckly face and his smile just as she remembers them. But the screen just fills with other suit-clad men who share his name.

She smiles at her own foolishness but still doesn't dare to search for his full name. She searches for other things instead, calls forth pictures of the place she once left. Where she had a friend who would be hers forever. *Fredrik, where have you been all these years?* She holds the chart to her chest.

The waiter is standing at her table again. He lifts the bottle and looks at it. Then he holds it out to her.

"It's not really allowed," he says. "But take it home with you if you want. This is too expensive to throw away. You have to go now."

Elin shakes her head, stands, and backs away from him. Then she turns and walks toward the door.

"Hey, hello, you have to pay before leaving!" He grabs her by the arm and pulls her back. She nods eagerly.

"Sorry, I . . ."

She digs in her bag for her card.

"Are you OK, has something happened? Is Sam OK?"

"Yeah, I think so. It's just . . . a little complicated. I probably just need some sleep."

The waiter nods and laughs out loud.

"We all do. Even here. Get yourself home now, tomorrow's a new day. 'The sun'll come out tomorrow, so ya gotta hang on 'til tomorrow.'" He sings the last sentence.

Elin gives a strained smile and nods. Heading for the street, she stops in the doorway, arrested by all the thoughts spinning in her head. She gets her phone out again. Taps a few words into the search engine, fingers trembling, and presses Enter quickly.

Statute of limitations homicide Sweden

Then

≡ ◈ ≡

"She was here yesterday too."

Gerd, the cashier at the shop, got up when she saw Marianne and Elin come in through the glass door. Elin stiffened and stopped in the doorway, but Marianne carried on in.

"Yes, and? I sent her, it's hardly the first time she's run in here on her own," Marianne muttered, taking a basket from the stack.

Gerd went over to Elin and gripped her shoulders gently.

"Are you going to tell her or should I?" she whispered right by her ear, with breath that smelled of coffee.

Elin shook her head and looked at her pleadingly, but Gerd ignored her.

"Missy here tried to steal a liter of milk."

"Elin! She would never try to steal anything, she had money with her to pay for it."

"Well, yes, she paid for one liter. But not for the one she had hidden under her sweater."

Elin saw Marianne's jaw clench. She walked around the shop, carefully choosing products and putting them into the basket. Her lips moved with each item added, as she calculated the cost. Elin remained tight in Gerd's arms. Gerd was soft and warm and breathed heavy, slow breaths. She smelled of hairspray, and her gray curls lay in a perfectly undulating mass across her head. They both followed Marianne with their eyes. In the end she came back and set the basket on the floor. In it lay a packet of macaroni, bread, carrots, and onions.

"You brat," she hissed, locking eyes with Elin. "We may be poor, but we don't steal. And that's that."

"How are things with you folks? Is it tough, now you're on your own? Do you have money for food?" Gerd stroked Elin's long hair.

Marianne turned her face away.

"She was just making mischief. Right, Elin? A good hiding's what you need. And that's what you'll get."

Elin nodded and looked at the floor awkwardly. The two women talked over her head.

"Are you looking after the girl properly? So she doesn't turn out like him?"

"Like him? What do you mean?"

"Well, a criminal. It can be passed down."

"Elin's not a criminal. What are you talking about? She made a mistake, but don't worry, she's not a criminal."

Gerd entered Marianne's shopping into the cash register in silence. Marianne followed the rising total with her eyes and fingered the coins in her little purse. She took the bread away, embarrassed.

"I just remembered, we have bread at home that needs eating first. You can take that out."

"If you say so," Gerd said with a smile, correcting the amount. Marianne held out a heap of coins.

"If it happens again, if Elin does something stupid, be sure to phone me right away. Just so I know."

"Yes, I should have called. It slipped my mind, that's all. It was just a pint of milk. But of course, she shouldn't be stealing."

Elin gathered up the shopping and stuffed it into the cloth bag. She hung her head. Gerd held out a lollipop for her, but Elin hesitated until she saw Marianne nod.

"How's the love life, by the way? I suppose you're trying to find someone new, now you're rid of Lasse? It can't be healthy to live alone."

"Find someone? Where would I be looking?"

"Someone will turn up, you'll see. Otherwise I guess you'll have to take Lasse back, when he gets out again."

"Take him back? What? But he's not . . ." Marianne stopped short and nodded toward the door. "Elin, you go ahead, I'll be out in a minute."

Elin went out through the door. Before it swung shut she heard the women go on talking, whispering heatedly.

"He's not all there, he's just a vile thief who frightens the life out of people. He almost killed her, and that's why he's in jail. If you ask me, he should stay there." Marianne sounded furious.

"Yes, you're right. He must have been drunk, men do such stupid things when they've been drinking." Gerd was trying to calm her down.

"You mark my words, we're better off now without someone staggering around, scaring us silly."

The door rattled as it swung shut behind Elin, and the women's voices fell silent. She sat on the upstairs doorstep of the house; the ground floor housed the grocery store. Some of the mortar had come away to expose the red clinker slabs beneath, just like the ones on the floor of the cold storage area. She picked at it, pulling off small pieces and throwing them toward a puddle in the road. Beyond the puddles lay the fields and the forest, and beyond them the largest farm in the area. The people there were so rich, they had an indoor pool in one of the wings of their house.

A few wisps of fog swept across the field closest to her. The combine harvester had left straw stubble where just a week earlier beautifully swaying rye had grown. It almost looked as though some tiny clouds had toppled down from the gray sky. The sunlight still managed to force its way through, making the vegetation shimmer before her eyes. She concentrated on the beauty of the scene.

Footsteps approached from behind her, making her heart race, and she heard the floor creak in spite of the closed door. She ran quickly down the stairs and disappeared around the corner of the building. From there she saw Marianne come out and walk toward the main road, and their home. She had the half-full cloth bag over her shoulder, and her gaze was fixed on the ground in front of her.

◆

When Elin came back into the shop, Gerd was crouched in front of the bread rack, stacking wrapped loaves on top of one another, and she dropped a whole pile as the door's bells tinkled. She smiled when she turned around and saw who it was.

"Hello, little one. What are you doing back here? Did Mama get terribly cross with you? Sorry. She didn't hit you like she said, did she? I had to tell her, you understand that, right?"

Elin shrugged. The lollipop stick stuck up out of her jeans pocket, and she took it out and pulled off the cellophane. Then she sat down on the floor beside Gerd with the pop in her mouth. She passed packs of bread to her, and Gerd put them in the right place.

"How lovely to have a little helper today, just when I needed one. Now there's rye bread for the Grindes and Skogaholm loaf for the Lindkvists and the Petterssons."

"How do you know who buys what?"

Gerd chuckled.

"I know quite a lot. Syrup loaf was your papa's favorite. And maybe yours too? Am I right?"

Elin nodded. Gerd held a loaf out for her.

"Take this one home, its date expires today. I always take loaves home and freeze them on the expiration date. They stay fresh then. I can give you bread every week, if you're having a hard time."

"But Mama will think I've taken it."

Gerd stroked Elin's cheek.

"Not if I tell her it's bread we'll throw away otherwise. You can freeze it in bags of four slices each and take them out when you need them."

Elin hugged the loaf tightly under her chin. Inhaled the faint scent of bread in one deep breath.

"I understand that it's tough at the moment, now that Papa's gone. He'll be home again soon, you'll see," Gerd went on.

"Mama says he'll never cross our doorstep again." Elin pressed her lips together sadly.

"Is that what she says? Well, perhaps that's the way it's going to be. But I'm sure he'll have his own doorstep. And you can cross it."

Elin nodded.

"Do you want to talk about it a little?"

Elin shook her head. Gerd gave her a hug and didn't let go until Elin wriggled free.

"They say Papa's a murderer and that he'll never come back," she said quietly.

"Who does?"

"At school. They say they've locked him up and thrown away the key. That he's a criminial or whatever you call it."

Gerd shook her head and laid a hand on Elin's cheek. It felt warm and rough.

"And what do you think?" she asked.

Elin shrugged. The lollipop was almost gone. She took it out of her mouth.

"What did he do that was so awful? Why won't anyone tell me?"

"Well, he didn't kill anyone, you can be sure of that."

Gerd laughed and looked over at the door. The brakes of a blue Volvo slammed just outside the door, and out stepped a tall man with a red checked shirt and a cowboy hat. He took the stairs in two great leaps and jerked the door open.

Elin leaned toward Gerd and whispered.

"Is it true they eat steak every Saturday at the Grindes' place?"

"You'll have to ask Micke about that. Or Fredrik."

Elin shook her head.

"No, don't say anything, it was just something someone said. It can't be true."

"You shouldn't listen so much to what people say. Let that be today's lesson."

Gerd lit up when Micke strode through the door. She followed him around the aisles, talking incessantly. Elin stayed where she was and played with the bags of bread. When he got there, she passed him a loaf of rye.

"Hello, kiddo. How do you know what I want?"

He sat on his haunches alongside her, with his arm leaning against the shelf. There was a large, dark, sour-smelling sweat patch under his arm. Elin looked up at Gerd.

"She's good at guessing, this little one." Gerd laughed.

"You can say that again."

He stuck his hand in his pocket and pulled out a five-krona piece. He fiddled with it and then threw it into the air. Elin saw it spin and glimmer in the striplights' glow. It fell toward her and she stretched out her hand to catch it.

"You take it, buy something nice just for you."

Micke turned his back on her, grinned at Gerd, and walked over to the cash register with his full basket. Gerd showered him with appreciation and listened carefully as he talked. Elin stayed where she was until she heard him leave the shop and climb into the blue Volvo. When the engine started, she went back to the milk section and took out a red carton. She took it up to Gerd and put it on the counter.

"I'd like to buy this. Can you write a note and tell Mama I haven't stolen it? And about the bread?"

Now

≍ ◆ ≍

The elevator creaks as it makes its way up through the building, as though the cables holding it are close to breaking. The mirrors show every part of her body; she sees her own image everywhere. She draws her hand across a small callus on her back, which can be made out through her dress, just above her waist. It appeared after she turned forty and refuses to go away. She bends forward and studies her face, searching for the beauty that used to be there, but she can see only dark shadows under her eyes and lines carving the skin of her cheeks. The elevator doors open and before her lies the bright white floor that signifies home. Elin takes a step inside and turns up the lights. On the sofa sits Sam, reclining, with his hands folded in his lap. His eyes are closed, his face relaxed. The corners of his mouth point upward slightly, even when he sleeps. He always looks happy, joyful somehow. That was what she fell for. The happiness, the confidence.

She sneaks past him with the heap of letters in her arms. Patters over to the desk and lays the letter from Sweden in the top drawer, the others in a pile on the tabletop. Then she sneaks back and curls up beside him. He groans slightly, as though he's just woken up.

"Sorry. It took a long time," she whispers, kissing him on the cheek. He jumps, as though the kiss is electric.

"Where have you been? What's the time?" he mumbles.

"What do you mean?"

"You smell of wine. You missed dinner with my parents. They're probably starting to wonder what you're up to."

Elin shrugs.

"I just had a glass, on the way home from the studio. I was on my own. The shoot took ages, the sitter was terrible. Egocentric actors, you've no idea."

She sighs deeply and leans her head against the back of the sofa, puts her feet up on the coffee table.

"You almost caught them. They just left."

"Who?"

"Aren't you listening? My parents. Don't you remember? We invited them for dinner to celebrate Alice and her dancing, her getting into the school. We even talked about it in therapy, that it was important to us."

Elin holds her hand up to her mouth as she suddenly remembers.

"Sorry," she whispers.

"You always say that. But do you ever mean it?" Sam shakes his head, looking concerned. Sighs.

"I do mean it. Sorry. I forgot. There's so much going on right now, you know how it is. The team, I can't just leave . . . everything depends on me. Without me there are no pictures. It's not like a normal job."

Sam flinches at her touch; he stands up and walks with shuffling steps toward the bedroom.

"I was waiting for you to say good night. At least. For you to talk to me, think about me." Sam shakes his phone at her.

"Sorry. I'm here now. I rushed home as soon as you texted, I wanted to say good night here. Is Alice still around? Is she staying here tonight? Please tell me she is."

Sam stops but doesn't turn around.

"She left at about nine, said she had a class early tomorrow. But I think she was disappointed; you should probably phone her."

Elin doesn't reply. She's already halfway out to the roof terrace. She sinks down into a chair and kicks her shoes off, pulls out her phone, and writes a message to Alice.

Sorry sweetheart, I was late home from work. Sorry.

She looks at the words she's just sent. Types a few red hearts, sends them too, and then puts the telephone upside-down on the chair beside her.

The wood under the soles of her feet feels warm. There's still smoke rising from the wood oven Sam insisted on building when they moved in. She shudders when she sees the smoke, gets up, and pulls the hatches across so they are tightly closed, smothering the embers inside.

❖

"What's this?"

Sam comes out to her. In his hand he's holding the star chart, which he waves in her face.

"I thought you were sleeping when I came in?"

"What does it say? What language is it?"

"I don't know." Elin shrugs a little.

"You don't know, but you hid it?"

Sam's face is pinched, disbelieving. Elin swallows with difficulty.

"I wasn't hiding it, I just put it in there."

"And you have no idea who sent it?" Sam sighs heavily.

"I really don't know, I promise. It must be some crazy admirer. A fan. I don't even know what language it is. Do you?"

Sam takes a step closer to the terrace railing and holds the chart out over the edge.

"And yet you hid it? I don't believe you. Tell me who sent it!"

Elin shakes her head.

"I don't know."

"So it won't matter if I drop it?"

Sam locks eyes with her. They look at each other. When she doesn't answer, he drops the chart and lets the wind sweep it away. Elin stretches her hand after it, but it moves too quickly. She sees it disappear down toward the street, follows it with her eyes, her hands gripping the terrace railing. The paper sways, twists, like a raft on stormy seas. They watch it fall until it disappears from view. Then Sam turns to her.

"So it doesn't mean anything?"

She tries to stay calm. Sam doesn't give in.

"I can see you're upset."

Elin shakes her head and holds her arms out to him.

"I don't know what you're talking about. Please, I've had a long day and I have to sleep now. I have to get up early tomorrow as well."

Sam backs away, pushes her hands away.

"It's Saturday."

"Please."

"That word would have suited me better."

"What do you mean?"

Sam doesn't reply. He turns his back on her and disappears into the bedroom. His steps pound the floor.

Elin doesn't follow him but sneaks into the hall and takes the elevator down. She's barefoot, and as she runs up and down the street looking for the chart, the asphalt scratches the soles of her feet. She can't see the paper anywhere. Maybe it got stuck on a balcony on the way down? She searches all the corners and doorways, in vain.

She cranes her neck, looking up at the building for the exact place Sam dropped it from and tracking its possible path with her eyes. Maybe it's blown around the corner, into another street? She runs toward Broome Street. As she makes the turn, she almost runs into an old woman. Her hair is gray and greasy; she's wearing a baggy green tracksuit with large stains on the front. In one hand she's holding the star chart, in the other a rolled-up blanket secured with a leather belt. Elin tries to take the chart from her, but the woman hisses, bares her teeth, high on something that isn't alcohol. Elin recoils.

"That's mine, please can I have it, I dropped it."

The woman shakes her head. Elin rummages for money in her pockets, but they're empty. She holds out her empty hands.

"Please. It's from a person who means a lot. I don't have any money to give you, I can go and get some if you wait. But please give it to me," she pleads helplessly.

The woman shakes her head and presses the paper against her chest. Its corner has been crushed against her body. Elin shakes her head.

"Please be careful with it. It's from someone I . . . someone who means very much to me. Please."

The woman looks at her with a sorrowful expression; she nods.

"I see, I understand, I understand. Love, love, love," she mutters, dropping the paper so it drifts down to the ground at Elin's bare feet.

Then

=== ◆ ===

The main road was deserted. The edge of the asphalt was uneven and broken, split by the spring's ground frost. Long cracks snaked across the road, and its white lines were faded and scraped. Elin jumped from one marking to the next. The empty cloth bag on her arm fluttered after her in the wind. She jumped with great concentration, landing on her toes in the thin shoes.

Suddenly, in a flurry of laughter, someone appeared in front of her. He jumped farther than she did, clearing two road markings at a time, with his arms stretched high in the air. He was dressed in blue dungarees and heavy boots, and was covered head to toe in muck. He stopped and smiled at her. It was hard to tell the splashes of mud from the freckles on his face. Elin gathered her strength and jumped past him, over two lines this time. Almost.

"Come on, you weakling."

Stung by his mocking tone, she pushed herself even harder, jumped again, but still landed just short of the second line.

She glared at him as he roared with laughter.

"You'll never be stronger than me. Give up. I'm a guy, you know."

"I'll show you, one day," Elin shot back, and stuck her tongue out at him. Then she cut across the road and started running toward the shop.

Outside the door was a tractor with a trailer full of wooden crates containing potatoes, carrots, and rutabagas straight from the ground. Micke came out through the door and glowered at the children.

"Hello, Elin. Fredrik, you're working, come on, no games," he called, his voice rumbly as though the words came from deep inside his stomach.

Fredrik tugged Elin's hair gently as he ran past her. From the trailer he took two large crates, which came up above his nose. He stooped under their weight.

Elin took hold of the top one, trying to take it from him. "It's too heavy, let me help you. I'm not in a rush."

Fredrik shook his head.

"Papa'll go crazy. Let go. I can do it, I have to do it myself."

Elin did as he wished, letting go just as Micke came out the door again. He talked without pausing in his work, lifting three crates a time, his shirt straining across his chest as his muscles tensed. Through the gaps between the buttons, she could see skin covered in curly black hair.

"I've done three rounds and you're still standing here, flirting. A farmer's son has to put the work in, you know that. Nothing gets done by itself," he snapped.

Fredrik reeled up the steps with the heavy crates, unable to see where he was putting his feet. Elin ran alongside him and held the door open. When he passed her, he whispered:

"Run now before he gets cross at you for being in the way. I'll see you later. Listen out for the tune."

One round more, then they were gone. Elin heard the tractor start and drive off. The crates they'd left were stacked high by the vegetable racks. Muddy footprints made a trail from the door, like a reminder of the food's origin.

❖

Elin was awoken by someone whistling a soft melody. She quickly jumped out of bed and pulled on her jeans, the worn bell-bottoms she'd inherited from a neighbor a little farther down the road, and a tight green T-shirt with a four-leaf clover on the front. She cast a quick glance at herself in the mirror and smoothed down her hair, which fell in thick tangles over her shoulders; she fixed her part so it cut sharply down the center of her head. She opened the door cautiously and looked both ways down the hallway before going out. There was no one there. The door to her brothers' room was closed, the light off. She crept over to the stairs without turning the lights on and peered down between the banister to where Marianne sat bent over the kitchen table, a gray wool blanket wound tightly around her. There was a scent in the air, but Elin couldn't see a lit cigarette, or cloud of smoke. Marianne sat perfectly motionless, as still as the late evening.

Elin crept down, careful to land both feet on each step before attempting the next. Marianne didn't react; the only movement in her hunched body was her heavy breathing. Elin could hear the air whistling strenuously through her nose. Apart from that, the house was silence itself. Elin tiptoed the last steps to the front door, her feet spread wide apart so her pant legs wouldn't rub together and make a noise.

◈

A cold, hard sea wind sucked at the door as she opened it. She held on and closed it carefully, one millimeter at a time. Then she ran quickly across the yard toward the little forest road. The whistling had stopped and the only thing she could hear was the crash of the waves. She stopped still in the pitch-black night and listened attentively. Whistled a few notes herself. There was no response, but she thought she heard someone approach, steps crunching on the gravel. Her pulse quickened.

"Fredrik? Is that you?" Elin called. There was no reply, and the footsteps had stopped.

She started to whistle again, the same melody again and again. In the end, it was answered by a single high note that slowly ebbed away.

"Don't be afraid, come out!" Elin looked around; the juniper bushes and the tree were filled with threatening shadows that hung over her. She spun around, craning her neck anxiously. Suddenly he jumped out right in front of her, with his hands in the air, and she screamed and punched him hard on the shoulder.

"Stop it, you frightened me!"

"Scaredy-cat, are you afraid of the dark?" Fredrik laughed at her and started running along the road. Elin ran after him. They knew the area inside-out; they didn't need eyes to guide them in the dark evening. Suddenly he stopped dead and took her hand, pulling her into one of the gardens they passed.

"What are you doing? Aren't we going to the beach?" she protested, struggling.

"Shhh," he whispered. "Look: Aina just put a light on. Come on, let's play a game with her."

They ran toward Aina's outhouse. They could see a soft glow from the heart-shaped cutout of the door. A power cable dangled from the branches of the trees, running the electricity out from the house. Fredrik crept around behind the privy and opened the hatch that concealed the bucket. Elin kept her distance, wrinkling her nose and flapping her hand to ward off the smell. Fredrik held a long stick out to her.

"Shhh, she's coming, not a sound," he whispered with a giggle.

Aina was the oldest person in the village and used a wheeled walker. They heard it squeaking as she rolled it over the paved garden path, and she groaned as she made her way up the little step. The whole outhouse swayed as she sat down with a thud; then there was a loud rumbling. Elin and Fredrik looked at each other and smothered the laughter that bubbled up in their bellies.

"Now," Fredrik whispered, stretching the stick toward the hole. Elin took hold of his arm and shook her head.

"No, it's mean. What if she gets angry?" she whispered.

But Fredrik didn't listen. He poked Aina gently on the bottom with his stick, and when her terrified shriek filled the night, he couldn't keep the laughter down any longer. He guffawed until he almost wept as he and Elin vanished, quick as shadows, into the dark forest.

"You horrible little scamps!" Aina shouted after them. Elin snuck a look back and saw the flab on Aina's arm wobble as she stuck it out the door and shook her fist.

"That was mean, Fredrik. What if I'm not allowed to go there now, what if she doesn't want to read to me anymore?" Elin admonished him.

"It was funny, though. She'll never think it was you, she loves you." Fredrik chuckled as he wiped away tears of mirth.

Elin couldn't contain herself when she heard his infectious laughter. They laughed all the way to the sea and their secret spot between the rocks, the place they had their campfire. Fredrik gathered sticks and dry grass and laid them over the charred remnants of their last fire. Elin lay on her back and studied the yellowy-white explosion of stars in the sky.

"It's so clear. Tonight we'll definitely be able to see everything," she said.

"Hmm, almost everything. Not Venus. Unless you want to stay up until five, that's when it's meant to come up, over there behind the cliff." Fredrik struck his knife against the steel. The sparks lit up the night.

"Five. We don't have school tomorrow. Why not?" Elin put her hands behind her head. The stones felt knobbly and hard beneath her back.

"Dad gets up at five. I'd better be home by then or he'll go crazy." Fredrik struggled with the steel, but none of the sparks caught. Elin stuck her hand out and grabbed a few pine needles.

"Here, light it with dry needles, that might work," she said, scattering them over the sticks.

"Ah, what do you know about fires? You can probably light one only with matches and newspaper. I can do this, just wait a minute."

"Dad used to light fires with pine needles. He was good at it, he was good at everything. Well, until he turned into one of those . . . you know . . ."

"Don't think about it now. You're having a nice time here with me, right? I'll get the fire lit, I promise."

Fredrik carried on feverishly scraping the knife against the steel, and at last the dry grass started to glow. He blew carefully. The flames turned yellow and took hold. He stuck in a few extra sticks and then lay flat on his back a short distance away.

Elin stretched out her hand and put it on his arm. She left it there, like a link between them, and felt the warmth from his body against her palm.

"Can you see Cetus?" He pointed up at the sky with his free arm.

"No, where?"

"There, in the southwest, can't you see it? It's really bright tonight."

Fredrik inched closer and took hold of her hand, pointing it toward the constellation.

"I can't find it, it's too hard." Elin sighed and pulled her arm back again. She went on quietly studying the heavens above them. "I can see something there. It's Castor and Pollux. That's Gemini, right?"

"Good, you're learning."

"What is a cetus anyway?"

"It's a whale, dummy."

"But whales are called whales, not cetuses."

"You think too much. Stop thinking." Fredrik threw a little stone at her, which bounced off her stomach and then fell back among the others on the beach. Elin gasped.

"Did you see! Three at once," she whispered.

"I saw."

"Do we get three wishes each then?"

"Yeah, of course. One for every shooting star."

"Though you only need one."

"What do you mean?"

"I wish all my wishes would come true."

Fredrik groaned loudly.

"But they're not going to." He sighed.

"Why not?"

"Because you said it out loud, of course."

Now
═◆═

Elin wakes early. Sam is lying far over on his side of the bed, with his back to her. He's sleeping deeply. She reaches toward her bedside table and feels for her phone. When the screen lights up, she sees that she's got a reply from Alice. *OK,* it says. Just two letters. She sighs and sits on the side of the bed to send a swift response.

> Sorry. I really mean it. Can we have dinner soon? You choose the place. I love you.

Two against one again, she thinks, and rubs the sleep from her eyes. She looks at the screen, studies the words she just wrote. Then she clicks away from the thread with Alice and her bad conscience to read another message. It's from Joe, her assistant.

> I'll pick you up a bit earlier, 7:15. The drive takes longer than I thought. Hope that's OK?

She looks at the clock and is suddenly wide awake. Barely half an hour from now. She struggles out of her nightdress on the way to the shower.

Sam is still sleeping when she sneaks past the bed and into the closet, feeling her way among the hangers without turning the light on. She chooses black on black, a blouse and pants, and gets dressed in the hallway on the way to the elevator. Sam doesn't wake up. Or he doesn't let her know that he knows she's leaving. The last few sessions with the therapist have mostly been about her job, about how he wants her to take a step back, to be more present. Once upon a time he was the one pursuing a career, but now he seems to have grown tired of it. For Elin, her job has never been about having a career. It's been something else altogether. When she's taking photographs, time and thought cease.

◈

In a little more than half an hour she leaves the building. Joe's jeep is double-parked, and he's leaning out through the open window. His arms are covered with tattoos and his T-shirt is tight across his shoulders. He holds out a large cup of cappuccino and she gratefully takes a big gulp.

"Let me guess. You didn't see the message until you woke up." Joe laughs.

Elin is hiding behind large black sunglasses. She steps out into the street, between two hooting taxis, and quickly climbs into the vehicle.

"Maybe, maybe, but I'm here now," she says, smiling as she sinks down into the soft seat.

"But you know where we're going, right?"

The old jeep lurches as Joe releases the clutch and pulls away.

"Out into the bush." Elin sighs.

Joe changes gear, and the engine's vibrations spread inside the jeep. There's a strong smell of gasoline. Elin screws up her nose.

"What?" Joe pats the dashboard. "This is a priceless treasure. Don't you start complaining about my ride."

"We can talk about it when we get there. *If* we get there." Elin sighs. "Why didn't you take my car?"

She winds down the window a little and leans her face into the breeze, shutting her eyes against the bright morning light.

"Who are we shooting today again?" she drawls.

Joe turns toward her, a little too long, so that the jeep swerves slightly.

"Are you kidding me? Are you still asleep?"

"What do you mean?"

"You've never forgotten who we're shooting, or where. You look a little out of sorts. Are you unwell?"

Elin keeps her eyes on the street and shakes her head vaguely.

"Yeah, I'm kidding, I do remember," she says, so quietly she can barely
be heard above the engine.

◆

When they arrive, the garden is already full of equipment and people
purposefully crossing the lawn. The rest of the team is there. Reel after
reel of cable is unwound to power the lights arranged in front of a luxuriant flower bed. On the drive there's a trailer, and outside it, beneath
a protective canopy, the woman who'll be the subject of the portrait is
being made up. Her long hair is in curlers, and she's tilting her chin and
gaze upward, so the makeup artist can line her lower eyelid with kohl.

It's a novelist this time, but Elin hasn't read her books. She hardly
ever finds time to read these days, even though it used to be her idea of
heaven. In her jacket pocket is a piece of paper with a short summary
of the book, but she hasn't read that either. The star chart is in the same
pocket, folded four times. She can feel the folds against her chest.

The publisher wants flowers in the background. The portrait should
feel pastoral and warm, which is why they've left the city and made their
way to this garden in the suburbs.

Elin holds the camera and moves around the house, followed closely
by Joe and two other assistants. Here and there she puts the camera to
her eye, looking for backdrops. She settles on a flower bed at the back of
the house, where masses of marigolds and asters are clustered together.
Behind them are two low apple trees, branches loaded with round red
fruit.

"We'll do it here, this will be better. Move everything."

Joe stares at her. Four flashes are already rigged up; everything's
plugged in. But he doesn't protest, and traipses off with the assistants to
start breaking down and moving the heavy equipment.

Elin wanders on alone. On the edge of the garden is a little shed,
hidden behind a wall of bushes. The door is blue. Shining cobalt blue.

She reaches a hand toward it, strokes her fingers across the surface. It's uneven, hand-painted with a brush. Between the brushstrokes, streaks of black show through. A rusty old-fashioned key has been left in the keyhole. She turns it, this way and that. Feels the chill of the iron in her hand. Suddenly she can't move. She remembers another door. Details from another time wash over her. The front wall of the house, with plaster coming off in big chunks. The flower bed, where the rosebushes grew wild and unpruned, their branches tangled. The scent of moldering leaves and damp earth.

She backs away a couple of steps and takes a photo. But the light is bad and the color doesn't come out properly. She uses her phone camera instead. Then she stands, still as a statue, staring at the door.

◈

Someone comes and takes hold of her arm. She shakes off the touch. They're talking around her but she doesn't hear any words. There's a muted ringing in one of her ears. She's tiny and barefoot. The door she's standing in front of is suddenly her own.

Then

=⸺◆⸺=

Elin heard the blue front door slam shut, then everything was quiet. Marianne's joints often gave way, from exhaustion. When that happened, she would curl up in the fetal position on the doormat, or wherever she happened to be at that moment. Her jacket was spread out behind her, like a pool of brown mud. Her forehead was touching her knees and her cheeks were pale. When Elin went up to her and stroked her hair, she mumbled that she just needed to rest a little, that she'd get up in a minute. That Elin should go away.

Elin left her reluctantly, after putting a soft sweater under Marianne's head, and went back to the kitchen table. It was covered with drawings. Just flowers, wildflowers in gentle pastel colors. It was Gerd who'd taught her how to draw flowers, a long time ago. She started with four small circles, close together, a green stalk and two green leaves. She practiced in the shop, day after day. And when the results got good enough, Gerd let her draw a flower on the front of her datebook, on the first page. She made it yellow. Yellow like the sun. Yellow like Gerd's smile.

Now she could breathe life into all kinds of flowers: clover, lady's bedstraw, chicory. She would draw the leaves carefully with a pencil, down to the tiniest vein. There was often a bouquet on the table at home, in a well-worn glass vase. Now there were hardly any flowers left to pick; only a few kept growing into the autumn, slightly withered and drooping.

◆

Dusk was falling when Marianne at last stood up and joined Elin in the kitchen. She opened the fridge door and stared at the shelves. The skin on her cheekbones was rough, and the darkness made the shadows in the scar sharper. It was because of The Angry that she looked like that. Not her own, but his. It came when he drank. Marianne got angry sometimes, but not like Lasse. The children could wind her up, but the storm always passed. Lasse got so furious that his rage had a name: The Angry. The Angry's coming. Elin shivered at the memory.

It was The Angry's fault that they came, that the police came and took him. They didn't know that there was another side to him, they didn't know about his warm hands and his cuddles. How could they?

She missed him, but not The Angry. Things were calmer now.

Elin saw him dragging Marianne across the yard by her hair that evening, when her cheek got rough. She saw Marianne's dress get ripped up and one of her legs get colored with dark-red blood as her skin-and-bones body was dragged across the ground. Elin was little then, standing on tiptoe by the kitchen window. The voices, the screaming, the despair on Marianne's face. When he finally let go and staggered drunkenly away from the farm, Marianne crawled toward the door, toward the children inside. Toward Elin and Erik. That was how it always went when they fought. Marianne stayed and Lasse went. When he finally returned home, he'd be his normal self, kind and full of cuddles, with big warm hands that stroked your back.

◊

"There's milk?" Marianne's voice roused Elin from her thoughts. The sound was weak and reedy, as though she hadn't spoken in a long time. She turned to Elin and held up the carton.

"Yes, I didn't steal it. Micke gave me five krona the other day. I had a few krona left so I bought it today."

"Micke did? Grinde's Micke? How come?"

"Dunno."

"We don't need alms."

"Alms, what are they?"

"I'm going to give it back to him. Say no next time."

"But we need milk, don't we? It's good, isn't it?"

"Stop arguing. Water does just as well, we'll none of us die from drinking water."

"I just thought . . ."

"Well, don't. I'm tired, I can't handle any more, damn it. Water's free and it's good enough for us." Marianne was glaring at her.

"You swore."

"Yes."

Elin grabbed a pen from the table and added a line to the tally on a piece of paper taped to a kitchen cabinet. There was one for each of them, but Lasse was crossed out with a thick black line.

"You've got the most now, not counting Papa," she said.

"Aha. Good. Damn, damn, damn, damn, damn, damn, damn. Now I have even more," Marianne said, indifferently.

"What are you doing? Do you want to lose? You were the one who came up with the idea of tallying it up."

"So you'd stop swearing at school. So I wouldn't get any shit from your teacher."

Elin turned to the paper and put another mark under Marianne's name.

"It's your fault. It's you and Papa who taught me."

"Oh, be quiet. It's mostly your papa who swears, and he's not our problem anymore." Marianne picked up a shirt and threw it in Elin's face. Elin caught it and cautiously threw it back. Something sparked in Marianne's eyes, a light. She grabbed the cushions from the bench and flailed her arms about. Elin swung back. The kitchen, always so quiet and still, was filled with fumbling, rising laughter.

"What are you doing?" Edvin shouted, running down the stairs. Marianne and Elin waited quietly, and when he came through the doorway, cushions rained down around him. All three of them landed in a heap on the floor. The cushions were spread around them. Elin lay close to Marianne, head on her shoulder. She smelled of smoke and the sweet perfume of her soap. Edvin wormed his way on top of them. They were red in the face from the exertion and longed-for laughter. Legs tangled together. Hair full of old bread crumbs and dog fur.

"We still have a good time, even without men and milk and other people's money." Marianne pulled both children close and hugged them hard.

"What, aren't we allowed milk anymore? Damn," Edvin cried. Marianne and Elin laughed.

"Yeah, damn, damn, damn, damn," Marianne said.

Elin got up and walked over to the tally again, putting one mark under Edvin and four under Marianne.

"Mama, you're going to lose."

"I know." Marianne pushed Edvin aside and stood up again. She sat on a chair and lit a cigarette, blew the smoke out into the room. "I'm such a loser."

The room was silent. Elin lay back down on the floor, her head on one of the cushions, and stared up at the ceiling as she listened to the sound of the wall clock's second hand and the heavy breaths that filled the room with a smoky haze.

❖

Elin ran fast from pine tree to pine tree, following a couple walking slowly along the pebble beach. When they stopped to embrace, she crouched behind a bush and watched them intently through the yellowing leaves. She squinted to see who the man was, but she could see only his back. His body was hidden by a baggy jacket and on his head he wore a dark-blue hat, pulled down tight. The two stood close together, her hands stroking his back. Their heads moved rhythmically in a passionate kiss.

Looking away, Elin raked the earth with her hand and found a stone, which she threw at them as hard as she could. It clattered against other stones where it landed, and the couple let go of each other.

"What was that?"

Elin held her breath for a few seconds; then she heard, and recognized, the man's voice. She got up and ran, crouched over, as quickly and quietly as she could, up toward the forest. Her feet flew over the needle-covered ground, dodging roots and swerving around the bent, stunted pines as though they were poles in a slalom. She stopped and listened. From the beach came only the sound of the waves and the crunching of feet wandering farther along the pebbles. No voices. No one chasing her. Relieved, she squatted and pulled a well-thumbed piece of paper and a stub of pencil from her jeans pocket. Unfolding the paper, she added a few lines to the scrawled paragraph:

> Mamas found someone else. I thought you should know. Your sitting there, rotting in prison while she kisses someone else. Gross. You shud be hear. But I guess you already know that. I hope your sorry. Sorry for all the drinking. Mamas the best. Do you understand that. Soon itll be too late.

She stared at the words, reading them over and over, then returned to the start of the letter, the questions she'd piled up, one on top of another:

> Dear Papa. Why dont you write to me? Dont you miss me? Dont you miss Erik or Edvin? Dont you wonder wot were up to? Dont you ever think about us? I can tell the police your kind sometimes.

She screwed the paper into a little ball. She thought about throwing it away, but her arm froze mid-motion and her fingers locked around it again, clinging stiffly to the words she needed to get out. She stuck the letter back in her pocket, along with the chewed yellow pencil stub, then lay down and watched the wind playing with the clouds. Seagulls flew high above, sailing forth with their wings outstretched. She would have so loved to be a bird. To fly, to float, to dive. To escape all her thoughts. She stretched her arms out to the sides, flapped them up and down, and closed her eyes.

❖

"Elin! Elin! What's happened?"

The voice woke her from her daydream. She sat up and saw Marianne running up from the beach, on her own now.

"Have you hurt yourself?" Marianne got down on her knees beside her. Elin swatted away the hand that stroked her cheek.

"Stop it!"

"I thought you were dead. It looked like that." Marianne's eyes were wide. "I was scared. What are you doing here?"

"Nothing. What are *you* doing here?"

"I was just taking a walk. It's so lovely by the sea. But now I want to go home. It's cold."

Elin stood up and started walking away quickly, and Marianne hurried after her.

"Wait, Elin, we can walk together."

Elin didn't reply. She sped up until she was running. Faster, faster. Her jacket was flapping in the wind like a superhero's cape.

Tears were running down Elin's cheeks. The pebbles made her feet hurt through the thin soles of her shoes, but the pain didn't stop her. She didn't know why she was crying. Maybe it was because the end had suddenly become so apparent. The end of their family. The end of the only bit of normality she'd ever had. She stopped, out of breath from crying, braced her arms against a tree trunk, and kicked it as hard as she could, over and over again. It hurt her toes, which got little protection from her canvas shoes, but that wasn't why her tears kept coming faster and faster. She was crying because the tears needed to come out. She was crying because there was no longer space for them inside her. Because her soul was full to the brim with shit.

❖

At last Marianne caught up with her, and soon Elin was wrapped in her arms, surrounded by her soothing noises.

"My love, why are you so sad? What's happened?"

Elin didn't respond, but her crying increased in force, bubbling up through her eyes and nose, tears running down her cheeks and into the corners of her mouth. She wiped her face on her sleeve. Marianne held her close. Shushed her, hushed her.

"Come on, let's go home. I can make you some hot chocolate."

"We don't have any milk." Elin sniffed loudly. Her cheeks were streaked with dirt from her hands where she'd wiped away the tears, and still they kept coming.

"Aha. I slipped some packets out from the café."

Elin met Marianne's smile with astonishment.

"You've been pinching stuff?"

"Yeah, I've been pinching stuff. We belong in prison too. The whole bunch of us. Scumbags, that's what we are."

Elin smiled uncertainly.

"But Mama . . ."

"We deserve hot chocolate. Both of us. And the best thing about the stolen packets is that they don't even need milk. Just water. Regular water. Free water."

Elin dried her eyes once again, with her damp sleeve. A cup of hot chocolate. She couldn't remember the last time she'd had one. Cautiously she took Marianne's cold hand and they walked home, hand in hand, as though Elin were a tiny child.

Now

⇒ ◈ ⇐

> Have you got time to eat beforehand? At that little Italian
> place, the one you like?

Elin sneaks a look at the message that makes the screen light up. Before-hand? Before what? She can't remember what Sam means, what they're supposed to be doing. Joe nudges her discreetly in the side and she jumps and raises the camera again. Before her is a still-life arrangement of white porcelain tableware, and beside it, the designer sits dressed in black, with her arms crossed. Her hair is cropped into a bob that slants forward slightly, her forehead covered with short bangs, sharp and straight as though cut with a knife.

Elin takes a few pictures, calling out instructions. The woman shifts position, the stylist adjusts the porcelain by a few barely discernible mil-limeters. The only thing Elin can think about is what it is she's forgot-ten. Her phone lies beside her computer on the table next to her, but the screen stays dark.

"That's a wrap," she says, although she doesn't know whether the photo has really come out well. The woman slides down from the table carefully as the other people in the room begin to disperse. Elin excuses herself, takes her telephone, and goes to the bathroom. Once there she reads the message from Sam again and glances at the clock: almost one. She phones him. It rings at the other end but no one answers. She tries again, but a text message interrupts the call.

I'm already in the waiting room, hurry up.

Suddenly she realizes what it is she's forgotten. She throws open the door and almost collides with Joe, waiting outside.

"What's going on with you? The client's asking questions," he whispers.

Elin takes a deep breath.

"Can you take them out for lunch? An hour would be good, entertain them a bit?"

Joe shakes his head uncomprehendingly.

"Lunch? But there's food here, we don't have time to break for lunch, there's loads left to do. Didn't you see the crates that arrived? It all needs to be shot."

"I forgot a doctor's appointment. I have to dash off for a while now. I have to."

Joe tilts his head and looks concerned.

"Nothing serious, I hope?"

Elin shakes her head emphatically, locking eyes with him.

"Tell you what. I'm going to sneak off for a while, you're going to sort it out. OK?"

He doesn't have time to answer before she's disappeared around the corner and out the door. Taking the steps two at a time, she continues into the street. When she gets to the therapist's office a few buildings down, the waiting room is empty. It's past one. She walks over to the consulting room door and opens it carefully. Sam is sitting on the sofa, the therapist on a chair opposite.

"Elin. How nice that you could make it," the therapist says in an exaggeratedly calm voice.

Elin is out of breath, her heart racing after the speed-walk, and her brow is covered with sweat. She nods to him.

"Let's do this," she says, with determination and a big smile. She sits down close to Sam, places her hand on his thigh.

"See? This is the reason she's so hard to live with. She's married to her job as well. I promise you, she has a whole team standing around waiting for her in the studio right now."

"Is that the case?" The therapist turns to Elin, taking the pen from behind his ear and writing a few words in a notebook.

"I thought we were here to talk about me and Sam, not about my job?"

Sam gives a strained laugh. He turns to her and strokes her cheek gently.

"How many people are waiting for you? Five? Ten?" he asks.

Elin takes a deep breath.

"More like ten," she whispers.

"See? She won't listen to anything you or I say." Sam sighs.

"She's not there now, she's here," the therapist says in a level tone.

Elin's gaze falters. In her pocket her phone is vibrating with messages, probably from Joe.

"Can we get to the point now? Start talking. Yes, we both work hard, but that's not what we're here to discuss, is it? What are we actually going to talk about?" Frowning, Elin turns to face Sam.

He tenses his jaw and his eyes darken.

"She's not really *here* at all, do you see? We may as well cancel. Go back to the studio, Elin. I can have a solo session this time."

Elin stands up as though the sofa is suddenly burning her.

"Are you sure?" she says, her face lighting up with a smile.

Sam stands up too.

"I'm sure. Go on," he says.

Elin forces herself to hug him. He's stiff, but she lingers a moment in his embrace, meeting the therapist's gaze over his shoulder.

"This is why I love him so much. He always understands," she says.

Then she lets go and runs out the door without looking back.

Then

═◈═

The steps up to the hayloft were dizzyingly steep and had no rail. Fredrik went first, then Elin, both concentrating hard to keep their balance. There was a strong smell of grass up there, so strong it tickled their noses. The loft was full of freshly cut hay, bound in rectangular bales and stacked in uneven heaps. It would be enough for the sheep for the whole winter. The animals were out in the pasture now, but as the chill came creeping in, they'd move into the barn again and fill the farmyard with sound and scent. Fredrik carried on, high up on the stacked bales. Elin lay down on her back, with her hands underneath her head, and watched him climb.

"If you fall now, you'll crush me. Come down!" she scolded, but he went on jumping from stack to stack, making them wobble alarmingly. Elin fiddled with pieces of hay, pulling one out and popping it in her mouth.

Muted squeaks caught her attention.

"Ugh, can you hear that, there are rats here. Let's go down to the beach instead." A shudder passed through her.

Fredrik stopped and sat down, listening as his legs dangled over the edge of a hay bale.

"That sound isn't rats, it's something else. Have a look around, you'll see."

Elin stood up and looked, checking every crevice between bales of hay. In the end she realized where the sound was coming from. It was Crumble, Elin's beloved cat, and she wasn't alone. Elin knelt down.

"Five tiny ones, oh, hurry, come and look!"

"I told you it was something else," Fredrik said smugly.

"But they look like rats."

Fredrik came up behind her and peered behind the bale where Crumble had made a nest for herself and her kittens. Two brown ones, a ginger, and two tabbies. He laughed.

"Yeah, they're not exactly cute. What do you think they should be called?"

"Vega, Sirius, Venus . . ."

"In that case, this one has to be called Sol." Fredrik picked up the red one carefully. It was so little, it fit in the palm of his hand. It mewed faintly.

"Put her back, she needs her mom." Elin reached for the kitten but Fredrik pulled his hand away.

"How do you know it's a she?"

"He, then. I don't know. It. It needs its mom. Put it down now."

Fredrik did as she said, placing the cat down carefully in the same spot.

"One more to name, the darkest one. We can call it Pluto," he announced.

"Vega, Sirius, Venus, Sol, Pluto," Elin recited as she pointed at the little bundles.

They lay on their stomachs, watching the little kittens crawl around for a long time. Crumble lay on her side and let the kittens feed from her. Fredrik rolled onto his back. They heard the rain pattering on the metal roof of the barn.

"I think they're going to get divorced," he said softly.

"Who?"

"Mom and Dad, of course. Who do you think?"

"Why do you think that?" Elin picked up one of the kittens and held it close to his cheek. "Feel how silky it is."

"They argue all the time. About money." Fredrik batted away the hand holding the kitten and sat up.

"Ah, them too? I thought you were rolling in it, so they can't have much to argue about, can they?"

Fredrik snorted weakly.

"Ah, I don't know. It just feels that way. I hear them at night."

"Do they fight?"

"What?"

"Do they hit each other?"

"Fight? No, of course not. They just argue loudly, shouting. They're angry all the time. Dad's angry." Fredrik sighed, wrapped his arms around his legs, and leaned his forehead against his knees.

"I saw him the other day, with . . ."

Elin fell silent mid-sentence. She reached out and stroked a kitten's back tenderly. It was so soft, like velvet beneath her index finger.

"Who? Dad?"

"Oh, it was nothing."

"Come on. What's he done?" Fredrik reached up and put his hands behind his head.

"Nothing, I said it was nothing." Elin lay beside him. They remained there quietly for a while, staring up at the roof.

"It's cozy up here. We should move here in the summer. Escape all the other stuff." Fredrik lifted his head and looked out across the loft.

"Mmm, Crumble's chosen a good spot."

"Are you going to keep them?" he asked.

"Yeah, of course. They're really sweet. Crumble needs a bit of company, she's always so lonely. But don't tell anyone they're here, don't tell Mama."

"Why not?"

"She might decide to sell them."

"No one buys kittens, they're running around everywhere," Fredrik scoffed.

"She might give them away, then. Is that what you want?"

"No, OK, we won't say anything. I know, they can be ours," Fredrik said, and his face lit up in a smile.

"Our cat babies. Then we'll be a real family, you and me and all the cat babies." Elin giggled, scaring Crumble and making her jump.

She put her hand to her mouth and stifled the rest of the laugh as Fredrik grabbed a handful of hay and threw it at her.

"You're such a weirdo. You dingbat."

"Why did you call me that? What is a dingbat, anyway?"

"Someone like you. Cute but weird."

◆

Marianne was sitting on a chair in the hallway when Elin came back into the house. Darkness was falling and it was murky downstairs, but she hadn't put any lights on. She had one hand on the telephone, a heavy old thing that lived on the telephone table, as though she was waiting for someone to call. The phone was bright green, with a curly black wire and a silver dial. When Elin came in, Marianne got up and went into the kitchen. She took some potatoes out of the bucket in the larder, black, earthy ones, straight from the potato fields. Holding a handful under the tap, she scrubbed them carefully with a coarse brush until Elin came up alongside her and took the brush from her.

"Let me help you."

Marianne nodded and dropped the clean potatoes into the pan. She put plates out on the table and with them, tall wineglasses.

"Scrub lots, it's just potatoes and sauce today."

Elin smiled.

"Why are you putting out wineglasses, then?"

"It's more fun that way, drinking tap water. We can toast and pretend it's champagne and fizzy pop."

"It's fine, Mama. It's no problem."

Marianne sat down in her favorite chair and lit a cigarette.

"I should stop smoking," she muttered. "It costs too much."

Elin didn't answer, just nodded as she went on scrubbing. She knew what cigarettes cost.

When the telephone rang, Marianne ran back over to it. She was whispering but Elin heard every word she said.

"I miss you so much."

"Can we meet soon?"

Silence. Happiness in the form of little suppressed giggles.

"Come as soon as you can. The kids will be in bed soon."

◆

There were many toasts around the table. Edvin stood on the bench and gave a speech, pretending he was king of Gotland and the others were his guests. He laughed and lost track of what he was saying, had to start again. His cheeks flushed in embarrassment as he cleared his throat and continued.

"I hereby declare this dinner open. Everyone may eat, as long as you eat nicely. Close your mouth and use your knife and fork."

Marianne nodded in agreement and applauded loudly. Erik joined her. Elin sighed.

"Give up. We'll never get to eat with the king," she muttered sourly.

"Give up yourself, don't spoil it when we're having fun for once," Marianne whispered, and pinched Elin hard in the side. The pain stayed long after she'd let go.

◆

Elin was awake when he arrived. She heard the front door open and close, heard whispers and the smack of a kiss. Creeping out of bed, she peered through a crack in the door and watched as they headed toward Marianne's bedroom as though they were one person, tightly entwined, Marianne walking backward with her mouth on his. Elin crept over to the stairs and stood there a long while, looking down in fascination at their feet kicking about, sticking out from under the covers. In the end the groaning got too loud, and she tiptoed back to the bed and clasped her hands hard over her ears. She held her teddy bear close, the pale yellow one she'd had since she was born, hugging it tightly, but she couldn't sleep and couldn't make the sounds disappear. Her eyes stared emptily at the door. In their bunk beds in the next room, Erik and Edvin were sleeping soundly. Erik was snoring, she could hear it through the thin wall, so she tried to concentrate on that sound instead, tried to make it take over. But she couldn't. The noises from Marianne's bedroom were too intense. She heard her mother's cries: short, high shrieks that carried through the house. Was he hurting her? Should Elin run downstairs?

She took a deep breath, her eyes fixed on the door and her ears on the sounds beyond it, sounds that only seemed to grow louder. She picked up her pad and pencil from the bedside table and spelled out two words in big capital letters:

BED SHREEKS

Then she tore the top sheet off the pad and folded it up, bending down and reaching her hand under the bed. There were rows of containers: glass jars and tins in different colors and shapes. She collected them, then filled them with things she found and made. One of the jars contained pieces of paper with sounds she didn't like, and she lifted it onto the bed, unscrewing the gold lid. There were already a lot of notes inside, carefully written out. There were things like *DENTIST DRILL, ANGRY FOOTSTEPS, SKWEEKING FAN BELT, ANGRY SHREEKS, SMASHED GLASS, CLOKKS TIKKING.* She added *BED SHREEKS* to keep the other noises company and then screwed the lid shut again. She shook the jar up and down, wishing she could put a stop to the sounds forever. One day she'd set fire to the notes, let all those disgusting noises burn. But not yet; she wanted to save them a little longer.

She tiptoed down the stairs, crept carefully past the kitchen, with the jar under her arm. The noises from Marianne's bedroom had stopped, and Elin could hear her talking with the man who was in there. The man whose voice she recognized so well, the one who really shouldn't be there.

In the hall, the jackets hung in a row on heavy wrought-iron hooks. She took Marianne's thick brown one down and pulled it on over her nightshirt. She wanted to get out into the quiet, out to all the sounds that made her feel safe. The ground was cold, and the gravel scraped the soles of her bare feet as she ran quickly across the yard to the barn.

Above her head swooped the bats that lived under the eaves, on their nocturnal insect hunt. She half-crouched to avoid them.

The building looked like a great dark colossus, deserted and ghostly. She turned the key and went in, shining her flashlight's flicker into all the corners while her heart turned somersaults in her chest, which made the thin fabric of her nightshirt vibrate. In one corner someone had built a wall of old junk, which reeked of damp and mold. As she climbed over it and jumped down on the other side, her nightshirt caught on a nail, and she inched back and freed the fabric. The nail left a ragged round hole.

The floor was covered with a thick layer of hay, dust, and earth, which she brushed away with her hand to expose the rough floor beneath. One of the planks was loose, she knew, and she wiggled several experimentally before finding the right one. She had watched her father open the floor many times before; this was where he kept his bottles, the ones he didn't want to show Mama. She lifted the plank carefully and reached down, feeling the cold, rounded glass surfaces. There were four bottles, each half full of liquid of various colors. She took hold of the jar of notes and added it to the stash, right at the bottom, screwing it down into the soft damp earth so only the lid and the top part of the jar could be seen. Then she put the plank back and brushed hay and earth over it.

"Stay there and don't ever come out again," she whispered.

Now

⚍ ◆ ⚍

NEW YORK, 2017

Footsteps move back and forth over the floor of the apartment, in an endless pattern. Elin sits before the mirror, carefully dabbing dark-purple shadow onto her eyelids. Her hair is already done, a high, glossy knot high on her head. The steps seem to grow louder. Sam is talking on the phone; she can hear him walking and talking, as he always does when something has happened at work. He sounds agitated, focused. She gets up and goes out to him, wearing only her black tights and bra. She catches his eye and points to the clock on the wall. He's wearing dress pants and a shirt, which has a large damp patch on the back. His forehead is beaded with sweat.

"Go away," he mouths, and carries on discussing figures whose meaning is a mystery to Elin. His voice increases in intensity.

"We have to go soon," she mouths back, irritated, but is met with only a fierce shake of the head and an outstretched palm.

Sam continues his wandering. The heels of his leather shoes strike hard against the wooden floor, sending echoes through the room and making her shudder with discomfort. The footsteps sound angry. She turns up the music in the bedroom and steps carefully into the long green Selman dress delivered to her by courier earlier in the week. The shoulder straps are trimmed with pearls, which feel hard and cold against her skin, and the silk fabric clings to her body, shimmering beautifully. It's low-cut, emphasizing the contours of her breasts. Looking in the mirror, she twists around, studying herself from the front and the back. The color of the dress reminds her of lush grass. The grass she and Fredrik used to run across barefoot in the spring, the grass that smelled so good. She smiles at the memory, and her reflection smiles back.

She lowers the volume of the music on her phone; the voice out in the living room has fallen silent, but the steps have resumed.

"Sam, are you ready? The car will be here in ten minutes," she calls, as she slides her feet into a pair of high-heeled sandals.

"Do I have to come?" Sam peers in through the door. He's taken the sweaty shirt off, his torso bare and tan and his hair damp and ruffled. Elin nods and smiles at him.

"It's important."

"How can a Louis Vuitton exhibition be *important?*"

"That's not the main thing. You know that. Don't start this again, please."

"Start what again?"

Elin stops talking, looks back to her own reflection. Her hair is smoothly coifed, but she suddenly sees it loose and wild. Fluttering in the wind as she runs. She laughs.

"You're right. It's superficial, this stuff, I almost look like I'm in costume. But . . ."

"You have to . . ."

Elin turns and spins in front of him, the delicate silk rustling. She holds out her arms.

"You're going on a date with a lawn. That can't be so bad."

Sam can't help but laugh.

"Sometimes I wonder what on earth we're doing." Elin sighs.

"What do you mean?"

"All this." She gestures to the room.

"What? Is there something wrong with this?" Sam's brow furrows.

"No, I just meant . . . Oh, never mind."

"Come on! Tell me. You never tell me anything these days, you just clam up."

"Don't go on at me. We have to leave now." Elin groans.

Sam sighs and walks over to the wardrobe.

"OK, what do you want me to wear? It's probably best if you decide."

Elin stands in the doorway and watches as Sam rummages irritably in the wardrobe. He holds a suit out in one hand and a shirt in the other. She nods approvingly and holds out a pair of sunglasses with green frames and two thick silver rings.

"Of course, we have to match," he snorts, and puts the frames on the end of his nose.

"Hurry up, please," she says, and looks at their reflection as they stand there, side by side. He in his suit pants and sunglasses, she in all her finery.

◈

They sit in silence in the limousine, at opposite ends of the back seat. Sam sips a glass of wine, his gaze fixed on the street outside. Elin taps at her phone. When the limo stops and they step out, she smiles and smooths her dress. He holds his arm out politely, and they walk slowly up the red carpet. The sharp, white flashes of the camera sting their eyes, but they still turn patiently in various directions and pose for the photographers who shout loudest. Sam puts his arm around Elin, and they put their heads close together, look at each other, and laugh.

"Half an hour, max, then we'll go and eat somewhere nice. There's just a few people I have to say hi to," Elin whispers, as they walk into the gallery and are each given a glass of champagne.

"You always say that."

"You're the businessman; you should know how important it is to have the right network."

Sam smirks.

"Just be honest, you love this stuff. The luxury, the attention."

Elin lets go of his arm without responding and with a smile sets off to greet the people mingling in the hall. Sam trails after her, holding his phone like a defensive weapon.

◈

She eventually finds him out on the street, after wandering around the gallery for a long time. It's been hours since they last saw each other. Sam is pacing back and forth, his phone pressed to his ear, his shirt unbuttoned at the throat. The red carpet is no longer surrounded by photographers, and the floodlights have been dismantled. People are starting to leave the party, and life on the street is returning to normal. Sam's voice is agitated again, stressed. She stops in front of him, her feet hurting after hours in uncomfortable shoes. Sam changes direction without acknowledging her and keeps pacing. In the end she takes hold of his arm and nods toward the street. He shakes his head, holds a hand over the microphone, and whispers:

"Got to go to the office; you'll have to go home on your own."

"Weren't we going to get something to eat? Wasn't that why we were going to leave early?" Elin sighs and turns away from him.

He leans closer and mutters, "Perhaps you haven't noticed, but I've got a crisis to sort out at work. See you in the morning."

"I'm working early," she says, but her voice bounces, unnoticed, off his back as he walks away. He goes on talking heatedly to the person on the other end.

She takes a step out onto the road, waving down a taxi. When the driver asks where she's going, she hesitates.

"I want to go somewhere quiet and dark. I'm so sick of this," she says.

"I can drive you to the park, but it's dark and dangerous at this time of night."

"Where are you from?"

"India. Not so quiet there either. And you?"

She hesitates.

"Orchard Street. It's probably best if you drive me there, drive me home."

He laughs and turns quickly out into the traffic.

"You can crawl in under the bed and put your hands over your ears. Like children do when they're hiding from monsters," he says.

Elin asks him to stop before they're all the way there, at the nearest deli. Inside she orders hot chocolate with whipped cream in a large paper cup with a lid. She takes it with her and walks slowly toward the apartment. It's still warm out, but the breeze gives her bare arms goose bumps. Above the buildings the moon shines big and clear and white, and she stops and tips her head back, glimpsing faint stars in the sky, shining through the pollution and city lights. Her heart races. She starts to run, haltingly on her toes in the high heels, toward her door and the elevator. Some chocolate splashes out from the little hole in the lid and spatters the expensive silk dress. When she gets up into the apartment, she hauls the blankets from the sofa out onto the terrace. She sits on one of the sun loungers, wrapped in warm wool, and studies the few stars that shine brightly enough to be seen, hunting for constellations and murmuring the names aloud to herself. The hot chocolate is sweet and feels oily against her tongue. When it's finished, she fully extends the bed and lies stretched out on her back, eyes on the sky above her.

❖

It's the first rays of the morning sun that wake her, not the alarm on her phone. The light tickles her eyes and she opens them, squinting. It feels too early to wake up, so she closes them again. There's no sea nearby to lull her to sleep, only the noise of traffic. She listens to it while the sun slowly warms the chill from her body, as she tries to find her way back to the sleep she just left. She can't. In the end she gives up and sneaks back into the apartment. Sam's jacket has been thrown across the sofa, and on the table are a half-full wineglass and the crumbs from a sandwich. She creeps past the bedroom, stopping in the doorway, and sees him on the bed, spread right across it. Naked down to his boxers, with his arms and legs flung out to the sides. She smiles. His face looks so peaceful. She resists the temptation to kiss him and instead makes for the shower; then she carefully rubs off yesterday's makeup and replaces it with a new layer.

By eight she's dressed and on her way to the studio. The phone rings before she's made it there. It's Sam.

"Where are you?"

He's shouting, and she moves the phone away from her ear.

"I'm on the way to work. Why are you so angry?" she asks.

"You didn't sleep at home. Where have you been?"

"I fell asleep out on the terrace. Of course I was at home," she replies, just as angrily.

"Do you think I'm an idiot? Where have you been?"

Elin holds the phone a short distance from her ear and can still hear him shouting. He repeats the last sentence several times. When he finally falls silent, she says:

"Calm down! Look in the bathroom, my dress is on the floor. I was home, I got home before you. I just fell asleep outside."

She hears steps, angry steps, as Sam moves around in the apartment. He's silent but doesn't hang up, so she stays on the line, waiting patiently.

"Did you find the dress?" she asks.

He mutters something in response. She hears the street noise increasing as he goes out onto the terrace. The blankets are still on the sun lounger; she knows that.

"Why did you fall asleep out here?" His voice is a little quieter.

"I saw the stars, and the moon was so beautiful. I just wanted to look a little, to rest."

Elin's heart is still beating hard.

"You were looking at the stars? Alone?"

"Yes, I was. I have to hang up now, Sam, I have a shoot. See you this evening, we can talk then."

"Can we? You'll be late, I suppose?"

"I don't know."

"You don't know."

"No." She's whispering now.

"I managed to solve it, by the way. If you're interested." The volume of Sam's voice increases; the irritated tone returns.

"What?"

"Work. It can't have escaped your notice that I was having a crisis yesterday."

"Sorry, of course I noticed. What was going on?"

"Things were going badly with a deal."

"We can talk about it more later; I promise to listen when I have a bit more time. Sorry."

"Sure, that'll be fine."

Elin hears him sighing deeply.

Then

=≡ ◆ ≡=

Erik and Edvin sat on the kitchen bench, banging their spoons hard on the table.

"Food, food, food," they chorused between giggles.

Elin scooped porridge into their bowls, freshly made but thick as cement. The gray clumps clung to the spoon, so she banged it hard against the crackle-glazed china until the porridge fell off, then put the full bowls on the kitchen table. From the cupboard she took a hand-painted porcelain bowl filled with sugar, the one Aina had given to Marianne on her last birthday. Elin was about to sprinkle a little sweetness over the porridge when a dazed Marianne emerged from her bedroom. Elin turned away quickly and pressed the sugar bowl against her stomach, but it was too late. Marianne had already spotted it. She took it sternly out of Elin's hand.

"You'll have to have apples instead; we have to save the sugar on weekdays. You know that, Elin. The apples are sweet, they'll be fine for you."

"Sorry, Mama, it's just so much nicer with sugar," Elin said.

She opened the larder obediently. The apples were on the floor, in a lidded wooden crate. She'd recently picked them with her brothers from the tree outside. She took two and cut them into small pieces, which she shared among the three bowls.

"I made breakfast only for us. I didn't know when you were going to wake up," she said.

"You know I don't like porridge. Coffee's fine."

Marianne filled the percolator with water and coffee grounds and put it on the stove. The room soon filled with a bubbling, hissing sound. The gap in her dressing gown exposed her bare breasts underneath, pale and swollen, the nipples hardened in the cold of the room. She pulled the gown closer, tightening the belt around her waist when she noticed Elin's gaze.

"Can you walk to school today?"

Elin nodded.

"Is the gas all gone?"

"Not all gone, but you know . . . we should save it, so we can drive into Visby someday. You and Fredrik can come along if you want. As a reward, if you walk the boys to school the rest of the week. It's stopped raining today at least." She leaned forward so she could see the dark clouds beyond the kitchen window.

Elin lit up.

"Then maybe we can buy shoes for gym class? For Erik and Edvin at least; I don't mind going barefoot if we don't have the money. But they play so much soccer, and they get hurt."

Marianne ignored her question and started doing the dishes. Their dog, Sunny, wound around her legs and wagged her tail.

"Are you hungry, do you want some food too?"

Elin crouched down and scratched the black-and-white border collie behind the ears. The dog pressed her nose against Elin's cheek and licked her. Elin held Sunny close, scratching her back with her whole hand. The dog stood up with her paws on Elin's legs, as though she wanted a hug. Elin fell backward and lay on the floor for a moment.

"She feels so skinny. Do we have any food for her?" she asked.

Marianne had sat down on her chair with a cigarette in her hand. There was a steaming coffee cup on the table. She pointed at the larder.

"There's a bag in there. I took some from Grandma; they've got so many dogs, they won't notice if some disappears. I got a couple of packets of cigarettes too." She laughed and swigged her coffee.

Elin got up from the floor and took the dog bowl into the larder. She measured out the dry food precisely with a cup measure. When she put the bowl down on the floor, Marianne nodded at a smaller bowl alongside it.

"And that one? Have you seen Crumble lately? She hasn't been eating here," she said.

Elin shook her head. Sunny started eating before she'd even taken her hand from the bowl.

"Do we have some cat food then?" she asked.

"No, I guess we don't; maybe she's been getting by on mice and birds. But I wonder where the little beast has got to. Do you think she's been run over?" Marianne said.

Elin studied her mother's face. Did she catch a little smile, or was she just imagining it? The thought followed her all the way to school and refused to leave her in peace the whole day. Crumble was *her* cat, her very own.

❖

The morning's heavy rain had been replaced by increasingly scattered clouds, with sunbeams peeping through them. Erik, Edvin, and Elin played hide-and-seek on the way home from school. The rules were simple: they could hide only in the direction of home, and they took turns as the seeker. Edvin hooted with laughter when Elin found him high up in a tree. He climbed everything, as high as he could. Elin told him off.

"That's too high, you're going to fall and break your leg one day, I swear."

"Ah, he'll be fine. He's tougher than you think." Erik walked up and stood under the tree, beside Elin.

Edvin screwed up his eyes at them and jumped straight down, with his arms outstretched. Elin screamed, but Edvin landed successfully and grinned at her triumphantly.

"See? He's not just a monkey, he's a bird too." Erik laughed.

Edvin curled up by the tree trunk, put his hands over his eyes, and started to count out loud as Elin and Erik ran quickly ahead.

When they finally turned onto the track to the house, they'd managed to hide eighteen times. Erik always kept count, and Elin teased him, calling him a math genius. They were hot, and their cheeks were rosy from exercise and laughter.

❖

Elin saw the shadow behind the house as soon as they got to the farm. Someone was there, by her hiding place. She felt her pulse race and kept her eyes fixed on the house. The shadow was moving, as though it was digging, or playing with something on the ground. Elin swallowed. Maybe Marianne had found her jars, her hiding place.

Hopefully it was Fredrik, having arrived just before them.

She slowed down and let her brothers go ahead, running fast, swinging their school bags, and shoving each other.

Elin crept along the front of the house and peered around the corner. She screamed at the sight that awaited her. Marianne was holding one of the kittens, Sol, in her hand. It was wet from being plunged into the water barrel; its head hung, lifeless. Marianne threw it aside, onto a heap with two of the others. Then she bent down to a jute sack and took out another, Pluto, and without hesitation forced it down into the water and held it beneath the surface. Elin threw herself at her mother, who fell backward and smacked her head hard against the ground. Groping around in the cold water, Erin caught hold of the kitten's tail. She pulled it out and massaged the little body, but it was already too late: it was dead, its body limp.

Elin turned to Marianne, who had stood back up, and started kicking and hitting her.

"Murderer!" she screamed. "Murderer!"

Marianne grabbed Elin's wrists hard and twisted her onto her back. Elin didn't have a chance. Marianne fixed her eyes on Elin's.

"Now you be quiet. You hear?" she snarled.

"They're my cats, Crumble's mine, the kittens are mine. Murderer!" Elin screamed, writhing to escape Marianne's grip.

"We can't have five more cats. Don't you get that? You stupid little brat!" Marianne let go with one hand and slapped Elin hard. Her ears ringing and her cheek glowing red, Elin saw her chance to escape. Kicking Marianne hard in the shin, she grabbed the jute sack containing the last kitten, ran as fast as she could to the barn, and climbed up into the hayloft. Crumble was already gone; the nest, just a patch of flattened hay, lay abandoned. Elin sat with Venus on her knee and stroked the little kitten's back.

"I'll take care of you. You'll never die," she whispered, with tears streaming down her cheeks.

❖

The sole had come loose from the foot of one of her rubber boots, and every time her foot flexed midstep, water seeped in. That's why Elin always tried to keep that foot flat as she walked when it rained. She limped along with her toes stretched out stiffly. Her sock got soaked through anyway and made the rest of her body cold. She took a shortcut across the fields. *Floff, floff, floff,* the soles went as they stuck fast in the mud and then let go. She put her heel down first, so she wouldn't slip and fall over backward. Far off she could see Gerd and Ove's house. In one of her jacket pockets she had the kitten, which she could feel moving against her leg. Gerd would never drown it, Gerd would take care of it for her. She'd creep in and put it down in a place where they would easily find it.

❖

Elin crept along the building, keeping close to the rough, yellow-painted wooden walls. As she approached the corner of the house, she looked carefully in each direction and then ran as fast as she could to the veranda. She stood on tiptoe and peered in through the window. There was a light on inside, but she could see neither Gerd or Ove.

"What are you doing here?"

Ove's soft voice took her by surprise. He put his hand on her shoulder. She jumped but didn't turn around, just stiffened. Her gaze faltered, but her head was still facing the window.

"You're looking for a snack, I expect. Gerd's inside, run along in."

The kitten writhed in her pocket. Elin held her hand against the fabric and twisted her torso so Ove wouldn't see the movement. The door opened and Gerd came out onto the veranda.

"Just the visit I was hoping for!" she cried happily.

"Why's that?"

"I'm always so pleased when sweet little lassies turn up unannounced. Come in, I'm baking, there'll be warm buns soon."

She held the door open, and Elin pulled her jacket tighter, cupping one hand over the kitten before taking a step up the stairs. She was leaving a trail of mud.

"But those boots are not coming into my house. Sit down and I'll help you."

Gerd took hold of Elin's heel and pulled. The sole flapped open and bared her foot. Her white sports sock was wet and muddy, so Gerd pulled that off too.

"These boots are staying here," said Gerd. "Your mama needs to buy you some new ones."

Elin shook her head fiercely as Gerd held the boot high in the air and swung it, as though she were about to throw it out across the lawn toward the rubbish heap.

"No, they're mine!" she cried.

She jumped down quickly from the chair, grabbing the boot out of Gerd's hand just as she was about to let it go, and ran back down the steps. She shuddered as her bare foot touched the damp ground and hopped a few steps away on the foot that was still wearing a boot.

"My dear child, I won't take your boots if they mean so much. Come back and let's have tea. The buns will be done in a minute."

Elin put her bare foot down on the boot. Her jacket was quivering from the increasingly lively movements of the cat in her pocket. Gerd reached out her hands. When Elin didn't come any closer, she went down to her.

"Sweetheart, I'm not going to take your shoes away. I'm sorry." She put her arms around Elin but then pushed her an arm's length away.

"What's that moving? What have you got in your pocket, child?"

She shoved her hand into Elin's pocket and pulled out the little mottled-brown kitten.

"Christ, where did you find this?"

"Can you take care of her? Please? Her name is Venus," Elin whispered. "Mama's going to kill her otherwise; she's already killed the others."

Gerd held the kitten against her cheek, stroking its soft fur.

"Ove," she called. "Ove, come look, have you ever seen anything so sweet. We've got a new friend."

She winked at Elin and took her hand.

"I've always wanted to have a little cat. Imagine your knowing that, you're a clever one, you are."

Now

≡ ◆ ≡

NEW YORK, 2017

Elin is carrying a large armful of white lilies and a paper bag full of freshly baked croissants. She's on time for once, and breaks into a run as she gets home. The flowers' strong scent tickles her nose.

When the elevator doors open, she's met by Sam. He's wearing jeans and a cap and is on his way somewhere. He's holding his wallet and keys and looks surprised. She holds the flowers out to him.

"Oh, are you home already? And with flowers, were they a prop?"

"No, not at all. I bought them for you on the way home, you love lilies."

"Loved. That was a long time ago now."

Elin smiles and holds them out again.

"Do you remember? In Paris. You bought me lilies and I bought you roses. Though it should have been the other way around. Do you remember how many years it took us to find out who liked which best?" Elin laughs.

Something flickers in Sam's eyes.

"Sure, I remember," he says, nodding. "But I have to go now."

Elin doesn't move.

"Where are you going?"

"There's a match I want to see this evening. A few people from the office are going, so I was thinking of joining them. I'm tired of sitting at home on my own all the time."

Elin holds out the other hand, the one with the bag. The scent of fresh pastries floats up to them.

"I've got croissants. We were going to talk, remember? I was going to listen to you. I promised."

"I thought that was just something you said."

"No! I meant it. Please, can't you stay home, so we can talk?"

"Not tonight. I want to do something besides sitting around waiting for you."

Elin can hear his irritation growing with each word.

"I work too much," Elin says. She's still standing there, blocking the door. "It's true. I miss you."

Sam holds up his hands and grunts at her:

"That's enough, don't get sentimental. Move, I'll miss the match."

He forces his way past and enters the elevator.

"Don't wait up."

Elin kicks her shoes off, drops the bouquet and the bag, and pulls her dress over her head.

"Please wait. I'll come too, I'm just going to change. It'll take a minute, max. I'm fast."

Sam sighs loudly as the elevator doors start to close.

"It's too late, Elin, don't you get it? It's your turn to be home alone," he says. The gap gets smaller and smaller and he finally disappears, leaving Elin standing there in her underwear.

❖

There's so much to lose. Elin wanders from room to room in the silent, empty apartment. All the furniture, all the art. She stops in front of each canvas and studies the decor they chose together so carefully, she and Sam. The drab colors, the abstract patterns. Not one of the paintings depicts something real.

She's always loved art. What were once her own clumsy lines on thin sketch paper have become a world of oils, acrylics, and photography: valuable works by renowned artists.

Valuable works. She shudders at the thought and wanders on. Everything has its place, everything is considered. Objects are carefully arranged on tables and shelves. Figurines, boxes, lamps. Like little still lifes or installations. Forms and colors in harmony.

On one shelf are pictures of Alice dancing. Elin picks up one of the frames, the one with the photo in which she's youngest, just a few years old, and she holds close to her heart the little girl who no longer exists. In front of her, in another picture, a young girl dances with strong, precise movements. A part of her and Sam, and yet so unique. The most beautiful creature she's ever seen. She gets out her phone and sends Alice three red hearts to show she's thinking of her.

Elin inhales and sits down on the sofa, standing the picture of the child she once had on the table in front of her. Alice is so pretty, in a pink tulle skirt and a glittery white top.

Also on the table is a stack of books. One has her name on the spine, in large black letters: Elin Boals. It's a collection of portraits she's done of famous people. Beautiful people. Beautiful pictures. Where success and beauty walk hand in hand, in beautiful surroundings.

Stars.

But even stars can fade.

◈

Her stomach is cramping again. She puts her hand on it and strokes it gently, trying to massage away the pain. Outside the window darkness slowly falls. It's a long time since she's been home while it was light, since she's had time to think her own thoughts.

The surface of the coffee table is so alive; she's never thought about it before. The fibers in the wood, the notches, as though it's been chopped straight out of a thick tree trunk. As though a piece of nature has moved in.

She lies down on the sofa, pulling her knees up toward her aching stomach. When she closes her eyes she sees a whole forest of red-brown trunks and bushy dark-green treetops. Between them, someone is running, a figure that vanishes and reappears. Far away, close. She sees a face looking at her. Eyes serious and accusatory. Like a film playing out behind her eyelids. It's Fredrik. What does he want with her? Why has he turned up again, when he was just a distant memory?

The figure disappears and the trees sway in the wind like fragile blades of grass in a meadow. She follows them in her thoughts, lets them rock her to sleep.

◆

She doesn't wake until Sam returns. The apartment is dark; only the lights from outside are reflected on the walls. He's with a friend. Their loud voices wake her before the elevator doors have even opened. She's still wearing only her bra and panties. The guys sound happy as they walk into the apartment, talking and laughing. The right team must have won. Elin makes herself small, pressing herself against the back of the sofa, but she's in full view as they turn on the light. Sam's friend turns away, embarrassed, and Elin glares at Sam. He throws a blanket over her and laughs, clearly inebriated.

"You're home?" He sounds surprised.

Elin wraps the blanket around herself and quickly pads past them toward the bedroom and the closet. Her dress is still on the hall floor, but she doesn't bother to pick it up. She hears the men laugh again, and the sound of the fridge door, of beer bottles being opened.

◆

When she comes back, fully dressed and with her hair tied up severely, they're sitting out on the terrace. A cool draft finds its way to her through the open doors, and her skin prickles with goose bumps under the long shirtdress. She's on her way out to them, but she stops in the doorway when she catches sight of the fire. The flames reach up high, and glowing orange sparks spread through the air. Catching sight of her, Sam holds aloft a packet of hot dogs.

"Come out! Come and sit down and you can have some food too," Sam calls out happily, patting the chair beside him.

Elin shakes her head and takes a step back.

"No, I'll leave you to it. I've got a few jobs to do, I just realized. I'm going to the studio for a while."

◆

Elin sits with her datebook in front of her and Sam on speakerphone. She looks through week after week, suggests dates farther and farther into the future.

"These next few weeks are busy, it's impossible, I can't find the time. I'm sorry but you're going to have to keep going alone," she says resolutely.

"Alone? What do you mean? We can't stop therapy now we've started. It's important. Important if we're going to have a . . . future together."

Elin hums, distracted. She's closed the datebook now, and there's a picture on the screen in front of her; it's from the garden they were working in, the blue door glowing in the middle of it. She drags the slider, making the colors even sharper.

"Hello?"

Sam's shout startles her.

"Yeah, sorry. No, I can't. Why do we have to make everything more stressful by talking about it now?"

"Are you even listening?"

"Yeah, I think so."

"You *think* so?" Sam bellows this so loudly that she turns off the speakerphone function. She sees Joe squirming at his desk across the room, even though he's wearing headphones. She holds the telephone to her ear and gets up.

"You're creating problems that don't exist," she whispers. "If you need therapy you'll have to go alone, it's for the best."

"Oh, that's what you think, is it? I'm better off alone. Good, now I know how you see the situation. Now I know."

A silence, much too long.

"Hello?" Elin says at last, but gets no response.

Sam has hung up. She stands for a moment with her phone against her ear, as though she's expecting to hear his voice again. Then she goes back to the desk and the image of the door that fills her screen.

It's so similar, she's astonished by the details, by the memories they awaken. The flaking paint, the streaks of black between the brush-strokes, the key. It's Joe's voice that rouses her from her thoughts. He's standing at her side, nodding toward the staircase.

"Come on, let's go, didn't you hear them arrive?"

Elin looks up in a daze.

"Arrive? Who?"

"Oh come on, now you're scaring me."

Elin turns her head discreetly and peers over the railing, down onto the studio floor. When she sees, and recognizes, the actress who's standing there, head to toe in black, with dark sunglasses, she gets up so suddenly, her chair flies backward.

Then

=⬦=

They walked side by side along the main road, in the middle of the asphalt. It was quiet and deserted. Elin balanced on the center line with her arms outstretched while Fredrik kicked at small stones, pretending they were balls on a soccer field. Now and then he passed to Elin, but she carried on her balancing game and let the stones pass her by. They were silent. They didn't need words.

Suddenly a car came out of nowhere. It was Micke, driving fast, as per usual. When he caught sight of them, he braked hard, sending gravel flying onto the shoulder, and rolled down the window.

"Skipping school?"

Fredrik sighed.

"No. There's no school this afternoon."

"Hurry on home then, there's plenty to do at the farm."

Micke sped off and Fredrik threw a stone after the car, hard, smirking when it hit the back bumper.

"Why did you do that?" Elin grabbed his arm.

"He's an idiot. Everyone knows that."

"But he's your papa!"

"Yeah, so? Your papa's an idiot too, isn't he?" said Fredrik, raising his eyebrows.

"Maybe. But I wouldn't throw stones at him. I'd be glad if he came home again. He has a kind side. Your papa must have one too?"

Fredrik rolled his eyes and walked on a little ahead of her.

"Mama says we're going to move soon," he said. "She can't stand it anymore."

"So they're getting a divorce?"

"I think so. They were arguing last night and I saw some forms on the kitchen table," Fredrik said, stopping again.

Elin put her hand on his shoulder.

"You're not going to move away from here, though? You're going to stay in Heivide?"

"Don't worry. Me and Mama will probably live at Grandma and Granddad's. It's not far."

They went back to walking in silence, Elin balancing along the middle of the road, Fredrik keeping closer to the ditch, where there was a constant supply of new stones at his feet.

◈

When they came to the village, Elin stopped suddenly and dropped her backpack on the ground. She jumped lightly over the fence that surrounded Aina's house and motioned to Fredrik to do the same, but he hesitated.

"What if she knows it was us? The other night?"

Elin shook her head.

"Don't worry, it's only Aina. She'll have forgotten that, she's so old and muddled. I need a new book for school."

He jumped after her and they ran across the lawn. It was brown in patches with old moss. The thistles grew high and thick, like thorny statues. The purple blossoms had shriveled to expose round gray seedpods. Fredrik grabbed some as he ran and let them go, so they flew across the lawn. Elin took the steps in three great strides and knocked on the door.

There was a pause, during which they heard rustling footsteps and someone puffing from the exertion.

"Marianne? Gerd? Is that you?" Aina called from inside.

Elin took hold of the handle and opened the door, and Aina lit up when she saw who was standing outside.

"My goodness, what a rare treat. Here I was thinking it was Gerd with the food I couldn't carry home from the shop," she exclaimed, clapping her hands in delight. "No, a cup of coffee just won't do, not now. I'll have to get out the cordial and cookies."

Elin nodded as she took a step into the hall. The house smelled strongly of ammonia. Aina's housedress was covered in stains and on her chin sprouted a few long gray hairs.

Bookcases, crammed with books, lined the walls in both the hallway and the living room. Elin ran her hand along their spines; she had so many left to read. Aina always let her borrow books, as many as she wanted. And she always gave her cookies.

"Have you got any cookies with nuts?" Elin asked.

"Well yes, I baked fresh ones yesterday. I know they're your favorites. Come in, come in! Then we can play a game of Threes later, can't we? You have time, don't you? Gerd and Marianne are always in such a rush when they come over."

Fredrik and Elin each sat down on a kitchen chair and waited while Aina mixed some elderflower cordial in a china jug with red roses on it and put some cookies on a matching plate. She set it in front of them, and they each grabbed a cookie with eager hands. The chair creaked when Aina sat down with her whole weight. She took a pack of cards from the pocket of her dress and began to shuffle them carefully.

"Mmm, these are the best cookies in the world," Elin mumbled, with her mouth full. She pulled out the nut that had been pressed into the middle and popped it into her pocket. Edvin loved hazelnuts; she'd give it to him when she got home.

Aina dealt the cards onto the table and they each took their pile. The kitchen was silent for some time, apart from the regular ticking of the cuckoo clock on the wall. On the hour and the half hour, the little bird popped out and chirped.

Suddenly Fredrik stood up, looking panicked.

"I have to run home now. I promised Papa. He'll be mad at me."

He ran out the door with his jacket in his hand, one sleeve trailing after him. Elin and Aina stayed where they were. Aina shuffled and dealt, and they played on. The cookies on the plate grew fewer and fewer; the nuts for Edvin, more and more.

Eventually Aina got up and picked up a book from the sideboard.

"I finally found this one, you must read it," she said cheerfully, holding the book out to Elin. "But you have to be careful with it. I was given it by my mom when I was your age."

The book had a worn, yellowing cover, with a title in red capital letters. Above the title was a girl drawn in black and white, apart from her long hair, which glowed red in the same shade as the letters.

"What's it about?"

"A little lass, just like you. You remind me of her a bit, always so inquisitive."

"Inquisitive? What does that mean?"

Aina chuckled.

"It means someone who asks a lot of questions and gets along just fine by themself."

"She doesn't look very nice?" Elin looked at the illustration doubtfully.

"It's probably the illustrator who wasn't nice, because you're going to like the girl, I'm sure of that."

"Can I take it to school as a reading book?

"Yes, as long as you take care of it."

Elin put the book in her jacket pocket, where there was just enough space for it. Aina poured a little milk onto the empty cookie plate and walked laboriously with her to the door, then held the plate out to Elin.

"Could you put this on the steps for me, please? A little something for the littlest ones."

"But they don't exist. Do they?" Elin hesitated at the door.

"The littlest ones? The imps and kelpies? We'd better hope they do."

"Why's that?"

"Well, otherwise, who's been eating the treats I put out? And who's going to take care of me when I die, if they don't exist?"

She winked. Elin, still unsure, stood there with the plate in her hand.

"Do you always put food out for them? And do they always eat it all up?" she asked, bending down to place the plate on the top step.

Aina nodded.

"It might be the cats, have you thought of that?" Elin asked.

"Yes." Aina laughed, making a soft bubbling noise, as though the whole of her huge belly was full of liquid. She clutched her middle.

"Get ye home now, little bug. Your mama will surely be wondering where you've got to. And start reading that tonight, then you'll have something new to think about."

◈

Elin stopped in the kitchen doorway when she saw Marianne stubbing her cigarette out right on the pine tabletop, pushing it hard into the wooden surface until it crumpled and then flicking the butt into the sink. A new mark joined the other black spots on the worn pine. The lights were off, the kitchen full of shadows in the failing light. An almost empty glass with clear liquid in the bottom stood beside Marianne on the table. Elin backed away, in fear of the rage she could sense, and crept toward the stairs instead, up to where her brothers would be, romping about, filling the house with life. But she didn't creep quietly enough.

"Come in. Come and let me look at you," Marianne called, slurring her words. Elin went and stood in the doorway with her head bowed.

"Where've you been?"

"We stopped at Aina's awhile, played cards with her. Gerd says she needs company. She's alone all the time."

Marianne nodded.

"Will the cookies you had there be enough for you?"

Elin nodded.

"Mmm, I think so."

"Good. The boys can have a sandwich each, that'll have to do for today."

Marianne had a shiny red silk blouse on. Her hair was sprayed, and the back-combed bangs swept like a bridge over the top of her forehead.

"You look really nice," said Elin. "Why've you got makeup on?"

Marianne swept her hand over the table, over all the marks that formed a map of their life together: the anger behind every single burn mark, the joy behind every splash of paint, the scratches, the stain from hot coffee. The split from the knife that was suddenly there one day, plunged deep into the center of the table.

In the hall the mousetrap snapped shut over yet another wood mouse seeking shelter from the wet weather; Elin jumped when she heard the spring flip. There was no squeak to be heard this time. Sometimes they squeaked, poor little things.

"Well, that's that. One less for Crumble," Marianne said coldly, rising from her chair.

"Are you expecting someone?"

"Who would I be expecting?"

"Micke, maybe. What are you doing with him? He's Fredrik's papa."

"Don't stick your nose into things you don't understand."

"Fredrik says they're getting a divorce. His mama can't take it anymore."

"Does he, indeed?"

"Is it your fault?"

Marianne shrugged, took a step toward the larder, then stumbled and stopped. Her upper body swayed slowly, back and forth. She made a new attempt to get to the larder, taking two small steps and launching herself at the door handle. She tore at the things on the shelves, pulled out the round pack of crispbread, and broke off two large pieces. Crumbs fell to the floor and Sunny rushed to lick them up. When Elin turned on the overhead light, the harsh fluorescence showed that Marianne's eyes were brimming with tears, her eyelashes clogged with black mascara that was running down and giving her panda eyes. Marianne quickly turned her face away and wiped them with her index finger. Elin came to stand close to her, so close she was nudging against her leg. They stood quietly side by side while Marianne scraped the butter knife against the hard pieces of crispbread. She dug into the depressions to get the butter out, spreading it as thinly as possible.

"We'll be fine on our own, Mama," Elin whispered.

The butter knife's movements stopped.

"I'll have to get a job soon," said Marianne. "Anything will do."

Elin took the knife out of her hand and went on spreading. Marianne opened the fridge and took out the cheese. Edvin and Erik came and wriggled close to Marianne's and Elin's legs, filling the kitchen with questions, but Marianne didn't answer any of them and Elin pushed the boys out of the way, so they fought each other instead. Soon there were tears and screams. At last Marianne set the plates with the finished sandwiches down on the table, hard, and the slam silenced the children.

Marianne left the room without a word, shuffling unsteadily. Elin saw her let the beautiful silk blouse fall to the hall floor.

That was the last they saw of her that evening. Elin tucked Erik and Edvin into the same bed, then took the book she'd gotten from Aina and curled up under the covers. With the help of the thin beam of a flashlight she started her journey into the world of Green Gables.

◆

"Gerd! Gerd!" Fredrik shouted.

Elin ran behind him, trying to keep up, but he was faster. Gerd came out through the glass door, shielding her eyes with her hand to see who was making such a racket. When she caught sight of them, she walked down the steps and ran to meet them. Fredrik shouted her name again and again.

"My dear children, what's all this noise?" She held out her arms and caught them both, held them tight. Elin sniffed and burrowed her head into Gerd's warm body.

"Aina, she . . ."

"We went in . . ."

"She didn't open . . ."

"She's just lying there . . ."

"Not moving . . ."

They fell silent. Tears were running down Elin's cheeks and Fredrik was breathing hard. He pulled at Gerd's arm to get her to come and she started running too, stumbling along. Elin and Fredrik ran past her, jumped nimbly over the fence, and waited on the other side. When Gerd got there they took her hand and helped her over. Her breathing was ragged.

"It's quicker this way."

"Yeah, I guess you're the ones running all over the place the whole time. Today we're lucky you do," she said, as she struggled to get the other leg over. Elin grabbed her hand and didn't let go of it as they pushed through the high brown grass.

"She's on the kitchen floor." Fredrik stopped and sank down on the steps, burying his face in his knees. "I don't want to see her again."

Elin and Gerd went in without him, and Elin covered her eyes as Gerd leaned forward over the body. Her scream cut through the silence.

"She's dead!"

Then came the tears. Gerd was crying and wailing. Her throat clenched, she coughed and sobbed and gasped for breath. Reaching for the telephone on the hall table, Elin put her finger in the number-nine hole, pulling the dial back again to make it turn faster. Then the zeros, four zeros. And then the voice on the other end.

"Which service do you require?"

Elin had no words. Gerd rapidly backed away from Aina without taking her eyes off the body, took the receiver from Elin, and cleared her throat loudly. The voice on the other end became impatient.

"Hello, which service do you require?"

"I think she's dead, you probably don't need to rush."

Gerd gave the address and then let the receiver fall back into the cradle. Elin crept into her arms, and they stood and listened as the sirens from the main road came closer.

◈

More neighbors turned up when they saw the police car and ambulance. They came from every direction and stood quietly, watching the stretcher as it was rolled out. The round body swelled out over the sides. A blanket covered the head, but the bare feet sticking out were blue and swollen with thick, overgrown yellow toenails crusted with dirt.

Marianne had come too. She hugged Fredrik and Elin tightly and kissed their heads.

"She baked the best cookies in the world," Elin mumbled.

"Which ones did you like best? When I was little I used to ask for the vanilla dreams."

"Did you go there too?" Elin looked up at Marianne in surprise.

"Yeah, I went there when I was little, I remember we used to play Threes. And long before that, Gerd used to go there, when she was little. We've all eaten cookies at Aina's. Aina was our very own Cookie Monster."

Elin smiled through her tears.

"She was so cold. And now she's blue too, just like the Cookie Monster." Her voice cracked.

Marianne pulled her closer.

"That's what happens after you die, you know. The body cools down when the soul flies away. Aina's already somewhere else, it's just the husk that's left."

"She must have forgotten to put the plate out. That's probably why."

"What do you mean?"

"The plate for the littlest ones," said Elin. "Maybe they got angry with her."

"She probably died yesterday. The imps and kelpies will take care of her now. They'll be singing for her, beautiful songs that only the dead can hear. She's always taken care of them, so now it's her turn to be looked after."

"Promise?"

"I promise."

"She's never coming back?"

"No, she's gone forever."

Elin put her hand in her pocket and touched the book that was inside. The one she'd read all the way through under the covers by flashlight. The one she'd wanted so much to thank Aina for.

Now

≡ ◆ ≡

NEW YORK, 2017

There are bags in the hall. Not one, several. A box too. And the owl, the white one. The statue they bought together, long ago when they were traveling in Asia. Elin tiptoes carefully between the objects. The lights are off and she doesn't turn them on; the light from outside finds its way in through the big windows and illuminates the walls in broad strips. She jumps at the voice from the darkness.

"Where have you been?"

Sam's dark figure is suddenly visible, sitting in the armchair. Straight-backed, thin-lipped. She sinks down onto the sofa, smiles at him. She wants to kiss him, but he looks so serious.

"You're awake? It went on longer than planned, as per usual. Everyone always wants everything from me. It takes time, it took time today too. But it turned out well, want to see?"

Sam shakes his head.

"Don't you get it?"

Elin reaches out, tries to hug him, but he pushes her arms away.

"This isn't working anymore. I can't take it anymore," he says.

She shakes her head, baffled.

"What can't you take? I don't understand."

He says nothing, and they sit quietly for a while. The sound of sirens can be heard from the street. In the end, Sam holds out a key on a key ring swinging back and forth from his index finger.

"What are you doing? What's that?" Elin asks, smiling uncertainly.

"I've rented an apartment. I'm thinking of living there for a while."

Elin's smile falls. "Where? Why? What are you doing?" Her breath is coming in rasps and her chest feels heavier and heavier. Soon it feels almost like she's buried under lead, suffocating.

"We can't live like this anymore. Since Alice moved out everything feels lifeless, like the apartment is a ghost town. You're never here. Like you said yesterday, I'm probably better off alone."

"That's not what I said. I didn't say that, I didn't mean that."

Elin feels lost. She moves closer to Sam, curling up next to him on the sofa.

"I've had a lot on recently, that's all, big jobs. It will get better. I'm here now."

Sam shakes his head.

"It won't get better. It's never going to get better."

He pulls the key off his finger and closes his hand around it.

"Please," Elin begs him. She starts to rock back and forth, her arms folded tight across her chest.

"Now you don't have Alice to live for, you live for your work," he says. "You're never here with me, and when you are here, you're not *present*. And lately it's been feeling like you're hiding something, like you're a stranger."

"Why do you say that?"

"Because that's how it is. Eighteen years, Elin, eighteen years and I know nothing about you."

"What do you mean? You know everything."

"I know nothing. You're always smiling, but you're never happy. It's impossible to understand you. You never listen to me. You never ask me anything, never tell me anything. I've never even seen a picture of you as a child."

"They disappeared in Paris, you know that. Don't go. I can tell you more. What do you want to know?"

"It's too late."

"Don't go." Elin reaches out her hand, but he doesn't take it, just shakes his head.

"Sometimes I wonder if you even know who you are," he says.

"Don't say that. Why would you say that?"

"You orchestrate. Everything. Everything has to be perfect. You create fictions every day, every second. Not reality. It's as though all this is a backdrop in one of your shoots, as though we, me and Alice, are just props in something you're trying to create."

Sam stands up, straightening his pants, which have become hitched and wrinkled by however many hours he's spent in the chair.

"Are you leaving me?" she asks. She sinks down onto the floor in front of him, sobbing. Her breath still feels constricted, she can hardly draw air into her lungs. She puts her hands on his feet but he pulls them away, shiny brown leather slipping from under her hands.

"I've hardly ever heard you say you love me," he replies.

"I do."

"Say it then."

"I do. I promise. Don't go."

He turns his back on her and she hears him push the button to call the elevator, hears him load bag after bag onto it. He stands for a moment in the doorway, the owl underneath his arm, as though he's waiting for her. But she can't look at him any longer, so she looks outside instead. Out at the buildings, the roofs, the water tanks. Out at all the windows behind which other families are loving and fighting.

There's a scraping sound as the doors close. She hears the sound of the elevator fade and disappear. Then silence again. Silence and darkness.

Elin cries out and runs over to the elevator, where something's lying on the floor. It's a black notebook. Elin picks it up and opens it. No words, no sketches. Just smooth, untouched white paper. She calls the elevator back and goes down, but the street is already empty. He's climbed into a car, vanished. Where to? She doesn't know, she didn't ask. She calls him. The phone rings but no one answers. She tries again, and again. At last she hears his voice.

"Yes."

"You forgot something, a book. You have to come back," she says firmly.

"No. It's for you. I left it."

"Why?" she whispers.

"Don't you get it? It's empty, just like you. I think you need to listen to yourself."

The hardness in his voice wounds her, and she forces herself to swallow the lump that's formed in her throat. She can't find anything else to say, there's nothing there. They hang up. She's holding the book tightly, pressed to her chest. Everything begins to spin around her, and she sways and grabs hold of a newspaper stand to steady herself.

❖

The notebook is beside her on the bed, on Sam's side. She can't sleep. In the end she gets up, opens it, and glues the printed image of the blue door onto the middle of the first page. Now there's something in it, a part of her, a start. She puts the book under a pillow. The bed is empty, but it still smells of Sam. She flips the duvet so his side covers her, takes his pillow, and hugs it tight. It's four in the morning; in four hours she's due at the studio again. She doesn't want to go, can't stomach it. She closes her eyes and tries to press back the tears, but she can't stop them any more than she can stop her thoughts.

She gets out the book again and reaches for a pen, trying to think of something other than Sam. Single words come to her. She writes them down, in beautifully formed cursive script.

Barefoot. Gravel. Deluge. Horizon.

Then she puts the book down, closes her eyes, and waits for peace. Breathing deeply, she feels Sam's presence in the scents surrounding her.

Some time passes, but her thoughts won't go away and neither will the tears. She writes more words.

Star. Night. Stunted pine. Water fight. She smiles through the tears, at the memory of hands scooping up cascades of water. At the memory of friendship and love in a past life, when Fredrik was always at her side, there for her when no one else was.

The clock strikes five. Only three hours left. She closes her eyes, thinks of the sea. Sees the tops of the waves foaming as they crash in toward land. Feels the sensation of standing in them and being caught off balance by their power. She counts the waves. One, two, three, four. The roar of the street becomes ocean sounds in her ears. She sinks slowly into an unsettled torpor. She kicks her legs, twists, and turns.

❖

The wardrobe gapes empty on Sam's side. All his suits are gone, all his shirts. Only a few T-shirts remain: one red, a few black. She turns her face away. Her own dresses hang in perfect color order. Black, navy, light blue, gray, red. No other colors, just the ones she likes best. She reaches for a black dress but changes her mind and puts it back. Swaps it for a gray A-line she bought in Paris the last time they were there. Not that one either. She drops it on the floor, the hanger bouncing and landing a little way off.

Eighteen years. Alice was born right away, she's always been with them. Those years in Paris, when they were first in love, it's those years that have kept them going. She remembers it so clearly, the laughter of those first months, the late nights, all the parties they were invited to, with beautiful, successful people. The relief of no longer being alone and lost. And then the nausea and the joy over what their love had given them. From the first moment, she was determined to be the perfect wife, the perfect mother.

It's always been the three of them. Elin, Sam, and Alice. Not anymore. Now she's the only one left. Maybe Sam is right, maybe she's been so obsessed with being perfect, she's lost the ability to be real.

She runs her hand along the dresses, feeling silk, velvet, wool, and cotton under her fingertips. None of them are free from memories, each has been worn with the man she's now missing. In the end she closes her eyes and picks one. It's black silk, smooth and glossy. She pulls it over her head, ties the belt hard around her waist, and stretches. She has an important job ahead of her. A cover. It can't go wrong. In front of the bathroom mirror she pats her cheeks hard, trying to massage some life into her sallow skin. Her eyes won't wake up. The lids are thick and swollen. She smiles, tentatively at first, then wider and wider. Her eyes become slits. She does some yoga breathing. In through the nose, out through the mouth.

◆

At ten to eight she is hurrying toward the studio. On the way she stops at a deli, suddenly thirsty. A concrete ramp leads up to a glass door, its handle rectangular and shiny. She lays her hand on it and pulls, but the wind is pushing it shut and it won't budge. She lets go again and takes a step back.

◆

"One, two, three, four, five," she murmurs, remembering the steps leading up to another door. She takes a firmer grip and pulls. The wind reminds her of the storms, of the sea and the scent of sand and seaweed. She stands, eyes closed, in front of a fridge full of drinks. She breathes in the scent of fresh bread, sensing notes of plastic, printing ink, and freshly opened packaging. Of perfume.

Her telephone rings in her pocket. It's Joe, sounding tetchy.

"Where are you? Everyone's here. We're waiting."

"I'll be there in a minute. Start setting the lights up."

"Everything's ready. We were here at seven, like you said. Do you remember?"

"Seven. Yes, of course." She reaches for a Sprite, twists off the cap, with the telephone pressed between her shoulder and her ear, and takes a large gulp.

"Is everyone in a good mood?"

"Middling, to be honest. You should probably hurry," Joe whispers.

◆

Elin downs the whole bottle. It tastes too sour to be sugar soda, but it's close enough to make her remember the drink she used to love. Before she leaves she takes a photo of the glass door.

Then

≡ ◆ ≡

Elin jumped when the glass door opened with a jingling sound. A few metal bells were suspended by a string from the hinge mechanism so that Gerd, wherever she was in the shop, would hear when someone came in. This time it was Marianne, looking tired. She went straight to the register where Gerd and Elin sat, unpacking bags of candy.

"Give me a Bellman scratch ticket and a pack of smokes."

Marianne nodded tersely at the register. Elin held her breath. Gerd didn't move.

"Wouldn't it be better to put that money toward food? The mild cheese is marked down," Gerd said finally.

"Wouldn't it be better if you minded your own business?" Marianne snapped back.

Elin took a few steps back and eyed the newspaper rack. She squatted down and flicked through a Donald Duck comic. She would read there, sitting on the cold floor of the shop, and Gerd never told her to stop. She knew how much Elin loved to read and look at the pictures. And how much she missed books, now that Aina was gone and the door to her literary treasure trove was closed.

"You never win anything. It's just a dream, a castle in the clouds. All you ever win is pin money," said Gerd, choosing to ignore Marianne's threatening tone.

"Pin money for you, perhaps. For us every krona would work won-

ders. We need a little luck. Give me a scratch ticket, I can decide for myself what I buy."

The register slid open and Gerd lifted the note drawer, rummaging
through the tickets. Marianne turned to Elin.

"Come on, you can choose," she called.

Elin got up, stretched out her hand tentatively, felt among the scratch
tickets, then chose one. The scratch-off section was a novelty she'd seen
only at a distance. Marianne gave her a coin.

"You rub it off, my lucky little lass."

Elin carefully scraped away the foil covering, every trace. They hadn't
won. Gerd nodded sadly.

"Don't say a thing," Marianne hissed.

"There's a lottery draw too, so keep the ticket. On the twenty-fifth."

"Shit."

"Hmm."

"I should have bought milk for the children instead."

Gerd said nothing.

"Next time, I'll do it next time. Next month. It'll be the twenty-fifth
soon. We'll get a little money then."

"You could still win."

Elin continued to hold the comic in her hand.

"You take that home, sweetheart," Gerd whispered, stroking her hair.

Elin looked up at her, wide-eyed.

"They're going to be sent back tomorrow anyway, there's a new issue.
They'll get one too few, and we'll cross our fingers no one notices."

Elin grinned and clutched the comic to her chest. Marianne shook
her head.

"You spoil those kids, Gerd."

"Yeah, yeah. Kids should be spoiled whenever possible. It makes the
world a better place, I always say," Gerd announced happily.

"Really? Sounds insufferable."

"Not at all. Don't you worry. And a kinder child than Elin would be
hard to find."

Outside a powerful gust of wind made the glass door fly open and slam shut. Elin buttoned her coat as high as she could and pulled the hood up. She leaned all her weight against the door, but the wind resisted. Marianne reached over Elin's head to help.

"Autumn's coming, and the storms. Now we'll have to put up with messy hair for the next six months." Gerd laughed as the wind caught Marianne's hair, obscuring her face. She pushed it away with her hand.

"Messy hair, I have that for at least twelve months of the year." She sighed. "Try having three kids, even for a week, and you'll see."

"Nonsense, with all that time to spare you should be able to comb your hair. Make sure you do a bit of job hunting now. Call around. You'll find something soon," said Gerd.

As she left, Elin let go of the door and let it swing toward Marianne. She held the comic as if it were made of china and smoothed the glossy pages from time to time with her hand. When she got home, she'd read aloud from it so Erik and Edvin could hear.

❖

Erik and Edvin lay on either side of Elin, with their legs hanging off the side of the narrow bed. Elin sat curled up against the wall. In her hand was the copy of *Anne of Green Gables,* and Erik and Edvin were listening attentively as she read aloud from it. This was the fourth time she'd read it, and in some way it made her feel as though Aina were still alive. She couldn't stop; she'd read it again and again, and now her brothers would get to meet that willful Anne too.

"Why did they want a boy? Are boys better than girls?" Erik asked suddenly.

Elin slammed the book shut.

"No, of course they're not. Aren't you listening? But imagination probably is better than reality, I think Anne's right about that."

"But I'm hungry in reality," Edvin moaned. "And you can't imaginate that away."

"It's 'imagine,'" Elin corrected him.

"I'm hungry too," Erik groaned, rubbing his tummy.

Elin went down to the kitchen but stopped in the doorway. Marianne sat motionless on a chair turned toward the window; a tiny gray bird was sitting on a branch outside. The branch swayed as the bird burrowed its little head in under its wing and preened. Suddenly it paused, turned its head, and listened to some far-off sound. One of its eyes shone in the low evening sun. After a moment it flew off from its perch, but Marianne didn't react, just stared emptily ahead.

"What are you doing, Mama? Are you sad?" said Elin, going up behind her and putting a hand on her shoulder.

Marianne sprang to her feet, as though the contact had caused her pain. She turned away from Elin and walked off, head bowed, but Elin beat her to the doorway.

"It's almost evening. Aren't we going to eat? What were you planning?"

Marianne shrugged. Elin opened the fridge and looked at the empty shelves. There was half a parsnip and a few carrots. The bucket of potatoes was in the pantry.

"What do you say to baloney soup?"

She held up a few carrots. Marianne nodded and took them out of her hand.

"Sure, but we don't have baloney. Baloney soup without baloney."

She started peeling the carrots under the running water. Elin fetched some mud-caked potatoes and put them in the sink.

"That's OK, it will be tasty anyway!" Elin smiled and started slicing the carrots thinly.

"We can drink hot chocolate afterward, if we're still hungry." Marianne didn't smile back at her, but Elin laughed.

"Thief chocolate, you mean. How much did you take, anyway?"

"Enough. We're a real bunch of bandits, have you thought about that? Just wait till Erik and Edvin get going."

Elin eyed her in alarm. Marianne suddenly lit up, a grin spreading across her face.

"Mama, that's not funny."

"You're a fine one to talk, stuffing milk cartons down your top. Little burglar."

Elin fell silent. Marianne filled the pot with water and started peeling the potatoes. Elin tipped in her carrot slices.

"At least we don't rob shopkeepers with rifles," she muttered.

Marianne stopped what she was doing.

"So you know now?"

"Everyone knows. Everyone whispers about it. You talk about it too, do you think I don't hear?"

"You're right, it's not funny," said Marianne. "I'm going to get a job, a good job, I promise. As soon as I've got a job, I'll stop stealing. Pinkie promise."

She held out her little finger and Elin hooked her own around it doubtfully.

"Does that mean I can lift as much milk as I like? Until you've found a job?"

Marianne turned off the running water and took Elin's face between her hands. She kissed her forehead.

"No, sweetheart. The two scoundrels we already have in this family are quite enough."

Elin pushed her hands away and went back to slicing the last carrot.

"Does that mean we're still a family?" she said. "You, me, Papa, and the others?"

"I guess we'll always be a family, in one form or another. I'm your mama, he's your papa. That will never change."

"But do you love him?"

Marianne said nothing. She took the parsnip from the counter and peeled it quickly with long, rapid strokes.

"Do you love him?"

Marianne turned to Elin, dropped the parsnip and the peeler in the sink, and gripped the countertop.

"Elin, he robbed a shop with his hunting rifle. Do you understand? He shot the cashier with it. She could have died."

"That hasn't got anything to do with it. Do you love him? Answer me."

"It's got plenty to do with it."

"Answer me!"

"No."

"You used to."

"Maybe. But not now. He's too dangerous, he gets dangerous when he drinks. Do *you* love him?"

"Yes, of course. He's my papa and he's kind when he's not drinking. You know that too. Don't you remember? The cuddles, and when he used to sing for us. We used to laugh so much."

"But I don't want to have him here anymore."

"You'll never get him, you know that, right?"

"Who? Papa? I don't want him."

"You know who I mean. That other guy, Micke. Don't think I don't know. He doesn't give a shit about people like us."

"I don't know what you're talking about."

❖

Elin dropped the carrot, ran out of the kitchen, and left the house. She ran to the chair behind it and sank down beside the four small crosses on the kittens' graves. The rain had stopped falling. She took the paper ball out of her pocket and carefully uncrumpled it, then wrote a few words at the bottom:

> Behave nicely in prison so you can come home soon. Otherwise youll screw it all up. Please come home. We miss you.

Now

≡ ◆ ≡

It doesn't look like a restaurant. A large neon sign on Essex Street leads you into an unpretentious store selling antique jewelry from tatty display cases. Alice is standing by one of them when Elin arrives. She looks up and their eyes meet, for the first time since Sam moved out. Elin's are pleading, Alice's accusing. She turns her back on Elin without a word and moves farther into the store. At the back wall stands a well-built man, wearing a leather jacket and black sunglasses; he looks them up and down. When they get to him he nods discreetly and pulls open the door behind the counter. Beyond him, a whole new world opens up. It's like walking into a country manor, with an elegant staircase leading to the upper floor and the dining room. Alice walks ahead of Elin; the girl's denim skirt is so short and tight, Elin thinks she can see a glimpse of underwear. With it Alice is wearing a baggy red T-shirt with a wide neck, which has fallen askew and bared a shoulder. Her hair is gathered in a messy knot; there's no makeup on her face. Still, she fits in with the surroundings somehow. She glows, she looks youthfully cool.

A waiter shows them to their table. The music's so loud, it's hard to hear what he's saying. Elin pulls her chair closer to Alice, and Alice moves away the same amount.

"Are you enjoying college? How's the dorm?"

Alice sighs.

"I thought we were here to talk about you and Dad?"

"Yeah, maybe, but more than that we're here to celebrate you. I missed that dinner with Grandma and Grandpa, you know."

"I'm guessing that was the last straw for Dad, you missing that dinner. How could you just not bother to turn up?"

Alice holds the menu up, hiding her face; only her hair is visible above it.

"It's not that I didn't bother . . . I . . ."

Alice looks around the side of the menu, eyebrows raised.

"You didn't want to?"

"Alice, I was working." Elin is pleading for understanding, but Alice has already vanished behind the menu again. When the waiter comes she casually orders an appetizer and an entrée. Elin hasn't had a chance to look at the offerings yet.

"I'll take the same, that'll be fine," she says, pushing the menu aside.

"They're plates for sharing. It's better to order four different ones," the waiter says.

"I don't want to share with her," Alice says tightly, slamming the menu shut and handing it to the waiter, who leaves.

"Alice, please, can't you just try? Can't we try to have a nice time?"

Alice shakes her head.

"This dinner isn't going to be nice, however much you try. You and Dad have separated. If there's anything we should be talking about, surely it's that?"

The waiter comes back to the table and pours water into their glasses. The pitcher is made of white porcelain, and a solitary pink rose decorates the crackle-glaze surface. Elin reaches out and touches it, and the waiter puts it down in front of her, looking almost apologetic. Then he disappears again. Elin arranges the pitcher and then gets out her phone to take a photo.

"Are you working now, even while we're eating?" says Alice, watching her.

"I'm not *working*. It's beautiful, it reminds me of something, that's all."

"What?"

"Something. Nothing. Please, tell me how things are going at school. I miss you so much at home, it's so empty."

"It's good. It's hard. We dance. My feet hurt all the time. So, now you tell me. What's with the pitcher?"

"You're stubborn. Just like your dad."

"Aha, is that a problem? Are you going to divorce me too?"

"But I haven't — I don't want to — we're not going to . . . what has Dad said?"

"That you're always working and that he can't bear being home alone."

"Did he really say that?"

"No. But that was what he meant."

The first course arrives, two identical dishes. Elin leaves her plate untouched as Alice scoops the thin slices of tuna sashimi into her mouth, seemingly swallowing them whole. When she's finished, she eyes Elin's plate.

"Aren't you going to eat anything?"

"No, I'm not hungry. Take some of mine too if you want."

Elin pushes the plate toward Alice, who hesitates, but then begins to help herself greedily. Piece after piece disappears. When the plate is almost empty, she looks at Elin.

"I get angry when I'm hungry," she says.

Elin nods.

"Do you get hungry from all the dancing? Is it hard?"

Alice reaches for the last piece of fish.

"Mmm, that was so delicious," she says. "Now let's talk about something else. Tell me about the pitcher. What does it remind you of?"

"Elderflower cordial." Elin smiles.

"Cordial? I've never seen you drink that."

"It was a long time ago. When I was little. Someone used to give it to me."

"Who?"

"I don't remember. But I can remember the pitcher."

"You've never talked about when you were little. Can't you tell me more?"

Elin turns and sweeps her gaze nervously across the other tables.

"Does the music have to be so loud?" She sighs.

"Could you stop complaining? This place is good, I've wanted to come here for ages. And anyway, you can't orchestrate everything so it turns out exactly like you want it to."

Elin's eyes return to Alice.

"You've been talking to Dad."

"I hardly need to talk to Dad to know that. Lose control for once, Mom. Jump in a puddle, dance, play with a dog. I don't think I've ever seen you even interact with an animal. It's weird. *You're* weird. You don't have any interests besides your job. What makes you happy?"

"It was an old lady, a neighbor, who used to give me cordial. And lend me books, OK?" Elin doesn't look at her daughter.

"Good. What else?"

"Nothing else. It was good cordial, and she had it in a lovely pitcher like this one." Elin reaches out and strokes the porcelain surface.

"Where? In Paris? There's something else, I can tell," Alice says.

Elin folds her arms and shudders.

"This is hard for me too, your dad moving out."

Alice looks up and meets her gaze.

"It's your fault, Mom, don't you realize that? To be honest, I can understand him being tired of you always working. I am too."

❖

It's raining when they leave the restaurant. Warm, damp summer rain that falls on their heads and shoulders. They're not talking. Neither seems to have more words to share. They had eaten the rest of the meal in silence, paid, and left. Now they're standing side by side on the sidewalk.

Reflections of the street lamps glitter in the puddles, and everything shimmers. Elin hails a taxi and opens the door for Alice, who climbs in and pulls the door shut without looking at her. Elin stands alone and watches the red taillights disappear into the night, along with the most precious thing she has. Or had. Everything seems to be slipping out of her hands. Everything she fought so hard for.

Then

=⬥=

Elin had been standing behind the lime tree, eavesdropping for a good while, when the little group of people disappeared, one after the other, in through the glass door. Her breathing quickened. She was holding a handwritten list and a fifty-krona note. She stuffed both into her jacket pocket and turned on her heel, then ran as fast as she could along the gravel shoulder of the main road. The gravel slowed her down, so she stepped out onto the road instead. Took long strides on the asphalt, swinging her fists up to her face as though she were running a race. Faster, faster, faster. She crossed toward the hedge without slowing down; she slid through the hole, getting mud on one of her pant legs. She tore the door open and rushed in with her shoes on. Marianne didn't stop her. She was sitting on her chair, cigarette in hand, with her hair rolled in huge curlers. Elin stopped short in front of her, panting. Her hair was disheveled and full of leaves from her slide across the lawn, her pants and shirt muddy. Marianne looked at the ashtray and stubbed out her cigarette, pressing it down so the butt wrinkled into a little lump that disappeared down into the sand, along with her fingertip. Then she looked up.

"The state of you. What have you been doing? Where's the eggs and butter?"

Elin shook her head, couldn't get any words out.

"My God, child, what's happened? Has someone else died?"

"Gerd and Ove, Aina . . . ," she managed at last.

"What about them? Has something happened to them?"

"Money."

"Have you stolen money from Gerd and Ove?" Marianne stared hard at her. Elin shook her head eagerly; she was stammering and could hardly get the words out.

"Money, they've . . ." That was all she could say before there was a knock at the door.

"Take your shoes off and brush off that mud," Marianne muttered. She got up slowly and walked over to the door. A thin shawl was wrapped around her shoulders, and she was hunched as though cold. Elin followed her. As the door opened, she looked into the solemn eyes of someone she'd just seen outside the store.

"Are you Marianne Eriksson?"

Elin saw her mother nod and suspiciously pull the door toward her a little. She touched her hand to her head cautiously and pulled out the curlers.

"Yes, who's asking?"

"May we come in?"

"What is this about?"

"We've got good news, can we do this inside?"

"Of course." Marianne took a few steps back and let them step into the hall. There were three of them. Two men in brown suits and a woman in a full skirt and neat blouse. None of them took their shoes off. The woman had a folder full of papers in her hand, just as she'd had when Elin saw her outside the shop. They sat down at the kitchen table, and Marianne folded her hands over her stomach.

"What do you want? Is it Lasse? What's he done now?"

The three visitors looked surprised.

"Lasse?" said one of the men. "No, we're here to talk about Aina. Aina Englund. Our condolences."

Marianne nodded and took a few steps backward until she was leaning against the kitchen counter. The woman took a piece of paper from the folder and cleared her throat. She read aloud:

Aina Englund, Will
15 August 1979

I can feel the life running out of me. This is my last will and testament. I die alone. Without children or close relatives. I wish for all my possessions to be divided evenly between Gerd Andersson and Marianne Eriksson. The girls who have always been there for me.

Witnessed by
Lars Olsson
Kerstin Alm

The woman looked up again and lowered the paper a little. Marianne laughed out loud.

"Aina! And she wrote this just recently?" she said. "Well then, there can't be much. She was the last one in these parts who still went to the privy to take a shit."

Elin elbowed her, but Marianne shrugged and laughed again.

"What? It's true. And she even ate the rind of the ham, always said the fat was good for the brain."

One of the men cleared his throat loudly and the woman took out another piece of paper.

"Mrs. Englund actually had a fair amount of money. I understand she concealed it well. It was family money, it's tied up in stocks and bonds. She left behind . . ."

The woman paused and pushed her large wine red plastic glasses up the bridge of her nose.

"Almost three million krona." She paused again. "And then there's the house."

Marianne stared at her. The woman passed her the piece of paper.

"But you're not the sole benefactor. Half will go to Gerd Andersson."

Marianne took the sheet and stared in astonishment at the rows of figures. She turned, smiling, and Elin could see the delight in her eyes. They were sparkling.

◆

Erik and Edvin were jumping around upstairs, shouting. They pounded the floor, but Marianne, humming to herself, seemed unconcerned. No one was fighting, no one getting hurt. Their loud laughter and singing poured along the walls and filled the whole house with joy, as though an entire orchestra was tuning its most beautiful notes. Elin sat at the kitchen table. She was holding the lists they'd written earlier that evening, filled with everything they lacked, everything they wanted. *Star Wars* toys, games, bikes, clothes. Not all at once; Elin was careful to point that out to Marianne. But as soon as possible.

"And you, Mama," Elin said. "You haven't written anything, is there anything you'd like?"

Marianne took the pad and the pen and started writing her own list:

> *Canary Islands.*
> *Makeup.*
> *Clothes.*
> *A new pair of shoes.*
> *Two new pairs of shoes.*
> *Three new pairs of shoes.*

She laughed and her eyes glittered.

"We're not dreaming, are we?" Elin watched her mother studying the document the lawyers had left behind.

"No, it doesn't seem that way. It will be more than a million krona after tax. It's unreal. But true."

Elin saw her counting and thinking, her mouth moving and her lips forming silent figures.

"We'll have enough to get by on for a long time, if we live frugally. Even if I don't get a job."

"It's gone very quiet." Elin nodded toward the stairs.

They quietly ascended and peered into Erik and Edvin's room. The boys lay close together in bed, under the flowery cover, flicking through a catalog. Elin crept up behind them, putting her arms around both brothers' shoulders. Erik flicked through the pages while Edvin pointed out items of interest.

"Can we get real fishing rods now, Mama?" Edvin whispered. He still had his lisp, and his hazel eyes looked at her full of expectation. Marianne sat on the edge of the bed, leaned forward, and studied the page he was pointing at.

"I want this one, can I have it?"

She nodded and held him closer. They lay there together, one big heap of family, pointing and wishing and dreaming.

"What do you say to a trip to the Canary Islands over Christmas and New Year?" Marianne asked all of a sudden. "Wouldn't that be fun, a little warmth and sunshine?"

"Flying in an airplane?" Edvin asked.

"Obviously, dummy, how else will we get there?" Erik shoved him so he fell sideways. Edvin whined, but Marianne pulled him close and kissed him on the forehead.

"Come here, my little treasure," she said, hugging him tight. "Don't fight, boys. I'm not joking. We can go, we can afford it. So let's do it, shall we? We'll stay in a fancy hotel with a swimming pool, so you can swim around like fish all day long."

"But what about Father Christmas? How's he going to find us if we go away?" Edvin asked sadly.

"You know what, maybe he won't. But I don't think he's been doing his job all that well the past few years. It probably won't make any difference if he doesn't come." Marianne tried to stop herself from laughing, but she couldn't; it bubbled up as she tried to smother it. Edvin pressed his hands to his ears.

"Then I'm not going," he screamed. Elin stroked his back.

"Mama's just joking," she soothed him.

Marianne stopped, her face growing serious again.

"I think Father Christmas will find you one way or another. Maybe you can write him a letter and tell him where we're going to be?"

Edvin jumped down from the bed and ran quickly to the desk. He rummaged around in the mess of pens and paper and started to write, in big, untidy capitals with great concentration, stopping to carefully fold an old drawing into an envelope .

"I need an address," he called out after a while.

"Write Father Christmas, North Pole. That should be enough." Erik sniggered. Elin threw a cushion at him.

"It was probably Aina who used to be Father Christmas. So Father Christmas is dead now!" Erik's voice was muffled under the pillow, and Elin pressed it down.

❖

The first tentative rays of the dawn tickled Elin's eyes. She squinted at the window and caught a glimpse of the sky, beautifully streaked with red. She closed her eyes again, turned onto her side, and pulled the covers around her shoulders. She heard whispers fill the house. Someone was there again. She wrapped a blanket around her and crept over to the banister. From there she peered in through the door to Marianne's bedroom. The covers on the bed were moving, and giggling voices could be heard from underneath.

"Go on now, hurry. The children might wake up."

The words were smothered. She heard the sound of lips sucking tight to each other. She saw a naked back, hairy, roll over Marianne's struggling body.

"I'm never going to leave, you're too lovely."

More noises. Wilder movements.

"I think I love you. I love you."

His voice. Muffled and deep, it sent vibrations through the house. Her reply:

"You're crazy. Go on now, before the children see you here."

Elin sank to the floor. She pulled the blanket tighter, up over her head, so only her eyes and nose remained uncovered. Hardly dared breathe for fear of being discovered.

Micke left the bed. She saw his face now. He was naked, his buttocks shining white in the morning sun. He stretched his arms above his head and groaned loudly, too loudly. Marianne was quickly there, naked too, and silenced him with her lips. Her breasts jiggled as she moved. He cupped one in his hand, leaned forward, and took her nipple in his mouth. She leaned her head back. He let go and kissed her throat. Elin closed her eyes and held her hands tightly over them.

In the end Micke left the house through the bedroom window, wriggling his way out and jumping down into the flower bed. Elin slunk back to her room. She saw through the window how he staggered off across the farmyard, toward the car that was parked there. In his stocking feet and with a boot in each hand, he hopped from one foot to the other and wiggled them into the boots as he went.

Downstairs, the rare sound of Marianne's laughter could be heard. She too was watching from the window.

❖

Elin crept closer to the cliff edge, holding her breath and taking one cautious step at a time on the bare ground, legs and arms stretched wide so her clothes wouldn't make any noise. Right on the edge sat a white-tailed eagle in stately profile, its pale-yellow beak elegantly curved. It turned its head and looked out across the sea, folding its wings tightly into its brown-speckled body. She wished she could capture the beautiful image forever, the light was so perfect.

When Elin was ten meters away it was no longer possible to sneak up undetected. The bird quickly spread its wings, their span greater than Elin's entire height, and cast itself away from the cliff. In front of her hovered another. Like two warplanes the eagles flew, patrolling the coast. Elin ran along the path, trying to keep up and watch, but the birds were too quick. Soon they were no more than dots in the distance, then they disappeared. Elin sat on the edge of the cliff with her feet dangling down, as she often did. It was dizzyingly high. Ten meters down she could see the limestone slabs of the seabed, like an irregular patchwork quilt under the clear green water. On a sunny spring day you could see the sea trout and cod swimming after sticklebacks and other small fish. She loved sitting there, just watching everything silently in the gorgeous

light. It still hadn't rained; the air was cold and clear, but the clouds were
stacking up on the horizon, black and threatening.

◆

In the pocket of her pants she had a new letter on pink writing paper.
She'd found the writing paper in the drawers in Marianne's room. Now
it was folded three times into a little flat package. She wrote a little every
day, just a few lines. Sometimes the letters ended up in her desk drawer,
sometimes burned in the stove. She thought she ought to tell Papa about
all the money, that she should put a letter in the postbox, addressed to
the prison. But she couldn't find a good way to tell him. She had a feeling
that the money would tempt him home, make him find a way to get out of
prison. But how? She didn't know. Was it still possible to dig your way out
of a cell? To slowly, slowly gouge a hole in the stone wall and squirm out
to freedom on the other side, one night when all the guards were sleeping? Or to use a fork to break the main power switch so the electricity
in the high fence around the prison shut off? Papa was good at electricity; he used to do all the wiring for the farm himself. Then he could just
climb over and run. He was quick and strong, Elin had seen that for herself when he'd nimbly swung himself from branch to branch in the climb-
ing tree, the few occasions he'd taken the time to play with his children.
He wouldn't even need to swim home, like the prisoners in Alcatraz did.
He'd easily be able to hide in one of the Grinde trucks. Elin was astonished by the brilliance of that thought as it drifted by. She started writing, with the chewed yellow pencil stub she'd taken home from school.

> Papa, you don't have to be a scandrull. Theres money here.
> Lots of money. Old Aina died and gave it all to Mama and
> Gerd. Come home as soon as you can. Hide in one of the
> trucks going to Grindes then you wont be discuvered on
> the boat. I can hide you here when you come.

She folded the paper carefully and shoved it in her pocket. No one
in the Eriksson family would ever need to be a scoundrel again. They

wouldn't even need to steal hot chocolate. Now they too would be able to eat fillet steak and Hasselback potatoes every Saturday, every day even, not just when there was a celebration. They'd finally be like everyone else. They'd even be a little better off than everyone else.

Elin looked out at the faint line that divided the sky from the sea and observed the reflections of the light in the water, the rough surface with small irregular crests, the clouds' dance with the wind. The sun that struggled to get through. She saw it glimmering, like a yellow diamond beyond all the darkness.

A rumble far off over the ocean made her jump up in a hurry. Soon the lightning and the storm would come closer; then it would be dangerous to sit there. As she walked along the path toward the forest, she felt the first small drops of rain landing softly on her head. They became heavier and heavier until, as she reached the letterboxes on the gravel track, the downpour came. It was as though the heavens had opened, the drops hitting the puddles with such force that they bounced. She pulled up her thin cotton jacket to protect her head and ran until a car pulled up alongside and tooted. It was Gerd.

"Quick, jump in, you can ride with me for the last bit," she called through the rolled-down window. Elin heaved open the door and sat alongside Gerd. She was shaking from the cold, and the water from her wet hair ran down her cheeks.

"Poor darling, you're freezing. You mustn't go out without a raincoat, you know what the weather's like this time of year."

She reached over and pulled out a blanket from the back seat. Elin took it gratefully and wrapped it around her shoulders. The engine coughed and big clouds of exhaust fumes puffed out, finding their way into the car. Elin wrinkled her nose. "You can buy a new car, now you've got all that money," she said, coughing.

Gerd laughed out loud and pressed the horn a few times. "Oh no, she'll do fine for me, old Silvia."

"Like the queen of Sweden? Is that why it's called that?"

"Yes, only the best for us."

"Everything's going to be better now, isn't it?"

"What do you mean?"

"Well, with the money."

"Of course, you're not poor anymore. Aina was a master of surprise. Just think what a secret she was sitting on. It's crazy."

"But I miss her. I'd much rather have her here with us."

Gerd stopped the car. She switched off the engine and reached out to Elin's cheek, stroking it with her warm hand.

"That's life, little one. We're born and then we have to die. And in between we have to go on living the best we can. And you can get your cookies from me in future."

"How did you know about that?"

"How did I know? I used to go there myself, as a child. And your mama too. Aina's always given the children in this village cookies and cordial. That was how she was. I think that was how she found company. Otherwise she'd just be sitting there at home, on her own, waiting for time to pass."

"She was so kind . . ." Elin fell silent and twisted her hands in her lap.

"Yes, she was that. The world's kindest."

"What's going to happen to all her books?"

"Well, I guess we'll have to drive them to the dump. They're not much worth having, just a lot of fantasies." Gerd winked, then laughed.

"I can take them. If no one else wants them," Elin said.

"Yes, I'm sure that will be fine. That way you'll have something to do for years to come. I've never understood all that."

"Aina understood it."

"Yes, she did. I'm sure she's living in a library in heaven, what do you think?"

Elin lit up at the thought of Aina in a lovely old library.

"By the way, why didn't Aina ever get married and have children? Why was she so lonely?"

"Well, I guess she took the answer to that with her to the grave. Not everyone is lucky enough to meet someone." Gerd suddenly looked sad, and fiddled with the shiny locket she wore around her neck. Elin had opened it many times and seen the pictures inside.

"But you did," Elin said.

"Yes, I have my Ove. I'd never want to be without him. Make sure you find someone to share your life with, someone who'll be your very best friend," Gerd said, giving the locket a quick kiss.

"You're taking care of Venus, aren't you?"

"Of course we are, dear. Would you like to come and see her? We can go over to our house now if you'd like. No, you know what, let me phone your mama, let's have dinner together tonight. You all can come over to our place."

Elin nodded and wrapped the blanket even tighter around her body. She was shivering, her lips purple. A bolt of lightning lit the road and the thunder came soon after. Gerd turned the key and restarted the car as Elin looked out the window nervously.

"That wasn't even a second away from us! Imagine if we got struck by lightning."

"Are you scared?" Gerd reached over and patted Elin's leg.

Elin nodded.

"A bit."

"There's nothing dangerous about thunder. It's just the angels in their bowling alley in the sky." She put her finger to her lips. "But don't tell anyone. It's the angels' secret."

Elin smiled at her. "You're just kidding," she said.

"Oh no, Aina will probably be at it too. That's why it's particularly loud today." Gerd laughed.

◆

They sat quietly for the last stretch and listened to the thunder. Elin gazed at the thick greenery that grew in the roadside ditch and saw the water spraying up as the car cut through deep puddles that formed in the potholes. Accordion music streamed from the radio, the doors juddering when the music got especially loud.

◆

Ove was bent over his saxophone, blowing so hard his cheeks were red and marking the beat with his foot. His eyes were closed. He was playing "Take the A Train," and everyone was caught up in the cheerful melody, Gerd clapping her hands and Marianne humming along. The table was full of pots and pans and scraped-clean plates, and Elin was sitting on the kitchen bench between her brothers. All three were fascinated by Ove and the sounds he was making with the golden instrument. When he finally took his lips off the mouthpiece, Edvin and Erik jumped up and down on the bench and begged him to play more, but he set the instrument aside and pulled his chair up to the table.

Their dreams expanded to fill the room as they talked, eyes glittering and laughter flowing.

"Shouldn't we be a bit sadder about Aina?"

Elin's sudden question made everyone around the table stop. The candle flames, in the light breeze from the window, were the only things that moved.

"Aina was so old, my love. It was time," said Gerd, tilting her head at her.

"But of course we miss her," Marianne added.

"It's just hard not to be happy about all the money." Gerd smiled broadly.

"Yes, you must understand that? We miss her but we're happy at the same time. Because now everything's good again. Aina made everything good."

Marianne poured more wine into the adults' glasses. They drank quickly and got redder and redder in the face. Ove fetched more glass bottles of sugar soda from the plastic crate on the veranda and put them out for the children, who were allowed as much as they wanted, given it was a celebration. Elin sucked up the cold liquid through three thin straws, unaccustomed to the feeling of bubbles on her tongue.

Ove picked up the saxophone again, and Erik and Edvin danced before him as he played, bobbing up and down and bumping hips, their arms above their heads.

It was after eleven when they finally started making their way home. Erik and Edvin were too tired to walk, so Marianne let Erik climb up on her back and Elin carried Edvin. He wrapped his skinny limbs around her and burrowed his face into her neck as she hummed the song Ove had just been playing: *Summertime, and the livin' is easy.*

Marianne was walking so fast, Elin couldn't keep up with her. Suddenly Marianne stumbled on a stone and Erik fell off, landing hard on the ground. He burst into noisy tears, and their happy mood was replaced by an irritated hushing. When he didn't stop, Marianne left him there and swayed onward alone, holding her arms out to the sides for balance. Edvin called after her, but she didn't turn, even though the word "Mama" cut through the air. Elin put Edvin down and took both her brothers' hands.

"Let her go. We'll be fine, it's not far. Hold on to me, I know the way even in the dark."

They walked along the gravel road, Erik and Edvin in the tire tracks that shone white in the light of the full moon, Elin on the line of grass that ran between them. Elin began to sing, the same line over and over again. In the end, the brothers joined in too:

> This little light of mine, I'm gonna let it shine.
> This little light of mine, I'm gonna let it shine.
> This little light of mine, I'm gonna let it shine.
> Let it shine, let it shine, let it shine.

Now

The notebook is no longer empty. She keeps sticking images into it. The pitcher is there, alone on a page with a beautiful frame around it, drawn with many flourishes from Elin's fountain pen. The white porcelain vessel reminds her of the taste of elderflower in a far-off place. She smooths her finger over it, remembering.

On the next page she has drawn from memory a freckled face, a smile with large, uneven teeth, sparkling eyes that look at her, pleading. The face is surrounded by little stars. She is filled with a curious longing.

Perhaps she'll stay in bed. Just one day on her own. There's no one there, nothing she can or has to do. She puts the book aside and pulls the covers up to her chin, gripping them hard with both hands. She takes out the book again, opens it, and finds the image she printed out yesterday. A single dandelion in a crack in the asphalt. Yellow as the sun. She remembers all the dandelions they had to pull up and throw away. Beautiful yellow flowers destined only for the compost. Perhaps she herself is a dandelion? A weed in the wrong place. A country bumpkin in the city. She closes her eyes.

The telephone rings, for the third time. It's her agent, and she's clearly not giving up. Elin answers.

"You're late. There's a whole team waiting for you, and time is ticking by. Why aren't you picking up?"

The woman is shouting at her. Elin sits up, suddenly wide awake.

"I don't have anything on today — it's empty, free."

"Look again. You fucking do have something on. Like a shoot for fucking *Vogue*? You don't just forget that. We talked about it two days ago."

Elin gets out her phone and pulls up the calendar, opening her eyes wide as she realizes her mistake.

"I'll be there in a quarter of an hour. I thought it was tomorrow."

"Five minutes. They've already been waiting too long. It's not like you to be so forgetful."

No shower; she doesn't have time. She runs to the closet and grabs a black jumpsuit. Below it is a pair of red sneakers; she eyes them doubtfully and in the end chooses them. Alice gave them to her for her birthday a long time ago, but Elin has never worn them. She unties them and shoves her feet in. It feels strange, too comfortable, as though she were en route to the gym. She checks her reflection in the mirror quickly, pulls her hair back, and fastens it in a bun. Then she runs the few blocks to the studio.

The door is locked, so she rings the bell. There's no one there. She pulls her phone out again and looks at her diary. The shoot is in Central Park. She gives a little shriek of frustration, suddenly remembering all the planning. The lake, the boat, the model standing in it, wearing a long pink dress. Elin's assistants have been struggling for days to find anchors to hold the boat still.

Elin remembers everything now, especially how important the shoot is. She runs out into the street and hails the first taxi she sees.

◈

The lawn is full of them, even though autumn is on the way and their season should be long over. Unwanted little yellow suns in the lush green. In front of her, everything is a stage set. Behind her, everything is a memory. She pulls her shoes off and stands barefoot in the grass, feeling the damp chill of the earth against the soles of her feet. The model standing on the boat stretches, arches her back, and pouts her bold red lips. The full skirt of her dress is taped to the stern of the boat to create the illusion of wind blowing. The makeup artist is standing in the water, with his pants rolled up to his knees, ready to jump in and correct the smallest hair that settles out of place; there's a comb in his back pocket and a powder puff in his hand. Two assistants are holding the studio lights to stop them from blowing down, and behind Elin stands the rest of the team: the stylists, the art director.

She holds the camera to her eye, wiggles her fingers in the air, and asks the model to look at them; she pulls her hand to the side, has the model follow the fingers with her gaze.

"Your face too, turn a little, just a little. Chin up."

She walks closer, taking pictures from different angles, then asks one of the assistants for a reflector. He holds up the shimmering gold surface so it reflects the impression of sunshine onto the model's pale skin.

"There. It's a wrap. We've got it."

There's a wave of protest, but she lowers the camera. The model remains standing in the same stiff position. Elin waves to her.

"You can come in, relax, we're done. Pull the skirt off there, it's only tape."

She puts the camera straight down on the grass and picks up her shoes, then walks off slowly across the lawn. Her tears spill out. It feels odd. The team is standing behind her, watching.

"She hasn't started drinking, has she?" she hears one of them whisper, but she still doesn't stop. She starts running, flying across the grass, carrying on until the grass becomes asphalt. It's hot under her feet, warmed by the sun. She runs down Fifth Avenue, shoes still dangling from her hands. Past the hawkers, past the souvenirs, past the tourists studying their unfolded maps in bewilderment. One street hawker has put out a blanket on the sidewalk and is selling bracelets braided with small colorful beads. They are displayed in rusty metal tins. Elin stops and stares at them.

"How much do you want?" she asks.

The man nods and holds up a few different-colored bracelets on his finger. He twirls them in front of her.

"Five dollars, ma'am, five dollars," he says.

She shakes her head.

"Not the bracelets. The tins, I want the tins. All of them."

"Sorry, ma'am, they're not for sale."

She takes a wad of notes out of her pocket. Gives him one after another: 50 dollars, 70 dollars, 80 dollars, 130 dollars. The notes run out. He stares at her and then without a word rapidly empties all the tins, letting the bracelets fall onto the blanket. She gathers them up, four rusty tins just like the ones she once owned.

Then

≡ ◆ ≡

HEIVIDE, GOTLAND, 1979

The darkness and silence enveloped Elin as she lay wide awake on her bed, fully dressed. The hands on the alarm clock glowed green in the darkness; it was almost midnight and everyone else was sleeping. She heard Fredrik from a long way off. Not his whistling, but his footsteps; the gravel crunching under the soles of his feet. She quickly crept out of bed and downstairs, and found him waiting on the swing seat. He looked gloomy.

"Have they been fighting again?"

Elin sat beside him. The cushions weren't there, so the taut steel fibers on the seat's base cut into her thighs and buttocks.

"We're moving," he said.

"Where to?"

"Visby." He swallowed audibly.

"But you'll be here sometimes, won't you? Is Micke going to move too?"

"I don't know, I don't really understand. It's got something to do with money, we haven't got any money."

"But everyone says you're loaded. Aren't you? Isn't it true?"

"Come on, let's walk." Fredrik acted as if he hadn't heard her question. He took her hand and together they walked down toward the sea. The cold limestone made the path glow white against the black backdrop of the autumn night. Fredrik was carrying a book, the one about stars that they liked to look at. Elin had matches in her pocket and a thick blanket under her arm.

"How many do you think we'll see today?" she asked.

"Shooting stars?"

"Mmm."

"Enough. But I guess you've got enough already? Is it true your mama got Aina's inheritance? I heard Mama telling Papa."

Elin hesitated, then decided not to answer. They continued on in silence. She lifted her right foot automatically as she came to one of the thick roots that stuck up out of the path. Even though it was dark, she knew exactly where it was. Fredrik tipped his head back and looked up at the stars as they walked.

"I wonder if she's sitting up there right now?"

"Who, Aina?"

"Mmm, maybe she's become a big, bright, golden star."

"Gold would really suit her." Elin laughed.

"Just imagine her pretending to be poor even though she was so rich. Why would someone do that? It's weird."

"Is this the last time, do you think? That we'll sneak out and watch the stars?" Elin's question stopped Fredrik in his tracks. He held the book out to her.

"No, of course not. I'll come to stay with Papa sometimes, obviously. You can keep the book here. I'll never look at the stars with anyone but you, I promise."

There was a flash in the corner of his eye. A little drop of sorrow ran down his cheek, leaving a winding trail of moisture on his freckled skin. He ignored it.

When they got to the beach they lay on their backs under the stars. The roaring sea washed in over the stones. Elin held the book close to her chest. Her thoughts were full of Micke and Marianne, but she dared not reveal to Fredrik what she knew. She didn't want to make his sorrow any heavier.

"Being an adult seems so hard. They just fight and get divorced and get sent to prison and cry. When I grow up I'm going to marry someone just like you," she whispered.

"Promise?"

Fredrik rolled over onto his side and stretched out his little finger. She hooked her own around it.

"Promise we'll always be friends. Whatever happens," she said.

A shooting star flew across the sky, leaving a pale pink streak.

"Let's wish for it. Then it will happen," Fredrik said, pointing at the sky.

"Dummy, you said it out loud."

"OK, worrywart. I promise we'll always be friends. No matter what happens."

❖

The only thing she could think about was that this was probably exactly what being a thief felt like. To be able to just grab what you wanted without needing to think about it, taking a little here and a little there. Elin stayed a few meters behind the others as the family walked around the shop, Erik and Edvin running back and forth in ecstasy, around and around Marianne's legs so she nearly stumbled. They couldn't keep still, they jumped around, pulling at everything they passed. Edvin stopped occasionally, winding his way around the racks of clothes. They bought bikes, balls, toys. All the things they'd always been lacking. All the things other people had, but they'd only dreamed of.

"And you? What do you want?" Marianne turned to her. Elin shrugged.

"Too much to choose from?" Marianne let out a peal of laughter. "Don't choose, then. Take everything you want. And when you're done, take a little more. It's all on Aina."

"Stop it!" said Elin.

"You don't understand. We're rich now, we can buy everything we've ever wanted, everything we need. You don't need to think twice. Take the first thing you see that you like."

Elin eyed the shoe racks, where a pair of low-heeled leather shoes glowed white. She picked them up, inspected them, then put them quickly back on the shelf.

"White will get dirty in the forest, it's not very practical," she said.

"No, neither are heels. But take them anyway. You might get invited to a disco sometime. Get a nice pair of Velcro sneakers too, you can wear them for school. Everything's changed now. You need tops too; all of yours are too small."

Elin tugged at the red T-shirt she was wearing. Marianne was right; it was tight across her stomach and barely covered the waistband of her pants. She always stretched her tops when they were damp after the wash. First widthwise, as far as she could, then lengthwise. They ended up a funny shape from this rough treatment; the seams twisted around her body rather than hanging straight. She swept her hand over the row of T-shirts, some in single colors, some with prints, and put two pink ones and a purple one into Marianne's basket. Marianne nodded in approval and then held up a gray sweater.

"Take this too, get some more sweaters. And pants. You need clothes."

Elin went on dropping item after item into the basket. After a while she stopped.

"But what about you, Mama? Aren't you going to have anything new?"

Marianne smiled.

"You're always thinking about others, Elin. It's nice, but think of yourself too. Moms mostly need dresses, blouses, and things like that. And you get those in other shops, not here at the Co-op."

"Are you going to wear dresses at home?"

"Yes. I am. From today on, I intend to wear dresses and red lipstick. Every day. Just because I can."

It seemed reasonable. Unnecessary, but reasonable. Elin smiled at her. Anxiety had lost its grip on Marianne. The worry lines had filled out. Her cheeks and mouth were no longer as tense, her skin was rosier and less sallow. She knew now that worry wasn't just a feeling, buried deep inside the psyche. Worry could be seen, almost touched. Marianne reached out and stroked Elin's long hair.

"What are you doing, that tickles!" said Elin, shaking off the unfamiliar caress.

"I just wanted to touch your hair, it's so pretty and shiny. You're so lovely."

"You are too, Mama."

"Not like you. No one's like you. You've got a heart of gold, and the light from it shines out of your eyes."

"Oh, you're so silly. My heart's red and blue and purple, just like everyone else's."

"No, not yours. It's special."

"What about us? Aren't we lovely?" Edvin protested loudly from the skateboard he was riding back and forth along the aisles.

"You too," Marianne said. "All three of you. You're my aces, my three aces. A little trio of joy, what would I do without you?"

Marianne picked up the overstuffed baskets at her feet and took the escalator to the cash registers. Elin followed her. At her side she had a new pink bicycle with dropped handlebars. She carefully stroked the gleaming white saddle, the frame, and handlebars, blinking away the tears that stubbornly filled her eyes.

"Thank you," she whispered.

"I would have given you all of this long ago, if only I'd been able."

"I know, Mama, I know."

❖

That evening they cooked together, all four of them. Chicken, on a bed of onion and potato, with thick creamy sauce. The kitchen filled with warmth and scent. They ate until they were full, and when they were full, they ate a little more.

Elin and Marianne washed up, and then Marianne disappeared into her bedroom. Elin saw her pulling a silvery new blouse over her head, smooth silk with a bow at the throat, and pairing it with a corduroy bell-shaped skirt that fit snugly around her waist. She painted her lips red and swung back and forth in front of the mirror, observing her figure from the front and the back. When the house had fallen silent and the lights were out, the car came. Elin heard it a long way off. The low growl of the engine, the car door slamming, the door to the house opening, Micke's voice.

Then came the shrieks again, the bed shrieks she hated so much.

◆

The swing seat squeaked a little. Elin was lying on the worn cushion with her hand hanging over the side. She was holding on tight to a tuft of grass and pulled on it now and then to speed up her swinging. Through the holes in the shabby beige plastic canopy she could see gray clouds in the sky. It would start to rain soon. She pulled on the tuft. Back and forth. The cloud formations came and went as she listened to the creak and groan of the wind in the treetops.

"Are you out here all alone? Aren't you cold?"

Marianne lifted Elin's legs and squeezed in at one end. Instead of replying, Elin turned in to face the back of the seat and pulled up her jacket to cover half her face.

"Maybe we should chuck out this old heap of trash now, it's barely standing."

Elin peeped out at her mother as she stretched up and touched the canopy. The plastic had eroded, and flakes peeled off and floated to the ground.

"When's Papa coming home again?"

"Elin."

"Why do you say that? Why do you say 'ELIN' every time I ask about Papa? Don't you think I have a right to know? I'm ten, I'm not some little kid like the others."

"OK. He's not coming back. Not to this house in any case. And maybe not even to Gotland. It's over. We're better off without him."

"But he can change, can't he? Can't scoundrels ever be good again? He's our papa. We need him."

Marianne shook her head.

"We don't need him."

"In that case you don't need anyone else either. In that case it's just the four of us."

Neither said anything. Elin pulled on the tuft of grass, but Marianne's feet on the ground stopped the swing's motion. Elin went on pulling until the grass was torn from its roots.

"Go away, I was here first," she hissed.

She felt Marianne's hand nudge her back and tried to shake it off. Marianne held her hand there, calmly, as Elin went on thrashing like a dying fish.

"Go away, I said!" She kicked hard against Marianne's leg with both feet.

"Ow. Stop that!" Marianne stood up and walked away. "Don't stay out here too long, you might catch something. The rain will come back soon. The sky's getting pretty dark, look."

Elin didn't reply, just let her mother disappear back into the house, back to the kitchen table and her cigarettes.

The swing seat slowed gradually. When it stopped there was silence, just the odd squeak when the wind set it in motion again. The raw chill brought in by the wind made her shiver. She wondered if the rain was this persistent in Stockholm, if the sun shone as rarely, if it was possible to see the sky from a cell, if they were looking at the same clouds, she and Papa.

A soft whistle roused her from her thoughts. She peered over the edge of the seat and saw Fredrik running up the path. He sat down on her stomach, making her flail her arms and legs to get free. At last he moved, taking the spot Marianne had just left.

"It's going to rain soon," Elin said.

"Great, that means we can skip the shower," Fredrik said, and got the swing going so fast the stand swayed.

◆

"Promise me we'll always be friends. Whatever happens."

They sat beside each other on the pebble beach, gathering small white stones and taking turns trying to hit one of the large stone blocks at the water's edge. The surface was white with chalk from all the stones that had struck it and disintegrated.

"Why do you always say that? We've always been friends, and we always will be." Fredrik shoved Elin, making her fall sideways. She got up straightaway and gazed at him intently.

"Whatever happens?"

"Whatever happens. And what could happen here anyway? Nothing ever happens. Nothing at all."

Elin took out a little pocketknife and quickly cut a nick in her finger. She held the knife out for Fredrik.

"What are you doing?" he exclaimed.

"Blood pact."

"You're crazy! You know that, right? Is this something you've read about in one of those books?"

"If you're chicken I can help you make the cut," she said.

She reached out, but he shook his head, took the knife, and held the little blade to his finger. Then he shut his eyes and pushed the point in. A dark-red bubble of blood welled up on the skin, and Elin quickly put her finger on his so their blood mingled.

"No one can break a blood pact. No one and nothing. We'll always be friends. Always. Whatever happens. Swear."

"Visby's only twenty miles away. And I'll be staying at Papa's sometimes." Fredrik pulled his finger away and put it in his mouth, sucking the rest of the mingled blood off it.

"Whatever happens. We'll always be friends. *Swear*," Elin repeated, and threw a stone. It missed the big rock and hit the water with three rapid bounces. Fredrik laughed.

"And you've never even managed to skip a stone before. It must be a sign. What comes in threes?"

"Crazy parents!" Elin laughed.

"Only three? Which of them isn't crazy then?"

"Your mama," Elin mumbled.

"Shows what you know. Last night they argued so much, Papa took off. She was running after the car, totally naked. I saw her from the bedroom window. He put his foot down and sped off, and she ran and ran and ran. She didn't stop until she'd gone halfway down the avenue."

"Do you know why she was so angry?"

"All I know is what she was screaming 'You're not going to her place,' over and over again. *To her place.* Maybe that's why they're getting divorced, because he's in love with someone else."

Elin stood up and walked to the shoreline, gathering a heap of flat stones on the way. She stood sideways to the water, throwing stone after stone and trying to make them skip. Every one sank to the bottom.

"Come here, I'll show you how to do it." Fredrik stood behind her and put his arm on hers so they were holding the stone together. "Bend your knees, start with your hand low, look at the surface, follow the surface with your gaze as you throw."

He let go and she threw again; the stone bounced once and she punched the air.

"I did it!"

"Course you did. You can do anything if you want to."

◆

Outside the window the storm swept in, whipping up gravel and flying leaves. The dawn sun pushed its way through dark clouds, coloring the whole farmyard with a golden glow. Inside, it was warm from the crackling fire in the woodstove. When Elin came into the kitchen, Micke was sitting there, leaning back on one of the kitchen chairs, legs akimbo, in just his underpants and an unbuttoned checked shirt, which bared his sweat-slicked hairy chest. She stopped in the doorway and turned, but it was already too late. He'd seen her.

"Hello, missy. Awake already? Nice to see you."

"What are you doing here?"

"Is that the way you greet a stranger?"

"Where's Mama?"

"In bed. She'll be out in a bit, you'll see. She didn't get much sleep last night." His booming laughter filled the room. He took a piece of bread from the cutting board, threw it high in the air, and caught it in his mouth. On the table were some half-full cocktail glasses, covered in greasy fingerprints, and a bowl of peanuts. Elin turned her back on him, opened the larder, and took out the plates. She cleared away the dirty glasses and put the plates on the table, all on the kitchen-bench side, none on Micke's.

"Erik and Edvin will be down soon. You should go now."

He looked offended.

"Go? I'm not going anywhere."

Elin went on clearing up in silence, and soon Marianne opened the bedroom door and hurried in. She yawned and stretched up to the ceiling. Her purple robe was tied tightly around her waist and her hair was disheveled, sticking out like a back-combed halo around her face. The skin under her eyes bore traces of sooty black mascara. When she caught sight of Micke, she stiffened.

"What are you doing here?" She tried to smooth her hair, embarrassed.

He took hold of her shoulders with both hands. He tried to mouth the words at her, but he wasn't quiet enough and Elin heard him say:

"I think we should tell Elin. She's big enough."

Marianne shook her head. She took his hand and pulled him with her, back into the bedroom. They went on talking in low voices; then the bed creaked as two heavy bodies fell onto it. Elin crept up the stairs to her brothers' room and into Edvin's bunk. He'd wriggled halfway down the bed in his sleep, and she sat above him, curled up on the pillow, with her hands clamped over her ears.

❖

It was one of those rainy, stormy nights, when shoppers hesitate before going back outside. Gerd gave them hot coffee in paper cups and crumbly little oat cookies. A few wet rain slickers were hanging up by the door, and the floor of the aisles was covered with muddy footprints from the day's customers. Elin was helping to sort the magazines and papers: the old ones were being bundled up and sent back and the new ones had to be brought into the shop and put out on the shelves. She sat on the floor by the newspaper stand and read the dates on the covers carefully before sorting them and filling in the issue numbers and quantities on the return slips.

There was a flash from the sky, then a low rumble. Elin saw Marianne come running along the main road, with Sunny loping along after her, head low and ears back. Marianne smiled when she came in through the glass door. Wet tufts of hair were slicked across her face. She shook herself like a dog, making the drops from her jacket fly through the air. Then she hung it up with the others and ran straight up to Gerd. They hugged. Elin crept closer and tried to hear what they were saying, but she only caught a few words. *Move in. He loves me. Happy.*

She moved closer, out across the floor, hiding behind the candy rack. Now she could hear as well as see. Gerd was shaking her head.

"She's only just moved out. And you're going to move in right away?"

Elin's lips parted. She stared at Marianne, and the long wait for her reply made her heart beat hard in her chest.

"He loves me," she whispered at last, earning a guffaw from Gerd.

"He needs a wife. Someone to work on the farm. Don't go wasting your life again now."

"You don't understand."

"I understand more than you think. Much more than you think. With you, he even gets money thrown in."

"How dare you suggest . . ."

Marianne turned on her heel and Elin jumped, banging her head on the shelf. The sharp edge sent a shock of pain through her, and she let out a shriek.

"Are you eavesdropping?" said Marianne.

Elin shook her head.

"I've told you not to run around in here. Gerd needs peace and quiet to work. This isn't a playground."

Gerd stepped between them, put her arm around Elin, and pulled her close. Elin felt the warmth and safety of her soft stomach.

"The lass is helping me. And she gets some pocket money for it."

"There's a whole heap of things to help out with at home too. Especially now we're moving."

Elin felt for Gerd's hand. When she found it she squeezed it hard. Gerd stroked her thumb over the back of Elin's hand, comforting her.

"Shouldn't you give this a little more thought before you make your mind up?"

Marianne pulled Elin's hand out of Gerd's and led her toward the door. She looked down at her.

"You heard me, don't look so shocked. We're moving to the Grinde farm and that's all there is to it. Where's your jacket? We're going home."

"Marianne, I'm not saying it isn't love. I'm just saying you should think it over a little before you decide. Think of the children."

Marianne jerked open the glass door and went out into the rain without putting on her jacket. Elin turned and waved as she followed her.

"I'll take care of these last few, you'll get your money still," Gerd called after her.

◈

Marianne was walking a few steps ahead of Elin. The wind came in gusts, making it hard to balance. Leaning into it, they struggled on through the storm.

At last Elin dared ask the question. "Why are we moving?"

Marianne didn't stop or respond. She sped up and the distance between them increased; Elin saw her take the shortcut through the hedge. Micke's car was in the farmyard, parked behind their own, the shiny blue paintwork glowing through the hedge's bare branches. She heard the front door slam, and through the kitchen window she saw Marianne falling into his arms. Edvin and Erik were there too, sitting on the kitchen bench, following the adults' movements with fascination. Elin stood outside for a while. The rain streaked down her cheeks like tears, but she just felt cold and empty inside. She went around the corner, to her chair. She pressed herself against the wall for shelter from the rain, and took out her paper and the stubby pencil.

> Now its too late. Were getting a new papa. You dont need
> to come home anymore.

She underlined *dont need to* with a thick, hard pencil line. Then another. And another.

Now

≡ ◈ ≡

NEW YORK, 2017

Alice is sleeping on the sofa, curled up under a blanket, when Elin gets
home. She carefully stacks the four tins just inside the door and then
sits down close beside her daughter. Alice's feet stick out from under
the blanket, and her toes are red, swollen, and bruised. Elin takes them
in her hand, caresses them, blows on the damaged toes. It's been a long
time since Alice was home; in the beginning she came back all the time,
but since Sam moved out it happens rarely. Alice turns over and Elin
strokes her forehead tenderly.

"Is it late?" Alice murmurs.

Elin shakes her head.

"No, it was quick today, just one picture. It's still afternoon." Elin
takes her phone out to show her, but Alice turns and hides her face in
the back of the sofa.

"That's lucky, I would've slept too long otherwise."

"I'm so glad you came over. It turned out all wrong at the restaurant."
Elin lies down beside her, her arm around Alice's middle.

"I don't know who to go to."

"What do you mean?"

"Who out of the two of you. If I should go to Dad's place or to yours.
It's so weird, all this." Alice clasps her hands nervously, making her
knuckles whiten.

"You can stay with both of us, can't you? You needn't choose. Alter-

nate, or do whatever works best. Come to the one you're missing most."
Elin untangles her daughter's fingers, strokes them gently.

"It just feels all wrong. I miss him here and you there. He should be here, you should both be here. I want everything back to normal."

Elin hugs her. They lie quietly. Everything is still.

After a while Elin reaches for her phone on the coffee table. She puts a song on and the sound of Esperanza Spalding fills the apartment. Alice nods her head.

"Thanks. I love her — what a voice, what great rhythm."

"I know," says Elin.

"Have you always liked jazz? Why?"

"Hmm. I don't know, it's music that gets into my soul somehow."

"How do you mean?"

"I feel it, it's like it creeps inside me, under my skin, into my blood."

"I get what you mean." Alice nods, then grimaces, lifting her legs in the air.

"My feet hurt so much."

Elin moves to the other end of the sofa and lays Alice's legs across her lap. She picks up one foot and blows on it.

"That's the price you have to pay."

"The price for what?" Alice scowls, then flinches as Elin touches her toe.

"To get where you want to go."

"I don't know if I want to get there anymore. It doesn't feel worth it."

"You were dancing before you could walk. You used to stand up and rock back and forth on those chubby little legs. You've always danced."

Elin reaches for the framed photos on the bookshelf, takes one down, and angles it toward Alice, who smiles and reaches out to take it. She looks at the little child for a long time.

"Yeah, maybe," she says finally.

"Not maybe. Tell me, how do you feel when you're in the middle of a performance?"

"Like life doesn't exist. The other stuff. It's just me and the music. The steps, the moment."

"See? That's what it's like for me when I'm taking photographs. That's probably how it is for everyone who has a passion."

Alice places the photo facedown on the coffee table.

"But what if it's just an escape?" She sighs.

"An escape?"

"Yeah, an escape from reality."

"In that case, I don't need reality."

"Ugh, don't say that, Mom, it sounds so tragic."

◈

A taxi pulls up to the curb and Elin drags Alice toward it. She shuffles along on in her flip-flops, protesting wearily.

"Can't we just order takeout instead? It was nice on the sofa."

"What was that place called outside Sleepy Hollow? The farm. You remember?"

"Stone Barns? Why do you ask?" Alice furrows her forehead.

"Drive to Sleepy Hollow," says Elin, leaning in toward the driver. He accelerates and pulls out right in front of a truck, which beeps.

"But Mom, come on, I don't have time for this, forget the food. I need to study tonight. And rest." Alice leans forward again. "Stop at Broadway and Broome, please; I'll take the subway home." She puffs up her cheeks and exhales heavily, laughing and shaking her head.

"Stone Barns. Mom, what are you thinking? You don't even like the countryside and you hate animals. Stone Barns is a farm. What are we going to do there?"

"They have good food. We went there once when you were little and you liked it. Please?" Elin tilts her head, pleading.

"I'm not little anymore. You're just being weird now. What's past is past. Let it go."

"Well, we can do something else then, go for a walk, go to an exhibition."

"Mom! You're doing it again." Alice sighs loudly.

"What?"

Alice extends her foot toward her mother, lifting it so it's almost touching her chin. Elin's nose wrinkles at the sight of the crusty scabs.

"Have you already forgotten? I can't walk. You're hopeless at listening, you know that?"

She puts her foot down again as the taxi pulls to the curb. As Alice wriggles out onto the sidewalk, Elin leans across the seat.

"I'm sorry! Come back, we'll eat someplace else," she calls, but Alice has already limped away. Elin gazes after her.

"Ma'am?"

The taxi driver is giving her a questioning look, but she hesitates, sits in silence a moment. Alice has disappeared from view and all she can see is other people walking past, a fast flow of thoughts and unknown destinations.

Impatient, the taxi driver sounds his horn loudly, making her jump.

"Stone Barns," she says. "Just outside Sleepy Hollow. Please."

"It's a long way. It'll cost you," he replies.

"That's fine. Just go!"

❖

The taxi journey lasts forever; she manages to fall asleep and wake up and fall asleep again. When they finally arrive, she sticks her Amex in the card machine and gives the driver a generous tip, even though the total is already dizzyingly high. Then in front of the gray-brown stone barn she steps out onto the gravel, which she can feel through the thin soles of her ballerina flats. Taking them off and holding them in her hand, she carefully walks barefoot around the buildings, letting her toes spread and focusing on the pain as the sharp stones dig into her feet. In the paddock behind the farm a few large black-faced sheep are grazing. She walks to the fence and climbs over, into the paddock. There are black clumps of droppings on the grass, but she lets her feet get dirty, drawing in the stench through her nostrils. It's early evening and the sun is setting slowly behind the tops of the trees. She takes photos with her phone: of the grass, the trees, the feed racks. Her own feet walking on the grass. She sits down on a rock at the forest's edge and listens. It's quiet. She hears birds twittering, leaves stroking one another in the wind. She lies on her back on the grass, closes her eyes, and lets the mild rays of the evening sun warm her skin.

❖

The pink-lilac evening sky gets darker and darker. The stars begin to shine above her, in their thousands, their millions. She recognizes many of them, knows the names of the constellations: knowledge she's kept buried in her memory for many years. She lies there on the grass for a long time, watching them. In Manhattan there's no real darkness at night. No stars. No blackness. Just artificial points of light.

And no *peace.* Everything is noise. Sirens, cars, music, shouts. Not like here, where her own breath sounds loud to her.

It's late in the evening when she stands up, makes her way back to the road, and manages to stop a car. The man at the wheel lowers the window and reproaches her:

"A woman shouldn't be hitching on her own. You should be glad it's me that stopped and not some crazy person."

"I *am* glad. Can I get a ride with you?"

Elin jumps in. He's playing country music, and without asking she turns the volume up. The music, a lone voice and a guitar, fills the car. The man sings along, glancing at her now and then.

Just call me angel of the morning . . .

The road winds through the dark landscape. It's lined with tall trees, which cast long shadows in the glare of the headlights. Here and there, beautiful white wooden houses lie nestled in the greenery. She suddenly longs to be far from the city that's been her home for so long. She yearns for her own flower bed, for roses and grass damp with dew.

"Do you live here?"

He nods and turns the volume back down.

"A little farther up. And you, where are you from?"

"I live in town. But it's complicated."

"It generally is. I'll drop you off at the train station in Tarrytown, is that OK? You can get to where you're going from there."

She nods. They fall silent again.

◈

The station is empty and desolate. She walks slowly up the steps to the platforms, aware of the gritty remnants of gravel and earth between her feet and the insoles of her shoes. There's a bench on the platform and she sits down. Forty minutes to the next train; the minutes tick by on the station clock. Her phone has lain untouched in her pocket since she used it to take photos on the farm, and when she gets it out, she sees missed calls and messages. From Joe. From her agent. From the client.

> Where are you? We need you in the studio.

> The client's not happy. We have to shoot again in the morning. 7:00 in Central Park. OK?

> Elin where are you? Pick up!

> We need you to be there. Can you confirm. Hair and makeup are booked. We're rigging from 5:30.

She responds briefly to the last one, with a thumbs-up. Then she swipes to delete the messages, one after another. She calls Sam, who answers sleepily.

◈

"I miss you," she whispers, and the echo of her words spreads across the paved platform.

"Elin, where are you? They've been looking for you." He suddenly sounds more awake, as though he'd been lying down and has now sat up.

"I'm OK, I just didn't look at my phone. What are you doing?"

"Why are you calling?"

"We need to talk."

"You never wanted to talk before."

"But now I do."

"We need a break. Don't you get that? *You* need a break."

"We're a family."

"There is no we, no us right now. You are you and I am me. You have to live with that."

"It's too hard. I can't do it. I'll never manage it."

"You have to try. We need breathing space."

"I don't want to."

"You have to."

He hangs up, and all is quiet again. Elin sits and stares at the phone in her hand, and when the train rolls into the station, she stays on the bench. She can't make herself get on. The train leaves the platform and the numbers on the departure board change. Another hour until the next one. She flicks through the photos she took at the farm, uses her fingers to zoom in and out. Tightly cropped, they show a place different from the one she just visited. Grass, gravel, a sheep's hooves, her own bare feet, a kitten in the high grass.

Joe calls, his face smiling at her from the screen. She lets the phone ring, looking at his unruly hair and broad grin in the black-and-white photo she took. The ringing stops and the face fades and vanishes, replaced by a photo of a fence. Texts start to pop up.

> We have to talk about the clothes. The pink dress doesn't work. They want a black one. That means different light and we have to talk about it. Call me.

Black. She sighs. So many photos over the years, so many anxious, black-clad people. Another message.

> Please call me. I have to sleep now. I can't stay awake any longer.

His pleading wears her down and she calls him. They speak for a long time, right up until the train finally comes. She hangs up, gets on, and settles into the PVC seat. Before she closes her eyes she writes a message to Sam.

♥ you.

The emoji heart glows, red and warm and rounded. The train is cold, chilly night air streams in through gaps in the windows, and she pulls her sweater tight around her shoulders and shivers, exhausted. There's no reply. She doesn't get a heart back. Only silence.

Then

=⟐=

There was hardly space for Elin on the little chair she'd built from branches and planks all those years ago. The seat was too narrow now for her broad hips. She sat in it anyway, although the juniper-wood armrests cut into her legs, making her buttocks and thighs bulge over the sides. The rough surface chafed her skin even through thick denim. She held three stones in her hand, the number of children she'd have one day. Three of a kind. She had a piece of dried-up yellow grass clenched between her molars, and when she sucked on it, the sweet taste mixed with her saliva.

She got up and leaned against the wall of the house, lifting one thigh at a time to get circulation back into her numb legs.

"Is it hurting you? Fatty." Fredrik lay in front of her, stretched out on the ground with his feet up against a tree trunk. Two towels, one pink, one blue, hung drying on a branch.

"It's too hot," she sighed. "I'm going to die. I wish a few clouds would blow in from the sea."

"Don't wish too hard. Soon it'll be autumn and too cold to swim. Then I'll have to move back to Mama's in Visby."

"I love it when you're my brother. I wish I could move too. I miss home."

"You *are* home!" he said.

"I mean back here. I want to live here again."

"Do you really?"

"What do you mean?"

"Were you happier here? All of you? Was Lasse a better papa to you than my dad?"

Elin didn't acknowledge Fredrik's question. She turned and peered in through the window, on tiptoe. No one had lived there since they'd moved to Grinde's. Fredrik and his mama had moved out, Marianne and all the children had moved in, and they'd become siblings. Stepsiblings.

The house looked just the same as the day they'd left it, apart from the layers of dust and cobwebs. No one wanted to buy it, so it stood there, abandoned, the "For Sale" sign like an eternal ornament on the lawn. Elin beckoned to Fredrik.

"Come on, I want to show you something."

He stood close behind her, rested his chin on her shoulder, and looked in.

"What?" he asked impatiently.

"Can you see the kitchen table in there?"

Fredrik nodded. His chin dug sharply into her shoulder, and she cried out in pain as he wiggled it back and forth.

"Ow, stop it! Can you see all those black marks?"

He nodded again, dug his chin in even harder. She pushed him away.

"Stop it! Why are you always starting fights? I want to tell you something important."

Elin pulled her towel down and hung it around her neck, then set off running toward the sea. Barefoot, she stepped gracefully between the pinecones and the stones. Fredrik ran after her.

"Wait! I saw them, the black spots. What is it you want to tell me?" he called. He caught up with her at last, grabbed her arm, and pulled her toward him, so they both fell over and landed among the flowers along the roadside ditch. They lay there quietly awhile, side by side, watching thin streaks of cloud trail across the deep blue.

"Actually, I always wondered . . ." she began, then stopped.

Fredrik held up his finger and made small movements in the air, as though he was sticking little dots onto the sky.

"Ah, it was nothing," she continued. "I just remembered something, a memory from when we lived there. You know, when everything was normal."

"Which you wanted to tell me?"

"I did, yeah, but then you wounded me with your beardy little chin."

"Take that back, I'm not beardy."

"Sure you are." Elin reached over and stroked his chin. "I can see you've started shaving."

"Well, so what? Come on, let's swim. It's too hot lying here."

He stood and pulled Elin up, and she brushed pine needles and bits of grass off his back. They ran the rest of the way to the sea, pulling their clothes off as they went and then diving in. The water was pale green and lukewarm, the sand on the bottom striped by the motions of the waves. They dived down, again and again, so deep their heads almost hit the bottom. Elin did a handstand and Fredrik pushed her over.

◈

When they finally left the water, they lay on the sun-warmed sand to dry, and Elin's wet hair, mixed with fine grains of sand, looked white.

"Mama says we should enjoy all this now, while we're young. Because afterward everything goes to hell."

"And what do you think about that?" Fredrik threw a pebble at her stomach.

Elin jumped and picked up the stone, which was shaped like a heart. She held it tightly in her hand.

"It's probably true. What do I know? Being a grown-up doesn't seem that fun. Not here, anyway."

"Oh, come on. We'll always have a good time, you and me. Even when we're adults. We're smart enough to make sure of it."

"Well, I'm going to be famous and move away from here. I just know it. And rich." Elin nodded firmly.

"Famous!" Fredrik burst out laughing. "What are you going to be, a pop star? How are you going to do that?"

Still laughing, he scooped up a handful of sand to throw at her. Elin fell silent and locked up her dream inside herself, embarrassed.

◈

Fredrik was balancing on some boulders by the water's edge, jumping from one to the next with his arms out. Elin watched him. His back was a dark tan, his hair cut short on top and long at his neck, with sun-bleached ends. She lay on her stomach on a towel and dug her fingers into the warm sand. Beyond Fredrik the glittering sea seemed endless. His arms and legs were covered with bruises and grazes from working in the fields. Micke acted as if summer vacation was a labor camp.

Other people rarely found their little beach. It was remote, hidden behind high cliffs; you had to climb over boulders to get to it. But nestled between the stones was a narrow open stretch of sand and limestone slabs, the perfect size for two people.

Fredrik bent down and splashed her, and the cold droplets startled her.

"Stop throwing things at me all the time," she complained.

Fredrik took a couple of steps out to where the waves were cresting, and allowed seawater to wash over him. When he stood up again, droplets flew out around him, dancing and glistening in the light. He called out to Elin and then dived in again, striking out toward the horizon. With a few powerful strokes he was far out. Elin stood, then followed him. Her long brown hair was loose, and she was wearing nothing but little yellow bikini bottoms. As she ran out into the water, the flat rocks felt smooth beneath her feet, and as soon as the water reached her thighs, she dived in, her hair fanning out around her head.

"Come back!" she called after Fredrik when he came up to the surface. "Watch out for the drop, the currents are strong!"

He flipped onto his back and thrashed his legs so that great cascades of water rose like a fountain. They swam together, with strong, rapid strokes. It turned into a competition. Now and then Fredrik plunged down, then suddenly popped up somewhere else—right in front of her, behind her, to one side. Each time he startled her, she shouted and splashed him. When he dived down and tried to grab her legs, she kicked out at him, laughing and begging him to stop.

◆

Shivering, they returned at last to the beach and the remaining dry towel. Elin pulled at it so they both had a little bit to lie on, though it was hardly big enough for their heads and backs. Their bottoms and legs had to make do with the hot sand. Beads of water shone like silver on their tan bodies.

Fredrik poured sand onto her stomach.

"Stop it!" She batted away his hand.

"You've got breasts."

Elin flinched and covered her chest with one arm.

"I have *not*."

"Sure you have."

"Have not."

"Have too."

She felt for her T-shirt with the other hand, sat up, and quickly pulled it over her head. The small bumps were still visible under the thin cotton fabric. They felt like hard balls and they hurt, so she had to massage them each night before going to sleep.

"Can I touch them?"

Fredrik reached a hand out, but she pulled back.

"Are you stupid or something?"

"I just want to see what they feel like. Please. I've never touched a breast before."

"I told you, they're not *breasts*."

"You're thirteen. They're breasts. Everyone gets them. I wonder what yours are going to be like. I bet they'll be big and bouncy, just like Aina's were."

"Shut *up!*"

Fredrik reached out again, and this time she didn't stop him. He gently stroked his thumb over one of the buds. She winced.

"Does it hurt?"

He sounded surprised. She nodded and tugged at her T-shirt to make it baggier. He leaned forward and gave her a quick kiss on the cheek, his breath warm on her skin.

"Sorry," he whispered.

Jumping up, Elin ran toward the rocks to start the climb back. He ran after her and stopped her by grabbing hold of one of her bare feet.

"Stay here. It's nice, you look really nice."

"Shut up, I said."

"They're only breasts. That's just the way it is. There's nothing wrong with it."

She smiled at him. *That's just the way it is.* That was the way he always thought. About everything, even when things really weren't right. She sat down and let her legs dangle off the boulder she'd just climbed.

"Yes, there is. It means we're becoming adults," she said seriously.

◆

Elin held both hands out in front of her, palms up. Once soft and white, they had grown callused and discolored, with a thick yellowish-gray lump at each finger joint. When she stroked her thumb over the lumps, they felt hard, the surface rough like sandpaper. She turned her hands over and inspected the backs instead, letting the hands rest on her lap. Her nails were short, gnawed right down to the quick; the backs of her hands were tan, and the fine hairs shimmered white. She took the glass of milk that stood before her on the kitchen table and emptied it in one go, gulping greedily.

Marianne sat down beside her. Coffee was dripping through the filter on the counter. She rested her own hands on the table, one on top of the other. They were traced with thick, dark purple veins, and they looked swollen. Elin reached over, ran her index finger over the back of her mother's hand. It was dry and rough, the skin on her fingertips cracked.

"That must hurt," she said.

Marianne pulled her hands away, stood up, and poured coffee from the half-filled pot into a blue clay mug. There was a hiss as a few drops landed straight on the hot plate. Gingerly, she took a sip, and then leaned against the kitchen counter. Elin was doodling on an envelope, forming a delicate chain of daisies without lifting the pen.

"Don't spoil it," said Marianne.

She moved the envelope away from Elin, poured the rest of her coffee into the sink, and walked out toward the barn again.

"Come on, you too. We've got a lot left to do out there."

On the table was a vase filled with blue, pink, and yellow wildflowers, which Edvin had picked at Marianne's request. She always wanted those colors. She said blue stood for the peace she was always seeking. Yellow for joy and laughter. Pink for love. Chicory, clover, and lady's bedstraw. There were different flowers each time, but she was dead set on the colors, and each had to be included in the bouquet.

Elin eyed the pile of papers where the envelope had landed. It had been carefully slit open with a letter opener. A few pink petals had floated down onto it, and it was dappled with pollen from the bouquet. She picked it up again, blew the surface clean, and turned it over. She stared at the handwriting that had written Marianne's name and address, the old address. It couldn't be . . . ?

"Come on then! I need help with the hay bales!" Marianne called from outside. Elin stuffed the letter into the side pocket of her work pants, stood up, and went out to her. The goats had become their project when they'd moved to the farm. The goats and their cheese were meant to be the farm's new source of cash under Marianne's leadership. But right from the start they ran into problems. The goats were there, ready to be milked, but there was no equipment: the milk needed to be pasteurized and made into cheese, and the finished cheese had to be packaged. Marianne had invested Aina's money in the project, and Elin had seen the big withdrawals listed in the bankbook.

❖

The goats bleated a welcome as Elin turned the heavy iron key and opened the door. She took the pitchfork and heaped on a little more hay, they gathered eagerly around the feeding rack, and all was quiet again. One goat was trying to get her attention, snapping at her pants and step-

ping on her feet. Dairy goats were always hungry. She patted it quickly
on the head but then withdrew. The goats were used to people, used to
her, but far from tame.

Marianne was efficiently mucking out the pens. Elin swapped her
pitchfork for a spade and went to join her. They worked side by side in
silence. Marianne looked tired. The early mornings on the farm had put
thick, wrinkly bags under her eyes. She didn't wear those pretty dresses
anymore, the ones she'd bought with Aina's money when they were still
happy. Now she wore plain cotton tops, spattered with muck, and heavy
work pants. Her hair was gathered in a messy knot under a kerchief, to
protect it from the worst of the farmyard's stench. Elin had a matching one.

◈

When they were finished and Marianne had gone back to the house,
Elin sank down into the straw, leaned against the wall of the stall, and
pulled out the envelope. The letter was written on a sheet torn from a
notepad. A tatty edge remained where it had been pulled from the spiral binding. She read:

> Dear Marianne,
>
> I have something I want to tell you. I want to tell you
> that I did it for all of your sakes. For you. For the children.
> I never wanted it to turn out like this, the gun went off by
> mistake, I never meant to hurt her, just scare her. I didn't
> want the family to be split up. Our family. I did it for us,
> to get a little money. For us. You and me and the children.
>
> Do you remember when we met? Do you remember
> how we could never keep our hands off each other? Do
> you remember how we said it was you and me forever? It
> was a promise. I've never forgotten that. Have you?
>
> I've been released now. They say I'm not to contact
> you, but I want you to know. I have a little apartment here
> in Stockholm, and I have a job. I know you don't want to

see me again. But the children, I really want to see the children. And I'd do anything to get you back. Tell me what I
have to do. I'll come as soon as you ask me, please ask me
soon.

Yours always,

Lasse

The handwriting was untidy, as though a child had formed the words
with great effort. The letters were in mismatched styles, and they sloped
in different directions. Elin's hand shook as she lowered the letter to
her knees. He was thinking about them, he was thinking about her. He
wasn't behind bars anymore; he was free. She looked at the address
again. Didn't he know they lived at Micke Grinde's place now? Didn't he
know anything about it? How could that be possible? On the back of the
envelope was a return address: Tobaksvägen 38, 12357 Farsta. She read
it over and over, then she stuffed the letter back into her pocket and ran
toward the fields where Fredrik and Micke were working.

❖

The sign hung lopsided in front of the shop. It had come loose at one
corner, and it squeaked as the wind took hold of it and swung it to and
fro. The chains were brown with rust from the autumn's rain and the
winter's endless storms. Fredrik stretched up to reach it, but he couldn't.
He climbed up onto the fence, balancing with his feet curled around a
narrow metal bar, and his hand pressed hard against the building's front.
Elin held his leg steady, but he shook it to make her let go. Gerd peeped
out through a crack in the door.

"Don't fall," she implored.

Fredrik got hold of the chain and managed to secure it again. He
jumped down and clapped his hands.

"What would I do without you?" Gerd smiled. "You can certainly get
things done, you two. Come in."

"Can we sit in the stockroom for a while? It's so hot everywhere."

Gerd nodded.

"You know where the cookies are. I'm guessing that's why you're here."
Fredrik smiled broadly and nodded. Elin gave Gerd a hug. She
smelled strongly of hairspray, the gray curls on her head as stiff as plastic. Gerd stroked Elin's back gently.

"Little lass, how happy it makes me when you come. Even though
you stink of farmyard," she whispered, wrinkling her nose.

◈

The stockroom shelves were empty. Everything sold out in the summer
months, when the many tourists swelled the number of customers. In
one corner was a thick pile of cardboard boxes broken down for disposal, and the two lay on the flattened cardboard with the cookie tin between them. The room had no windows, but the great fan on the ceiling
cooled their warm bodies. The door was ajar, and they had a clear view
of the register. Customers came and went. Gerd chatted with them and
Fredrik and Elin listened.

After a while it was Marianne standing at the counter, wearing her
farmyard clothes. Elin sat up to hear them better. Marianne was balancing a tray of cheese packages in her hands, and Elin saw Gerd shaking
her head.

"There are too many," she protested.

"They're milking well now."

Marianne held the tray out to her, and Gerd pressed her lips together.

"I can't take them all, no one buys that much cheese. I end up having
to throw it out."

Marianne put the tray on the counter and took half the cheeses away.

"How about that? What do you think?"

Gerd sighed.

"My dear, I just don't know. Not many people buy it, it's too expensive."

Gerd walked away from the register, out of sight of Elin. Marianne
stayed where she was, tapping her foot on the floor.

"What do you mean? You don't want to buy any at all?"

She picked up the cheeses she'd just put down. Gerd came back, carrying a few packs of bread, and put them down on the conveyor belt.

"I think you need to get yourself a new hobby soon."

"Hobby?"

"Yes, you're lucky you don't need the money too desperately. This is not exactly something you can live on, is it?"

Marianne looked cross. Suddenly she dropped the tray, spilling all the cheeses onto the floor. Gerd looked from the mess to Marianne, and then back at the cheeses spread across the worn linoleum. With an effort she bent down to pick them up, one after the other. Her belly got in the way, and the exertion made her breathe hard.

"You can keep the crap, no one buys it anyway," Marianne snarled as she walked to the door. Elin heard the little *pling* as it opened and closed. Twice — Gerd went after her. Then silence. Fredrik got up from the heap of boxes.

"Best we go home now. They'll want us to work, if that's the mood they're in."

"I don't want to." Elin stayed where she was. She lay back down, put her hands behind her head, and stared up at the ceiling, following the turning blades of the fan with her eyes and listening to their monotonous drone.

"We have to." Fredrik took hold of her arm and pulled her up again.

"Why? We're just children. It's summer vacation. What's going to happen if we say no?"

"You know what. Why are you even asking?"

◆

The door opened again. Marianne and Gerd came back. Marianne looked like she'd been crying, her cheeks streaked with tears and dirt, and Gerd had her arm around her protectively. Fredrik peered out, then hurried back, sat down beside Elin, and put his finger to his lips. Marianne and Gerd walked past them, into the office. There was only a thin wall between the two rooms.

"I'll put some coffee on. Sit down for a while," they heard Gerd saying.

"We need money." Marianne's voice was shrill, cracking with emotion.

"No problem, I'll buy the cheese, if it's that important to you. But you have loads of money, don't you?"

"It costs a lot to run a farm. You have no idea."

"Have you given all your money to Micke?"

"We run the farm together. It's ours, we're a family."

"Do you have that in writing?"

Marianne sat silently. She played with her car keys.

"Aina would . . ." Gerd hesitated and fell silent again.

Be turning in her grave. Fredrik whispered the words in Elin's ear, and she mouthed the word *ghost* back. They giggled.

The chair scraped against the floor as Marianne got up quickly.

"Aina would what? Be turning in her grave? Do you know what? Aina doesn't even have a fucking coffin to turn in. She's just some gray ash in an urn. Let me take care of my own life, please. And you can take care of yours. OK? I'm sick of you having to know everything. Stop sticking your nose in."

◆

Marianne stormed out but stopped in her tracks when she realized Fredrik and Elin were in the stockroom. They got up immediately, standing in front of her, eye to eye. She took a step closer and stood with feet wide apart, in heavy work shoes.

"Get home! I've told you not to loaf about here! How many more times?"

"We were just on our way."

Gerd stood at the children's side.

"Now, don't take it out on the children. They're helping me. I don't mind having them here."

Marianne grabbed Elin hard and pulled her along.

"There are plenty of things to help with at home. I told you, stop sticking your nose in everything!" she barked.

Now

≈ ◆ ≈

NEW YORK, 2017

Everything happens mechanically. Arms and legs move, the camera changes position. Finger on the shutter releases. Eye squints to assess the composition. Microscopic adjustments to the angle, creating a whole new vision. Elin directs the model into new poses, turning her face, up and down and to the side, pulling her shoulders back, angling her body sideways. It's the same young woman from the previous day, but she's dressed in black now, a full, diaphanous evening dress. Her skin is pale; she has strong, smoky eyes; her lips are blood red. As she stands with one foot on the prow of the rowboat, her leg shakes with the effort and sets the boat vibrating. The placid surface of the lake quivers slightly, spreading rings farther and farther, creating contrasts in the photograph Elin takes. Elin challenges the model, instructs her to put more and more weight on the leg. The stern of the brown wooden boat lifts out of the water.

"It's magical. So much better than with the pink dress," Joe whispers. He's standing right behind Elin, looking at the computer screen and the images that pop up as she takes the photographs.

The whole time, Elin's thoughts are somewhere else; now and then she sneaks a glance at her phone, lying face-up at her feet. Neither Sam nor Alice has replied. Just emptiness and silence. She shivers at the thought of Alice's anger, of how she's pushing her away, accusing her. There must be some way she can get through to her; she can't lose her too.

Joe nudges her lightly in the ribs and she jumps, jerked out of her thoughts. He nods discreetly at the magazine's art director, who has put his thumb and forefinger together in a sign that he's happy, that it's a wrap. Elin lowers the camera without saying anything and holds it out to Joe.

"Elin, what's wrong? You seem so sad," he whispers, and puts his hand on her upper arm. She shakes her shoulder lightly to shrug it off, forcing him to take the heavy camera.

"Nothing. It turned out well. You can take the rest of the day off, just drop the equipment off at the studio first. I'm going home," she says, her voice a sorrowful monotone.

The model is wading toward shore with a disgusted expression on her face, the dress hoicked up so her narrow thighs and underwear are exposed. The stylist breathes in sharply.

"Watch the dress, careful, don't slip, it's muddy," he repeats over and over. "That dress is worth thirty thousand dollars."

The model looks stressed. She picks her way forward slowly, shuddering each time a foot sinks into the sludge.

Elin walks over to her.

"Perhaps it's Mary we should watch out for, not the dress," she says. She earns a weak smile from the model, who with her support takes a step up onto the lawn. The stylist rubs the shivering model's legs dry with a rag.

Elin backs away. The art director shows up at her side. He talks, but she's barely listening to the words streaming from his mouth. She just nods now and then, watching Joe and the others dismantle all the equipment.

"We'll have to work together again soon," she says when he finally stops talking.

He takes a step toward her, much too close. She takes a step back.

"Didn't you hear what I said?" Suddenly the irritated tone from yesterday is back, now that he understands Elin hasn't been listening. "We have to take a close-up of the dress too, a detail so you can see the fabric."

Elin nods.

"Of course, Joe can do it. It will probably be best in the studio."

She nods at her assistant. The man in front of her shakes his head and sighs.

"First a reshoot and now you're not even going to finish the job," he says. "We're paying a lot to have you, far too much if you ask me. I expect you to take the picture here, in the same environment, not let some . . . assistant do it."

Elin grits her teeth, pulls the camera roughly from the bag, and walks over to the dress, which is on the hanger hooked over a branch and swinging in the wind. She twists it with one hand, so the sunlight makes the surface shimmer, and snaps four frames. When she lowers the camera, her eyes have fixed on the tree trunk behind the dress, where a long line of ants is wandering up and down the uneven bark. She holds the dress aside and steps closer.

◆

Alice, what are you doing? Have you finished rehearsal? Please call. It's important.

Elin walks with her phone in her hand, staring at the screen. Alice isn't picking up when she calls, or answering texts. She checks the time, and types:

Call me. Now! Something has happened.

Alice phones less than a minute later, sounding tense and breathless.

"Mom, what's happened? Is it Dad?"

"No . . ." Elin pauses.

"What is it then?"

"Nothing. I was nearby, and I've finished work. I thought we could grab a coffee?"

Alice sighs.

"I was in the middle of a difficult position I've been practicing all afternoon. You interrupted me. And scared me. Why did you say something had happened?"

"You don't reply otherwise," Elin whispers.

There's silence at the other end.

"Alice, please," Elin pleads.

"Where are you?"

Elin looks around.

"Almost at the bottom of the park, east side."

"OK, go to Brooklyn Diner on Fifty-Seventh and Seventh and wait there; one of their milkshakes would be good. I'll come as soon as my lesson's finished. I'm just going to take a quick shower afterward."

◆

Elin orders a cappuccino while she waits. The foamy surface is decorated with a chocolate heart, and she takes the spoon and drags points of it out toward the lip of the china cup. It turns into a star. She stirs rapidly, mixing beige, brown, and white. She makes another heart, cutting through the thick foam, then letters, an *A*, an *E*, an *F*.

F for Fredrik. Maybe that was a sign, that he turned up just as Sam abandoned her. She eyes the clock. It's evening where he is. She wonders what he's doing, if he's alone too.

When Alice finally arrives, Elin is still playing with the spoon. The coffee has grown cold, the foam has almost melted.

"Mom, you scared me." Alice plumps down into the chair opposite with a thud. She grabs the menu. "Can I order some food? I'm so hungry."

Elin nods.

"Have what you want."

A tear runs down Elin's cheek. She swipes it away and bites her lip hard to refocus the pain. Alice lowers the menu.

"Oh, Mom, what is it? What's happened?"

"I'm just so tired."

"Are you sad?"

Elin nods.

"Yes."

Alice takes a deep breath, as though she suddenly needs more air. She picks up the menu again.

"I know what you need." She smiles and points at a line on the menu. Elin leans forward to look. *The Chocolatier*, she reads.

"It's incredible, it has chocolate ice cream and fudge and big chunks of chocolate. You'll love it."

Elin smiles cautiously.

"Well, that's what we'll have then. Chocolate always works," she says.

"Maybe it'll work out? Between you and Dad?"

"I don't know, I don't know anything at the moment." Tears fill Elin's eyes again.

"Let's talk about something else instead. Can you tell me something from when you were little? I'd love to hear."

Elin closes her eyes, but Alice ignores her, goes on asking questions.

"Why is it so hard to talk about? I don't understand. It's so simple. Were you a good girl, or naughty? Did you have any pets?"

"Yes." Elin looks up eagerly.

"What? Did you?"

"Yes, a dog, we had a dog. A border collie, black and white."

"In town? Isn't that one of those sheepdogs that need fields to run around in and stuff?"

Elin nods.

"Yep, that's the one. She used to run, fast as lightning across open fields. It was her favorite thing."

"I didn't think you liked dogs, you always seem to be complaining about them barking."

Elin bursts out laughing.

"Yeah, all the spoiled, yappy little city-dog fluff balls. I could really do without those."

"But yours must have been a city dog too?"

Elin avoids the question. She draws the spoon across her coffee, but there's too little foam left to draw anything.

"Sunny, her name was Sunny, and she was the sweetest dog in the world. She used to sleep with her head on my pillow."

"What? She got to sleep in your bed? Gross." Alice shudders.

"Yeah, maybe it was. But pretty cozy. I had a cat too, all my own. She was called Crumble."

"Like the dessert? Cute. Do you remember what you said when I was little and wanted to have a cat?"

Elin shakes her head.

"No, I don't actually."

"That it was better not to have animals, because it was so sad when they died. Such a weird thing to say to a child, I've never forgotten it."

"But it's true, isn't it?"

"What do you mean? Should you avoid loving people too then? Because anyone might die, or leave."

Then

=≡ ◆ ≡=

The rocking chair squeaked softly, the sound filling the empty house. Elin sat on the bottom step and listened. Marianne had been sitting there almost all day, just staring ahead and rocking. Back and forth, back and forth. No lunch had been prepared, no afternoon coffee. Not a word had crossed her lips. Not a smile. Not even when Elin had stuck her head in and met her gaze.

She'd had to look after the animals in the barn all by herself. Micke and Fredrik were out in the fields. On the days when there was extra work to do, they didn't come home until late in the evening. She could hear the eternal ticking of the kitchen clock and the infernal grumbling of her stomach. She'd lost track of time.

Erik and Edvin. Where had they gotten to? They needed food. She listened but couldn't hear anything from upstairs. She went out to the farmyard, stumbling over the gravel in her clogs, twisting her ankle but limping slowly onward, looking everywhere. At her heels padded Sunny, who had been out on her own all day. When Elin stopped and scratched behind her ear, the dog squirmed in gratitude and laid a paw on her arm.

Right in front of them on the gravel lay Edvin's bicycle, with the chunky red saddle he was so proud of.

She eventually found them in the tractor shed, behind heaps of junk they'd fashioned into a den. Long, irregular planks, damaged by the sun and water. Rusty bits of corrugated tin. Oil drums. A tractor tire and a sack of hay had been turned into a sofa and they both lay in it, with a well-thumbed Donald Duck comic between them. Elin stopped a little way off, listening to Erik reading the speech bubbles to Edvin with great effort. Edvin was resting his head on Erik's chest. Between them lay an open packet of crackers. She crept up to them and squeezed in next to Erik, took the comic, and went on reading where Erik pointed. Erik and Edvin each took a fresh cracker and crunched on it. The heat shimmered under the tin roof and their bodies were clammy and warm. On one of the roof trusses a pigeon sat cooing. In the grass along the walls the grasshoppers chirped.

Edvin turned the cracker packet upside-down, sending crumbs raining down all over his top.

"Elin, I'm still hungry," he moaned, clutching his belly.

"Me too. Mama's tired today, so we'll have to make our own food."

◆

Elin fried some fish fingers in the cast-iron frying pan and boiled some quick-cook pasta. When she put the pans on the table, Marianne came shuffling over and sat down at one end. In one hand she was holding her bankbook, its corners torn, the pages yellowing and full of handwritten figures in blue and black ink. She flicked through it, staring at the numbers. Elin set a plate down in front of her.

"Is money tight again now? Is it, Mama?"

Marianne raised her eyes and quickly met Elin's. Then she lowered them again and slammed the bankbook shut, resting her hand on it like a protective cover. She took her fork and dipped it in the open jar of mayonnaise. Let the sweet, oily condiment melt in her mouth.

"I'm sure it'll work out. Micke says it will. We've got a good harvest coming," she said finally.

She gathered the bills that were spread across the table into a pile and put them and the bankbook in one of the sideboard drawers. Then she went back to the rocking chair, leaving the children alone at the table. Elin served up the fish fingers, three each, and Erik and Edvin ate greedily.

◆

It wasn't until later that evening, with the sound of the tractor approaching, that Marianne found her way out of her fog. She came into the kitchen and grabbed the dishes with their dried-on food, the empty milk glasses, the scraped-clean pasta pot, and the greasy frying pan. Elin was still sitting on the kitchen bench, her nose deep in a book. She observed her mother's movements as she submerged the dishes in hot soapy water, noticing how she stood up straighter and pulled a hand through her hair when Micke's and Fredrik's shuffling steps could be heard on the veranda. Micke groaned as he used the bootjack to kick off his muddy boots. When he came into the kitchen, his half-pulled-off sports socks danced around like tails on the ends of his feet. His cheeks were muddy; even the stubble on his chin bore traces of dried-on dirt. He grabbed Marianne's behind hard and kissed the back of her neck, pushing himself against her. Fredrik rolled his eyes and made straight for the stairs.

Micke wouldn't let go of Marianne. He bit her on the ear, making her let out a little shriek. Embarrassed, she met Elin's gaze and tried to push him away. Elin slammed her book shut and stood up. Micke never gave up, she knew that. He turned Marianne to face him, and she held her wet hands high in the air and closed her eyes as he kissed her.

Elin walked past them, with her eyes on the floor. She turned around on the first step, saw him lift Marianne by the hips. A glass fell to the floor and smashed. Elin sped up, taking the stairs two at a time.

The noises from the bedroom shortly afterward made all the children leave the house. Erik and Edvin snuck back to their den in the tractor shed, each with a blanket under his arm. Elin and Fredrik climbed out the window and down the ladder that was propped outside, and then ran, hand in hand, toward the sea and the stars.

◈

The fat package felt heavy in her jacket pocket. It had come in the mail earlier that day, and she'd recognized the handwriting immediately but hadn't dared open it. In the firelight she took out the padded brown envelope and showed it to Fredrik. He understood immediately.

"Is it from him?"

She nodded.

"Open it, aren't you curious?"

"He hasn't written to me for four years. Not a word."

"Have you written to him?"

Elin thought about all the words, all the things she'd told her papa. But none of it had ever been posted. She shook her head and had started to pick at the sealed flap of the envelope when Fredrik took it from her, tearing it brutally right across.

"There, now you can look."

Elin stuck her hand in and took out a black plastic box and a pair of headphones. She looked at it doubtfully.

"It's a Walkman. Wow, I heard everyone in Stockholm has one."

Elin turned it over, running her fingers over the buttons.

"What do you do with it?"

Fredrik put the headphones over her head and pressed the button. She smiled when she heard the music and bopped her head to the opening bars of "Eye of the Tiger."

Fredrik pressed Stop and took out the tape to show her.

"It works with any tape, with all our mixtapes."

"Can I see, what does it say?"

Elin took the cassette and read the narrow label.

Elin's musical treasure trove

He'd written the words carefully and that was all. There was no other message. Four years of silence and then a mixtape. Elin flung the Walkman aside, and Fredrik barely saved it from hitting the ground. He stuffed the lump of black plastic safely in his back pocket.

"Look, we can carry it everywhere with us."

"But how would you be able to listen to the music then? If there's only one set of headphones, you can't share them."

"I can borrow it, can't I? We're not together all the time, are we?"

"Pretty much."

"I'm going to Mama's tomorrow, you know that."

"Stay here."

"You know I can't, she's coming to get me early. But I'll come to visit. I promise."

Fredrik gave her a little shove on the shoulder. She curled up and put her head in his lap, looked up at the sky, and sighed.

"When you're gone all the stars go out. It's all black."

"Then you'll have to be the moon, and let the sun's rays reach you. Light up all the blackness. Never forget that the sun is always there, beyond the darkness."

"You're starting to sound like a poet, where did that come from?"

"What? It's true. Never let the darkness eat you up. It's not worth it. Fight back."

Elin stretched her legs out and rolled over onto her stomach. Little stones dug into her elbows as she rested her chin on her hands.

"Have you noticed that Mama's gone back to how she used to be?"

"What do you mean?"

"She's somewhere else, she just stares ahead of her. Like she used to do before we moved here. It's almost impossible to reach her. She never smiles."

Fredrik snorted.

"They haven't got any money, that's why. It's always like that at this time of year. Papa throws it away, he just spends and spends. My mama always used to get angry about it, they used to fight about it. I think that's why she left. But everything will sort itself out, you'll see, they'll get money from the harvests soon. Then it will be party time again. That's how it works."

"Aina's money is all gone now. I saw it in Mama's bankbook. That was meant to make us happy."

"We'll have to find other things to make us happy. Stuff all that, anyway. Stuff the money, stuff the grown-ups. Come on, let's go for a swim."

He stood up and started to take his clothes off, throwing off each piece one after the other until he was wearing nothing but his underpants.

They raced to the water. The horizon was still a soft pink-purple, like a reminder of the sun that had just set, and the lapping water shone black and silver. Elin dived in first, deep under the surface. She took long, powerful strokes underwater and came up close to where Fredrik was standing with his arms crossed, shivering, drops of water glistening on his chin. She tried to push him over, but he was too quick, and vanished below the surface.

They dried themselves on the blanket, the wool one that jabbed their skin like a thousand tiny needles. Then they built a new tower of dry twigs in the fireplace that was theirs alone, and lit it with matchsticks from the worn matchbox they kept hidden there, under a mountain of stones.

At night everything was so simple. From either end they rolled themselves up in the damp blanket and let the fire warm them.

Now

≡ ◆ ≡

NEW YORK, 2017

Only minutes to go. Elin waits by the red staircase in the opera house's lobby, watching the entrance expectantly, longing to see Alice's curly hair and beaming smile. She reluctantly advances up the stairs and checks the time. From the orchestra pit she hears stray notes from instruments being tuned, and all the people who so recently thronged around her have disappeared into the auditorium to find their seats. She hears doors closing; the instruments fall silent.

She's wearing an emerald-green dress of delicate lace, cut close to her body, with a silk slip underneath. Around her neck is the diamond necklace Sam gave her, long ago, when they were first in love. Her hair is loose, freshly blow-dried and curled specially for the evening, one she's been longing for.

But the doors to the entrance remain closed. Elin sighs heavily and takes the two tickets out of her handbag. She drops one behind her, and it floats down the staircase as she heads toward the stalls.

"Mom! Wait!"

The familiar voice makes her stop: Alice is behind her. She turns around slowly. Alice stops and hangs over the banister, exhausted but waving, gasping for breath. Her curly hair stands up like a halo around her head. She's sweaty and wriggles out of her overfilled backpack and gray knitted sweater with great effort. Underneath she's wearing a neon-green top with big black lettering spelling out the word *power*. Her jeans have rips in both knees, and her white sneakers are covered in stains. Elin sighs deeply and motions for her to hurry. Alice reaches for her hand.

"Sorry, Mom! I had to run straight from my class. I lost track of time and there wasn't a minute to go home and change."

Elin doesn't reply. She points to the ticket that's lying on one of the steps. Then she turns and keeps walking, without a word. Alice snatches up the ticket and runs to catch up with her.

"It doesn't matter, does it? It's just a regular performance, not opening night. And anyway, we match," Alice sniggers, pulling her T-shirt to touch Elin's dress.

Ignoring her, Elin carefully opens the door to the stalls. The lights are already down in the auditorium. The velvet curtains part, silencing the hubbub immediately, and the orchestra's strings guide the audience into a little attic apartment in 1830s Paris.

Elin and Alice stand stock-still, side by side. The stress of Alice's late arrival has made Elin's heart beat extra hard; sweat has broken out on her forehead and under her nose. She wipes it away awkwardly. Alice reaches for her arm, strokes it, and whispers an apology.

A man with a flashlight emerges from the darkness and shines it on their tickets. He looks displeased as he points toward row eight, and mouths: *In the middle.* Elin and Alice creep forward and pick their way apologetically past the people already seated. Alice puts her heavy backpack on her lap, hugging it as though it were a cushion, and fixes her eyes, enchanted, on the scene before them. After a little while, she plunges her hand into her bag and rummages around, making a rustling sound. Elin slaps her wrist. Undeterred, Alice fishes out a chocolate bar and offers it to Elin, who slaps her wrist again, harder this time.

"Ow," Alice whispers loudly.

"Be *quiet*," Elin whispers back.

The man in the next seat shushes them, and they sit in silence for the rest of the performance, including the intermission. Alice eats her chocolate; Elin walks to the restroom alone and comes back to the auditorium just as the lights are lowered again.

The music finishes at last, replaced by rousing applause. That too falls silent. The auditorium lights come up and the seats empty. Elin and Alice don't get up. Finally, Alice breaks the silence.

"Are you not going to speak to me all night? Just because I ate a little chocolate?"

Alice stands. Elin sighs and leans her head back, studies the golden circles on the ceiling. She senses her daughter's gaze but doesn't acknowledge her.

"Oh well, I guess I'd better go then. If I'm not good enough."

Elin turns her head to face her. The diamonds around her neck glitter, as do her eyes.

"What do you mean? If you're not good enough?"

"Well, that's what you think, isn't it?"

Elin puts her hand to her forehead and closes her eyes.

"Stop it! You mustn't think that," she says.

"What should I think then?"

Alice grabs her backpack and leaves the row of seats. Elin stands and follows her.

"Of course you're good enough! It would have been nice if you'd dressed up a bit and been on time, but you're lovely as you are. You know that's what I think. I've been looking forward to this, longing for it."

Alice stops short, and Elin bumps into her back. Alice doesn't turn around.

"I told you I didn't have time. I'm studying. This is what students look like; maybe you don't remember that, Mrs. Perfect. I came here and really enjoyed the show. Isn't that enough? It's not some fucking fashion show. It's culture. And I doubt Puccini would have minded."

Elin smooths her hands over her dress, closes her eyes, and slowly counts to ten.

"Sorry." She looks Alice right in the eye.

"Have you considered that it might be you who's overdoing it? Clothes don't matter, you know that. Look around you. People don't go to the opera in ball gowns anymore. And it's OK to eat a bit of chocolate. No one cares. No one apart from you."

"It's a special evening."

"How so? It's a regular Thursday, a regular performance. It was really good, and I'm glad I came, but can we go and eat now, so I can go home?" Alice rolls her eyes.

"It's a special evening because I'm spending it with you. I miss you every day," Elin whispers.

Alice says nothing. Then she laughs.

"But then why are you so cross when we do see each other? OK, I look the way I do, but I'm still me."

Elin nods.

"I gave you money to buy some new shoes last week. You look like a poor person," she whispers, pointing at Alice's scruffy shoes.

"Yes, but I don't need any new shoes. These are fine for me. I gave the money away instead. To children in Tanzania. *They* need new shoes." Alice emphasizes this sentence as she slowly rises up onto her toes.

Elin holds her breath again, counts silently in her head again. She looks at Alice's disheveled hair, curls going in every direction, and at the bushy eyebrows that have never been plucked. She's so wild and yet so beautiful.

"Can we start over? Please? I've got a pair of jeans in the studio, it's not that far. Let's swing by and I can change. And then we'll go and eat at . . . some simple place. You're right, I overdo it sometimes."

Alice nods.

"Did you wear that for my sake or for Dad's?" She nods at the necklace. Elin lays a hand over it.

"I just wanted to wear it today," she murmurs.

"Does it really mean that much to you? Ugh, how sad. I don't understand why you live apart when you clearly still love each other so much."

"I don't understand either."

"Are you blaming Dad?"

"Yes."

"Then I think you need to reconsider. You haven't been at home with him for years. All you do is work. And if you're not working, you're thinking about work. Or talking about it. Talk about something else instead, something interesting. You should try it next week, when we go for my birthday dinner. Tell him something he doesn't know."

Elin turns away from Alice and goes down the red staircase, through the empty lobby, and out into the dark night. Tears well up in her eyes. Her high heels echo against the paving. Alice runs after her, walks close, stubbornly pushing her arm in under Elin's. When they get to Columbus Avenue, Elin steps out into the street and hails a taxi.

"Jeans, then. Blue. You promise?" Alice puts on a smile with her chin thrust forward in an exaggerated underbite. She wiggles her head from side to side.

"I promise. I have a pair. Stop making that face, it's scary." Elin laughs, and the movement forces a tear to leave her eye and roll down her cheek.

"I'll believe it when I see it." Alice catches the tear tenderly with her index finger.

◈

Alice dances her way across the white-painted floor of the studio, doing pirouette after pirouette, from one wall to the other. Elin captures her movements with the camera, still dressed in the emerald-green dress and heels. She follows her daughter's rhythmic, supple body in fascination. Alice stops and bends her neck and spine backward in an arc. As her curls graze the floor, she steadies herself with her hands and lifts one leg toward the ceiling. Her jeans creak and she falls, laughing, to one side. The spell is broken, and Elin lowers her camera.

"It's the jeans, I swear," she laughs, still lying in a heap on the floor.

"Sure, blame it on the jeans." Elin puts her camera aside and leans over the computer. She flicks through the images she's just taken, selects one, crops it, and shifts the color scale a little.

"Here, would this do for a profile picture?"

Alice leans over her and studies her own image. She's caught in motion, blurred, her hair wild. The text on her T-shirt stands out.

"Wow, it's perfect. You're magic, I don't understand how you do it."

"You're the one who's magic, it's you moving your body. I just capture reality as it is."

Elin adjusts the color scale a little further to sharpen the text on the T-shirt.

"Ah. Your reality is not reality. You mean all your fancy portraits in *Vanity Fair* and *Vogue* are real? No wonder people get complexes."

Elin shuts the laptop and turns toward Alice.

"Come on. Even in reality there are different types of light. Even you look better in some, worse in others."

Alice protests. "No, stop, don't start defending retouching. Every re-touched image should come with a warning." She holds her hands up in the air.

"Please, let's not have this conversation now. We've already talked about it a thousand times. Most of the people I photograph are more at-tractive than average from the start. And with good light and makeup it's even better. But you can get magical light in reality too, on a beach at sunset or at a meadow in the mist. In certain lights everyone's more beautiful. Every *thing*'s more beautiful, not just people."

Alice says nothing. She opens the screen again and studies the pic-ture, comparing it with the original.

"Yeah, yeah, you're right, it is better. Thanks for the picture. But don't retouch it any more now, it's fine as it is. Lovely, magical. Though not particularly realistic," she says, wrinkling her nose so her whole face scrunches up into a grimace.

Elin grabs the camera and quickly presses the shutter.

"Here, a perfect profile image. Totally real," she says.

Alice smirks.

"No thanks, I'll skip it. Surely I'm allowed some kind of advantage, having a star mom."

"You could be a star yourself. It's clear you've been training a lot, you're really one with the dance. It's lovely."

"Yeah, yeah, don't even try it, we both know which of us is the star." Alice sighs. "Go and get changed now. Jeans, you promised me jeans. I'm starving and I want pizza. And Coke."

Elin vanishes up the spiral staircase that leads to the studio's office as Alice reclines on the sofa. Elin stops and looks at her against the backdrop of buildings and bridges over the East River, through the gigantic windows. The music that had just filled the room has stopped, leaving space for the high, steady hum of engines and sirens from the street. Alice stands up again and walks around the studio. White floors, white walls, white cupboards, white tables. Only the light stands, covered with black-and-white fabric slipcovers, interrupt the brightness.

"Where's the stereo, Mom, have you thrown it out?"

"Stereo? I was playing music from my phone, from Spotify."

"Put it on again, then."

"In a minute, I'll be down in a minute. I haven't got my phone up here," she calls.

When Elin comes back from the office, she sees Alice sitting with the black notepad in her hand and Elin's handbag beside her. She is flicking slowly through the crowded pages.

The steps creak and sway as Elin runs down them, two at a time. She's changed into narrow jeans, an open-necked white shirt, and high brown motorbike boots. Her hair is pulled into a ponytail. Alice slams the book shut when she hears her coming. Elin runs across the floor and grabs it out of her hand.

"That's private, it's mine. Come on, let's go," she says, stuffing the book into her bag and gripping it close to her body.

"Are you writing a diary?" Alice is still sitting on the floor, astonished.

"It's just a project, you wouldn't understand. It's . . . notes," says Elin, aware that her voice sounds tight and stressed. She reaches out a hand and pulls Alice to her feet.

"It looked like a totally different world. What was that house, a farmhouse?"

"It's just a game, I said. Let's go." Elin turns her back on Alice.

"A game? Just now it was a project."

"Yeah, yeah," Elin sighs, "a project then . . ."

"There was so much nature: trees, flowers, farms. I thought you hated the country?"

"Yeah, I do, I hate the country. I'm a city mouse. Come on now, I'm hungry."

Elin turns off the ceiling lights; the glossy floor of the studio is covered with reflections from the streetlights. Alice lingers.

"You're not going mad, are you?"

"Why do you ask that?"

"Something feels weird. You're not yourself."

Elin shakes the keys, making them rattle loudly.

"I'm locking up now, are you staying here?"

Alice pulls on her sweater and her backpack. She points at Elin's boots and the tight pants, which have rhinestones on the back pocket.

"Those aren't jeans."

"What? Sure they are. What's wrong with them?"

"You still look like you've just jumped out of a page in a fashion magazine. Can't you ever just be normal?"

"At least I haven't been retouched."

Alice rolls her eyes.

"No? If my face is that smooth when I'm nearly fifty, *then* I'll believe you."

Then

≡ ◆ ≡

HEIVIDE, GOTLAND, 1982

Micke heaved open the door without knocking. Elin pulled the covers over her head and pressed herself against the wall, but it was too late: he could see she was there, and he pulled the covers off roughly. She was naked, apart from pink cotton underwear, and she flailed with her hand to grab the cover again. He didn't let go. She pulled stubbornly.

"It's almost eleven," he said firmly, tapping his watch with his eyes fixed on her.

"I don't feel like waking up today."

Elin turned her back to him, her arms wrapped tight around her to protect her nakedness.

"I mean it. Come on, up with you, this is not a hotel. Marianne told me she had to look after the goats all on her own this morning. You know that's your job."

Elin turned around again and reached for the cover.

"Give me the cover, please! You're not my dad." Elin raised her voice and pulled hard at the flowery fabric he held in his hand. Micke dropped it nonchalantly on the floor, so that she lost her balance and fell back onto the bed.

"You little . . . you should be fucking glad you get to live here and not in that rat hole you came from."

"Rat hole!" Elin sat up straight, her embarrassment forgotten, her naked brown skin shining in the sunlight coming through the window. Micke leaned over her.

"Rat hole, yeah. Perhaps you don't remember?"

"What are you talking about?"

"You and your mom were nothing before you met me. Nothing."

Elin felt her heart racing in her chest.

"What are you talking about? You wouldn't even have a farm if it hadn't been for Mama and Aina's money. We were the ones with the money. Remember? And now it's gone. Don't you think I know that?"

"You shouldn't talk about things you don't understand. You hear? And I bet you're just as much of a slut as your mother was. Who knows what you and Fredrik have been getting up to, when you get so depressed as soon as he leaves. You're siblings, for fuck's sake." He gestured to her budding breasts and snorted. Elin picked the cover up off the floor and wrapped it tight around her.

He locked eyes with her and then turned on his heel and left the room. She put on a short T-shirt and ran after him.

"Don't think for a minute I want to be here," she screamed. "I hate it here. I could move back home. I could move home today if you want to be rid of me."

Micke stopped a few steps down and looked up at her over his shoulder. Marianne shouted something from her rocking chair down in the living room, but they neither heard nor responded to what she said.

"Now you shut your mouth, little girl, do you hear me? Shut it!"

"You're no more than a simple thief. You've taken our money. Don't think I don't know."

"I told you not to talk about things you don't understand."

He took a step up again, and she took a step back. For a long time they just stood there, staring at each other. She saw beads of sweat shimmering on his forehead. His threatening look made her think thoughts she'd rather not. She backed away again, but then he banged the banister hard with his palm. She jumped in terror. He came close, and the smell of sweat and chewing tobacco nauseated her. His wheezing breath echoed against the bare walls.

Elin took a hesitant step forward again, toward Micke. Her heart thumped hard against her ribs. He held his fist up in the air, waved it threateningly at her. Around his mouth she could see tense little wrinkles. She stopped.

"Let me past. I want to go down to Mama."

He raised his eyebrows.

"To Mama. Got you scared?"

She twisted to the side and darted around behind him, but he pressed his body back, hard, trapping her against the handrail. She struggled for breath.

"Let me go," she managed to gasp. His muscular body cut into hers. She felt the blood rising in her face, felt the veins in her neck filling.

"Mama!" Her scream came out as a reedy little squeak. Micke gave a loud, fake laugh. He leaned even more of his weight against her. Elin pulled one of her hands free, managed to turn it around, and dug her fingers into his back, pinching as hard as she could. He jumped and suddenly the pressure was gone. She fell in a heap on the stairs, gasping for breath.

"Goddamn brat. See what you made me do." He came close, stared her right in the eyes. His front teeth were speckled with brown chewing tobacco.

"You're not allowed to hit me!" Elin met his gaze, suddenly unafraid.

"What are you going to do? Phone social services? Call your dad in prison?"

"My papa never hit me."

"He hit your mom."

"Maybe he did, but not me."

Micke smiled contemptuously. His breath made her gag and turn her head away.

"You call that hitting?"

Elin nodded.

"You're not touching me again. You're not my dad," she said, at first whispering but increasing in volume. She took a few steps toward him, and now she was screaming.

"You're not touching me again. Get it?"

Micke attacked her so fast, she almost didn't manage to react. His palm struck her cheek and her whole head flew sideways. A sharp note rang in her ear and sent her reeling into the banister again. She rubbed her hand over her cheek in astonishment. Her skin stung, as though his hand was still there.

"Not a murmur about this to Marianne. You hear me? If you do she'll get it, and it'll be ten times worse than this."

He bent over her and held his fist close to her face. She crouched down and backed away so that she was pressed against the wall once more.

"Not a murmur. You hear? And in the future you'll get up on time and help out here on the farm. You're not on vacation, if that's what you were thinking. You're old enough to work," he said.

Elin pushed past him without a word and ran down the steps. She took them two at a time. Tears streamed from her eyes. She left the house barefoot, in only a T-shirt and underwear.

◈

The ground in front of her was blurry. She kept her eyes on the path, the narrow one that wound through the forest's stunted pines down to the sea. Her eyes swam with tears, her nose was thick with mucus. The briar thickets had grown close over the summer, and they tore at her legs, but she didn't care. Her bare feet pattered on in a straight line across the earth, jumping over stones and roots. From the sea blew a wind that cut through the summer heat and gave her bare legs goose bumps.

Elin didn't stop until she reached the beach and fell down on all fours, panting from the exertion. Her breaths came shallow and fast. Panicking, she gasped for oxygen. Her head was spinning. She curled up in the fetal position and watched the sea and the faraway horizon. The waves were dotted with white crests; the beach grass was hunched. Now that the forest was no longer sheltering her against the wind, she was cold.

She lay there a long time, softly humming a melody, their melody, hers and Fredrik's. The notes were drowned out by the sea's roar. No one could hear her, no one was there. She was safe in her isolation. Her breathing became calmer.

By the time the sun hung just above the cliffs, her tears had stopped falling. She could tell it was late in the afternoon now, and soon it would be evening. She stood up and began to gather dry twigs in her arms: crooked ones, rotten ones, healthy ones, long ones, short ones. She carried them all the way to the campfire site and threw all the sticks into the firepit.

Their blanket was still there, thrown over a large stone. And the book about the stars, the one they'd flicked through in an attempt to understand the infinity that surrounded them. The pages were well-thumbed and the spine was held together with tape. She sat on the stone and considered the pile of sticks. It covered the entire base of the firepit, but she wasn't satisfied. She took another walk, filling her arms again. And another. And another. The wood rose up over the edges of the pit, enough to create a great bonfire. She put everything she could find onto it. Great heavy branches from the woods, ones that had fallen in the early storms and dried in the sun. It wasn't cold, but she was freezing; the wind made her body tremble. She longed for warmth. Soon, soon she'd light it. She was just going to gather a little more, to make the fire a little larger.

Now

=⧫=

The studio is covered with purple velvet, long shimmering bolts of it. They're draped along the wall, across the floor, and over the chair, in the camera's viewfinder. The waves of cloth look like water, soft and rolling. A stylist and her assistant are crawling around on the floor, adjusting everything, making the fabric float. Between the bolts they lay out pink flowers. Pink and purple, a little girl's dream. A child sits at the makeup table. Not any child, though. A full-fledged child star, with her own agent watching over everything the makeup artist is doing. The girl's red hair gets corkscrew curls. Her face is powdered. She looks more and more like a porcelain doll. Her lips, painted dark pink, pout sulkily. She stretches her hand out as her nails are painted a pale pink. Elin stands behind the chair and studies her in the mirror.

"Don't put so much powder on. I want to see the skin's structure. She's just a child, it has to feel real."

The makeup artist looks from Elin to the agent and back again, confused. She holds the powder puff still in the air. The agent waves at her to continue.

"Make her perfect. She has to be perfect," he says definitively.

He turns to Elin.

"What was that? Is it suddenly up to you to decide now?"

Elin turns and walks over to the spiral staircase.

"Do what you want, it normally turns out fine. Everything else is set up and ready to go. Call me when *she* is. Call me when she's . . . perfect." She hesitates before this last word, as though she's not sure it's the right one.

◆

On the screensaver, images of Alice flicker past. Sam is in some of them too. He smiles at her, smiles at the camera, smiles at Alice. She clicks the mouse to get rid of him and opens her search engine. She types the name Fredrik and presses Enter, opting to see only image results. Thousands of men in shirts and suits smile at her. She scrolls down; it never ends. They're all different men but all the same in some way. She does a new search, types in his surname, and holds her finger on Enter without pressing. She studies the letters. Fredrik Grinde.

She deletes Fredrik and makes do with an initial search for Grinde. This time, only sailboats come up. Boats bearing his name.

Someone calls her from the floor below. She takes a few deep breaths and then goes down. The girl is already sitting on the chair. She's wearing a simple white cotton dress and holding her chin high. Everything about her is false. Made up right down to her bare arms. Her hair looks like a blazing fire. Elin walks up and adjusts the bolts of purple fabric around her. She runs her hand over the soft surface. The girl grows impatient.

"Go over to your camera instead," she whines. "*I'm* ready."

Elin stands up and turns to the agent.

"I can't do this."

"What do you mean?"

"It's sick. She's just a child. She looks like a doll."

"That's the point."

"Who are you trying to fool?"

"What do you mean?"

"Why can't she just be the way she is? I want to see her freckles. Wash all this stuff off her."

"OK, Mrs. Star Photographer, that's enough. We're the ones paying here. Take the picture and don't try to interfere with our strategy." The agent crosses his arms and stares at her.

"Perhaps the strategy should be to give her a good childhood? Instead of this . . . sick facade."

The girl's mother gets up from the sofa where she's been sitting with a book, walks over to the agent, and whispers something to him. He pushes her away.

"I'm in control. Let me take care of this."

The mother glares at Elin, who turns her head away. The agent takes a step closer.

"The pictures shouldn't be *real*. I don't know what's going on with you, I've never seen you like this before. Her next film is out in a month. We need these pictures. So press the damn shutter and make your magic happen. Be yourself."

Throughout the conversation, the girl sits perfectly still, not a trace of emotion on her face. She's still holding her chin high, and the dress sits exactly as the stylist draped it. Elin walks over to her. She starts close. Takes pictures that show nothing but the girl's large green eyes and then slowly backs away. The agent, stylist, and makeup artist are all standing at the computer, as image after image comes up on the screen. Elin gets caught up in the girl's incredible presence and soon forgets the artifice.

❖

That evening she falls asleep with a piece of the purple velvet against her body. It reminds her of a blanket she once had. The one that soothed her so well, when the skin on her cheek was streaked with red and stinging with pain.

❖

She can hear the sea so clearly. The waves roar in her ears, crashing again and again over the beach. She ducks under blackened branches and creeps forward between the tree trunks. It's deserted and everything is burnt, everything is gone, turned to charred remains. She can't find the sea, though she can hear it. She's searching everywhere. The sound grows weaker, then stronger. She runs. The ground is black and covered in ash, and as she tentatively places one foot down after the other, they sink into the hot and soft material. She sees flames licking her bare legs and runs even faster. The flames climb up from the earth, higher and higher, reaching out for her. She dodges between them, throwing herself from side to side. The sea is close again, she can hear it clearly. Water splashes, roars, murmurs in her ears. She looks up. Above her is nothing but thick gray smoke. A thick bubbling mat that presses down onto her. No sky, no stars. She hears a distant voice whisper:

"I'm here."

It's him, it's Fredrik. She shouts his name.

"Brother, where are you? Show yourself."

She spins around, searching for him. The flames rise up around her body. She feels no pain.

"Fredrik, come out."

The flames are reaching her face now, they flicker before her eyes. The voice comes closer.

"The star. I've lost my star," it whispers.

"Fredrik. I can hear you. Come to me! I'm here."

She reaches out her arms. He's there, she can see his face through the flames. He smiles. Water drops from his chin. The fire hisses around him. His hair is burning. She screams.

◆

Elin opens her eyes suddenly. She's soaked in sweat, and the silk sheets cling coldly to her body. It's still night. Shadows dance across the wall as the plants out on the terrace sway in the breeze. Her heart is racing, and she's breathing as if she's just been out for a run. She pushes the piece of purple velvet, now wet, aside. She pulls off the camisole she sleeps in and drops it over the edge of the bed. Her body feels damp and rough. She pulls Sam's side of the covers over her and turns on the light. She hasn't washed the bedding, and the cleaner hasn't been allowed into the bedroom since Sam moved out. She can still smell his scent, but it's getting weaker and weaker every day.

She takes out her notebook and flicks through to an empty page. She starts to draw, sketching flowers, and it makes her feel a little calmer. Oxeye daisies, bluebells, clover. It turns into a bouquet. She gathers it in a vase, draws stalks down into it, a narrow pencil line from each of the flowers. When it's done she tears out the page and writes in Swedish:

Thanks for the star. Here's a summer bouquet for you.

Then

=⧫=

The fire wouldn't light. Elin struck match after match against the box and held each one to the kindling; soon, all the matches in the secret supply were gone. The first flames from the dried grass subsided quickly. She kicked a stone, kicked at the branches. Then she threw the matchbox onto the heaped wood.

She pulled at her T-shirt in an attempt to make it longer, but it barely reached the waistband of her underwear. She grabbed the blanket and wrapped it around her middle. It was stiff with saltwater and rain, which had dried in the strong sunlight. Soon she was back on the path again, running with the blanket fluttering behind her, her bare legs peeping through the gap in the fabric. When she was level with the store, she left the path.

Gerd laughed at her when she came in through the glass door.

"What's all this about? Is it some new fashion?"

Without replying, Elin stood just inside the door and scanned for the matches with her eyes. She found them on the shelf behind the register.

"You look freezing. Do you want some hot chocolate? I'm closing soon, but there's time for us to have a drink."

Elin nodded. When Gerd went into the kitchen, she quickly grabbed a few boxes of matches and hid them under the blanket, in the hand she was using to hold it closed.

"Here, get this down you." Gerd handed her the steaming cup and placed a flowery plate of vanilla dreams between them on the counter. She picked up a cookie gratefully and put the whole thing in her mouth. Her stomach was aching from hunger after a whole day without food.

"Almost as good as Aina's," she mumbled, her mouth full of crumbs.

"Almost, yeah. But it's not good enough. I don't know what it was she put in the dough to make them so lovely and crisp. I've searched the whole house for the recipe."

"Aina never used any recipes. She did a bit of what she thought best, she knew it all by heart."

"Yeah, I guess she did. She was magical, wasn't she?"

"You're magical too. Your cookies are just as good." Elin took the other cookie too. This time she nibbled at it and let the sweetness melt in her mouth.

"How are things at the farm? Are you sad now Fredrik has gone?"

Elin didn't reply. Gerd went on talking, as though she already knew the answer.

"Of course you are. You two, you've always belonged together. I was scared something might change . . . you know, when . . . But you stayed together all the same. Friendship must be at least as strong as love."

"Friendship is love too, isn't it?" Elin turned to face Gerd.

"Of course, I suppose it is. Are they nice to you? Marianne and Micke? Do you have to work hard?"

Elin held up a hand, showed her the calluses on her palm.

"Oh, Lord. You know you can always come here if there's something you need to talk about."

Elin nodded. Gerd babbled on.

"It's so lovely when you come, it brightens my day."

"Yeah, but now I have to go again." Elin took a last gulp of hot chocolate and stood up.

"You young people are always in such a rush. Stay a while longer and you can eat some more. There are nut cookies too."

Gerd opened the cookie tin, but Elin was already on her way out. Gerd held out a cookie to her.

"Take this with you."

Elin turned and took it. She put it straight into her mouth, still hungry.

"I hear that Lasse's come out now, have you heard from him at all? Is he coming back?"

Elin shook her head.

"I'll be fourteen soon. I don't need a dad anymore. Not Lasse and not Micke."

"If you say so."

"Yeah, I get by just fine."

"He'll turn up soon, your papa, don't you think? You must miss him?"

"I don't know. I have to go. By the way . . . do you have any lighter fluid?"

"What do you want that for?"

"Micke asked me to ask you, I don't know what he wants it for," she lied, averting her eyes.

"I've got half a bottle, if that. But it's his if he wants it."

Gerd disappeared again and Elin bent quickly over the candy racks. Two packs of toffees, mint and chocolate, joined the matchboxes under the blanket. She jumped when she heard Gerd's voice from the basement stairs and pulled the blanket around her body to hide the stolen goods. The packets rustled and bulged. She gathered the blanket and pressed her arm tightly across her stomach.

"It's pretty old, I don't recognize the brand. But it says methylated spirits here," Gerd said, peering at the label over the top of her glasses.

"It doesn't matter, I'm sure it'll be fine." Elin grabbed the bottle and quickly made for the glass door.

"I'm shutting up now, I can drive you home."

Gerd walked after her with the key in her hand, but Elin pretended not to hear and let the door slam shut behind her.

◈

Through the trees she could make out a faint light in the dusk, coming from Aina's house. Someone was there. Stopping on the gravel track, Elin stiffened, unable to move her legs or arms. The blanket was trailing on the ground. Who would break into a dead person's house? She dropped everything in a heap, the blanket, the matchboxes, the candy, and the lighter fluid, and crept up to the fence. The light was coming from the living room window. One of the lace curtains was hanging askew, and thick layers of cobwebs shone like silver in the white glare from the striplights on the ceiling. Shadows flickered back and forth across the pale walls. There was someone inside. She stared at the window, listening to the noises coming from within. Someone was going through the things left in the empty house.

A car stopped in the drive, and Elin ran around the corner of the house and hid. She climbed up on the garden furniture that was stacked along the side of the house and peered in. She could make out a face behind the thin curtains: Marianne's. She was moving uncertainly around the room with a cigarette in one hand, a cloud of smoke around her. With the other hand she was rummaging through drawers and cupboards.

She jumped when she heard a voice. Elin did too, almost losing her balance, and she had to grab the windowsill to avoid falling to the ground. It was Gerd, who apparently had also seen the lights. She stormed into the living room. Her voice sounded tinny and weak through the filter of the windowpane.

"Marianne, what are you up to? I thought there was a burglar."

Marianne and Gerd stood eye to eye in the bright room. Objects lay spread across the floor: silver cutlery, vases, china. Marianne looked like a twisted abstract painting. Sweat on her forehead and upper lip, tears in her eyes, hair ratty, lipstick outside the natural contours of her lips, creased and unbuttoned shirt hanging to one side, exposing a shoulder and her camisole. She dropped what she had in her hand, a vase and a silver spoon, and the vase smashed to pieces. Elin reached her hand out reflexively. It was the vase Aina had always filled with blue anemones, the one that stood on the kitchen table in spring. As she saw Gerd bend down and pick up the shards, Elin felt the stack of furniture sway beneath her feet.

"We have to clear this place sometime. It can't stand here abandoned; someone has to move in. The place is too empty. We have to sell it now."

"What were you planning to do with all this?"

Gerd went around looking at the objects that had been spread around the place.

"Sell it. The silver's real, that'll be worth a bit. And the crystal glasses. There should be some jewelry too, but I haven't found any."

"Jewelry? Aina only had costume stuff."

"How do you know? She was rolling in it. Those big stones she used to dangle around her neck might have been real."

"Have you looked in the cellar?"

Marianne nodded. Gerd sat on the old blue-velvet sofa, the one Aina never used because she thought it was too fancy. Bits of the stuffing, small clumps of dry gray foam, fell out onto the floor. Marianne sat down beside her. Elin saw their heads poking up over the sofa back. They leaned against each other. She could no longer hear what they were saying; they were talking too low. Suddenly Marianne stood up, seemingly angry. She walked to the stairs, dragging on the cigarette between her fingers.

"Don't tell me how to live my life," she shouted at Gerd. Then she dropped the cigarette butt nonchalantly on the floor and disappeared upstairs.

❖

As Elin jumped down, a chair slipped to the ground. She grabbed her things and ran fast toward the beach, the sea, and the bonfire that wouldn't burn without Fredrik. The clouds piled up on the horizon, pinkish in the setting sun. The waves had subsided in the light evening breeze. Elin shivered and rubbed her legs to stay warm.

She squirted lighter fluid over the branches, using every drop in the bottle until the dry wood was stained dark. Then she took out the matchboxes and lit the matches one by one, dropping them carefully, deep into the woodpile. It crackled, and the flames climbed high, upward the trees. Warmth enclosed Elin's body, flushing her cheeks. She lay down, wrapped herself in the blanket, hugged her knees to her chest, and rested her eyes on the red flames until she fell asleep.

Now

≡ ◆ ≡

NEW YORK, 2017

Ten minutes late, but here she comes. Elin sees her darting between puddles down on the street, a newspaper over her head as protection from the downpour. The water splashes up her legs, striping her pale jeans with damp. Elin sees her wave cheerfully at the concierge before she disappears from view. The studio is full of people. She needs Alice for a picture, and Alice has promised to help out. Joe laughs when she comes running in through the door.

"Voilà! Your mini-me is here at last," he calls to Elin. Both Elin and Alice look offended.

"I don't look like . . ."

"She doesn't look like . . ."

They protest simultaneously, then both laugh.

"You do, apart from your clothes, I guess," he says.

Alice sighs.

"Don't you start, Joe. Mom already hassles me enough. Cool clothes aren't important to me."

"I didn't say you weren't cool. What I meant was that you're the cool one." Joe runs his hand through his blond hair and glances at Elin. Alice smiles with delight.

"Thanks, at least someone's on my side."

◆

When Elin turns her back, Alice leans toward him.

"Mom's going crazy, I swear. Have you noticed anything weird?"

Joe nods.

"I can *hear* you." Elin whirls around.

"She lost it when Dad moved out," Alice continues.

"Shh," hisses Elin.

Joe looks from one to the other.

"Sam? Has he moved out? How come?"

"Alice, you were late and we've got work to do. Let's get going now. Joe doesn't need to hear about that."

Alice mouths to him: *Hasn't she told you?* He shakes his head.

"Joe works with you every day," says Alice to Elin. "How could you not tell him you and Dad have separated?"

Ignoring her, Elin walks away, and Alice follows her through the studio. The models — men in suits — are standing around, waiting. An enormous bunch of colored balloons has floated up to the ceiling. Joe jumps up and pulls it down. He walks over to the white backdrop and waves at the models to follow him. They stand next to one another, stiffly. One at the edge of the backdrop holds the balloons. Alice takes off the clothes she's wearing, revealing a pale-pink ballet costume underneath. She stretches carefully, warming up her stiff legs and arms. Elin walks across the backdrop and gestures.

"I want you to jump in front of them, high in a grand jeté, your arms stretched out gracefully and your head tilted back."

She turns to the men.

"And you stand stock-still. Try not to move at all; you almost need to hold your breath just as she jumps. Look serious. You and you look sideways," she says, pointing at two of them. "The others look straight ahead. OK?"

The models nod. Alice tries a jump. She lands softly and Elin nods approvingly.

"My princess, this is going to be perfect."

◈

Alice and Joe are each lying on a sofa. The photo is done, and the models have left. Elin sits with the computer on her lap and tags the best images. Now and then she turns the computer around to show them. She's happy.

"Alice, can you run up and fetch my sketchbook? I want to show you. It turned out just like my sketch, almost better."

Alice walks over to the stairs. She's still wearing her ballet shoes and she trips along, sway-backed. The tulle tutu flips in the draft. She dances a few steps to the peaceful music streaming from the speakers, does a solitary pirouette, spinning turn after turn.

Elin takes her place on the sofa. She stretches, her back aching after many hours with the heavy camera. Just as she closes her eyes, she feels a piece of paper land on her face. Her eyes snap open and meet Alice's.

"Is this yours?" Alice asks.

Elin takes it and looks. It's a page torn out of a notebook. She quickly folds it twice and places it on the keys of the computer. Then she closes the lid.

"What language were you writing in?"

Elin shrugs.

"It must be something someone left here."

"Stop it. I'd recognize your flowers anywhere. What does it say?" Alice reaches for the computer, but Elin twists it out of her reach.

"I don't know. Stop asking."

"You don't know? You're so ridiculous." Alice raises her eyebrows and sighs.

"No, I don't know."

"You've written it, it's your handwriting. But you don't know what it says?"

Joe clears his throat awkwardly and sits up. Alice sits down beside him. She slaps her hand on his leg.

"See? Crazy. Now she's started speaking a language she can't even understand. Weird, huh?"

Joe shrugs and wanders off to start dismantling the equipment. Alice moves closer to Elin.

"Just let it go." Elin's voice is sharp.

"Come on, tell me. Fredrik? That's a name, I get that much."

Elin tears the paper into pieces. Turns it into tiny flakes and releases them. They float slowly through the air and land like confetti on the floor.

"Why did you do that? Who's Fredrik? If you've met someone new, you can tell me. I want you to be happy," Alice says, tilting her head to one side.

"Another day perhaps. Not now. I want to go home, I need to sleep." Elin stands up, hugging the computer tight to her stomach.

"Does this have something to do with your project? What is it you're doing?" Alice won't give up.

"I'm just longing for nature, it reminds me of something I miss."

"You've always detested nature."

Elin shakes her head.

"I take a lot of walks in Central Park. And I like being at the beach."

"The park is hardly the country, there's asphalt, you can hear the cars. And when we're at the beach you just lie by the pool while Dad and I swim in the sea."

"Let it go now, I'm telling you. Please."

Elin walks away, beckoning to Joe, who follows her up to the office, leaving Alice on her own on the sofa. She stands and picks up her backpack.

"You haven't forgotten our dinner tomorrow, right? The usual place. Eight o'clock," she calls.

Elin stops on the stairs, her face blank.

"Mom!"

"Oh yeah, right. The twentieth. Your birthday."

"Yeah. Dad's going to be there. Are you coming?"

"Yes, of course. I'd never miss your birthday."

"You have before. When you had a really important job. Don't you remember?"

"But I won't miss this. I promise."

Elin blows Alice a kiss. She catches it.

"I love you," Alice says, with the kiss caught in her fist.

Elin smiles at her and waves.

"Ditto," she whispers.

◈

Elin waits awhile at the entrance to Alice's student dorm. Young people come and go. Alice is right, everyone looks like her, dressed in jeans and worn-out sneakers. With curiosity she walks toward the door, but the doorman stops her.

"Residents only here."

"I'm visiting my daughter."

He looks her over.

"Are you really old enough to have a daughter living here?" He grins.

She nods and pulls out her driving license. He signs her in and she takes the elevator up. She's only been here once before, when they brought all of Alice's bags and boxes into the little bare room.

The door is ajar. Outside, young women run from room to room. The corridor is full of music and chatter and laughter. Elin pauses in the doorway. The walls are covered with pages torn from magazines, mostly pictures of dancers. A red helium balloon in the shape of a heart is tied to the end of the bed, and she wonders who gave it to Alice. The bed-clothes are crumpled, a pile of dresses on top. Alice is staring at her own reflection. She's so young. Elin looks at her watch and starts. Only five minutes now. Five minutes to seventeen years. She puts a hand on her stomach, remembering.

Alice's curly hair is carefully brushed and gathered in a bun at the base of her neck. Around her neck hangs the gold heart she got when she was born, the one she's worn every birthday since. Her face is lightly made up with mascara and red lipstick. She's wearing a duck-egg-blue dress. The draped neckline clings across her bust, and the diaphanous fabric floats out into an ankle-length skirt.

"Happy birthday," Elin whispers just as the minute hand moves. Alice turns around.

"Are you here already? We were going to meet . . ."

"I thought we could walk there together, you and I. You look like a dream."

Elin kisses Alice's cheek, careful not to ruin her hair and makeup. Alice takes a step back.

"And you look . . . totally normal." She laughs and flies at her mother in a tight, hard hug. Her bun loosens a little, a tendril of hair escaping. Elin catches it and carefully tucks it back in.

"I'm trying," she whispers.

❖

They walk arm in arm to the restaurant. Elin is tense, her eyes searching for Sam. She spots him a long way off, hurrying along in a black suit, as though he were late for an important meeting. He cruises along through the people on the sidewalk. When he sees them he stops and walks the last few steps, his eyes fixed on Alice. His brow is coated with droplets of sweat, and his hair is slicked against his head.

"Sorry I'm late." He kisses Alice on the cheek and nods curtly to Elin. She feels a sharp pang of longing in her stomach.

"If I'm even late," he goes on, twisting his arm to see the face of his wristwatch. "Ha, no, I'm not, why am I apologizing?"

Sam puts his arm around Alice's shoulders and pulls her along with him. Elin is left behind. She sees them lean toward each other familiarly. He says something, Alice laughs. They've always been close, always talked in a way she can't really understand.

They are seated in a corner, around a circular table. However they sit, Sam and Elin will end up next to each other. Elin pulls her chair closer to Alice. They sit in silence.

Alice entreats them. "It's my birthday . . ."

"Perhaps we can talk about the weather," Sam says, in an attempt at humor.

Elin closes her eyes and takes a deep breath.

"Can we just order. And eat. And get this over with," she says in the end, sorrowfully.

"Get it over with? Mom!" Alice glares at her.

"Elin, it's Alice's birthday," Sam scolds, shaking his head.

"I didn't mean it like that," Elin whispers. "Please don't fight."

Alice tries to change the subject.

"Can't you tell us about your new project, Mom? About the note-book and all the pictures?"

Sam leans across the table.

"Oh, so you've started? Tell us!" he says.

Elin sighs.

"It's nothing, just a few images and a bit of text."

Alice looks from one to the other.

"Started? Do you know what she's up to, Dad? It's not just pictures, it's like a totally different world, a farm, wilderness."

Sam shakes his head and looks at Elin. She squirms.

"Stop it now, Alice, you weren't supposed to see it. It's private. Stop it, both of you."

Elin stands up quickly, so quickly her chair falls backward. She just catches it with her hand. The other guests at the little Italian restaurant fall silent, and several pairs of eyes turn in their direction.

"Excuse me." She rights the chair, embarrassed, tears burning in her eyes. "I just need to go to the ladies' room."

She hears Alice whisper to Sam, loud and clear, as if she'd screamed the words right into her ear.

"She's completely lost it, you really need to come back home."

❖

The rain is hammering down when they finally leave the restaurant after a quiet, tense dinner. Sam leaves after giving them both a quick hug. Taxi after taxi passes, but none of them stop for Elin's outstretched arm. In the end she takes a step back.

"I guess we could also walk. Together. Via your place and then I can walk home."

"Mom, it's the wrong side of town and more than seventy blocks from your place. It's raining."

"I'd like to walk you home in any case. I'll get a taxi later," Elin insists.

"I'm not twelve."

"No, geez. You're seventeen. Do you know what I was doing when I was seventeen?"

"Let me guess. You were already a star, earning more than the GDP of Gambia," Alice says.

"Lord above, do you have to turn everything into politics?" Elin stops. "I was planning to tell you about my first great love, but if you'd rather talk politics, go ahead."

"Love. How can you even think about that after this evening? Thanks for destroying my birthday, next year I think I'll celebrate on my own."

Alice's eyes start to shine, tears welling up and spilling over the rim of one eye. She turns on her heel and starts walking in the wrong direction, fast, as though she's trying to escape from something. Elin is left standing, watching her disappear past all the other people hunched over against the rain. Her blue dress glows beautifully. She sees her tug her hair out of the bun as she goes, the curly hair standing up again like a halo around her head, extra frizzy from the moisture in the air. Elin smiles when she sees the soles of the white gym shoes she's been hiding under the beautiful long dress all evening.

"Wait!" Elin walks after her, but she's already far too far away. She starts running. The black pumps she's wearing make the balls of her feet hurt with every step. She limps the last few meters and manages at last to get hold of Alice's shoulder.

"Hey, sorry! It's your birthday. Can we start over, please?"

Alice turns to her, arms by her sides.

"Now? It's the middle of the night. It's too late. This birthday is already over and it's ruined as well. Sometimes I wish I didn't have any family at all. It's better to celebrate with friends."

Elin shakes her head. Now they both have tears in their eyes, one from sorrow and one from anguish.

"Don't say that. Never say that. We'll always be your family, you'll never lose us," Elin says.

Alice is crying. She looks at Elin with a resigned expression.

"I'm actually glad I've moved to school," she says, with a voice that gets thicker and thicker.

"Please, my love, come home with me. You can sleep at home tonight. I'll make you some hot chocolate, mom-chocolate. Please."

Alice doesn't answer for a while.

"If you promise me one thing," she says at last.

"What?"

"That you'll tell me what you're up to. About that notebook. There's something weird about it, and I want to know what's happening. And I want an honest answer."

Elin takes a deep breath and blows the air out again. She closes her eyes. The ground sways beneath her feet.

"Mom, promise," Alice goes on.

Elin nods, almost imperceptibly.

"I promise," she says, under her breath.

◈

They shake themselves like dogs in the elevator. Alice's dress is so wet, her nipples are visible through the thin fabric. She puts her hands over them in horror when she catches sight of her reflection. They fall laughing into the hallway when the elevator doors open. They're wet and hopelessly disheveled after a long walk and then a taxi journey for the last few blocks. Alice points at the mirror in the hall.

"Look, aren't we gorgeous. Totally natural."

"Some more than others," Elin giggles, at which Alice wriggles out of the wet dress and lets it fall to the floor.

"Totally natural," she laughs.

"I thought it was only back in my day we would burn our bras."

"You try fitting a bra under that dress; I haven't been able to breathe all evening. I don't understand how you manage wearing fancy clothes all day, every day. When you're working. You really should try jeans and a T-shirt. There's nothing better."

Elin fetches a dressing gown and hands it to her.

"I was young once too. I promise. I've even run home at night, barefoot after swimming in the sea."

Alice sinks down onto the gray-blue sofa. She pulls her legs up under her and wraps herself in a blanket.

"You, barefoot, night-swimming . . . I'll believe that when I see it." She pats the spot beside her. "Come sit down now. And tell me. Why are you so obsessed with farms and tractors?"

Elin hesitates. She stands quietly, thinking.

"You're the most stubborn person I know," she says at last. Alice nods expectantly.

Elin has a lump in her throat. She swallows hard, walks over to the desk, and picks up the black notebook. Stroking the cover with her index finger, she carefully opens the first page. She sits down beside Alice, the book in her lap, and starts talking. The words that leave her mouth come out as whispers. Alice turns to face her and listens.

"This door, the blue one . . ." She stops and looks at the image for a long time.

"Yes, what about that door? It looks shabby, like it's attached to a shack."

"It was, this one. But not the real one, the one I remember. I grew up a long way from New York."

"Yes, in Paris. You told me about it. About your modeling career and the fancy apartment with the view of the Eiffel Tower. And the bookshop that belonged to your rich, flighty mom, Anne. What a shame she died. I think I would have liked her."

Elin shakes her head. She clears her throat, her throat catches, her heart beats rapidly. When she starts speaking, her voice breaks.

"Behind this door lived my real mother."

"What do you mean, real?"

"I grew up in Sweden. On an island, in the country. On a farm, to tell the truth."

"What do you mean?"

"These images are my memories. The language you saw on the drawing is Swedish. I was writing to a friend. I drew the flowers for him, flowers that grow where we used to live."

"Sweden?" Alice shakes her head, unable to comprehend.

"There are so many memories resurfacing, I can't run away from them anymore. It's as though Sweden has come here. I can't stop it."

Alice takes a deep breath.

"Have you been lying to me all my life? And to Dad, your whole relationship? What about Paris? We've been there and you knew your way around the whole place."

Elin shuts her eyes and clutches Alice's hand. Alice stands up now and stares down at Elin.

"I had to," Elin whispers.

"No one's ever forced to lie, Mom. You told me that yourself."

"I had to. Because I ran away from there and decided never to return."

"But didn't anyone look for you? Your mom?"

"I ran away to my dad's place, and she found out. To Stockholm. Then I headed to Paris, not long after. I was discovered on the street in Stockholm. Swedish girls were popular in Paris; I got an agent and they arranged a place for me. I worked hard, swallowed all my tears and all my heartbreak. And then it was exactly as I've told you."

"Apart from your mom."

"Yes, but she did exist, she was a friend. Perhaps I dreamed of having her as a mother."

"So I'm half-Swedish. Not half-French," Alice says.

"Yes, you're half-Swedish. But I haven't been to Sweden since I was sixteen."

"Like I am now."

"You're seventeen. Or have you forgotten?"

Alice smiles, but her expression soon turns serious again.

"Why have you never said anything? What's so terrible about being Swedish?"

"There's nothing terrible about that. It was just so long ago. France became my new home; I had a totally different life when I met your dad. I was so scared of losing him."

"But don't you get it? You keep us, the people closest to you, so far from the truth that it's impossible for us to love you. For you to love us."

"What do you mean?"

"You're just one big question mark. To us and to yourself. A question mark is always just half a heart, have you ever thought about that? You can't love someone whose heart is full of secrets. You just can't."

Tears are running down Elin's cheeks. She flicks back and forth through the pages of the notebook.

"I should have told you."

"Yes, you should have told us. Why didn't you? Why did you tell so many lies?"

"It wasn't easy, there were a lot of things that weren't good. We were poor, I think I was embarrassed. I was afraid he'd leave me if he found out how things really were. I wanted him so badly, I fell so deeply in love with him, he made me feel safe."

"So you pretended to be perfect for his sake. All these years, your whole marriage. That's sick, Mom. Sick."

❖

Elin wanders slowly back and forth across the living room with her fingers in her mouth. She's chewing on her pale-pink nails and listening to the rain through the open terrace door. The force of it is so strong, she can hear the drops drumming on the patio furniture. Far off there's a rumble of something that could be thunder, but in New York you can never really be sure which sounds are nature's and which are artificial. She pulls the door shut, blocking out the storm.

"Thunder," she says.

"Hmm, the angels are having fun again," Alice replies.

She's still sitting on the sofa, the notebook on her lap. She's flicked through it, but now it's shut. She runs her hand over it.

"I really don't understand anything. It's just pictures. It means nothing to me."

"I understand that. But it means a lot to me."

Alice starts leafing through again, and Elin leaves her to it and goes to the wardrobe. She needs to get dressed, brush her hair, paint her face. Get herself back. She chooses a long gray dress she bought one time in Paris. It's comfortable, a supple flow over her slender body.

Paris. It's such a beautiful story, and she wants, more than anything, to go on clinging to it and to never let it go. A mother who loved her more than anything. Who, even though she wasn't perfect, was a creative genius. Who knew everything a well-read person should know, who'd read all the classics and had daily discussions with all the artists, authors, and philosophers who visited her bookstore and attended her dinners. Elin has given Alice many books from there, books she's saved and now forces her to read too. Books that really exist.

But the mother doesn't exist; she never has. It was just a woman in a shop. And Elin was just one of many customers who became close friends with her. She has told so many lies. She rubs her eyes hard, the remains of her mascara leaving black streaks across her face.

"Can you tell me more?"

She jumps at Alice's voice, shudders in discomfort at the thought of the truth.

"Don't say anything to Sam. Please."

"You have to tell him too."

"I will. But I need to work out how. Please understand."

"If you tell me."

Elin nods and picks up the book. Alice points at a word.

"Is that Swedish?"

Elin nods. Alice pronounces the word awkwardly.

"*Mar-tall.* What is that?"

"It's a tree. A regular pine, but stunted by the wind."

"Was it very windy on the island?"

Elin nods and runs a hand over her hair.

"The whole fall and winter. Our hair was always a mess."

"Is that why you like to have it so smooth?"

Elin shrugs.

"I don't know. I've never thought about it."

Alice points at a picture of a car. It's an old blue Volvo, rusty. Brown patches run along the bottom of the chassis, as though someone has taken little bites out of the paint. One of the doors is crooked, hanging at an angle. The car almost looks like a hat from the side, the hood as long as the trunk and a mound in the middle for the passengers.

"Whose was that?"

"Everyone's. In my childhood almost all the cars were Volvos. They differed only in shape and color."

"Did your real mom have a Volvo?"

Elin nods.

"Mmm, and my stepdad. His was the nicest, blue and shiny."

"And your real dad?"

"He got to ride a Volvo to prison."

"What? He was in prison?"

"It was black and white. With big letters on the sides. I'd prefer to forget that Volvo. The slam when the door shut. And the look he gave me through the window. His eyes staring into mine. The blue lights flashing."

"Why was he in prison? Where is he now?"

"He'd done something, robbed someone, I think. He's dead now, he died young, just a year or so after I went to Paris."

Alice goes on turning pages and stops at a picture of a barn's interior. Through gaps between the planks, small strips of light dance across the worn floor. A bird has found its way in, its wing movements blurred.

"What was in the barn? Did you have animals?"

"Sheep. And cattle. And goats. There were lots of barns, in different places. It was always so hot inside, the animals generated heat. And it stank, the smell got into your clothes and hair, which reminded everyone we met that we were farmers."

Alice laughs.

"I really can't picture you as a farmer. It's impossible."

"Well, I wasn't really. I was a child. A child on a farm."

"Is your mother alive?"

Elin takes the notebook out of Alice's hand. She puts her finger on an image and slowly follows the path shown in it.

"There were paths everywhere. Deep furrows that cut across lawns after years of use. They were surrounded by thousands of daisies in the spring. White and pink dots in all the green. I used to walk barefoot."

Alice interrupts her angrily.

"You didn't answer my question. I want to hear about the people. I don't understand why you were forced to deceive me into thinking my grandma was a creative, intellectual woman. When in actual fact she was a farmer. You've even said I reminded you of her. You're lying. Everything is a lie."

"You do."

"But she doesn't exist!"

"No. But you're creative and intellectual. You've turned out the way I described her. Just as fierce and just as inquisitive."

"Socialization," Alice mutters.

"Huh?"

"We've read about it at school. I've embodied your values, your norms, your fantasies about me with no genetic influence at all. I've become your lie."

"Please, don't fight with me."

"You owe me the truth. How can you lie to your own child? Tell me about your family."

Elin sits in silence. Tears run down her cheeks. She wipes them away over and over again but they won't stop falling.

"I killed them," she whispers at last.

Then

≡ ◆ ≡

HEIVIDE, GOTLAND, 1982

The noise woke her. She could feel it pressing against her back. The wind was blowing directly inland, and the waves had grown higher in the night. But that wasn't where the noise was coming from. A cloud of smoke made her cough, and she opened her eyes and looked over to the fire. The great bonfire was burnt to nothing but charred remains, some peeling and white, others glowing faintly in the night. The booming sound came from behind her, as though the sea and the forest had swapped places in an uncanny storm.

The forest. An inferno. It was burning high, it was burning everywhere, and the night sky was orange-red. Flakes of black ash were floating in front of Elin, and as she caught them in her hand they crumbled into dust. She ran toward the flames, screaming. Her stomach flipped, as though she needed to vomit or shit, she wasn't sure which. She stopped and bent over, heaving, but nothing came up. She went on running. The houses were on fire. Gerd's house, Aina's too. Flames from the dry grass licked at her legs. She pulled off her top and held it over her mouth. Fire everywhere. She shouted for help. The fire she'd lit to warm herself had spread.

"Wake up! Wake up! Gerd! Fire! Wake up!"

She screamed through the thin cloth of her T-shirt, but her voice was drowned in the fire's threatening roar and the words came out as a whisper.

◆

She ran as fast as she could. Far away she could see the buildings at the Grinde farm rearing up like black shadows in the night. The avenue was already in flames. She headed across the fields, where the fire couldn't take hold. Fought her way across the porous earth that buried her feet and left thick, sticky traces between her toes.

"Edvin! Erik! Mama!"

She screamed their names. Screamed until her voice broke. The forest around the farm was burning. It boomed. The light of the flames was like a train shining its way along the tracks. Like ten trains. It was so dry, it went so fast. She approached the buildings, which looked like they were still unharmed. She'd be able to save them! She ran, her feet flying through the air.

◆

She banged hard on all the doors and shouted continuously. On the stairs she met a dazed Marianne, just out of bed. She wrapped her dressing gown around her and locked eyes with Elin.

"What's all this about? What are you screaming for? It's the middle of the night," she grunted.

"Can't you smell the smoke? It's on fire. Everything's on fire. The whole forest is on fire, the barn's on fire."

She pushed past Marianne and went on shouting. She ran into Erik and Edvin's room but their beds were empty. She called their names again and again, pulling at their bedclothes in the weak glow from the night-light.

"Erik! Where are they? Edvin! Erik! Edvin!"

Marianne came up to her and shoved her aside.

"Let me look."

She felt about with her hand. There were no children there.

"Bloody kids, come out!" she shouted. "Where are you?"

Elin had already left the room. She ran out into the farmyard, Marianne close behind her. The fire had engulfed the barn: half the roof was on fire, flames licking the sky. The doors were wide open, and cows and goats were wandering about nervously on the gravel. Micke was standing at the bottom, throwing buckets of water from the rain barrels. The fire hissed gently, as though it were mocking the tiny amount of water he was trying to put it out with.

"The children are gone!" Marianne screamed at him. He went on throwing his buckets, moving closer to the fire. Now the flames were consuming the walls, and there was a great boom as the beams gave way and the remains of the enormous roof crashed to the floor. A burning beam fell right toward Micke. He sheltered himself with his hands and backed away, but he couldn't escape. Marianne screamed and ran toward him. The beam lay right across his back. Blood was running from a great wound on the back of his head. Marianne pulled at the burning-hot wood and tried to pull the beam aside. She tipped buckets of water over him. Micke groaned in pain.

"Help me!" Marianne shouted. Elin ran toward the tractor shed and the boys' secret den. One of the walls was on fire, and the whole building was full of smoke. She coughed and shouted her brothers' names as she made her way in, past the tractor and the combine harvester. She clamped her T-shirt over her nose and mouth.

From the farmyard she heard a roar of boundless rage followed by a drawn-out moan and the nervous yelps of the animals.

Elin went farther in. Flames burned above her head. Then, on their tractor-tire bed, she saw small naked feet sticking out from behind the oil drum. They were Edvin's. She pulled at them.

"Wake up, Edvin, wake up, hurry," she said, shaking his limp body. Erik lay alongside, just as still. She kicked him with her foot as she hauled Edvin's body up into her arms.

"Erik, wake up, you'll have to walk by yourself. You have to get out!"

He whined a little, and she saw a strip of white as one of his eyelids opened a few millimeters. He was alive. They were both alive. She held Edvin close to her body and ran with him. Toward the fields. Toward the open fields no fire could reach. He looked at her, dazed, one arm hanging down, bumping against her back. She kissed his cheek without stopping.

"You have to be brave now. Promise me."

He murmured faintly, no words; she couldn't hear what he was trying to say.

"Can you smell the smoke, can you see the fire? It's all burning. It's burning so much. We have to get out, fast. We have to get to the sea, to the water; we'll be safe there."

He nodded. He put his little bare feet down into one of the furrows of the field, but his legs would not carry his body. He fell in a heap, his hands clutching at his face as though they were cramping. He was rocking back and forth. His face was deathly pale, with trembling blue lips.

"I'm just going to get Erik. I'll be back soon. Here, hold the T-shirt over your mouth. Breathe as little as possible."

She gave him her T-shirt. Now she was naked again, apart from her underpants. But the night was no longer cold. The raging fire spread a heat, the like of which she'd never known. When she got back, everything was in flames. The barn, the tractor shed, the farmhouse. She couldn't see Marianne. She couldn't see Erik. She couldn't see Micke. Just flames and smoke and darkness.

"Erik!" She screamed his name, screamed, just screamed. But it was too late. It was burning, everything was burning, and charred remains were falling to the ground in a shower of embers. She went back to Edvin. He was sniffing.

"It's burning everywhere, Elin. It's burning so much, why is it burning so much?" He sniffed.

"Shh, don't talk, don't waste your energy." She stroked his forehead.

"We can't go anywhere, we're shut in. Can't you see?"

"The ground won't burn. There's no trees here, no grass. We're on the biggest field. We're safe here. We won't burn up. We'll sit here for a little while; come, my love. Listen, the fire engines are on the way, we'll be rescued soon."

She let him lie with his head on her lap. The sirens wailed from the main road. A helicopter buzzed overhead; it was approaching quickly. She slowly stroked his hair and forehead. He shrieked as she touched his cheek, which had been burned. Her eyes stung from the smoke. Sweat was running from her legs and arms. The heat and lack of oxygen made her vision fuzzy. Elin coughed. She pulled off Edvin's T-shirt and pressed it to her mouth. His bloodshot eyes looked at her pleadingly.

Clouds of red sparks from the trees spread into the sky. Soon the flames blew out the kitchen windows and licked the front of the house with their long tongues. Edvin tried to stand up, wanting to run, but she held him down. He screamed and put his hands over his ears as she clutched him to her.

"Don't look, Edvin, don't look. Just lie totally still. Shh, don't look."

"Where are we going to live? Where are we going to go?" Edvin's voice was despairing.

Elin closed her eyes and lay down beside him. The ground felt hard and uneven against her side. Edvin was soft and warm. She held him close to her, hugged him tight. Closed her eyes until his body became heavy and still.

"I'm sorry," she whispered, barely audibly, then she let go of him.

◈

The glow from the burning buildings lit up the sky and turned it orange as Elin stood in the middle of the field and watched a fire engine and an ambulance arrive. She saw men in black jumping out and running across the farmyard, calling to one another as two of them rolled out the hoses. She heard distant sirens from more fire engines, farther away. The helicopter was flying between the sea and the fire, dropping water from great containers over the forest. Elin waved her arms over her head and shouted, but her voice didn't carry far enough. From a distance she saw them trying to pull away the beam that was covering Micke's charred body until one fireman held up his hand, stopping the others. Micke was already dead. Elin could barely breathe. Fredrik's papa, dead. She fell to her knees, croaking Erik's name. No one was looking in the tractor shed. She knew it was too late, the building had already burned down, but she couldn't stop whispering his name. The tin roof lay on top of a glowing heap of lumber, which hung askew over the vehicles inside. Everything had collapsed. And underneath lay Erik. All alone.

❖

Elin saw a firefighter trying to put a blanket around her mother's shoulders, but she batted it away and waved her arms around, agitated, pointing at the house. Elin waved at her but couldn't make herself move forward; her feet seemed to be fixed to the earth. Everything that was happening in front of her was a nightmare, like standing in the middle of a horror film.

Now Marianne was running toward the house, her dressing gown flapping open. The firefighters stopped her, grabbing her shoulders and pulling her toward the ambulance, lifting her feet off the ground. The paramedics came to meet them with a stretcher, and they heaved her up onto it.

Elin couldn't breathe anymore. The air was thick and heavy, the smell so acrid, her nostrils ached. The firemen had masks over their faces, and she could see that Marianne had been given one. Elin stretched her arm toward them, but her body seized up and she fell flat on her face.

❖

When the ambulance reversed in order to turn around, its headlights lit up the field. Suddenly it braked, and the paramedics jumped out and ran toward Elin, whose arm was still stretched, pleading. Her mouth was dry and full of earth, and the men looked blurry and seemed to be swaying toward her. She saw their faces draw close but couldn't hear the words coming out of their mouths. She whispered Edvin's name, wanted to point behind her, but her arm wouldn't move. The paramedic put his ear right up to her mouth, in an attempt to make out the words. They carried her toward the ambulance, their uneven steps jolting her. Everything went black.

❖

Black had turned to white. Elin was lying in a bed, the covers pulled up to her chin. She blinked in the uncomfortably strong light. A tube was hooked up to her arm, leading to a drip on the stand beside her. When she moved her arm, the needle attached to the inside of her elbow pulled slightly. Someone came running over and she closed her eyes again as she felt a cool hand on her forehead.

"Are you awake?"

She murmured and squinted. A nurse with a blond perm was leaning over her, her face very close.

"Are you an angel?" Elin asked her softly.

"You're in the hospital. Don't worry. Do you know what happened? Can you remember?"

"Mama?" Elin said, the last syllable hanging on her lip, making it tremble.

"Your mama is here too, on another ward."

"I want to see her."

"Not now, you have to wait awhile. First you have to get stronger."

The nurse sat down on the side of the bed and took Elin's hand.

"You're weak, but you were lucky. You only have a few burns on your legs, nowhere else."

Elin looked at her. Her eyes welled up. She remembered.

"It was burning so much," she whispered.

"You were caught in a forest fire. It's still burning out there."

"Erik? Edvin?"

"Who are they?"

"My brothers. Edvin was there with me. In the field. He was lying on the ground. He fell asleep." It was hard to get the words out. Her voice was cracked and hoarse from all the smoke.

The nurse let go of her hand, sprang up, and ran out of the room. Elin heard voices from the corridor, raised in agitation. The tears were spilling down her cheeks.

"Mama!" she called, as loud as she could.

The nurse came back. She took her hand again and stroked her forehead.

"We're in touch with the firefighters, they'll find your brother."

Elin shook her head.

"It was too hot, there was too much smoke."

"They've put a lot of it out, I'm sure he's made it, it hasn't been that long."

"And Erik."

"What happened to Erik?"

"He was in the tractor shed. It collapsed."

The nurse crept closer, pulled her legs up onto the bed, and put her arms around Elin. Her cool hand stroked Elin's face.

"Is Mama angry? Doesn't she want to see me?"

"Her lungs aren't very well; she's in intensive care. You can see her when she's better. We need to keep her there for the time being."

"Is there anyone else here? Who survived?"

The nurse shook her head cautiously. Her eyes too were shining with tears.

"Sleep now, my dear. Go to sleep, and you'll feel better when you wake up."

Elin closed her eyes. The nurse rose from the bed and left her alone. Elin opened her eyes a crack as she left and saw her discreetly wiping her eyes.

❖

One sound after another captured her attention. Beeps and clicks, footsteps in the corridor. There was no clock, so she had no way of knowing whether minutes or hours had gone by. Every time a nurse came in, she asked after Edvin. Every time they shook their heads.

Micke. Gerd. Ove. Erik. Edvin.

It couldn't be true.

She heaved herself up to a sitting position. Her hands were working; they felt strong. She clenched and released them, clenched and released. Her legs felt OK too, although her ankles were wrapped in white gauze. It hurt to put her feet down onto the floor, but she stood up. The tube in her arm followed her wherever she went, so she took hold of the stand and rolled it toward the bathroom, taking small, cautious steps. She felt dizzy, the floor swaying in front of her, and the hospital-issue gown was too thin, making her shiver and hug herself with the other arm. In the bathroom she drank directly from the tap, swallowing the cold liquid greedily. Then she filled her hands with water again and again, rinsing her face. Her hair still stank of smoke, so she put her whole head under the tap, letting the water rinse it out.

There was a girl in the other bed in Elin's room, sleeping peacefully behind drawn curtains. Elin watched her through a gap. The girl had a bandage around her head, and her arms were resting on her stomach. Her hair was lank and greasy. Her clothes hung in an open cupboard alongside her bed: normal clothes, jeans and a college sweatshirt. At the bottom of the cupboard was a pair of black canvas shoes. Elin pulled the tube from her arm, and a dark bead of blood welled up on her skin. She licked it off, sucking hard, tasting the tang of metal in her mouth. She pressed her thumb hard against the vein to stanch the blood.

The girl moved uneasily in her sleep, but soon lay still again. Elin crept over to her cupboard, holding her breath as she eased the clothes from their hangers. They were too big for her, but she put them on anyway, the jeans slipping down over her hips. The reverse was true of the shoes, which were too small, and her toes were cramped at the tip. She looked in the mirror one last time, wiped away her tears, and smoothed down her wet tufts of hair. Then she crept carefully out of the room, with one hand clutching the waistband of the jeans, before hurrying out of the hospital building.

Now

≡ ◈ ≡

Alice shrieks and runs out into the rain on the terrace. Elin follows her, reaching out to her, but Alice flails and pushes her hands away, still wailing. She backs away from her mother and presses herself against the terrace railing.

"Don't touch me. Don't touch me," she spits.

"There was a fire. Let me explain what happened. Please, come inside."

Alice shakes her head. She has the blanket wrapped around her, her hair wet from the rain. She is trembling.

"Did you murder your whole family?"

Elin shakes her head. She holds out her hand again.

"Please, come here. It's not what you think at all. I'll tell you, I want to tell you."

Alice accepts the hand reluctantly, her expression still earnest, reproachful. Elin sits down on one of the rattan armchairs, and the moisture from the seat seeps through the thin fabric of her dress. She shivers. Alice lets go of her hand and sinks down beside her, pulling her knees up to her chin. The raindrops bounce off their heads and run down their cheeks.

"Micke, Edvin, Erik, Gerd, Ove," Elin says at last, without looking up.

Alice stares at her.

"What did you do to them? Who are you?" she whispers.

"I'm Elin," she replies. "I'm your mom."

"I don't know if I want to hear it." Alice gets up and goes in, and Elin follows her as she moves listlessly from room to room.

"But I want to tell you now," she says.

Suddenly, it all runs out of her, all the memories. She tells her about the house where she lived with Marianne and Lasse, about her brothers, about the shop and Gerd, about poverty then prosperity, Aina, Micke, the fight, the blow.

By the end, Alice is sitting quietly on the sofa with her hands resting in her lap and her mouth half-open. Elin sits down close to her, without pausing in her story.

"I lit a fire one evening, down on the beach. And then I fell asleep in front of it. The fire spread. Everything burned."

"What do you mean, everything?" Alice put her hands to her cheeks.

"There was nothing left. Everything burned down. The trees, the buildings. And everyone died. Everyone apart from me and Mama."

"But I don't get it, what happened then? Where's your mom now?"

"I don't know. I ran away from the hospital where we were both being treated and since then I haven't heard from her."

Alice frowns, confused.

"But surely she missed you? Where did you run away to?"

"To Lasse, to my papa. He was living in Stockholm then, I knew his address, because we got a letter when he came out of prison and it was written on the envelope. Mama got a letter."

"But didn't anyone come looking for you?"

"No. Papa told them I was there. No one wanted to know anything about him after what he'd done. And I guess no one wanted to know anything about me either. I'd killed my mother's new husband, my brothers, our neighbors . . ."

Elin is struggling to breathe now, her breath rasping in her chest. She gasps for air, her nose blocked, her eyes swollen.

"But your mom might still be alive, my grandma. Maybe she's always wondered, always missed you. It was just an accident, wasn't it?"

Tears are streaming down Elin's cheeks. She shakes and sobs.

"Edvin was so sweet, my littlest brother. He had hazel eyes that glittered when he smiled and curly, golden hair. I rescued him from the flames, but he was left there, they left him behind when they rescued me from the field."

"Was he alive when you left him?"

Elin nods.

"But there was so much smoke. It's the smoke that kills."

Elin stops. She breathes deeply, as though she still can't get enough air.

"So how did you end up here? In New York?" Alice asks her.

"You know that."

"So Paris is just a lie?"

"No, Paris isn't a lie, not at all. Just the part about my mother. I lived there, just like I told you. I was discovered as a model on the streets of Stockholm and got to move there and work. I told you that. My papa was nothing special, so I left again."

"What do you mean, nothing special? How can you say that about your own dad?" Alice shakes her head.

"I know, it's hard to understand — for me too. He tried, he did. He made sure I had clothes and everything I needed for school. But he drank too much. He loved alcohol more than he loved me."

"That sounds awful."

"Yeah, it's not something I was in a hurry to get back to. Paris saved me. I learned to take photographs while I was there too, and I was much happier behind the camera than in front of it. And after a while I met your dad. The woman in the bookshop really existed too, she was a friend. And she was just as I've described her. She just wasn't my real mom. I often wished she had been. She was so smart, she taught me about life, she believed in me. No one had done that before. Not in the same way."

"How can I trust you now? You've been lying so much, all my life."

"It's just the first thirteen years, everything else is true."

"Just the first thirteen years ... Mom, do you hear how nuts that sounds?"

The dawn light finds its way in through the apartment's windows, painting pale stripes across the white floor. Elin and Alice sit quietly, surrounded by all Elin's suppressed memories and all the thoughts tormenting them both. The sounds of the street grow louder; trucks stop and unload, taxiscabs toot. Alice takes Elin's hand, braiding her fingers into her mother's.

"Oh, Mom, I want to go there. I want to go to Sweden with you. You need to go home again," she says.

Then

=⧫=

The trucks were already lined up down on the harbor, protected by a tall fence and manned barriers. One or two cars drove up, the drivers showing their tickets and joining the queue for the ferry. Elin crept along the fence. There was barbed wire at the point where it met the sea, but if she climbed out around the edge of the dock, she would be able to get under it. If only these jeans weren't so hard to maneuver in. She crossed the asphalt to a cluster of shipping containers and found a flat plastic packaging band on the ground, which she pulled through the belt loops. The smooth surface made it hard to tie, so she frayed the ends and knotted the narrower shreds together. The jeans stayed up. She ran back to the fence and looked in all directions — no one had seen her. She eased herself down, clinging tightly to the small stone blocks sticking out from the dockside, and climbed sideways, one careful step at a time. Soon she had passed under the thick coils of barbed wire, and she heaved herself back up and ran over to one of the trucks. She picked one that was dark blue, the same color as her clothes, and squeezed her way in between the driver's cab and the trailer. From her hiding place she could see the seamen crossing the harbor in their yellow jackets, directing the vehicles as the lines grew longer and longer.

⧫

She balanced on the heavy tow hitch when the vehicle finally began to move. The asphalt flickered beneath her feet; she held on for dear life, so hard her knuckles whitened, but her body still swayed from side to side.

The truck shook as it drove up the ramp, making the grooves in the metal clink and clang. One of Elin's knees buckled, and she lost her balance, hanging by her hands alone for a terrifying second until she was able to pull herself up again with the aid of the cargo lashes, scrabbling for a foothold. The black asphalt under the wheels had been replaced by green-painted metal, with broad yellow stripes marking the lanes, and the truck slowed down. Elin held her breath, standing in the narrow gap, pressing her whole body against the trailer. No one noticed her. She heard the door to the driver's cabin open and close. Everything was vibrating. Then there was silence.

She didn't move. It wasn't until all the vehicles had grown quiet, with no more doors slamming, and the low rumble of the boat's engines filled every nook and cranny of the car deck, that she let go and climbed carefully down from her hiding place. The burnt skin around her ankles stung and ached.

Realizing there were people still in the next car, she gasped and instinctively crouched down. But they didn't see her; their seats were reclined and they were sleeping.

Brushing off the dust and debris from her pants and top, she walked along, straight-backed, as though she'd come from a car. Now she was onboard, and the boat had already left the harbor; she didn't need to hide or be afraid anymore.

The lounge on the upper deck was full of people, sitting in armchairs around circular tables. Families with children who clambered over the chairs and crawled across the carpet, couples with thermoses and homemade sandwiches, young people laughing and toasting each other with their beers. She walked past them all, toward the large windows. She stood there a long time and looked out. She didn't have a krona in her pocket; her luggage consisted of the clothes she stood in. In her head she rattled off the address in Farsta, the one she'd make her way to once the boat landed in Nynäshamn.

Calmly, she watched the place the boat was leaving behind. The towers and steeples of Visby gleamed in the sunlight, and the cliffs shone white against the dark backdrop of forest. The coast grew longer and longer, the island smaller and smaller. In the end it vanished completely over the horizon, and there was nothing but sea.

❖

The passengers left the boat in a steady stream. Elin followed them, limping. Her feet were hurting in the undersized shoes, and she was cold. Outside the terminal, a long line formed as people waited for the bus to Stockholm. Others carried on down the street. Perhaps they lived in Nynäshamn, or perhaps they were going somewhere else. Elin stood and observed the scene. A few cars had stopped at the pickup area, and people vanished from the sidewalk one by one, as though they were sticks in a game of pick-up-sticks. She and Fredrik used to play it, with regular twigs they'd gathered in the forest. Now they might never play together again. The thought made her feel even colder; shivers spread through her body. Would he miss her, would he look for her? She hugged herself, hunching her shoulders.

Her fellow travelers vanished one by one until only she and a solitary car remained. No one came up to it; the vehicle seemed to be waiting in vain.

Plucking up courage, Elin rapped on the window, two careful knocks. The man in the car reached over the passenger seat and wound the window down. The car was full of smoke, which belched out. Elin coughed and took a step back.

"Are you lost?"

The man raised his eyebrows.

"A little," she admitted, folding her arms tightly across her chest.

The man nodded to the seat beside him.

"Jump in if you want, I can drive you to the commuter train."

Elin hesitated.

"Aren't you waiting for someone?"

The man laughed.

"Always. I'm waiting for the love of my life, you know."

Elin smiled and put her hand on the door handle.

"Perhaps it's you," the man went on, and laughed again, but the sound turned into coughing. He put his hand over his mouth, his chest rattling.

Elin immediately let go of the handle and backed away, shaking her head.

"I'll walk, it's probably better."

"Better for you perhaps, not for me." The man chuckled.

His voice gave her a queer feeling. He stretched across the seat and pushed open the door, then patted the seat encouragingly. Dust sprung up from its plush surface.

"Come on, sweetheart. I'll drive you to the train. Young girls like you shouldn't be out on their own this late."

Elin walked away without a word. She chose the direction the stream of people had taken. She wasn't sure what a "commuter train" involved, as there were no trains on Gotland. But maybe it could get her to Stockholm? It was easy to dodge fares on trains; she'd seen it in films.

It wasn't long before the man in the car turned up again, crawling slowly alongside her. If she sped up, he did too. The light from the street lamps created faint yellow circles, and between them the street lay empty, a threatening darkness. She started to run, as fast as her legs could carry her, and the man drove alongside her the whole way. Suddenly he sounded his horn and called something through the window. She couldn't hear what he said, but he repeated himself.

"It's up there, turn right. I'll stay here until I see you've reached the platform. Do you need money for a ticket?"

Elin stared at him.

"How do you know that?" she asked.

"I know a runaway when I see one. I'm sure you've got your reasons, I won't ask. Here!" He held out a ten-krona note to her.

Elin walked hesitantly over to the car and took it out of his hand.

"Thank you," she said quietly.

"Hurry now, the train leaves soon and it's the last one." He grabbed hold of her wrist, hard. "And make sure you get in touch with the folks at home. Don't do anything silly."

Elin nodded and pulled her arm away. Her wrist ached, like a reminder of what he'd just said.

"I'm going to see my papa now, that's not silly," she whispered.

She turned on her heel without saying goodbye, and ran toward the platform. The train was there and she just made it through the doors before it set off. Through the window she saw the man in the car slowly driving off, exhaust fumes trailing behind it.

❖

The carriage was full of people with luggage; she recognized a few of them from the boat. Everyone looked hollow-eyed and tired. Elin chose an empty seat, leaned against the cold wall, and watched the buildings rushing by. When the conductor came, she held out the ten-krona note and looked him in the eye.

"Farsta, please," she ventured.

"You'll be wanting Södertörns Villastad, then," he replied, and gave her back a pile of coins as change, counting them out into her palm.

Elin closed her fingers on the coins and held them tensely the rest of the long journey. The train stopped now and then, and she read each sign carefully.

At last it came. The sign she'd been waiting for the entire journey: Södertörns Villastad. She got off and soon found herself alone on a deserted platform.

❖

Blocks of apartments in long rectangular rows, like gigantic brown shoeboxes. Neat lines of windows, in perfect symmetry. Doors with numbers above them, lit by weak lamps. Elin had finally gotten there after wandering the empty streets for hours, after taking directions from a slumbering alcoholic on a bench on the square at Hökarängen. And now here she was, walking toward Tobaksvägen. She stopped and looked up at all the windows, astonished that so many people could live in one building. Somewhere, behind one of these panes of glass, her father was sleeping. And soon he'd wake up.

◈

Thirty-eight. The number she'd stored in her memory since she'd seen it written on the back of the letter he'd sent Marianne. The door squeaked slightly when she opened it, echoing faintly in the stairwell, and a dog barked noisily behind a door. She stood still a while until it stopped. She was so tired, she was swaying from side to side. She was carrying the canvas shoes in her hand; her toes had been hurting so much that she'd gone barefoot for the past few hours. Her feet were cold, just like the rest of her, and the blackened soles of her feet stung. She tiptoed up the steps, reading the names on the doors carefully until she was standing before her own surname. She rang the doorbell without hesitation, rubbing the tiredness from her eyes as she waited for someone to open the door. It took a long time. She rang again, and again. At last she heard someone moving on the other side. She held her breath as the door was opened a crack.

"Number One, is that you?" The eyes that met her own were surprised, and the door swung open. Elin smiled as her papa stroked her cheek with his big warm hand.

He was wearing nothing but baggy white underpants. His stomach hung over the waistband, covered in curly black hairs. His chin was hidden under long stubble, his hair unruly. They stared at each other, neither of them sure what to say. In the end, Lasse stepped aside and asked her to come in. He moved quickly through the hallway into the only room, apologizing on the way.

"I haven't really got it shipshape yet." He gathered up bottles, rubbish, and beer cans until his arms were full. Then he pushed past her into the little kitchen and shoved the refuse into a plastic bag. The noise was cacophonous in the nighttime silence.

Elin took a few steps into the room and looked around her. There was a narrow bed with tattered sheets and a little table with a TV on it.

On the other side of the room was a single brown armchair, angled toward the window, and a large coffee table. The walls were bare, the window had no curtains, and there were no plants on the windowsill, only more beer cans.

Lasse came into the room again. He'd found a shirt from somewhere, but buttoned it up wrong, so the left side of the collar was pushed up toward his ear.

"Did your mother send you here?" He ran his hand over his head, smoothing the thick hair.

Elin nodded.

"Can I stay here awhile?"

"What do you mean?" Lasse sank onto the bed.

"Well, live here."

Lasse's eyes flitted around the room. He stood up stiffly and looked at her.

"You? Here?"

◈

When Elin awoke, the room smelled of cleaning fluid. Lasse had offered her his bed and she'd fallen asleep the second her head hit the pillow, exhausted from her journey. Now sunlight was flooding into the room. Lasse's head stuck up over the top of the armchair. His legs were stretched out, his feet resting on the windowsill. On the coffee table there was juice and bread and cheese, waiting for them.

Elin crept over to him and sat down with her back against the wall. Now it wasn't just the burns around her ankles that hurt; the soles of her feet were also wounded from her barefoot pilgrimage.

Lasse's eyes were closed, and the rattle of his breath was familiar. His scent reminded her of everything she'd longed for. She looked around. Everything had been cleaned up: heaps of clothes tidied away, the beer cans on the windowsill cleared, piles of newspapers thrown out. She smiled as she studied her father, who was wearing proper pants and a shirt, neatly buttoned right up to his chin. When he finally opened his eyes, he blinked several times.

"Number One, are you really here?"

"You've cleaned up so nicely. Have you been up all night?"

"Yeah, if you're going to live here it needs to be a bit tidier. I tried to phone your mother, but there was no one registered to that number. Hasn't she paid the bill?"

Elin shrugged and looked away.

"I sent a letter, in any case, when I went to the shop. Wrote that you'd arrived OK. So now she knows you're here," he went on, turning the chair to face the table and the tray.

Elin picked up a slice of bread and crammed it into her mouth in a few bites, with no topping.

"Are you that hungry?" Lasse cut a thick piece of cheese with the kitchen knife, passed it over to her, and watched as she stuffed it straight into her mouth.

"I didn't have any money with me on the boat. I've had nothing to eat for ages."

"What have you done to your legs?" Lasse gestured to the white dressings, now grubby.

"I burned myself, there was a fire . . ." Elin stammered and didn't know how she was going to explain.

Lasse interrupted her:

"Yeah, fuck, I heard about it. They called. Did you know that . . . ?"

Elin cut him off. "Yeah, I don't want to talk about it. Ever." She didn't want to think about what had just happened, just wanted to suppress it forever.

She reached for the juice and poured it into two glasses. Then she made two sandwiches, one for herself and one for Lasse. He made no attempt to force her to speak, just took a big bite of his sandwich.

"Look at that, I've got a maid into the bargain. This will be all right, this will," he mumbled, his mouth full.

"So I can stay?"

Lasse put both his warm hands on her cheeks and tipped her head from side to side.

"Well, yes, my little bug. I'll treat you like a princess. Tomorrow we'll find you a school. Today we'll fix up a mattress. And I'll sleep on that, you can have the bed, and I'll buy you the loveliest quilt there is. And teddies."

"But Papa, I'm too old for teddies." Elin sighed.

Now

⸻ ◆ ⸻

NEW YORK, 2017

Fredrik Grinde: Elin types his full name into the search engine and quickly presses Enter. An address in Visby comes up as the third result, a business address, along with a few articles in which his name is mentioned, but she doesn't read that carefully. He's on the results table of a half marathon too. But there are no pictures to show what he looks like. She keeps scrolling down.

He exists. He's alive. She holds her breath and then slams the lid of the computer shut.

His face was always so freckled in the spring, speckled as a speckled hen, she used to say. She wonders if that's still the case, if he still looks like that today. She remembers a boy, always happy, always smart. But now he's a man, a middle-aged man.

She's sitting in Sam's big brown leather armchair, staring ahead hopelessly. Her hair is greasy, and she's dressed in a loose-fitting gray tracksuit, her face not made up. She's been sitting there every day for a week now. All her jobs have been canceled. She's blaming it on illness, and so far her agent is going along with it. It's quiet and still in the apartment. She can't even be bothered to put any music on. The only things that can be heard are street noises and the humming of the fridge.

On the table in front of her, the star chart lies open. She has looked at it so much that the corners are getting worn. The folds have grown white and fluffy, cutting across the black background. Perhaps she should buy a star just next to it, and call it Fredrik, so they could sit together in the heavens and shine for all eternity, or at least until one of them went out. She hears the elevator moving through the building, the sound coming closer and closer, passing the downstairs neighbor. She hurriedly sweeps her hair up into a high knot, folds up the star chart, and puts it right at the back of the notebook. Then she starts clearing the junk from the table in front of her, but only has time to gather up a few boxes before the elevator doors open and Alice comes in. She looks happy, still dressed in her dance clothes.

"I rushed here straight from class." She throws herself onto the sofa and groans. "It's such hard work. What have I gotten myself into?"

"You're at Juilliard because you're a star. Only stars get in. It's the eye of the needle."

"I don't feel like a star. More like a clumsy oaf. You should see the others, they're so good. I don't compare."

Elin doesn't respond. She sinks down onto the brown armchair again, picks up the laptop, and reexamines the search results. Alice lies still, eyes closed, stretched out on the sofa.

Then she groans again.

"Oh yeah, I forgot. I brought food. I'm guessing you haven't eaten anything today, right? I haven't got the strength to get up, though."

She does so anyway, and serves up plastic containers of food on the table. Three kinds of salad, fresh tomatoes, chicken, avocado, and marinated carrots from the deli down on Broome Street. She puts the dressing to one side, along with a bottle of water and two Cokes. Elin's eyes flash when she sees the red cans, and Alice opens one of them and takes a large gulp.

"Mmm, *yum*," she says, with exaggerated enthusiasm.

"That stuff kills you from the inside," Elin grumbles.

"Well, doesn't everything?" says Alice. "Secrets, for example." Elin grimaces at her, but Alice goes on. "Stop nagging. I can drink what I want. It tastes good, and it makes me happy. You shouldn't underestimate that. I got you one too."

Alice picks up her phone and waves it at her mother.

"Look, I found loads of videos filmed on your island. It's so beautiful there."

Elin takes the phone from her and watches a few clips.

"It's even lovelier in real life. Who makes these films anyway? They're terrible!"

"YouTube is absolutely full of them. And people watch them. Not everyone cares about quality."

"It's weird," Elin says.

"What's weird?"

"How beautiful things are so much better."

"Than what?"

"Than ugly things, of course."

"What's beautiful and what's ugly are surely in the eye of the beholder?"

"That's true."

"I want us to go."

"What? You're crazy."

"Am I? Wouldn't you want me to come back, if I'd run away?"

Elin looks at her.

"You'd never run away. Would you?"

"No, maybe I wouldn't, but hypothetically speaking. If I had done that. Wouldn't you want me to come back?"

"I'd devote my whole life to looking for you. I'd search every millimeter of the earth. Of the universe if I had to." Elin smiles.

"How do you know she doesn't feel the same way?"

"Who?"

"Hello? Your mom. My grandma." Alice sighs.

"She hasn't lifted a finger to look for me. She knew exactly where I was. She could have come to see me, she could have taken me home. She could have picked up the phone and called me anytime. But she didn't. That says it all."

"It's so strange, all this. I don't get it." Alice waggles the phone at her again. "In any case, I've found us flights. For tomorrow."

"Tomorrow? You're crazy. It's impossible, I'm fully booked with work."

"No, you're not. You've canceled everything because you're 'sick.' I spoke to your agent yesterday, and I've taken some time off school."

"You haven't told her, have you? If you have, the whole world will know soon."

"Mom, the world doesn't end if you cancel a few jobs. And she doesn't care about your secrets. She and the rest of the world have got plenty of other problems. I promise you."

"If this gets out . . ."

"Yeah?"

"Then . . ."

"Then what?"

"No one can know."

"Don't be paranoid. Even if your agent knew, she'd hardly do anything to hurt you. She's on your side, you're on the same team."

Elin takes the phone and studies the itinerary.

"Direct flights," she says.

"Yes, to Stockholm, and then a domestic flight to Gotland. I've rented a car too, so we can drive around. And a hotel, the best on the whole island."

Elin's hands start to shake. She grips her stomach hard to make the trembling stop.

"Does she know that we . . . does she know that we're coming?"

Alice shakes her head.

"I don't even know what Grandma's name is, I don't know what the village is called. I know nothing. I only know we have to go there."

"She might not even be alive, she probably isn't." Elin's freezing now, her whole body shaking, and she places Alice's phone on the table, pulls her legs up, and puts her forehead on her knees.

"But the trees are alive, and the fields, and the sea."

"There was nothing left. The buildings burned down, so many buildings, so much forest. Who'd want to live there? We'll get there and it'll be deserted."

Alice sighs.

"It only looks like that in your head, in your memory. Give me your laptop." She reaches for it. "Password?"

Elin takes it back.

"I'll write it in myself."

"Why's it so secret?"

Alice hangs over her shoulder as she presses the keys: M i s s i n g A l i c e.

"Oh, Mom, I managed to read it," she whispered.

She takes back the laptop and opens the map.

"Tell me the name of the village."

Elin hesitates.

"I had a friend there too."

"What was her name? Maybe she's still living there. Or did she die in the fire?"

Elin shakes her head.

"He was at his mother's in Visby. I've missed him all these years. His name is Fredrik; he was the one I drew the flowers for."

"Ah right, that's sorted out. Let's go. I bet Fredrik still lives there. Give me your card, I'll pay for the tickets."

"Seems you can do it all, even if you are a tiny tot."

Alice throws a cushion at her.

"Ah, be quiet. I'm older than you were when you ran away."

"The village is called Heivide."

Alice falls silent. Listens as she repeats it.

"Can you spell it? What a strange name."

"Shouldn't you go home and pack?" says Elin. "If we're going on a trip?"

Alice nods, turns the screen toward her, and shows her a satellite image. Elin leans forward and studies the trees.

"They've grown again."

"Wounds heal."

Elin looks at her daughter. She's so smart. She gazes deep into her eyes, which are hazel, rimmed with gray. The eyes aren't Elin's or Sam's

—they're Marianne's. They're a gift from Alice's grandmother, a physical trace of everything Elin's been trying to suppress. She hasn't thought about it before, but Marianne has never completely left her. She's there, in Alice. Will she see it when they meet?

◈

Alice lies cuddled up under a thick blanket with her phone. She's awake and is inspecting every millimeter of Gotland's surface, with great curiosity. The fuzzy satellite images are hard to make out, but she meanders through the forest, swiping past isolated houses and farms. Elin lies beside her. Her light is off and she closes her eyes now and then, but sleep refuses to take hold; her thoughts are like a great black cloud around her whole body. From a distance she follows Alice's journey through the countryside, sees her zoom in on places whose names Elin instinctively knows. Their bags are ready and packed in the hall, the alarm is set, the tickets have been paid for. Tomorrow they'll be there, in what just a few months ago was a suppressed secret memory. She sits up and Alice reaches out, touches her arm.

"Can't you sleep? Tell me more. Tell me about Grandma, what was she like?"

Elin puts her hands over her face.

"She was everything I'm not."

"How do you mean?"

"I don't know."

"Tell me."

"I can barely remember. She was . . . quiet, sad, absent."

Alice laughs out loud.

"Absent! You mean you're not?"

"Not like that. She had no job, so she was almost always home. But she seldom laughed, seldom spoke. She was there, physically, but still she was far away."

"Depressed?"

"Perhaps. It wasn't something you talked about back then. She would get angry too, very angry."

"That doesn't sound like much fun."

"It wasn't."

"And your brothers?"

"They were so lovely. I'd wake them up in the morning, make them breakfast."

"Were you close?"

"Yes."

"You must have really missed them."

"They're dead. I haven't thought about them for a long time now. But of course I was sad for many years, thought about them every day."

"Maybe there's a grave we could visit. So you'd get a chance to say goodbye."

"You're so smart, Alice. How did you get so smart?"

"I have a good mom."

"An absent one."

"Not like that. I know you're there. You love your job a bit too much, that's all."

Alice gets up from the bed and goes into the bathroom, where Elin can see her shadow moving about. The shower starts and the sound of running water takes her to another place. She lies down and closes her eyes.

Then

=◆=

The wall in front of Elin was covered with sunglasses in lurid colors. She was wearing baggy stonewashed jeans and a matching denim jacket with rolled-up sleeves, and underneath she had on a pink top that matched the band in her permed hair. She was chewing gum frenetically and occasionally eyeing the exit, where a guy in a black leather jacket was waiting for her: John, a guy from school whom she was *possibly* in love with. She hadn't decided yet. He gestured impatiently to her. There were almost no customers in the shop, and the sales assistant at the cash register was looking the other way, so Elin grabbed a pair of sunglasses and slid them inside her jacket, in the space behind the pocket. Her heart was beating hard. She stayed where she was and took down another pair, turning them this way and that, as if considering buying them. Then she put them back and slowly walked toward the exit, getting a pat on the shoulder in greeting. She and John carried on with their walk through the mall as though nothing had happened.

She was just about to put on the sunglasses, which were pink to match her outfit, when a man stopped in front of her, blocking her path. He had short black hair and a Polaroid camera on a strap around his neck. He looked her up and down, and Elin lowered the hand holding the sunglasses.

"What are you doing? Move," she said boldly, trying to push past him.

"Wait a minute. Can I take a picture of you?" he asked, and lifted the camera to his eyes.

Elin recoiled.

"Gross," she muttered, and walked past.

"No, no, I don't mean it like that, I work for a modeling agency. Do you know what that is?" The man hurried after her and came back to stand in front of her again.

"Yeah, and?"

"You look fantastic."

John, who'd walked on without Elin, now turned and came back, glaring at the man. Elin drew herself up.

"OK, hurry up then, take the picture," she said sullenly, and looked intensely into the camera.

"Can you take off your jacket?" he asked.

Elin complied and handed the jacket to John, posing with one hand on her waist.

"Smile a little, I bet your smile is beautiful."

The man pulled a totally white picture from the camera and warmed it between his hands.

"Just wait a minute, I'll see if it turned out all right."

Elin watched curiously as shapes slowly began to emerge on the shiny surface. At last she was there, smiling, her eyes bright. The man nodded in satisfaction and handed her a pen.

"This came out really well. Can you write your name and telephone number on the white strip?"

Elin carefully wrote the details as requested, and the man put the photo in his pocket before disappearing into the crowds. Elin followed him with her gaze as he strolled along, carefully inspecting all the young girls he encountered.

"Pretty cool," John said, and put his arm around her shoulders. "So, a model, eh? I knew you were hot, but just think, you might get famous now."

Elin pulled away. The sunglasses suddenly felt heavy in her hand, and she put them in her pocket and pulled out a cigarette.

"I have to go now," she muttered, the unlit cigarette in the corner of her mouth.

John raised his eyebrows, but nodded.

"OK, see ya," he said, shoving both hands into the pockets of his jeans.

"Take this if you want," she said.

She held out the cigarette. Then she turned her back on him and ran fast along the sidewalk and down the steps to Sergels Torg. Just before she got to the metro station's ticket barriers, she took the cigarette packet out of her pocket and threw it in the trash.

❖

It was dark in the apartment when she got home. The blinds were drawn, and on the mattress on the floor Lasse lay sleeping, curled up like a little child. His pants had slipped down, exposing the crack between his buttocks. He was snoring dully, and the sound echoed in the empty room. Elin gathered up the bottles from the floor and put them in the wastebasket after dumping the remaining liquid into the sink. The room smelled rank, of beer and spirits, so she ran the tap for a long time to get rid of the stench.

They didn't have a TV anymore; it had broken. And no radio. It was always quiet. Sometimes she could hear the neighbors screaming at each other, but they seemed to be getting along better now. She sat down in the only armchair and switched on the lamp. On the table was a heap of library books, and she picked up the top one, but the words just blurred together and she couldn't be bothered to read. She hadn't finished a single book since she came to Stockholm. Just a few paragraphs here and there, when the mood took her. Aina used to say that reading was the secret: that if she just read enough, everything would work out in the end. Everything would be fine.

She laid the book in her lap, leaned her head back, and closed her eyes. She still hadn't found a place where she could sit in peace and just think. Nowhere like the place she had behind her house when she was little, or like the place she and Fredrik had on the beach. She often wondered if he still went there, if he looked at the stars on his own or with someone else.

The apartment was so small and cramped, she often felt trapped, like an animal in a cage. When Lasse was home it often stank of sweat and booze. And outside she was never really on her own. There were cars, people, noise everywhere.

She couldn't bear it any longer. In her pocket was a long letter she'd started writing, a letter to Fredrik. It never got finished, there was always more to tell him. But now it would have to do, now she was going to send it, ask his forgiveness for the fire, ask him for help, ask him to take her home.

It had grown late in the evening, and she had school the next day. But still she went out into the hallway and put her shoes on again, intending to get a stamp from somewhere. Maybe she'd be able to buy one off one of the alkies on the square, the ones who always hung out on the benches.

Just as she was about to open the door she heard Lasse's rumbling voice.

"You're not going out again, are you? It's dark." The words were slurred.

Elin rolled her eyes and slammed the door behind her, a little too hard. She ran down the stairs, holding the banister and swinging round each landing. Upstairs the door opened again and she heard Lasse's gravelly cough echoing.

"Elin! Someone was looking for you earlier," he called. His words weren't slurring as much now; his voice sounded clearer, more sober.

Elin paused, waiting for him to elaborate.

"Elin, come back up, I can hear you're down there," he called. Now his voice was sharp and firm.

She inhaled deeply.

"I'll be back in a minute, I just have to sort something out," she replied, and put her hand on the door handle.

Lasse's clogs clacked hard on the stairs. The sound came closer. She didn't dare open the door. When he came down, she was still standing in the entrance.

"The woman who rang said you were the most beautiful girl they'd ever seen. That they were going to make you a star. What have you been up to now, Number One?"

He wasn't angry. Quite the reverse. He smiled broadly and laughed so hard, his chest rumbled. Then he put his big warm hands on her shoulders.

"A model. Would you believe it!"

Now

≡ ◆ ≡

NEW YORK, 2017

It's been a long time since she lay sleepless for a whole night, but morning is here and she's still awake. Alice sleeps deeply beside her. The covers have slipped off and her top has ridden up, baring her midriff. Elin tenderly pulls the covers back over her.

It's dawn, and the small tufts of cloud in the sky are finely streaked with pink. From her bed she can see the pointed spire of the Empire State Building, shimmering beautifully in the morning sun. Elin rises, quiet and cautious, and Alice stirs a little but doesn't wake. Elin stands still, her gaze resting on her daughter's peaceful face. The bed is as it should be now, untidy and full of love. Alice often used to sleep in the bed with her and Sam when she was little. For too long, Sam thought, but Elin always told him a little extra closeness could only be a good thing. They used to argue about it a lot, but the lazy Sunday mornings together were always so much fun that they soon made up again. She wishes he was here now, that all three of them were in the bed again and that the room would fill with laughter when Alice woke.

But he isn't. She's standing there alone, in the middle of a nightmare, remembering what once was. Remembering only the good times.

The pipes in the walls rattle and the neighbors start to wake; the sounds of the city are growing more intense. She wraps herself in a dressing gown and goes out onto the terrace, picking withered leaves from the plants and throwing them over the edge of the building; they pick up speed in the wind and sail off. Just like Fredrik's present did. She wonders which magazine he saw her in, if he reads the American magazines, and if so, which ones. She's often to be found on the contributors' page, with a picture and a sentence about her, usually a reply to a silly question. Maybe he saw her in the pictures from some party or premiere. She wants to ask him, to talk to him about that, and about everything else that's happened since they last saw each other.

No journalists have written about her separation from Sam yet; no one knows about it. The thought makes her close her eyes and swallow hard. The headlines will come, she knows that. Nothing sells as well as the tragic lives of celebrities. She's never thought of herself and Sam as celebrities, but the papers don't care what she thinks. Through the years they've both become names that spark interest. She's the creator of portraits of the modern era, someone who gives the narcissists validation. He's a successful businessman.

❖

When Alice wakes, Elin is sitting on the sofa. Her face is carefully made up; the swelling around her eyes has been softened with a cold compress. Her hair is curled, falling with a beautiful shine over her shoulders. She is clothed in a severe black pantsuit, with a polo shirt underneath. Alice pulls on her baggy jeans and a plain top. Elin inspects her.

"Have you already showered?"

"I had a shower last night, that'll do."

She holds her hands up in the air, like a signal to stop.

"No comments on my clothing, thanks."

"I didn't say anything."

"But you thought it."

"Perhaps. But thought is free. Isn't that what you usually say?"

She detects a smile on Alice's lips.

"Let's go."

"Are we really going?"

"Yes, we're really going. Really."

Elin hides her eyes behind a pair of big black sunglasses with rhinestone-studded frames.

"Is that what you're wearing?"

"No comments on my clothing, thanks."

"Touché." Alice grins and pulls an oversized hoodie over her head.

"You look like a rapper," Elin says.

"No comments, you say? Seriously, how is this going to work?"

◈

They're flying business class, so the seats are soft and spacious. Elin sits straight-backed, with her sunglasses still on and her hands folded on her lap. Alice reclines beside her, with two cushions under her head and her feet pulled up on the seat. Dancing has made her as supple as a rubber doll. She pulls her earbuds out of her ears and hands them over to Elin.

"Listen, there are Swedish films. They speak so weirdly, *hoppety-hoppety-hop*. Can you talk like that?"

Elin takes the earbuds and puts them in. The familiar syntax makes her smile, and she follows the film on Alice's screen with curiosity. Alice pulls out one of the buds.

"Say something in Swedish."

"What should I say?"

"Say: 'Hi, Grandma, nice to meet you.'"

Elin says nothing.

"I can't remember."

"Can't you speak it anymore?"

"Yes, of course I can. It's my mother tongue. I still hear some Swedish: there are plenty of Swedes living in Manhattan, I've shot many Swedish stars."

"And what did you do then? Pretend that you didn't know Swedish, that you couldn't understand what they were saying?"

Elin nods and laughs.

"It's *'Hej, mormor, fint att få träffa dig,'*" she says.

Alice can't keep up.

"Again, slowly."

"*Hej, mormor.*"

Alice repeats the greeting, tripping on the rounded *r*'s. Elin goes on.

"*Fint att få träffa dig.*"

"*Hej, mormor, fint att få träffa dig.*"

"Excellent, that's it. You can say it now."

"Did they say anything stupid, thinking you wouldn't understand?"

"Who?"

"The Swedish stars."

Elin laughs.

"Yeah, it was actually pretty funny, their not knowing I understood."

"I want to learn Swedish; can you teach me some more? Please?"

"Later maybe. I need to rest now. I barely slept last night. Finish watching your film."

"No, please, can't we talk a bit more? I want to know what I should say to Grandma when we meet her. I want to know what she's like."

"But I don't know what she's like now. I don't know her. I just know she's called Marianne Eriksson and that, last I heard, she was still living in Heivide, where I grew up."

A lump forms in Elin's throat and she coughs, struggling to swallow. Alice gets up and calls the flight attendant.

"Water, can we get some water over here?"

The flight attendant comes running over with a glass of water. Elin takes two large gulps and then closes her eyes as Alice strokes her back.

"Can we rest now?" Elin pleads. Her voice sounds hoarse, weak, as though it's about to break.

Alice nods and returns to her film. But there's no way for Elin to relax. She stares ahead of her. In her head, the memories replay, one after the other. Fredrik is always there, always beside her, offering reassurance. Maybe that's what she's on her way toward; maybe the whole point is for the two of them to meet again.

Then

STOCKHOLM, 1984

Her suitcase stood ready to go in the hallway. It contained all the clothes she owned and still it was only half full. Two pairs of jeans. A few tops. An extra pair of white canvas shoes, the uppers so worn that the fabric over her big toe joint had ripped. Her passport was in her pocket, unstamped and new, collected just a few days ago. Lasse had moaned about the cost of the photos and she'd promised to pay him back.

"When you're famous," he'd said, laughing.

The two spare pictures were now clamped to the fridge with a blue magnet next to some home-store discount coupons. She was looking blankly at the camera, smiling weakly.

Lasse was still asleep, on the mattress. Beside him was a half-full bottle with the lid unscrewed.

He was snoring loudly and evenly. Those snores had become almost reassuring, like a metronome marking the seconds that passed in the vacuum of their home. Elin listened for a while, following each breath and rattling snore. She closed her eyes, took a deep breath, then picked up her bag and walked out into the stairwell without looking back. She stopped for a second outside the closed door, patting her pockets. Everything was there. Her passport, the tickets, the two hundred-krona notes she'd been given as pocket money by the modeling agency. Everything else would be paid for; they'd promised her that. Her metro card, which was still valid even though school had finished a few days earlier, would take her to the central station and the airport bus.

❖

Lasse had accompanied Elin to the Strand Hotel a few weeks earlier, where the French "mother agent" was meeting the teenage hopefuls. The woman sat in an armchair in the foyer, with assistants on either side. She didn't ask any questions, just examined them all, up and down. Some were asked to leave, a few were asked to fill in forms, others were led directly to another suite of sofas. Elin was one of the chosen who were moved to the sofas straightaway. Lasse, grinning proudly, sat straight-backed beside her. He'd dressed up for the occasion, in a shirt and tie and pointy-toed leather shoes with a stacked heel, a well-worn leftover from the 1970s. He had his arm along the back of the sofa behind her, and the sickly sweet scent of his cologne tickled her nose.

"If only your mother knew. Our little girl," he laughed, a little too loud, making Elin squirm. "You should probably call and tell her."

Elin nodded, distracted. The sofas around them had filled with more young girls, and all the others had their mothers with them. Lasse was still chattering away, but she wasn't listening. She kept her eyes on the waterfront outside the window, watching the boats coming and going, leaving passengers on the dock and the seagulls floating on the wind.

The water was the only thing separating her from her own mother.

❖

In Farsta there was no water. She struggled with her suitcase along To-baksvägen, toward the bus stop. Over her shoulder hung a tattered denim handbag, and inside it were the pink sunglasses. She wondered if the sun would be shining in Paris, and if the stars would twinkle as beautifully at night. Would she understand what anyone said?

An airplane cut through the air above the bus stop, its vapor trail like a string of bubbles across the dark-blue sky. She'd seen many like it before, from the beach in Gotland, and Fredrik had taught her everything he knew about planes. But neither of them had ever flown in one, and she barely knew what an airport was.

She unfolded the piece of paper she'd been given. The instructions

were in English, neatly divided into bullet points that gave precise tim-
ings. She would take the airport bus to Arlanda Airport, then fly to
Paris, and at Charles de Gaulle someone would be waiting for her, holding a sign with her name on it.

When the bus arrived, Elin was reading through the bullet points
over and over again, her heart hammering in her chest. She cast her eyes
over the field, toward Tobaksvägen 38 and Lasse's apartment. The sun
was too bright for her to make out anything, but maybe he was standing
there, watching her board the bus. Or maybe he was still snoring.

The bus doors opened and the driver nodded to her suitcase and
smiled.

"Aha, vacation time," he said.

Elin stretched and smiled hesitantly. It was going to be a two-week
trial period only. She'd probably be back soon.

"Yeah, I'm going to Arlanda," she replied.

Now

≡ ◆ ≡

The familiar scent hits her as she steps out of the plane. The scent of earth, sea, and rain. And the strong wind in her face. She stops dead and inhales deeply. Chaos ensues: Alice bumps into her cabin bag, and someone behind collides with Alice. But Elin is incapable of taking another step; it's as though she's taken root at the top of the metal stairs. Apologizing, Alice presses Elin toward the rail, to allow other passengers to move forward.

"Mom, you have to go down," she whispers.

"I feel like I'm going to faint."

"It's just a short walk, you can see the terminal over there. We'll sit down when we get there. We're not in a rush."

Alice takes Elin's hand and leads her down the steps. Slowly, Elin follows her.

The arrival hall is spartan, just a little room and a baggage carousel. There are no chairs. They stand there, along with many others, waiting patiently for their bags. Everyone is silent.

"Why is no one talking?" Alice whispers. "Is there a national vow of silence?"

Elin grins at her.

"City slicker," she says.

A couple standing in front of them are kissing passionately; the smacking of wet saliva echoes through the little room. Alice starts to sing, and Elin elbows her.

"What?" she whispers. "Someone has to do something. It's too quiet here. I'm going crazy."

Alice stops singing, but her hips are still moving to a beat and Elin can see her lips moving. There's always music in her, always joy.

❖

At last they're sitting in the rental car, all their luggage stowed in the trunk. Alice leans against the window, studying the passing landscape: the fences, behind which a few gray sheep are grazing the barren ground; the trees, the crooked little pines Elin has told her about. The houses, which are few and far between, surrounded by large plots of forest. Elin knows exactly where she's going; the roads haven't changed at all. When they get to the roundabout at Norrgatt, she turns toward Norderport, and Alice shouts and points as she sees the beautiful city wall. The buildings within look like toy houses, taken from another time.

"Do people live here?" she asks, astonished, making Elin laugh.

"It's probably a good thing we came here, so you can see something other than skyscrapers. Yes, people live in these houses."

It's barely three in the afternoon, but darkness is already falling. Light snowflakes float in the air beneath the glow from the streetlights. Elin winds her way through the narrow streets between the harbor and the hotel. Inside her body, her organs are twisting and heaving, and when she feels a wave of nausea she suddenly stops the car, leaning her head against the steering wheel. Alice unbuckles her seat belt and opens the door.

"No, we're not there yet," says Elin.

"Why did you stop then?"

"Why are we here?"

"Because you have to do this."

"I don't want to. I really don't want to."

The wind catches the car door, which blows open. Alice grabs it and pulls it shut, though not before the interior fills with cold, sea-scented air.

"Drive. Let's just get to the hotel and we can rest awhile."

"He lives here, I think. Just a few streets away."

"Who?"

"Fredrik."

"Tell me about him. Was he your boyfriend?"

"Just a friend. Almost like a brother."

"We can stop and knock on his door if you want."

Elin starts the engine again and drives off, the tires spinning against the slippery cobblestones.

"Are you crazy? Of course I don't want to."

❖

They sit in silence the rest of the way. They see only a handful of people, hunched against the icy wind, wearing thick coats and scarves, and hats pulled down over pale faces. This is where they live their lives, this is where they go about their daily business. She wonders what Fredrik does day to day, what work he does. He still lives on the island, so he can't have become an astronaut like he wanted to as a child. Maybe he has a wife, children. She wonders if he thinks about her often, if he missed her when she disappeared, or if he was angry at her for taking his papa away from him.

The thought makes her shudder.

❖

"Elin. *Är det du?*"

They're standing in the hotel lobby, surrounded by bags, when a staff member suddenly stops in front of them. Elin looks at her quizzically.

"It is you, isn't it? Elin Eriksson? I never thought I'd see you again."

The woman looks like she's seen a ghost. Elin puts her sunglasses back on, but Alice reaches over and pulls them off again.

"Yes, I'm Elin," she says in English, and nods at the woman. "Who are you?"

She starts hesitantly in English, but then switches to Swedish.

"It's Malin, don't you remember me? We were in the same class. Well, until you moved, after the fire. How lovely to see you here on the island after all these years. I've always wondered where you went. No one ever told us." Malin tilts her head and studies Elin. "You're just the same, and yet different."

Elin's face tightens, small wrinkles forming around her mouth. She avoids meeting the woman's eyes and reaches for her bag.

"I'm sorry, I don't remember you, you must be mistaken," she mutters in Swedish.

Alice prods her.

"What are you saying, who is that? Can't you speak English so I understand?"

"I don't know, I don't know her. Let it go."

Elin pulls her bag toward the reception desk, but Malin and Alice stay put. Elin can hear them talking, but she can't make out what they're saying. She checks in, eager to get to her bed.

"Mama, you have to stop running away now. Talk to her, you were in the same class at school, you must remember her. Don't be so rude," hisses Alice, who has now caught up with her.

Elin holds out a key card and turns her back on Alice.

"Here, you've got your own room. Do what you want, order room service if you're hungry. I need to rest awhile, be alone."

❖

She leaves the lights off in the room and sits down on the sofa. It's hard to switch off and rest when all the sounds and smells are so familiar. One of the windows is ajar, and gusts of cool sea air sweep in. It smells of salt and seaweed. It's so quiet.

Malin. Of course she remembers her. A quiet, kind girl who used to cast wondering glances at Fredrik now and then. How many more faces from the past will she see during these days on the island? Do they all still live here? Are they all friends?

A shudder goes through her body, and she falls to one side and curls up in the fetal position.

❖

There's a knock on the door, and Elin reaches for her telephone in a daze. Only half an hour has passed, but she still slept deeply. Alice must have lost the extra key already. She sighs as she goes down the spiral staircase of the duplex suite to open the door. She jumps when she sees who's standing outside. It's Malin. She has a tray in her hands, with a cup of coffee and a plate with a piece of golden-yellow saffron pancake.

"I thought you'd probably be hungry and tired after your journey." She smiles, holding the tray out.

Elin hesitates.

"You did recognize me, right?" Malin says.

Elin nods and eventually takes the tray.

"That's kind of you," she says quietly.

"I want you to feel welcome, we all missed you after you left. It was awful, what happened, and even more awful that she sent you away."

Elin shook her head.

"Who? Mama? No, that wasn't what happened, she didn't send me away," she says.

"There were rumors that you lived in the attic, that you were so badly burned that she hid you away!" Malin tells her.

Elin shakes her head again and laughs.

"Oh my God, no, of course that wasn't what happened. I went to live with my papa."

Malin laughs too.

"Yeah, I guess we knew that, really. But you know how children talk. We never heard anything, so our imaginations ran wild."

Neither says anything, and they stand there awhile until Malin gives a little shrug.

"Well, I guess I'd better be going. I just wanted to check on you quickly, make sure you were doing OK."

"Thanks, that's kind of you," Elin repeats.

Malin hesitates, as though she's hoping Elin will ask her to come in. But she doesn't. Elin slowly pushes the door shut, and when it's open no more than a crack, she raises her hand in a wave.

"I expect I'll see you soon," Elin says.

Malin cranes her neck to see her through the gap.

"I could invite a few people to my place if you want, we could have a reunion. That would be fun, right?"

Elin shakes her head vehemently and closes the door, sinking down with her back against it, her heart pounding.

◈

It's still night. Even though the clock insists it's early morning. Elin has barely slept a wink, and has given up trying. The black sky above her feels almost as though it's pressing her down into the cobblestones as she walks. She hasn't thought about the darkness for a long time, had forgotten how black everything could be here. All those times she walked home from school in darkness and stormy weather, along the main road with a weak flashlight in her hand, the cold and wind her only companions. They would find their way in through every fiber of her clothes; her jackets were always too flimsy, the pants grew stiff from the cold, and the shoes were too thin-soled to protect her from the ice. She remembers the white fingers and toes that she had to slowly thaw in front of the stove. They used to sting as the cold let go, sometimes hurting so much, she would cry.

In the harbor the moorings gape, empty, and thin floes of ice drift on the still surface, shielded from the waves by the breakwater farther out. She walks toward the park in Almedalen, past houses she's never seen before. New buildings, beautiful architecture with great gleaming windows. It's completely deserted and the sparsely distributed streetlights don't provide enough illumination. She feels the cold cut through her leather shoes and clenches and unclenches her toes to warm them. Her thick down jacket provides good insulation, and she only wishes she had something just as warm for her feet.

Elin walks farther up the promenade. Light starts to filter over the horizon: dawn is breaking. The wind takes hold of her; her upper body is forced to push forward, far ahead of her legs. The sea is ridged with large waves, and the seagulls are playing in the headwind. She sees them stop flying and float back, then fly again. Like a never-ending dance.

She breathes, slow, deep breaths. Fresh air fills her lungs. It smells just like she remembers. It's over thirty years since she last walked here, and yet almost everything is just the same.

She turns in through the Love Gate, the little opening toward the sea. She stops there and leans against the wall. She smiles at the memory of the times she stood there with Fredrik, how they joked about getting married one day.

If neither of us is married when we're fifty. Then we'll do it. You and me. We'll get married at sunset.

He'd say it like that, just like that, and she'd laugh at him. It feels so long ago. As far as she can remember they never actually shook on it. But now they were about to turn fifty: Fredrik in one year, Elin in two.

Fredrik. She walks away from the gate, but his face doesn't leave her thoughts. She sees his freckles, his big front teeth, his smile. His front teeth made his lip turn up toward his nose when he laughed.

She pulls her hat down over her ears and whistles a melody, their melody. She remembers every note, and her heart races as the memory washes over her. They always used to run, wherever they were going. They ran fast and barefoot, over stones and roots.

She starts to run, feeling the wind almost snatching her hat off her head. She runs fast along the shore, as though someone is chasing her. She loses control of her arms, lets them flail. She runs until the wall ends and is replaced by deep trenches; she runs past the great field that lies behind them. At the jetty by the hospital she stops. The long, ugly jetty, where the outflow from the hospital was said to have colored the water red with blood in the past. She carefully balances her way along its surface, which is covered with a thin layer of ice; every step requires total concentration. The waves' peaks throw small showers of seawater over it. Everything around her is swaying. The surface of the sea is black and menacing. She sits down right at the end of the jetty, and the endless sea surrounds her.

Her telephone vibrates in her pocket, but she lets it ring. Her pants are wet and she's so cold, her lips and shoulders are trembling.

How easy it would be to just fall to one side. To let the down in her coat become wet and heavy, and carry her and all her memories to the bottom of the sea. To lay her soul and her body to rest.

◈

A man is shouting at her, but the roar of the waves and the wind drown his words. She hears him and yet doesn't hear him. Her pants are soaked through now, her jacket too. She's shaking from the cold. The place she's sitting in is slippery and inhospitable. She doesn't dare turn around, nor stand up for fear of slipping.

She feels a hand on one shoulder, and then the other.

"You can't sit here, you'll freeze to death," he says, gently.

His hands go under her arms and pull her carefully to her feet. Crying, she walks slowly backward, led by him. He seems strong, and she feels safe. As they reach land, and the water on either side of the jetty becomes shallow, she turns and collapses into his arms. He holds her close and pats her back soothingly. She realizes that he's a policeman, in uniform; his car is parked by the road and his colleague is waiting on the beach.

"That could have ended really badly," he says sternly, pushing her away.

"I just thought . . . I just wanted to . . ." She stumbles over the now-unfamiliar language; she can't find a proper explanation.

"You're completely soaked through. Where do you live? I think it's best we drive you home."

She nods and follows him to the car. His colleague puts a protective hand on her head as she bends down to get into the back seat. It's a Volvo. She strokes the seat.

"My stepfather had a Volvo," she murmurs, but the policemen act as if they haven't heard her.

They want to know where she's going, and when she tells them the Visby Hotel, they chuckle as though she were from another planet.

"Fancy," one says.

"In the summer we have our fair share of crazy tourists here, but it's not so common in the winter." The other laughs.

Elin protests. "I'm not drunk, I promise, you can test me. I just needed to breathe a little."

❖

They enter the lobby with her. Her lips are blue and her face is pale. Her pants are clinging to her legs, and water drips onto the stone floor, leaving a narrow trickle behind her. Her shoes squeak from the moisture. She sees Alice, who shouts so loud, her voice echoes around the lobby.

"Where have you been?"

She looks to the policemen for a response, her eyes entreating them. They let go of Elin's arms and let her walk on her own.

"She says she's OK, but we're not sure. Do you want us to drive her up to the hospital instead?" asks one of them, in accented English.

Alice shakes her head; Elin leans on her.

"I'm so cold. Can we go upstairs now?" she whispers.

"What have you done, Mom?"

The English-speaking policeman hastily reassures her:

"She hasn't done anything. We found her at the end of the jetty by the hospital. The waves were splashing up over her legs; there's a storm outside. She would have frozen stiff if we hadn't brought her in."

"Thank you," Alice says fervently.

Elin heads for the lift without saying thank you or goodbye to the policemen. Alice apologizes to them and then runs after her. Elin is leaning against the wall, looking at her phone.

"Why has Sam called so many times? He never phones me."

She holds up the handset. She has eight missed calls from him. Alice shrugs and looks away.

"You could have died, Mom. What were you doing out there?"

The elevator doors open.

She answers Alice's question with one of her own. "You haven't talked to him, have you?" As Elin gets into the elevator, her hands are so cold that the phone slips from her grasp and lands on the stone floor outside the doors, cracking right across the screen. She swears, crouches, and reaches out of the elevator for it, struggling to pick it up with her stiff fingers.

"Yeah, he rang this morning," says Alice. "He was wondering where I was."

"He's already noticed you're not there?"

"He went to school, to say hello to me, and they said I'd taken some time off for a family emergency. It scared him."

"You didn't tell him?"

"I told him we were here."

"But not why?"

"I said I was helping you with a project. He already knew you were born here. How could he know that?"

"You can't hide everything. We got married; he saw it then. I told him they were just on vacation, my parents, and I just happened to be born here."

The doors close and the elevator ascends. Elin is trembling with cold, and Alice takes her sweater off and puts it around her mother's shoulders. Elin laughs.

"What are you doing? It'll only get wet. Just look at me."

"Wool keeps you warm even when it's wet. You're frozen, you're shaking all over."

"You're so sweet, you do so much to help me."

❖

They climb into bed, under thick down comforters. Elin has the suite, and the ocher-colored walls inspire a curious calm. Alice phones down for hot chocolate and cookies.

"Tell me more about the fire, Mom. What happened?"

Elin mutters and hides her face in the duvet.

"I saw the body," she says, then falls silent.

"Whose body?"

"Edvin was with me, behind me; he was lying there, in the field. I saw Micke, he was dead. And Mama was screaming, she was just bawling.

She was on her knees in the farmyard and I can still hear the noises she was making."

"Was that the last time you saw her?"

"Yeah, we were in the same hospital, but I didn't get to see her there."

"But why did you say it was your fault? I still don't understand."

"Like I told you before—we always used to make a campfire on the beach, Fredrik and I. That evening I was on my own, he'd gone back to his mother's place in Visby. I stoked it too high and then I fell asleep. I should never have fallen asleep."

Alice fills in the rest. "And the fire spread."

Elin nods, her voice growing thick and tears filling her eyes.

"Erik and Edvin were in their secret den, in the tractor shed. I couldn't manage both of them, they were too heavy, so I carried Edvin out first. The whole building fell down over Erik. I couldn't save him."

"Why did you run away?"

"Everyone I loved was gone and it was my fault."

"But your mom . . ."

"You don't understand, you'll never understand. She would have killed me; she used to get that angry."

"I can't imagine life without you. There's nothing that would make me leave you."

"It was different back then. She was young when she had me, she never loved me."

"How can you say that? About a mother and her child? Of course she did."

"No, that's how it was. I never heard her say it. The words. Not a single time."

"That she loved you?"

Elin nods and turns toward Alice, edges closer and strokes her hair. She doesn't say anything.

"You don't say it to me either," Alice says.

Elin starts, and pulls her hand back.

"Sure I do."

"No, you don't; you almost always say *ditto*."

Elin doesn't reply. She turns again, so she's resting on her back. They lie still, side by side. Elin's gaze follows the white molding on the ceiling, the jumble of patterns someone once carved by hand.

"Would you abandon me too? If you'd done something wrong?"

Alice's abrupt question makes her jump. She's about to speak when she's saved by a loud knock at the door. Alice disappears downstairs to answer it, and Elin expects her to bring back the hot chocolate. But she returns empty-handed and runs over to the bed.

"There's a man outside who wants to see you," she says.

Elin sits up hastily.

"Have you let a strange man in here?"

Alice shakes her head eagerly, disheveled wisps of her curly hair falling over her face.

"He's outside, waiting. Hurry."

Then

≡ ◆ ≡

Most days were OK, but not Sundays. Sundays were always the worst. That was the day the loneliness and longing got to her the most. Two weeks in Paris had become four months, the test shoots had turned into real jobs, and the pile of notes she'd earned grew and grew in the inside pocket of her suitcase, where she hid them so her roommates wouldn't get at them. Elin had quickly learned how to look into the camera to bring out her best features, how to squint a little with her lower eyelid and push her nose down to make her mouth fuller. The shabby clothes she'd brought with her from Farsta had been replaced with new ones.

There was no sea breeze in Paris — it was just as cramped and stuffy as Farsta. All buildings and asphalt. She went to the park every now and then, the Bois de Boulogne, but there were hardly any wildflowers there, just planted beds and neatly mown lawns. And someone had told her it was dangerous, that the forest was full of prostitutes and their clients.

She often walked along the Seine. The boats set the water in motion, and the lapping sounds reminded her of everything she longed for. But it smelled sour, and drifts of rubbish collected along the edges.

This Sunday she was sitting on a bench, hidden behind the pink sunglasses that reminded her of her old life. The autumn sun was no longer warm; the breeze suddenly felt colder. She was so tired.

People walked along the sidewalk in front of her. No one was alone; they strolled in pairs or together in whole families. Hand in hand, arm in arm. She heard laughter and speech she didn't understand. French was still a mystery to her. She could say hello and goodbye, simple phrases. But nothing more. The photographers spoke English, with accents as strong as her own. She longed to hear Swedish, she longed for the beach and for Fredrik. For Edvin and Erik. For a chance to let her hair get messy and not be constantly looked at.

Thinking about her brothers made something snap inside her, and tears over what she'd lost suddenly flooded down her cheeks. She had coins in her pocket. She used them once a week, when she rang Lasse. He was the one who'd told her school that she wasn't coming back, who'd given her permission to stay there. He was generally drunk when she rang, slurring his speech, not listening. Perhaps she should phone *her* instead, Marianne. Maybe next Sunday. She fiddled with the coins. Thinking about her mama made her cry even harder and she hunched over, shaking and sobbing. Her breath came in spasms. More than anything she wanted to talk to Fredrik, to hear his voice. But what would she say? Sorry, maybe.

Sorry I killed your papa.

She didn't see the woman arrive, just felt the thud as she sat down on the bench. She sat there in perfect silence to begin with, but her deep, even breathing still spread some kind of calm. She was wearing a green dress, a thick wool fabric. Her hands rested on her knees. They were knotty and wrinkled.

She said something in French. But Elin just shook her head. So she switched to English.

"I've seen you sitting here sobbing far too many times. Why are you crying so bitterly? What can be so terrible?"

Elin didn't reply, but the question set her weeping again. Then the woman stood up and took her by the hand, pulling her upright.

"Come with me, I can't let you sit here alone anymore. That's enough now."

Elin raised her gaze and was met by bright-green eyes and red curly hair. The woman wore no makeup, and the skin under her eyes was puffy. When she smiled, a fan of wrinkles formed at the corner of each.

"My name is Anne," she whispered, with her arm around Elin's shoulders. She pointed at the building in front of them. "And that's my bookshop, and inside there are books and hot chocolate. I'm convinced that you're in need of both."

◆

The walls were covered with built-in floor-to-ceiling bookshelves of dark wood. You needed a ladder to reach the highest shelves. On the floor between them were tables with more piles of books, and Elin ran her hand over them. Her nose still felt swollen from all the crying, and she sniffled now and then. All the books were in French. She quietly spelled out the titles without understanding their meaning.

"There are books in English too." Anne smiled and pointed to a shelf farther back in the shop. "But if you want to learn French, I'd recommend you start with a children's book and a dictionary. There's no better way to learn a language."

She moved away swiftly, the wide skirt swinging around her ample hips, and came back with a slim book in her hand.

"Here, start with this, you're going to love it. *The Little Prince.*"

She gave the book to Elin. The cover was yellowing and full of small stars, and a prince with golden-yellow hair was balancing on a very small planet. Stars! Elin clutched it to her chest.

"You can read it for free if you sit here," said Anne. "You can read anything you like in my shop. And you can ask me anything."

Elin nodded and opened the book at the first page. She ran her finger over the prince, the birds, and the stars, and a tear ran down her cheek. Anne stood quietly, watching her. Elin looked up and wiped her chin with the back of her hand.

"How did you know?" she said.

"Know what, my dear?" Anne didn't understand the question. She took her arm and led her to an armchair. On the table alongside was a dictionary. French to English.

"Do you have French to Swedish?" Elin asked hoarsely.

Anne nodded and climbed up one of the ladders. She held a well-thumbed little book up in the air, its spine broken and some of the pages dog-eared.

"This one's best years are behind it, but it'll probably do. Not everything in this shop is new." She laughed so hard it made her cough, then she climbed back down the ladder with some effort.

The armchair was very soft. Elin sank down into it and started working her way through the opening sentences. She looked up the meaning of every single word, learning how to say "hat" and "elephant" and "boa constrictor." Anne set a cup of hot chocolate down beside her, and the hot liquid warmed her from the inside. Anne laid a blanket over her legs, tucking her in thoroughly.

"You're better off sitting in here than out on that cold bench. And you can learn a thing or two here as well. Promise you'll come here next time, and not sit alone out there, crying. No one should have to do that."

Anne went on talking, to herself. Elin stopped replying, and the voice became more of a murmur in the background. Customers came and went. Some stayed, sitting in other armchairs, leafing through books.

There was a sign above the cash register. It read:

A home without books is like a body without a soul.

Now

≡ ◆ ≡

Garment after garment lands on the floor as Elin rifles through the clothes in her suitcase. Alice is standing behind her.

"Just grab something, come on."

In the end she pulls a black dress over her head. Her legs and feet are bare and her toes are still bluish, a reminder of everything that just happened.

"But who is it?"

"I don't know. He's waiting, come on. I didn't understand what he said. Your name and then a load of words. He looks nice."

"What did he look like?"

"I don't know, like a regular man, kind of. Big smile."

Elin stops. Holds her breath.

"He's going to have to wait a little longer," she says in the end, and then vanishes into the bathroom.

She pulls the brush through her hair, fastening it carefully in a knot. She powders her face with small circular movements and adds a little blusher to her cheeks. Alice paces nervously in the doorway, eyeing Elin's every movement. When she goes down the stairs at last, Alice is right behind her. There's another knock, and Elin pulls open the door. She almost manages to knock over the waiter who's standing outside with a tray. There are two steaming mugs on it, with a plate of cookies in between.

"Couldn't you have brought it up yourself? What did I have to get up for?" she groans, her heart still pounding in her chest. Her nervousness has been replaced by anger.

Alice puts her finger to her lips, shushing her. She takes the tray from the waiter, then nods her head down the corridor.

"It wasn't him, it was that guy," she whispers.

Elin looks out and there he is, leaning against the wall in jeans and a worn brown leather jacket. He isn't freckly, and his hair isn't sun-bleached and tousled: in fact, there's none of it left. His scalp is bald and shiny, and his chin is covered with a bushy beard. But he looks at her with the same eyes, and when he smiles there's no mistaking who it is.

All sounds cease, all thoughts fall silent. The distance between them seems to turn into a tunnel. They stare at each other.

"So that's how much a blood pact and promises are worth," he says quietly, and holds up one hand in a greeting.

They stand there staring at each other until finally he takes a step forward and holds out his arms. Then Elin throws herself into his embrace. It's not a reserved, polite hug. Not soft and reassuring. It's as though he'd just come back from the dead. She flies at him, holds on to him for dear life with both arms and legs.

"I never thought I'd see you again," she whispers in his ear.

"My little dingbat, why did you disappear?" he replies with a laugh, and strokes her back. He takes a deep breath. "Just imagine you being here now. At last."

Elin doesn't let go of him. She buries her face in his chest and feels his heartbeat against her cheek. His scent is the same, even after so many years. She inhales it deeply.

In the end he pushes her away. She meets his gaze when he takes her face between his hands and studies her.

"Why did you never get in touch?" he says. He lets go of her and leans against the wall again.

Instead of answering, Elin says, "How did you find me?" She reaches to touch his cheek, but he catches her hand and winds his fingers into hers.

"I saw your picture in a magazine at the barber's. It was just a coincidence. And then I started googling you. Elin Boals. Famous. Just like you said you would be."

"I mean now. How did you know I was here?"

"Aha. Visby's a small town. Malin phoned and told me you were here. So I expect everyone knows by now." He looks her up and down. "You look like a Hollywood star," he says.

"But I'm not."

"Well, now you're a star up there, anyway." He nods toward the ceiling.

"Thank you, it was sweet of you to do that. But you can't buy stars, can you? You can't own everything? Didn't you use to say that the stars belonged to everyone?"

"True. But I wanted to send something, and that was the best thing I could think of."

"In any case, we've always lived under the same stars, you and I."

"Not really. How could you end up so far away?"

"I'm sorry," she whispers.

"Sorry for what? I'm glad you're here. I've missed you."

"For the fire."

"What do you mean?"

"For starting it. For . . . killing them, all of them."

Elin shudders. She meets his uncomprehending gaze as he takes a step back.

"What? Were you the one who set fire to Aina's house? Why would you do that?"

She shakes her head vehemently. Alice pokes her head out the door, and Elin, flustered, looks anxiously from her to Fredrik.

"Aren't you going to introduce me?" Fredrik turns to Alice, his hand extended.

"Yes, sorry," says Elin, switching to English. "Alice, this is Fredrik, my childhood friend. And this is Alice, my daughter."

"Won't you come up and sit down? There's hot chocolate. Fredrik, you can have my cup."

Elin silences her with a gesture without taking her eyes off Fredrik.

"I didn't set fire to any houses; why would I? I made a great big fire on the beach, and it spread."

He laughs.

"Our little campfire, you think that started everything? No, no, the fire started in Aina's house and then spread to the forest and to Gerd and Ove's house. No one was home to raise the alarm, so it soon turned into a river of flames that ate up everything in its path. Well, you saw that, you were there. They were all in line with the wind direction, those three farms."

Elin sinks down onto the floor, putting her hand on the wall for support. Memories are flashing before her eyes.

"They weren't at home?" she whispers.

"No, they were having dinner somewhere; they'd gone out earlier that evening. When they came home everything was gone. Ove's motorbikes were totally destroyed and the house was a charred ruin. Terrible."

"The motorbikes? But I don't get it . . . are they still alive?"

"No, not anymore. They died, but it was quite recent, just a few years ago. Ove of a heart attack and Gerd just a little while later. She probably couldn't live without him. You know how they were, they stuck together, always."

Elin's gasping for breath, her throat is tightening, she can't get any words out. Alice bends down beside her, stroking her back.

"What is it, Mom, what's he saying? What are you talking about? Is Grandma dead? What's happened?"

Alice looks at them both, as if pleading with them to explain things to her. Fredrik bends down and hooks his arms under Elin's, lifting her carefully to her feet.

"Come. It is better if we sit down," he says in shaky English.

They enter the suite and sit on the sofa, Alice holding Elin's hand. The hot chocolate and cookies are on the table, and Fredrik smiles when he sees them.

"Can you not get cookies in America?"

Elin stares blankly.

"There were still so many who died," she says.

Fredrik shakes his head.

"No, not Edvin, he did not die. It was only Micke and Erik. But I probably should not say 'only.'"

"They found Edvin?" Elin's voice is almost inaudible.

"Yes."

He's alive. Edvin's alive. Elin almost can't take it in. There are so many thoughts racing through her head. Her little brother. All these years. Lasse must have known, why didn't he tell her? Why did he let her think they were all dead?

"He must be an adult now?"

Fredrik laughs, switching back to Swedish.

"Yeah, he's not that cheeky little guy with the squirrel eyes you remember."

Elin smiles. She turns to Alice.

"I have a brother," she says proudly.

"They still live out there, in Heivide. In your old house," Fredrik says.

"They?"

"Yeah, Marianne and Edvin."

"But Edvin is . . . doesn't he live on his own?"

Fredrik pulls out his phone, unlocks the screen, and scrolls through his contacts.

"No, no, you can't call her; don't tell her I'm here. Not yet, not now. Tell me about them instead. I want to know more."

Elin tries to take the phone but Fredrik twists it away from her.

"But you have to see her while you're here. You know that, right? She's never stopped talking about you."

Elin feels the tears well up and run down her cheeks. Fredrik reaches out his hand to wipe them away, carefully running his fingers over her cheek. His hands feel rough and dry, but warm. He smells of the workshop, just like Lasse used to, of wood and oil. She closes her eyes.

"You're just the same, you are. Sweet as sugar," he says.

"How do you know the fire started in Aina's house? There was no one living there." Elin's eyes fly open. Fredrik shrugs and pauses, holding her gaze, their souls in a kind of embrace.

"The investigation into the fire proved it; apparently they can tell. It was in the papers. The trees by the beach never got burned. So it absolutely wasn't your fault. I know that for sure."

"I've always thought . . ."

"That was wrong. You've thought wrong . . . Good God, is that why you've been gone so long?" He has raised his voice, distressed.

"I thought I'd murdered your papa, and you'd never want to see me again."

Fredrik sighs and strokes his bushy beard. He squirms, as though the sofa has suddenly become uncomfortable to sit on.

"I've never missed Papa all that much. Have you?" he asks her.

"It was so long ago. I barely remember him, just his anger."

"Yeah, right. The anger." Fredrik pulls her closer to him. "You were the one it was hard to lose; what you and I had was something much better than our dads. Don't you think?"

She leans her head against his shoulder. Alice, who has given up trying to understand them, sits deeply immersed in her phone in one of the armchairs. The room is silent. Fredrik rests his cheek on her head.

"I thought I'd never get to see you again," he murmurs, stroking her hair tenderly.

◆

Mother and daughter stay seated when Fredrik leaves. Alice lowers her phone as she hears the door close, and looks accusingly at Elin.

"Are you going to get together with him now?" she says crossly.

Elin recoils and pulls herself upright on the sofa, her head held high. She carefully smooths out the creases in her dress.

"He was my best friend when I was little, like a brother almost. Or you could say he *was* my brother . . . it's complicated."

Alice nods, her expression still pinched.

"Yeah, you really looked like great *friends*," she mutters.

Elin stands up and walks toward the bathroom.

"I need air," she says.

"I've never even seen you that intimate with Dad."

Elin stops short, turns around, and snarls:

"Now you listen to me! If it was my choice I'd be with your dad now, not here. You're the one who dragged me here."

Alice widens her eyes, startled by Elin's sudden rage.

"Mom!" she says.

Elin says nothing. Alice comes over and puts her arms around her, but Elin's arms hang limp at her sides. She's breathing rapidly.

"Mom, sorry, I just thought . . ."

"He was my best friend when I was little. My absolute best friend."

Elin pulls away from Alice's embrace and continues into the bathroom.

"We've got time to take a walk before we're due to meet Fredrik in Heivide. Do you want to come? I have to get out, I can't breathe in here," she says on the way.

Alice appears in the mirror behind Elin and nods. Elin pauses, with her hairbrush midstroke.

"Go to your room and get ready then," she says briskly, but Alice raises her eyebrows uncomprehendingly.

"I'm ready! I've got clothes on, haven't I?"

Elin strokes her daughter's head, tucking a few unruly curls behind her ears, but Alice shakes her head to get them out again.

"I like being messy. This is how I look, I can't be someone I'm not."

"You can't be someone you're not," Elin repeats under her breath, and smooths her hand over her own hair. It's sleek and tidy, but she pulls out the hairband and lets it tumble out, shaking it loose.

"Tell me more about your dad," says Alice. "Why didn't he live here?"

"My dad?"

"Yeah, you said he lived in Stockholm, before you went to Paris."

"I don't know where to start." Elin pushes past her and pulls her coat on.

They leave the hotel in silence, Alice a few steps behind her mother. Elin feels agitated; she has the urge to keep moving forward, to get away.

The sun peeps out between the clouds, and she squints. On Donners Plats a couple of men lean back on one of the benches. They are wearing thick jackets and scruffy shoes, with woolly hats pulled right down almost as far as their beards. Between them is a plastic bag. Elin stops and looks at them, and Alice comes up behind her and puts her chin on her shoulder.

"What are you doing? Why did you stop?" she asks.

"*That's* what my real dad was like," Elin says, nodding at the bench.

She sets off again, fast, so Alice has to run to keep up.

"What do you mean? Was he homeless?"

"No, but he was an alkie, I told you that before. He lived here on the island, he was a carpenter. He used to hang out in Visby sometimes, on those benches, drinking all his earnings. One day he took a rifle and went in and robbed a shop. As drunk as a lord. He accidentally shot the shop assistant. That was how he left the island, and us. In a prison van, to serve his sentence in Stockholm. And he ended up staying there."

Elin stops again and turns to face her daughter.

"Is there anything else you want to know?"

"Yes," Alice says earnestly. "Was he nice?"

Elin is taken aback.

"What kind of question is that?"

"A simple one. Was he nice?"

Elin considers for a moment.

"He had warm hands and big hugs. He called me Number One, as though I was the most important thing in his world."

"Perhaps you were?"

"No. Drink was the most important. Always drink, however hard he tried. And then he wasn't kind."

"But I don't understand. Didn't you speak to each other, didn't he speak to your mom? He must have found out what happened to his other children, to your brothers."

Elin sighs. She draws Alice close, holds her tight, and kisses her cheek.

"I don't know, Alice, I can't remember. I suppose he must have known, but he wasn't the kind to talk about things. We didn't talk. There's so much I don't understand."

"We can ask Grandma, when we see her."

"I don't know if I want to. I can't take any more. I just want to go home, I want everything to be back to normal. I want to take photographs again, to get back to work."

Alice wriggles out of her arms.

"Back to normal? You mean you want to go back to your lie?"

Then

=◆=

Elin ran along the street with an envelope in one hand and her bag dangling from the other. She was out of breath, and beads of sweat were breaking out on her brow. She couldn't stop smiling, and when she got to the bookshop she threw herself right into Anne's arms, making her stagger back a few paces, laughing. Elin pulled a piece of paper out of the envelope and waved it in front of her.

"I've got a job," she wheezed, leaning against the counter with one hand.

Anne didn't understand.

"But you work all the time, don't you? What's so special about that?"

"As an assistant." She grinned.

"An assistant to whom?"

"I'm going to be a photographer. I'm never going to stand in front of the camera again, only behind it." She grinned proudly.

Anne took both of Elin's hands in hers.

"But don't you love books? I thought I was going to convince you to study."

"Yes, but I love light more, magical light. Light is to photographers what ideas are to authors, you know that, right? And I plan to spend the rest of my life chasing light, the perfect light."

Elin was talking so excitedly, it sounded as though she was singing. Her French was more or less fluent now. Anne laughed at her.

"You sound so full of passion! That's good, passion is the most important thing. I believe in you, I always will. Just as long as you promise to keep coming here so I can make a fuss over you — you've become almost like a daughter to me."

Elin's face fell as Anne turned around and started automatically tidying the books on the table behind her. She arranged them in perfect stacks.

"And you're like a mother to me," Elin replied, barely audibly.

Anne didn't respond. She'd started talking to herself again, as she often did when she was working. Her red hair had started to go gray, and she wore it in a bun at the base of her skull. She moved about between the shelves, moving books, straightening books.

❖

Elin sank down into one of the armchairs with a thick, half-read book in her hand. The other chairs were already taken. The special thing about Anne's bookshop was that it also functioned as a library. She didn't seem to care much about sales and never seemed stressed about money. She taped up little handwritten notes about the books she liked the best. She helped students with their assignments. She held author talks in the evening. And she served hot chocolate with a drop of mint essence and marshmallows when you needed it most. But this afternoon she didn't bring Elin a mug. Instead, she had a stack of heavy books in her arms.

"If you're going to become a photographer, we're going to do it properly," she informed Elin, and put the entire stack on the table beside her.

"Here's a little history of photography. And here's a list of photographers you should know. Go through all of them. Study the light ... or whatever it is that's important."

She held out a handwritten note. Elin read through the names, delighted by Anne's enthusiasm.

"You can read your way to most things, but not all," she said, laughing.

Anne looked at her without comprehending.

"What do you mean?"

"I plan to have my own style, to be unique."

Anne nodded, pleased.

"Good, that's how it should be."

◈

At least this Sunday she had something to share. She phoned every Sunday, but if he was slurring too much she'd hang up without saying anything. The first telephone booth she tried stank of urine, the sharp stench making her turn in the doorway and walk along to another, farther down the street. She never called from home, always from a phone booth. It had almost become a ritual.

The phone rang, but no one answered. She hung up but stayed where she was. Another number flickered through her head, the one to her old home on the farm. She started to dial it, but stopped halfway through and tried Lasse's number again.

"Hello!"

The voice that answered sounded unfamiliar.

"Who's this?" she asked.

"This is Janne, who's that?"

"It's Elin, Lasse's daughter. Isn't he home?"

Silence.

"Hello, are you still there?" Elin said. She heard him clearing his throat. "Where's Papa?"

"Haven't you heard?"

Elin was baffled. What should she have heard?

"Has he moved?" she asked.

He cleared his throat again. She couldn't tell whether he sounded drunk or not. If he sounded friendly or if he was an intruder.

"He's gone now," he mumbled eventually.

"What do you mean?"

"Well, he's dead."

Elin was speechless. Dead. Gone. No more calls, no more questions. They'd never see each other again. She swallowed the lump that was growing in her throat and slowly replaced the receiver on its hook, without saying anything.

The sun burst out from behind the clouds above the telephone booth, a few rays finding their way through. She looked up and waved. God's lights. That was what Lasse used to call them.

"Bye, Papa," she whispered.

Now

Elin spins slowly around and around, watching the sea and the city wall disappear and reappear, feeling the wind on her cheeks. Alice is sitting in front of her on the beach, playing with the stones. After a while, Elin sinks down beside her. She's dizzy and her cheeks are rosy. Alice holds a pebble out to her. It's smooth and white.

"Look, it's a heart shape." She grins.

Elin takes it from her and puts it in the palm of her own hand, closing her fingers around it.

"Did you know that it was a stone just like this that made me fall for your dad?"

Alice raises her eyebrows.

"What do you mean? He's never been here, has he?"

"No, not here. But he bent down and picked up a heart-shaped stone on our first walk together. When he gave it to me, I knew."

"Knew what?"

"Ah, nothing."

Alice takes the stone back and puts it in her pocket.

"But why did you lie to him?"

"It wasn't that simple. I didn't lie at first. He got the wrong impression early on, and I just never ended up telling him how things really were. I was so scared of losing him, so worried he'd be angry with me. The months passed, the years. We became a family, and everything else became unimportant."

Elin stands up and puts her arms around Alice, and they slowly start walking.

"Sorry, Mom," says Alice, leaning her head against Elin's shoulder. "This is hard for you, and here I am asking you all these difficult questions."

Elin looks genuinely sad.

"You have to understand how my life was when I met your dad. I had Anne, I had my career, my day-to-day life in Paris. This was all so distant. But I guess that's how it goes; the truth always catches up with you." Elin gropes for the armrest of a park bench and crumples onto the seat, hunching her shoulders and folding her arms across her chest.

Alice sits down beside her, as close as she can get. They sit quietly, watching the ducks floating about on the edge of the little pond in the park. The sound of the sea is calming. There's no traffic noise; everything is still.

"Sam reminded me of all this in some way," Elin says at last.

"What? Of Gotland? You used to say he was a real city boy."

"Yeah, but he's still so down to earth in some way. So calm. He noticed all of nature's little details."

She reaches toward Alice's pocket.

"Give me the stone," she says.

Alice feels in her pocket and pulls it out. It looks maybe more like a triangle than a love heart, but the indentation is there, faintly, and the corners are gently rounded. Elin holds it in her hand and gets out her phone, takes a close-up, and sends it straight to Sam.

"I wonder if he remembers too," she says.

❖

The car follows the curves of the narrow country road much too slowly. A line of three impatient vehicles has already built up behind them. The November sun is low on the horizon, the light golden. There's a lot of green despite the season, the pine trees still growing densely in the forests they pass. Elin suddenly remembers the trips of her childhood, between countryside and city, how she used to pretend to hold out a knife that felled the trees as they drove past them. They fell invisibly behind her and she never dared turn around for fear the illusion would evaporate.

The road straightens and the cars behind them accelerate past, one after another. Elin shifts her foot to the brake and slows down even more. Her hands are gripping the steering wheel so hard, her knuckles are white. She pulls to the side of the road, her tires half a meter onto the white gravel alongside the asphalt. A compact silence spreads as the noise of the car's engine ceases. No outside sound finds its way into the car. Just a faint ticking from the warm engine as it slowly cools.

Elin turns the key again, backs into a narrow side street, and turns around.

"What are you doing? Fredrik is waiting for us," says Alice, suddenly alert.

Elin turns out onto the road and accelerates in the wrong direction. Alice tells her to stop, firmly, and she obeys, in the middle of the road. The car behind, forced to swerve, honks loudly as it drives past.

"I can't do this. Not today."

"You have to."

"It has to happen at my pace. That's the only thing I can't budge on."

Elin turns her head to Alice, who reaches out and removes her mother's sunglasses. Elin blinks away a tear, catches it with her index finger.

"It won't feel any easier tomorrow," says Alice. "You're just putting it off. She won't be angry, she'll be happy. You can stay here a little while, but then you have to turn around. You have to."

Elin leans back in her seat and closes her eyes. Her breathing gradually becomes deeper and calmer. Finally, she sits up again and puts both hands on the steering wheel.

"You can do this, Mom," Alice whispers.

◈

The car begins to move again, in the right direction. The closer they get, the more houses Elin recognizes; she can even recall the names of the people who live there, or lived there. Thomas from school, Anna, her teacher Kerstin. Soon they'll see the buildings of the Grinde farm towering up beyond the fields. Or whatever's there instead of the farm that burned down.

"Just imagine if she thinks it's my fault," Elin whispers, slowing down.

"It wasn't your fault. No one thinks that. Don't you get it?"

"That's what Fredrik says, I know, but sparks can travel a long way. And I made a huge fire."

"He's right, I think. You must be remembering wrong; you were only young."

"She was in love with him."

"Who was? With whom?"

"Mama, with Micke, Fredrik's papa. She worshiped him, even though life with him was hard."

"And you? What did you think of him?"

"He was difficult. He even hit me. I can still remember his big flat palms. It wasn't until recently that it occurred to me that not everyone knows how it feels to be hit."

"What do you mean?"

"That not everyone knows how your skin reacts, that tight, stinging feeling. That feeling stays with you, sometimes for several minutes. Not everyone knows how the blow sort of spreads through your bone marrow and that the pain can be felt in your whole body, not just where the blow landed."

"Oh, Mom, how awful."

"Those of us who know that, who know how it feels, we stand close together on the same dark ground. Completely unaware of each other."

"Does Fredrik know?"

Elin nods.

"Fredrik knows, of course; he had it much worse. He said he hasn't missed his father, and in a way I understand. Micke was much more difficult than my real papa. Papa used to hit us sometimes, but I got a lot more hugs than slaps."

"Men who use violence should be deported to Mars, the whole lot of them," says Alice.

"Women too," Elin replies.

◈

The fields that swish past are frozen and bare, the same fields Elin once ran across. In the distance she can see the avenue cut across them. The gravel drive that leads to the Grinde farm is still lined with bare trees, but they're lower and sparser than the old lime trees she remembers. She catches a glimpse of a house at the end of the avenue, white but unfamiliar. Her heart thuds in her chest as she drives past the turnoff.

"You should see the way it looks here in the summer. When the flowers are blooming all over the shoulder of the road," she says, pointing to the muddy brown roadside.

"Your flowers? They're the ones you're always drawing, right? I've always wondered, there are so few types I recognize. I thought they were imaginary flowers."

"I guess they may as well be." Elin smiles.

◈

Farther along the road, they catch sight of the store. The two-story stone building looks just like it did when she last saw it, beige stucco and red window frames. Now, just as then, the windows are covered with discount posters advertising cheap food. Fredrik's pickup is parked at an angle outside the building; it says "Grinde's Construction" on the side, in thick black lettering. When he hears them coming he gets out and walks over as Elin lowers the window.

"Took you long enough. I thought you'd got lost, that maybe you didn't know your way around here anymore."

"Imagine that, the store's still here," Elin says, astonished.

"Everything's still here; everything's just like normal."

"Nothing's like normal," she retorts as she steps out of the car. She's wearing high narrow heels, and they sink into the soft gravel. The black leather of her shoes is gray with dust. She pushes her sunglasses up on her nose and absentmindedly touches up her lips with a red lipstick from her bag. A cold wind blows in from the sea and Alice is hunched against it, shivering.

"Shall we go in and buy something for her? A box of chocolates?" Alice asks.

"Edvin likes salt *lakrits,*" Fredrik says. He tries to speak English but trips up and says the Swedish word for "licorice."

"What's that?"

"I can show you if you'd like?"

Fredrik gestures toward the shop and Alice follows him doubtfully. Elin stays outside and breathes awhile, listening to the branches in the wind, their familiar pattering sound. The roar of the waves. She inhales the scent of earth.

It's still the same door, the glass door. And there's a tug back as she pulls the steel handle, just as she remembers. She pulls on it hard and walks in. The floor is new, as is the shelving. The walls are painted a different color. But the smell is the same. Bread, meat, and brewed coffee, all fresh. Fredrik stands at the counter, talking to the cashier. He knows her; they smile and laugh. Alice comes up to Elin with a red box of chocolates. She takes it from her, turns it over in her hands, studying each side.

"We always had a box of these at Christmastime," she marvels. "Mama likes them, I remember that."

She walks on through the shop, runs her hand over the packaging on the shelves. Powdered mashed potato, béarnaise sauce, split pea soup, mustard, quick-cook macaroni. Familiar yet different. She goes over to the candy counter, takes bag after bag of the flavors of her childhood.

"You don't even eat sugar, do you?" Alice laughs.

"Today I eat everything." Elin's arms are full of candy, and she's smiling so much, her cheeks push her sunglasses up.

"It is pretty sunny today." Fredrik nods meaningfully at her, winks.

She shoves them up onto her head.

"Do you never wear sunglasses here?"

"Not in November. We're glad if we even catch sight of the sun now and then."

He takes her by the hand and pulls her farther into the shop, where the doors into the stockroom and the office are ajar.

"Come on, I want to show you something," he says.

She follows him up the stairs to the upper floor, which smells of dust and damp. There are boxes and cartons stacked on the floor, and the walls are covered with old posters, fixed with multicolored drawing pins. The old, heavy oak desk is still in the office, the one Gerd used to sit behind when she counted the money. Fredrik opens a cabinet; its interior is covered with taped-up pictures.

"Look at this. No one's forgotten about you here."

She moves closer. There are a few newspaper clippings from French magazines on the cupboard door. A young Elin, smiling innocently out at the reader.

"How . . . ?"

"Gerd knew exactly what was going on. When she heard you'd moved to Paris and become a model, she started buying French magazines. You generally weren't in them, but she spent so much money on those magazines; she ordered them direct from France. But now and then you'd turn up. Uncannily beautiful. I used to stand here and look at you for hours. I missed you so much."

"Has Mama seen them too?"

Fredrik closes the cabinet again and locks it carefully.

"I don't know," he says. "Presumably. Gerd always used to show me when she found a new picture. She was so proud of you. The neighborhood celeb."

"That was such a long time ago. I'm much happier behind the camera."

Fredrik stiffens and takes one of her hands in both of his, his tone suddenly serious.

"Hey, there's something I have to tell you. Before we go over to her place," he says.

Elin feels how her heart races from the sudden contact. She takes a step closer, their faces close; she can feel his breath, like a stream of warmth caressing her cheek.

"What?"

He backs away, averts his eyes.

"They found Edvin on the field, thanks to you. It was you who saved him. But he was never the same again. He got carbon monoxide poisoning."

"What does that mean?"

"His brain was severely damaged by the smoke. He has difficulty walking and speaking. He's a little . . . slow, you could say."

Elin sinks down toward the desk; he lets go of her hand.

"How do you mean, slow?"

"He's developmentally disabled. You'll see what I mean. I just wanted you to know before meeting him."

Distracted, Elin fiddles with a few brochures on the desk, and Fredrik strokes her back. She looks up at him.

"So he's not really there? Will he even remember me?"

"I think so; he's smart. He's still there, inside his head. It's just his voice and his movements that don't work. I think he thinks a lot."

"I've been thinking all the wrong things."

"Yes, you have."

He takes her hand again and brings it to his cheek, his beard tickling her palm.

"My girl." He smiles, meeting her gaze.

"I didn't know how much I'd missed you until I saw you," Elin whispers.

"It's easy to forget."

"No, it wasn't easy. I had to shut down completely to survive. The years passed and in the end all this felt like nothing but a dream."

Elin looks at the wall behind Fredrik. A rectangular obituary notice is pinned up. The newspaper is yellowing. She walks over and reads it.

GERD ALICE ANNA
ANDERSSON
26 March 1929–2 April 2015
Has now
found rest.
Much loved.
Much missed.
In death
as peaceful
as in life.
Marianne
In friendship

She runs her finger across the words. Gerd is gone now, dead and buried. Elin's sorrow wells again. So many days, so many years spent missing her and grieving unnecessarily. When she was here the whole time. Suddenly she sees Gerd's face before her. Her gray curls, her laugh, her rounded belly, all clear as day. Alice comes in, rousing her from her thoughts.

"Who was that?"

Elin doesn't answer, turning instead to Fredrik.

"She died so recently. How can she be dead, why didn't I get to see her?"

Alice and Fredrik both put their arms around her.

"Her middle name was Alice," Elin whispers to her daughter. "It was the most beautiful name I could think of when I was little, so I gave it to you."

Alice stiffens.

"How could you have named me after someone and never told me?"

"She meant so much to me," Elin says. "Just like you do. It was the loveliest name I could give you. I'm not asking you to understand. But I promise to tell you about her now, anything you want to know, anything I can remember."

❖

"Take off your sunglasses now," Alice whispers, grabbing hold of her mother's arm. "Please, it's evening, it's dark, we're in the country. You can't have them on when she opens the door." Alice goes on badgering her, walking close behind her.

Elin ignores her and keeps them on, pushing them up her nose so they cover her eyes completely. She cautiously picks her way across the mud, walking on the balls of her feet and jumping over the worst of the puddles. Her gaze is focused on the blue door. It's lighter than she remembers; perhaps it's been repainted? The stucco is just as worn as before, falling off in great chunks. One of the two lamps on the wall is broken, and inside the cracked shade is what appears to be a bird's nest, the twigs sticking out between the shards. The other lamp glows weakly.

She puts her hand on the door knocker but holds it there without knocking. Fredrik and Alice look at her in silence until Fredrik goes over and lays his hand over hers. They pull the door knocker out together and let go. At the same moment, the door handle turns. Someone has been standing inside, waiting for them. Elin takes two steps back, and as the door opens, she turns and walks quickly back toward the car.

"Mom, stop!" Alice calls after her. Then Alice's eyes fix upon the bent old lady standing in the doorway.

Marianne takes a step out, lifts her hand, and waves.

"Elin, is that you?" she calls. Her mouth must be dry, as the words seem to get stuck on her tongue.

Elin stops dead when she hears her mother's voice. She looks down at her feet, her shoes all striped with mud. Everything is damp, everything is cold, everything is wet, everything is as dark as night. Marianne calls again, imploring her to come back, and Elin turns on her heel and runs toward her mother. Water splashes up her legs with each step she takes; her heels sink into the soft ground.

"I'm here now," she says, coming to a halt before her mother.

They gaze into each other's eyes. Marianne is trembling with cold, but she leaves her arms hanging limp at her sides. There's no hug, no greeting. They just look right into each other. No one says anything. Alice nudges Elin's shoulder.

"Aren't you going to give her a hug? Aren't we going to go in?" she whispers.

Elin takes a step closer, without taking her eyes off her mother.

"I'm here now. I've come home. This is your grandchild, Alice." Elin pushes Alice forward.

Marianne nods and strokes Alice's cheek gently. Then she steps aside and motions for them to enter the hall. Fredrik attempts to give Marianne a hug, but she backs away.

"You do keep it cold in here," he says to break the silence, and reaches for the thermostat.

Marianne vanishes wordlessly into the kitchen, and Alice and Elin are left standing in the hallway as Fredrik adjusts the heating.

In the kitchen it's warmer; the woodstove is crackling. Elin shudders when she sees the blazing flames under the burners and smells the smoke. Marianne has prepared for their visit: her finest coffee service is out on the table, with cups and saucers in thin porcelain decorated with beautiful blue roses and a delicate pink napkin under each cup.

"That was a long trip you went on," she says, eventually taking Elin's hand in hers and stroking it again and again; her hand is rough and her fingertips are just as chapped as Elin remembers.

"Yeah, it ended up being pretty long," Elin whispers.

◆

They sit down, Elin and Alice on separate chairs but right next to each other, and Fredrik on the kitchen bench. It's quiet in the kitchen, apart from the crackling of the logs. Elin lifts the lace tablecloth cautiously: it's still the same table, the one she's eaten at hundreds of times. She runs her hand over the surface, feeling the scars with her fingertips, the cigarette burns.

"What are you doing, Mom?" Alice asks under her breath, ducking her head to look under the tablecloth.

Elin takes her daughter's hand and runs it over the wood.

"Can you feel them? Can you feel all those little pits?"

Alice nods.

"Mama made them with cigarettes when she was angry. She used to put them out right on the table."

Marianne turns to them. In one hand she has a sponge cake with thick white icing that's run down the sides, and in the other an old-fashioned coffee kettle. The spout is steaming.

"But I have stopped that now. I don't even smoke anymore," she says severely.

Elin's cheeks flush when she realizes Marianne understands enough English to get what she's saying.

"Then maybe you should treat yourself to a new table?" Elin smiles, but gets no smile in return and decides to change the subject. "The good cups, amazing that you still have them!" She lifts her cup and holds it out as Marianne pours the coffee. The lip is leaf-thin, and she blows carefully on the hot liquid before taking a mouthful.

"Yes, there were a lot of things I never took to the Grindes'. And it was just as well, since there wasn't much left there."

"Did everything burn?"

Marianne shakes her head.

"Not everything; they managed to put out a fair bit of the house. But most of it. Micke and Erik were burned alive. Did you know that?"

Her jaw is clenched and her voice is cold. She shows no sign of sorrow; it's more of a matter-of-fact statement. Elin swallows the lump in her throat, with difficulty.

"Yes, I saw it with my own eyes. I was there when the fire took them. Don't you remember? I'll never forget the image of Micke's charred body."

Marianne sinks down on a chair beside her and sighs deeply.

"It happened so quickly. Suddenly they were just . . . gone. All of them."

"Not Edvin," Elin protests.

"Yes, Edvin too. You'll see. He's resting now, you'll see him later. We had to stay at the hospital for months."

Elin reaches out, tries to touch Marianne's hand. But her mother pulls it away and puts it in her lap, intertwined with the other, then wrings them anxiously.

"Why are you here and not at Grinde's?" asks Elin. "I saw that the farm has been rebuilt."

"It was Micke's farm, not mine. It went to him." She nods at Fredrik.

"But didn't you own half? With Aina's money?"

She shakes her head.

"No, there was nothing on paper. And what difference would that make? It was all just debt and burnt rubble. Right, Fredrik?"

Fredrik nods.

Marianne goes on. "But Fredrik's never let me down."

"No, he's not like me," Elin replies quietly.

Pretending not to hear, Marianne rolls a corner of tablecloth between her fingers and looks down at the tabletop. Elin twiddles a silver spoon in her hand. The cake stands untouched on the table. In the end, Fredrik cuts himself a piece, then remarks on how delicious it is, but everyone ignores him.

"How've you managed? With Edvin and all. Did you meet a new man?" Elin tries to catch Marianne's gaze, but the older woman just looks down at the table.

"Fredrik has helped me out, all these years," she replies.

Elin drops the silver spoon on her saucer, the sound breaking the silence in the room. She gets to her feet, bumping against the table so the cups and saucers rattle.

"It's time for us to go now. We'll be here a few more days, staying at the Visby Hotel. You can find me there if you want."

Marianne reaches out to her.

"No, don't go. Please, Elin, you have to forgive me."

"Forgive you for what?"

"For not coming to Lasse's and bringing you home. I couldn't make myself do it. Days passed, months passed. I couldn't bring myself to talk to Lasse, I didn't want to see him. And then one day, when I finally phoned, you had already vanished out into the world. Alone in Paris. I got such a pain in my stomach when I heard, but Lasse assured me there were people looking after you."

Elin stares blankly at the floor, vacillating. No one ever told her they talked to each other, that Marianne cared.

"It's true, I had a good life there. Better than at Papa's in any case; you know how he was. Kind, but he never stopped drinking, as it turned out anyway, so there's no need for you to feel like that."

"You look so fancy," says her mother suddenly. "Like something from a film."

Elin fiddles anxiously with her sleeve. Then she takes a deep breath.

"Mama, I'm the one who should be asking for forgiveness. It might have been my fault all along. I lit a fire on the beach that evening. It must have been sparks from my fire that started the blaze. It was me who killed them. I killed Micke and Erik."

Silence falls over the room as they stare at each other. Fredrik walks over and puts his arms over Elin's shoulders.

"Stop it now, both of you. Stop trying to find a scapegoat," he says. "What happened, happened. You're here now. You'll have to start over."

Marianne reaches forward and grabs hold of Elin's shoulders.

"Was that why you ran away?"

Elin nods, and Marianne starts shaking her. Elin curls into herself, trying to protect herself from her mother's fury. She manages to get hold of Marianne's hands and pull them away.

"Mama, stop!" she says.

Marianne obeys. Her mouth is no more than a thin line, her breathing is labored. She leans against the counter and bursts into tears.

"We searched for you for days. Everywhere. We thought you were dead," she says between sobs.

"Mama, I'm sorry, I thought it was for the best, I thought you were angry, that I'd be blamed for the fire, for Micke and Erik's deaths. I thought everyone had died: Edvin, Gerd, Ove. That's what I've believed this whole time."

Marianne swipes tears from her cheeks.

"What? How could you think that? Why would you be blamed? You woke us up, you saved me."

"So you were never angry at me?"

"No, why would I have been? I was just sad. Sad when the letter from Lasse came at last and we realized where you were. Sad that you'd run away and left me when I needed you the most. When we needed you the most."

Elin stiffens and looks at Marianne accusingly.

"So why didn't you come and bring me home if I was so important?"

"Don't. It was so long ago," Marianne whispers.

Elin turns her back on Marianne.

"OK, I won't," she says, her voice thick. She switches to English to say, "Alice, come on now, it's time to go."

Fredrik goes over and helps Marianne, who seems about to faint, back to her chair. Alice pauses at the door.

"We'll come back, Grandma; we'll come back soon," she says before leaving the house.

◆

Elin puts her foot down before Alice has even shut the passenger door. Mud sprays as the tires spin. She accelerates out onto the road. It's very dark, and not even the high beams can light the way properly. Alice tries to calm her, but she's not listening.

"You see, she doesn't love me, she wasn't even happy when we arrived. We should never have come here," she says, then turns the radio up so high that conversation is impossible.

◆

Over thirty years. So many years have passed, carving wrinkles and scars into everyone's faces. Elin stares up at the ceiling, her head reeling from everything that's happened. The lights are off, and only a faint strip of light from the street cuts through the darkness. In the bathroom her clothes lie in a heap, the pant legs a muddy reminder of the countryside she so hastily left.

She fiddles with her smartphone, reading old messages from Sam. He hasn't answered at all. Perhaps he doesn't remember the heart-shaped stone, perhaps he doesn't understand why she sent it. She should write something else, but what? They don't have anything to talk about anymore. Only Alice. She tries to think of a reason to write, but the phone falls onto her chest and the text box stays empty. She should tell him everything but doesn't know where to begin.

◆

She's fallen asleep when the phone suddenly rings. The ringtone wakes her, the vibrations spread through her body, and she answers without checking the screen to see who it is.

"Sam?" she says hopefully.

"No, it's me, Fredrik. Who's Sam?"

"My . . ."

"Your husband? Are you married?"

"Alice's dad," she says, suddenly wide awake. "It's a little complicated."

"Isn't it always?"

She sits up and turns the light on.

"And you, are you married?" she asks, holding her breath.

He laughs, a rumbling sound; his chest rattles as he coughs, and he has to pause and catch his breath.

"Yes, yes, of course. I'm not going to live alone on a desolate island like this."

"What's her name?"

"Miriam."

"Do you have children?"

"Yes, lots of stones here."

"Stones? What do you mean?"

"Don't you remember? The stones we used to throw."

"It turned out different each time."

"Yes, I guess I added them all up. Five so far." He laughs again.

She holds the phone a little distance from her ear, waits before replying.

"Hello, are you there?"

"I thought you and I were going to get married," she whispers.

"Did you really?" Fredrik suddenly sounds serious.

"No, perhaps not. Or . . . I can't remember."

"It was lovely to see you. I've always longed for you, never stopped thinking about you."

"Me too, always."

Elin's eyes fill with tears. She breathes a heavy sigh.

"Though I guess we've never even kissed, you and I," she says.

Fredrik laughs.

"No, we were too little for that."

"But we came close, no? Am I remembering that right?"

"Yeah, you are. We came really close. It was you and me."

"And the stars."

"Yeah, you and me and the stars. Just remember all those nights on the beach, how great that was."

Elin wipes her tears away and changes the subject.

"Could I meet them? Your family?"

"Of course, that's why I was calling."

"It didn't go so well, at Mama's."

"You know how she is."

"No, I really don't. I haven't seen her for over thirty years."

"Give her a second chance, she deserves that. She's soft underneath that hard shell. She switches off, in a way, when things get hard. I know she's missed you all these years, that she's thought about you every day. She wants to invite you over for dinner. Miriam and I will come, and the children. Tomorrow evening. You didn't even get to see Edvin; he wants to see you too."

"He doesn't even know who I am, does he?"

"We'll see. He's smarter than some people think."

◆

They say good night and hang up, and the room is quiet again. Night has fallen, but Elin's thoughts are too chaotic for her to sleep; there's too much to process. She gets up and walks over to the window. The moon is reflected out to sea, the surface silvery and shimmering. She gets dressed, layer upon layer of warm clothes, and walks out into the deserted streets.

Tilting her head back, she studies the stars in the coal-black sky, a muddle of silver specks above her. It's so dark that she can see them; the streetlights barely illuminate the town. She whispers the names of the constellations, spinning around to see the whole of the heavens, discovering more and more. Like long-lost friends.

"Mom, what are you doing? Why are you out here on your own?"

It's Alice. She's out too, even though it's getting late. Her wool hat is pulled down over her ears, and the tip of her nose is red and moist. She has stopped a little farther up the road. Elin walks toward her.

"How did you know I was here?"

"I didn't. I went out to find a café for a cup of hot chocolate. Then I went for a walk. It's so beautiful here. It's like walking around in a fairy tale."

Elin burrows her arm in under Alice's.

"Isn't it just. Like wandering around in another dimension, another time. Do you want to keep walking a little while? I think I can still find my way. I can show you the church; it's a big one, really beautiful."

They walk off slowly, huddled close together. It's cold, and the breath that leaves their mouths turns into clouds of steam.

Then

≈ ◆ ≈

PARIS, 1999

The boxes were piled up on the sidewalk. Hundreds of them, full of books. A truck drove up and stopped in front of her, the engine spluttering as the driver turned off the ignition. He greeted her curtly, then went around and lowered the loading platform. Elin had her camera on a strap round her neck and carefully documented everything as the boxes disappeared, one by one, into the truck. The shelves of the bookshop were empty now; she walked slowly through it. It looked so small now that it was just a room. She remembered how big she thought it was the first time she stepped in through the door, like it contained the whole world and more.

The counter had been cleared of pens and notepads. She lifted the plaque from its hook: *A home without books . . .* Now it was a bookshop without books. Its soul would soon be gone.

She could clearly see Anne before her, just as she'd looked the first time they saw each other. When her hair was still red, her bust large and soft, and her dresses long and flowing. At the end she was thin and gray-haired, but her eyes never lost their luster and her heart was just as warm and open. She never stopped going to work, never retired. She just went to sleep one night and never woke up.

Now she was dead and the bookshop needed to be closed and emptied. There were several of them helping out: in her will there had been three names. None of them had been related to Anne, none knew one another all that well, but they were all her angels. That was what she used to call them. The lost souls who'd made her little bookshop their safe place.

The photography section was the last to be packed up. Elin kept one copy of each book, putting them carefully into a box with other mementos. Her own book was also there on the shelf, and Elin remembered how proud Anne had been when she saw the first edition. How she'd demanded that her dedication should be well thought out and personal, that Elin must take her time signing it.

Soon the sidewalk was empty again and the truck drove off. Elin's box, full of memories, was left on the floor for another day. She taped up a note to let people know the shop was closed and carefully locked the door. But she still couldn't make herself leave. She sat on the bench opposite the shop; her gaze turned to the river and the boats going by. It was the same bench she'd been sitting on when Anne came and fetched her the first time they met. Now she was sitting there again, alone and full of sorrow.

Along the wall, the hawkers stood with their paintings and postcards. Loved-up couples walked hand in hand and parents ran after their children. Her gaze followed them.

Her thoughts just kept coming. She gripped her camera on her lap. Then she stood up and started taking photographs, capturing the beauty of the light, freeing herself from her memories.

◆

He was leaning against the wall a little farther along the river, with his chin propped in his hand and his eyes trained on the water. Elin sneaked discreetly closer, hidden behind her camera. His brown hair was thick and shiny, and the light fell beautifully over his cheek, making the red-brown stubble shimmer like gold. He looked like a film star, and his slender shadow stretched across the sidewalk, a black silhouette against the gray. When a gap came in the stream of flâneurs and she managed to catch him alone, she let the shutter click. He was standing quite still. Perfect. Only the light changed as she carefully moved the camera, just a few centimeters at a time.

She moved a few steps closer and zoomed in on his face. Then he suddenly turned around, looked at her, and smiled broadly. She was still holding the camera to her eye, but her finger had slid from the shutter and she was standing absolutely still, caught in the act. He took a few steps toward her, his eyes glittering.

"Do you speak English?" he asked in faltering French.

She nodded and lowered the camera, embarrassed.

"Do you think it'll come out well?" he went on, nodding at the camera.

Elin's face grew hot and she couldn't meet his gaze, opting instead to stare at his shoes. They were shiny brown leather, worn with dark-gray suit pants.

"Sorry, I couldn't help it. It looked so nice with you standing there, it probably turned out perfectly," she said.

She glanced up and locked eyes with him. He smiled.

"Can I have a go?" he said, reaching for the camera. She reluctantly surrendered it and he held it up to his eye, but Elin turned away. He walked around her; she went on turning; he followed. In the end he gave up and lowered the camera.

"OK, you win. But you'd be better off in the picture than behind the camera. I know who you are. You're the daughter of that wonderful woman in the bookshop. I've seen you there; I recognize you."

Elin didn't reply; she'd never noticed him before. She would have remembered.

"I've always wanted to talk to you. You seemed to get on so well, you and your mom," he went on.

She nodded, sorrow suddenly washing over her again. She couldn't bring herself to tell him that Anne wasn't her real mother. He reached out a hand, as though sensing she was sad. She held out hers and he took it.

"I know she's gone now. I'm sorry. My company has bought the property. Elin, isn't that your name?"

She nodded.

"I saw it on the contract. Come on, let's walk a little," he said, holding her hand tenderly.

He took a few steps away from her and their arms stretched apart. She followed him cautiously.

"I'll get to see that picture sometime, right, when you've developed it?" he asked.

She nodded.

"Perhaps you can give me some reading recommendations too—I love books. What a dream to go for a walk with a bookseller's daughter. My name is Sam. Sam Boals."

Elin stopped, pulled her hand away from his.

"But the bookshop doesn't exist anymore. The truck just drove all the books away. Anne donated them to a school. The shelves are empty now. Everything's over."

Elin evidently sounded so sad that he stopped and laid a hand on her shoulder.

"But you have everything inside you, all the words you've read. No one can take them away from you. Your mom gave you the best thing you can give to a child."

Elin nodded. He patted her shoulder and his eyes were full of sympathy, but he didn't say anything. They stood in silence, side by side, leaning against the wall.

"What's going to happen to the shop?" she whispered at last.

He shrugged.

"I don't know. I work with property, buying and selling. Feelings don't really come into it. But this time it was harder. I've been to the bookshop so many times, I really like it."

He bent down, feeling for something on the ground. When he stood up again he had a little stone in his hand. He pressed it into her palm, closing her fingers around it.

"Put this in your pocket, and don't look until you get home. If you agree, let's meet again. Promise," he said.

"I don't understand." Elin furrowed her eyebrows.

"You will. Trust me. So, put it in your pocket now," he said, beaming broadly.

She did as he said and felt the weight of the stone settle in her coat pocket. Once again he took her hand and they walked along slowly, side by side. He asked about her favorite books, told her about his. They talked eagerly, the words just flowing.

It started raining, heavily, as though the heavens had opened, and he took off his jacket and held it over their heads. Elin drew closer, into his comforting scent. The street emptied of people but the two of them kept walking.

Now

≡ ◆ ≡

The table is laid with chipped crockery, the plates crowded together. Five at the long side by the kitchen bench, where the children are already sitting, waiting. They are blond, long-haired, disheveled, and happy. They sit crammed together according to size, from little ones to teenagers. They're all boys, and they all have pale freckles across the bridge of the nose. They are sitting still, but now and then someone gets an elbow in the side or a pinch on the thigh, and then the whole mass of bodies moves as one. Three plates are spaced along the other long side and one at each end.

Fredrik stands with his arm around his wife. They seem to fit together, as though they were one person. She's beautiful, with plump, rosy cheeks. She's wearing jeans and a simple striped cotton top, her stomach swelling gently over her waistband. Her hair is like Elin's when she's fresh from the shower and hasn't done anything with it: shiny and kinked, parted in the center. She's the one cooking, stirring the pot with a large wooden spoon.

The whole room falls silent when they enter, and Elin suddenly feels alone, even though Alice is at her side. The children look at them, wide-eyed, and Fredrik lets go of Miriam and locks eyes with Elin. She smiles and holds up a hand in a tentative greeting.

Marianne is standing behind them, shifting her weight impatiently from one foot to the other, as though she's trying to push Elin and Alice into the kitchen. Elin surveys the table, counts the plates, and turns to Marianne.

"Isn't Edvin going to join us for dinner?" she asks.

"He makes such a mess," Marianne replies.

"And he gets stressed out if there are too many people," Fredrik adds.

"It doesn't matter. I really want to see him."

Elin goes back out into the hallway.

"Where is he? Is he still in his old room?"

Marianne shakes her head and walks ahead of her.

"He can't manage the stairs. He has my old one."

It's only then that Elin notices that all the thresholds are gone. She feels her pulse rise as they approach the door.

Spotting a cabinet full of old photographs in the hallway, Elin dawdles awhile to look at them.

"Do you recognize yourself?" Marianne asks, picking up one of the frames.

It's a school portrait with a blotchy gray backdrop, in a little gold-colored oval frame. Elin had bangs back then, bluntly cut with Marianne's kitchen scissors. The tips of her front teeth are wavy and the few freckles on her nose are sharply defined, like dots of ink. Marianne strokes the photograph with her fingertip, running it down Elin's cheek.

"I've looked at you every day."

Elin takes the frame from her and places it facedown on the cabinet.

"Look here instead, look at me now." She takes Marianne's hand and brings it to her cheek. It feels cold and bony, the knuckles swollen. "I'm here now, Mama, I'm here for real."

Marianne pulls her hand back again. Elin sees tears well up in her eyes as she turns and heads for Edvin's room. Elin follows her.

He sits with his back to them, in a high-backed wheelchair. One of his hands is twisted in toward his body, and his elbow hangs out of the arm support. His head twitches slightly. When he hears them he starts making a noise, a monotonous lament. The room is cold. There is an adjustable bed with high railings and a red wool blanket across it. Marianne puts her hands on his shoulders and speaks loudly and clearly.

"Edvin, she's here now, your sister has come home at last."

He shrieks, high notes in and out with every breath. One foot stamps against the floor.

"Look how happy you are. Yes, just think how long we've been waiting for her," Marianne goes on. She straightens his wine-red cardigan and wipes his mouth with a piece of kitchen towel from the pocket of her dress. Then she nods to Elin, who takes a step forward, hesitantly.

"Hey, you, here you are," she whispers, and puts her hand on his. He looks at her with his hazel eyes, which light up with joy as he makes a lopsided smile. A string of dribble runs from a corner of his mouth, and Marianne wipes him again.

"Does he understand that it's me?"

Edvin stamps hard with his foot when he hears Elin; the smile disappears from his lips.

"I think so. You can see it, he understands what you're saying."

"But it was such a long time ago, how can he remember?"

The monotonous noise comes back, and Edvin looks down at the floor, the glint in his eyes gone out.

"Do you remember me?" Elin whispers, crouching down at his side. She leans in over the wheelchair and puts her head to his chest. "Do you remember how you used to creep up close to me, like this, when you were scared?"

He stamps his foot, puts his hand on her back, and pats hard. She hugs his hand and kisses him on the cheek.

"Oh, Edvin, I can't believe you're alive! Come and eat with us, come and be with us!" She takes off the brake and pushes the wheelchair toward the kitchen. Marianne doesn't protest; she lets them go past but stays awhile in the hallway, tinkering with the photographs on the cabinet.

Elin puts Edvin at one end of the table and sits close beside him. She can't stop looking at him, stroking his arm, his back, his head.

Miriam sets the pan down in the middle of the table. Steam rises from it and the scent spreads across the table.

"It's steak and chanterelle stew. All from Heivide."

Alice opens her mouth to say something, but Elin shakes her head and mouths in English: *Eat.*

"There's a vegetarian option too. You're not the only one with ideals," Fredrik says, nodding toward the kitchen bench. "I guess it's high time we introduced the team. This is Erik, vegetarian when it suits him; Elmer, eats only ham and Cheetos; Esbjörn, refuses cucumber; Emrik . . . Emrik's fine, he still eats most things. And little Elis. That was all the *E*'s, or have I missed someone?" Fredrik and Miriam both laugh.

"Do you speak English?" Alice asks Erik, who nods eagerly.

"I'm a gamer," he says in fluent English. "So I have a lot of friends in the United States who I play with."

A hum fills the room, which is so warm, the insides of the windows grow foggy. The pot slowly empties. Edvin bangs his spoon on his plate, and Elin helps him bring it to his mouth, carefully.

"Give him a little milk too, he likes milk," Marianne says, nodding at the empty glass.

"I know," Elin whispers.

◈

"Mom, Erik says there are cows in the barn. I've never stroked a cow. Can we go?" Alice calls across the table and gives Elin a pleading look.

Elis jumps up and down on the bench. His thin tracksuit bottoms have worn through at the knees and are hanging halfway down his bottom. Miriam pulls them up, almost lifting the little boy off his feet.

"Marianne, take the lass out, so she can meet the girls," she says.

"I'll come out, so I can translate." Elin grins. "Cows, huh?" She turns to Marianne and raises her eyebrows, questioning.

"Yes, not many, but they give us a little milk. We have to have something to live off, Edvin and I."

◈

They walk together across the farmyard, toward the little barn. Elin opens the door with a practiced hand, lifting it easily and turning the big chunky key. The warmth and the smell hit them as Marianne turns on the striplight on the ceiling. The cows low a welcome.

"Now they think they're going to get some food," she grumbles.

Alice and Elin wander past the cows' massive heads. A tongue reaches out suddenly and nudges Alice's hand, making her scream. The E-team laughs at her, and Elis climbs up on the fence and reaches his hand out to that cow's muzzle. The tongue comes out again, and he giggles when it licks him, long and rough.

"Alice has never seen a cow before," Elin explains.

Elis looks puzzled, as though someone had just told him Father Christmas didn't exist.

"They live in a big city where the buildings are taller than cliffs, where everyone lives on top of each other," Erik explains authoritatively, and mimes a tower with his hands. Elis shakes his head, baffled.

"Never seen a cow. It's a good job you came when you did," says Marianne, shaking her head. "The lass is almost grown. What's to come of her, if she's never been to the country and seen how things really work?"

◆

Elin runs out to the car and gets the camera she'd put in her handbag, the smallest one she owns. She feels oddly calm and no longer cares about the mud splashing her legs.

She photographs Alice alongside the cows, then Alice and Marianne close together and smiling. The boys, dangling from the rafters. She photographs details: walls, Marianne's clogs, halters hanging from hooks. She wants to capture everything, to save a moment that will otherwise disappear. She shows the pictures to Marianne, directly on the screen. Marianne inspects them with interest and happily poses for more, though she begs Elin in horror not to show them to anyone.

Alice and Marianne laugh intimately, as if sharing a connection. They can't really talk to each other; neither can fully understand the words the other uses to describe the world. But they're still communicating, with gestures, with smiles.

Suddenly a voice calls from the yard. It's Fredrik. The word "dessert" has all the boys stampeding back to the kitchen. Elin smiles when she sees Marianne and Alice walking together toward the door, side by side, arm in arm.

◆

Elin hangs back. She moves toward the wall, holding up the camera and trying to get a wider angle on the little barn and all the cows inside. Suddenly she stumbles over a sharp edge on the floor, wobbles for a moment, and steadies herself against the wall. She stares at the floor. Her pants and shoes are covered in dust and pieces of hay.

She bends down and slowly draws her hand over the boards, which are coarse and full of splinters that scrape the palm of her hand. She stops at a raised part, carefully wiggling the board. The liquor is still under there, the same liquor Lasse left so many years ago. She lifts the bottles out, one by one, untwisting the caps and letting the contents trickle out onto the packed dirt underneath the floorboards. The liquid gurgles hollowly against the glass, the smell so strong it tickles her nostrils. The liquor soon drains away, leaving only damp, dark earth.

Under the bottles is a jar, buried so deep that she can barely see the gold lid catching the light. She takes hold of it and tries to pull it out, but it's lodged, so she unscrews the lid instead. She sticks her hand in and fishes out the small, carefully folded notes she wrote all those years ago. The writing on them is so pale, it's barely visible, swallowed up by the paper's greedy fibers. She can see only half-words, the odd letter or two. What was it she hid here, so long ago? What were the secrets she didn't want to share with anyone? She can't remember.

She takes all the notes out of the jar and stuffs them into her jacket pocket.

◆

It feels as though she's sitting in a bubble. Elin looks at the people around the table, her eyes wandering from one to the next, but she can't make out what they're saying. They're all talking, all moving, all smiling. Small hands reach for the big bowl of ice cream, meringue, banana, and chocolate sauce. The children squabble over who's going to have the last of the sweet mixture, spoons scraping the china. Laughter rises above the other sounds.

It's the same table, the same walls. Even the picture they once painted together hangs in the same frame, in the same spot. The dog, the tree, the tractor tracks, the birds. There were four of them painting it; now Erik is missing.

Edvin looks so happy, not at all stressed that there are so many of them around the table. His head and hands jerk, but he looks as though he's listening, and his lips are stretched into a smile.

At one end of the table, Erik and Alice are talking about something they find amusing. They are laughing, and Alice is gesticulating. They look like they're the same age. She leans over to Fredrik.

"How old is Erik?"

He looks over at them.

"He'll be eighteen soon. And Alice?"

"Seventeen."

The two teenagers get up from the table at the same time. Alice stops at Elin's side.

"He's going to show me something outside quickly. We'll be back soon."

She nods as they disappear. Elin goes over to the kitchen window and watches their backs retreating slowly up toward the road in the low light from the yard lamp. They stop and look up at the sky for a long time. Perhaps he's showing her the constellations. She smiles.

Marianne stands by the sink, where there are towering piles of plates and bowls. She rinses one after another in running water. Elin stands beside her and passes them to her.

"My little helper," Marianne says without looking at her.

"Not so little anymore."

"No. It's been a few years."

The plates rattle and clatter. Elin doesn't know what else to say, and they stand side by side in silence. The youngest children have grown tired of sitting still and are careering noisily around the house; Fredrik and Miriam are sitting at the table with glasses of wine. They call to Elin and she looks over her shoulder, her hands still in the washing-up bowl.

"Elin, leave the dishes, Marianne can do that! Come and tell us about New York. Are all the buildings really tall? Is it true there are no trees?"

"You'll have to come and visit sometime." She sits down beside Fredrik. He puts his hand on her shoulder.

"We were best buds, me and Elin," he says to Miriam.

"Friends forever," Elin murmurs, so quietly that she's really only mouthing it.

"Forever ago," Fredrik says, as though he heard her anyway.

◆

Marianne's hands are still damp with dishwater when she suddenly grabs Elin and pulls her away from the conversation at the table. Elin goes with her up the stairs, into the room that was once hers. It's pink now: pink walls, pink quilt, pink curtains trimmed with pink lace. Even the wardrobe doors are pink.

"How lovely you've made it," Elin lies, suppressing a shudder.

It smells musty with old perfume and hairspray. On the dressing table, dusty bottles stand in neat rows on a crocheted doily. The oval mirror is mottled and shabby. Elin bends toward it and looks at her face. It's covered in black patches where the surface of the mirror is damaged.

"You can't put your makeup on here. We'll have to get you a new mirror," she says.

"Are you going to help me now?" says Marianne. "Is everything going to be OK again?" Marianne smiles but seems confused, her gaze darting around the room as she clutches the end of the bed.

"What do you mean?" says Elin. "It wasn't that good when I was last here, was it?"

"It was better."

Elin sinks down onto the bed and sits in silence, staring at the floor, studying the stained linoleum and scruffy baseboards. She remembers.

"Could it get any worse?" she mutters.

She reaches out and takes Marianne's hand, tries to get her to sit down beside her.

"No, come with me, I want to show you something." Marianne lets go of her hand and goes over to one of the wardrobes. When she opens the door, Elin gasps. Her things are still in there. Shelf after shelf of puzzles. Marianne takes out a thick bundle of drawings. She holds them out to Elin.

"Here, you did these. I've never stopped looking at them. They're so lovely, you were so talented, even though you were so young."

Elin takes the pile out of her hands and smiles as she looks at her work. Dogs, cats, trees, flowers, her beloved wildflowers. Drawings of the natural world, things that were so close then and are now distant.

"I carried on drawing flowers. I miss all the flowers we had here."

Elin holds up a sketch that's almost identical to the one she drew for Fredrik in New York just a few weeks ago.

"Just like the bouquets you used to pick for me. Do you remember that?" Marianne takes the picture from her.

"Yes. Yellow for joy, blue for peace, and pink for love. You had some funny ideas, didn't you?"

"It's ideas like that that keep you alive out here in the country." Marianne laughs suddenly.

"Hmm, ideas and dreams," Elin says, still flicking through the pile.

"I've only ever had one dream."

"And what's that?" Elin looks up, meets her mother's gaze.

"That you would come back," she whispers, as a tear escapes from her eye and runs over her cheek.

Marianne lowers herself onto the bed beside Elin, her breath whistling in her lungs, and Elin strokes her back.

"I don't understand. Why didn't you try to contact me?"

"Why did you leave me? Why did you never phone?" counters Marianne.

They fall silent. All the sounds in the room grow, the walls creak-ing, the wind whining outside the window, the children romping about downstairs. Marianne leans her head against Elin's shoulder, and Elin runs her hand over her mother's hair.

"I'm here now, Mama, I'm here. Let's try and forget, and start over," she whispers.

◆

In the end it's Fredrik who interrupts them, opening the door and sticking his head in.

"It's getting late. The kids need to get home and into their beds. The littlest ones, anyway; otherwise they'll start griping soon."

"The littlest ones," Elin and Marianne chorus, laughing at the shared memory of Aina's obsession with elves and imps.

◆

They go down together. Miriam is all ready to go, with the youngest boy in her arms. Elin strokes his head.

"It was lovely to meet you, all of you. We'd best head back to the hotel too. It's so dark all the time, I don't know how you stand it."

Elin takes her black coat from the bench in the hall and buttons it carefully, right up to the throat. Marianne follows her out into the hallway, standing very close. She's smaller than Elin remembers, and her hair is so thin, it looks almost brittle. Her cheeks and nose are covered in small broken veins. She reaches a hand out, hesitantly, and Elin immediately takes it in both of hers.

"Well, time for us to say goodbye, then," Marianne says. Her gaze wavers, not quite meeting Elin's.

"Bye then, Mama. But we'll see you again soon, we're staying a few more days, we have a lot to talk about," Elin replies.

Releasing her hand, she hugs her but gets no hug in return: Marianne's arms hang loose by her sides, and Elin can feel her trembling slightly. She lets go of her and embraces Fredrik and Miriam, while Marianne stays rooted to the spot and stares ahead blankly.

They can hear Edvin stamping his foot in the kitchen, louder and louder. Elin runs back in. Although the arm he reaches to her is stiff and slightly twisted, he's struggling to get closer to her. She bends forward and gives him a hug. His odor is strong, musty, as though it is a long time since he had a shower. He runs his hand across her back in hard, slow strokes.

"Bye then, little brother, I'll see you soon," she whispers, wiping a tear from his cheek.

◆

When Elin comes out into the yard, Alice and Erik are nowhere to be seen and don't reply when she calls for them. It's uncannily quiet outside, as though she is standing in an endless vacuum. She goes around the corner of the house where it's pitch-black, impossible to see your hand in front of your face. The ground is uneven. She eyes the back of the house, wondering what it looks like out there now. The light on her phone is too weak; she can see only earth and pine needles and the dense branches of the juniper bushes.

A weak light sways to and fro farther along the road. She sees the two teenagers stop a little way from the farmyard, where they think they're out of sight. She can hear them speaking but can't make out their words. Alice is given a quick hug and a caress of the cheek before Erik runs over to the waiting car. Alice waves as they drive off, in a minibus with space for all of them. Typical Fredrik, Elin laughs to herself, to make a whole soccer team.

Elin walks toward Alice across the uneven, wet ground. Alice grins when she sees who it is and reaches her arms out. Elin pulls her close and they stand a moment, looking at the buildings.

"I like this," Alice whispers, her cheek close to her mother's.

"What do you mean? The darkness?"

"Everything, your old life. It's lovely."

"Hmm, but dark. And cold. Let's get out of here."

◆

Elin turns up the volume in the car, but Alice turns it down again.

"Can't we talk a little?" she says.

"About what?"

"About all the things you were saying in there. I didn't understand anything. I've only been talking to Erik."

"It's not easy to talk about," says Elin. "Maybe I shouldn't have come; it's stirred up so many feelings for everyone."

"Do you really mean that?"

"No, I'm glad we came. It's just so sad. All of it. Don't you think so?"

"No, not at all. I love this. The cows and the farm. And Erik was so funny and so kind. He showed me the stars. We can come back soon, right? In the summer? Then I can see all your beautiful flowers for real, and swim in the sea. Erik wants to show me. It feels like I've got a new family." Alice smiles happily.

"It's just that she never called me, she never wrote; it's so strange. My own mother," Elin says softly, the words so sharp they cause her pain deep inside. She turns the volume up again.

Alice sits quietly beside her, strokes her hair now and then. It's messy from the wind and smells strongly of both farmyard and cooking.

"I love you, Mom."

At first Elin doesn't answer, but when Alice runs her hand over her hair again, she whispers:

"Ditto."

"You do exactly the same thing she does, you know?"

"Who?"

"Your mom, my grandma. You shut down. You're exactly the same."

Elin falls silent, but her head is spinning with thoughts. She puts her foot down and drives ever faster around the bends. It's not until she turns into Visby through the North Gate that Alice starts to talk again.

"I bet you're longing for your camera right now," she says.

Elin nods.

"You must realize that you hide behind it," Alice says.

"It's been good, working hard is good for you."

Alice snorts.

"You sound like an alcoholic."

Elin stops the car in the middle of the road. Unable to contain her emotions any longer, she bursts into tears and turns to Alice.

"I love you," she sobs. "I'm nothing like her, don't ever say that again."

Alice reaches over the gear stick and hugs her, and they hold each other close for a long time.

"Sorry," Elin whispers at last.

"Promise to stop running away now. Promise," Alice replies.

❖

They are traipsing through the hotel lobby with muddy shoes and messy hair when Elin stops in her tracks.

"I have to get something to eat, I hardly touched that stew."

Alice shakes her head.

"Not me, I have to sleep. I'm pretty much dead on my feet."

She yawns and points toward the bar as the elevator doors open.

"Oh look, see that guy over there? It could almost be Dad."

Alice presses the button for her floor, blows her mother a kiss, and lets the doors separate them.

❖

Elin stays where she is, her eyes on the bar. Alice is right: the short, thick hair looks like his, brown interspersed with streaks of gray. And his neck, the way he bends it toward the bar as he fingers the rim of his wineglass. The black shirt is tight across the shoulders exactly the way his are, the sleeves sloppily folded. Longing wells up in her, her loneliness suddenly very tangible.

Quiet piano music fills the room, and an espresso machine gives off a muffled hum behind the bar. Elin takes a few steps closer, hesitantly. The man is sitting alone at the bar, on a high stool. The other stools, empty, are neatly pushed in alongside his. The winter garden is almost completely empty of guests. Suddenly he turns his head and looks out across the room. Elin's heart leaps when she sees his profile, and she stops in her tracks.

"Sam, is that you?"

Her voice is too tremulous; he doesn't hear. She steps closer.

"Sam!"

He gets up as soon as he hears her voice, his face serious as he walks toward her. He stops right in front of her and puts his hand on her cheek. They stand in silence, looking at each other.

"I've never seen you cry before. Or seen you looking so untidy. You're so beautiful," he says at last.

"Why are you here?"

"You sent the heart."

"You never replied when I sent it."

"No, but it stirred up some memories. I phoned Alice and she told me everything."

"So you know now?"

Sam nods and takes a deep breath.

"Why, Elin? Why have you never told me?"

Elin squirms.

"I don't know, it just worked out that way. But I'm here now, I'm home again," she says quickly, on an inhalation.

"No, you're not, not quite," he whispers, kissing her on the cheek. He pulls her close and strokes her back. "*Now* you're home."

~ ~ ~ ~

So much happens in a life.

Events that become memories that are gathered within us.

That build us up. That change the way we are and the things we do. That shape us.

Words someone said to you.

Kind ones.

Mean ones.

Words you said to someone else.

That you can never forgive yourself for saying.

The first kiss.

The first betrayal.

The times you made a fool of yourself.
The times someone else made a fool of themself.
We remember the little details. And the memories engrave
    themselves on us.
Some gain strength, year by year. Some affect us forever.
Maybe more than we realize. Maybe without reason.
Can you be sure you remember things as they really were?

ACKNOWLEDGMENTS

To work on a novel is to be invited on a journey through the winding thoughts of your characters. They're not always clear, not always logical. They're often easy to hear, but not always easy to understand. Thanks to Karin Linge Nordh and Johan Stridh for helping me navigate and find the right direction. Thanks to Julia Angelin and Anna Carlander for always believing in me, always supporting me in the right way. Thanks to everyone at Forum and Salomonsson Agency for working so hard and so enthusiastically on my books. Thanks to Carl, for inspiration and brilliant thoughts. Thanks to Mama, Papa, Helena, Cathrin, and Linda for being there to support me. And thanks to my wonderful, lovely Oskar, for putting up with an absentminded mama.

ABOUT THE AUTHOR

Sofia Lundberg is a journalist and former magazine editor. Her debut novel, *The Red Address Book*, was published in thirty-six territories worldwide. She lives in Stockholm with her son.

Don't miss the global sensation—published in 32 countries around the world!

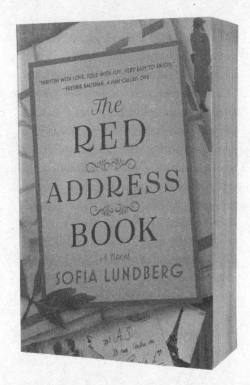

"In a reader's lifetime, there are a few books that will be companions forever. For me, *The Red Address Book* is one of them. It will comfort you, and remind you of all the moments when you grabbed life with both hands. It is also an homage to the wisdom of women who have lived longer than most of us. One is never too old to learn that love is the only meaning of life—let's listen to these women."

—NINA GEORGE,
author of *The Little Paris Bookshop*